10/06

The Taos Truth Game

The Taos Truth Game

Earl Ganz

University of New Mexico Press ~ Albuquerque

Printed in the United States of America

12 11 10 09 08 07 06   1 2 3 4 5 6 7

LIBRARY OF CONGRESS CATALOGING-IN-PUBLICATION DATA

Ganz, Earl, 1932–
The Taos truth game / Earl Ganz.
p. cm.
ISBN-13: 978-0-8263-3771-9 (ALK. PAPER)
ISBN-10: 0-8263-3771-6 (ALK. PAPER)
1. Brinig, Myron, 1897–1991—Fiction.
2. Luhan, Mabel Dodge, 1879–1962—Fiction.
3. Wells, Cady, 1904–1954—Fiction.
4. Jewish authors—Fiction. 5. Closeted gays—Fiction.
6. Taos (N.M.)—Fiction. 7. Novelists—Fiction.
8. Gay men—Fiction. I. Title.
PS3557.A52T36 2006
813′.54—dc22

2005025595

"Opus 40"by Emanuel Morgan a.k.a. Harold Witter Bynner from *Light Verse and Satires* by Witter Bynner. Reprinted by permission of the Witter Byner Foundation for Poetry.

"Snake" by D. H. Lawrence from the *Complete Poems of D. H. Lawrence*, edition by V. de Sola Pinto and F. W. Roberts, ©1964, 1971 by Angelo Ravagli and C. M. Weekley, Executors of the Estate of Frieda Lawrence Ravagli. Used by permission of Viking Penguin, a division of Penguin Group (U.S.A.), Inc.

"Song of the Sky Loom" from *The Songs of the Tewa* by Hernert Spinden. Appears courtesy of Sunstone Press, Box 2321, Santa Fe, NM.

Permission for the use of lines from Gertrude Stein's poem "Lifting Belly" was granted by the estate of Gertrude Stein through its literary executor, Mr. Stanford Gann of Levin & Gann, P.A.

Book and Jacket design and type composition by Kathleen Sparkes

This book is typeset using Trump Mediaeval, 8.5/12; 26P
Display type is Gothic 821 Condensed.

Thank you's

To the Beinecke Rare Book and Manuscript Library at Yale University for the unpublished manuscripts "Derision is Easy," *Water of Life,* and "Una and Robin in Taos" by Mabel Dodge Luhan, and for access to the letters of Myron Brinig.

To the University of New Mexico's Center for Southwest Research for the letters of Myron Brinig to Frank Waters in the Frank Waters collection.

To Lois Rudnick for her biography of Mabel, *Mabel Dodge Luhan: New Woman, New Worlds,* University of New Mexico Press, 1984.

Although many characters, places, and events of this novel are factual, this is a story of what may have happened or could have happened. . . .

Prologue

The Closet

"WHO LET YOU OUT?"

Ignoring the question, Myron continued around The Closet's circular bar to his spot at the back. Years ago Carmen had dubbed him Captain Midnight. Myron didn't give a shit. He liked to watch who came in and out and be near the bathroom.

"Where is everyone?" he asked. There were just two men and they seemed to have eyes only for each other.

"It's early." Carmen was in front of him with a gin and tonic.

"Thanks." Myron laid the book and a five-dollar bill next to the drink.

"What's that about?" asked the bartender, returning with change.

"Olden times." Myron pushed the book forward.

"Mabel Dodge Looohan," the man read. "*New Woman, New Worlds*." He looked up. "Who's Mabel Dodge whatsits?"

"Someone I used to know."

"Oh?"

Myron pulled the book back, found a page of photos, and again pushed it forward. On the right-hand page were two shots, one of the poet Robinson Jeffers, his wife, Una, and Mabel herself, the other of the Jefferses' stone house in Carmel. On the left-hand page was a large photo of a man on horseback. Myron pointed to it.

"Who's he?" asked Carmen.

"Me."

Carmen looked down again, then up at Myron. "So it is." Then down again. "You were a handsome devil, Mike." Up again. "If I'd been alive back then I wouldn't have minded you in my bed at all."

"Ugh," said Myron.

"Ugh to you!" said Carmen and left him for the two men at three o'clock.

Myron pulled the book back and closed it. On the cover was Fechin's portrait of Mabel looking like a dowager empress. The world doesn't remember you either, he said to the portrait. But it was obvious from the book's existence that somebody did. So he raised his glass to Mabel and took a long sip. He was thirsty and hadn't realized it. That's what happens when you get old, he thought. Your body stops telling you what it wants. You just have to keep asking. So he finished the drink quickly, then thought he should slow down. He didn't want a buzz, at least not before George got off work and could take him home.

"Here you go," said Carmen and set another in front of him. "Compliments of the boys." The bartender nodded toward the two men, who were hardly boys. They raised their glasses to him. "I told them about your picture. They wanna see it."

"Sure." Myron picked up the drink, raised it toward them, then reopened the book to the right page and handed it to Carmen.

"You were a handsome guy, Myron Brinig," said one of the men. He had read Myron's name in the photo's caption.

"You're still handsome," said the other. "How old are you?"

"Eighty-seven this December," answered Myron. It was June.

"I don't believe you," said one.

"You're kidding," said the other.

Myron smiled. He loved it when people said they didn't believe how old he was. So he asked them what they did and it turned out the small one was an art dealer and the one who said Myron was handsome was his assistant.

"I know about this lady." The art dealer was looking at the cover. "She's the one who did the Armory Show with Gertrude Stein, right?"

"That's her," said Myron and remembered Mabel saying that Gertrude Stein had had little to do with it.

"And you knew her?" the man asked.

"Yup."

"Wow. It's hard to believe," said the dealer. "That was a long time ago."

"1913," said Myron. "Over seventy years ago." Even he was amazed at the number.

The two men slid their drinks counterclockwise and were beside him.

"Did you see it?" asked the dealer, who was closest.

"The art show?" asked Myron.

The man nodded.

"No. I didn't get here until 1914."

"The beginning of the First World War!" noted the assistant, who was standing beside his boss.

"Not for America," said Myron and extended his right hand to the art dealer. "Here," he said, "shake my hand."

"Aw Myron," said Carmen, "lay off."

"He's not going to fart or anything?" the man asked.

"No," said Myron. "I'm serious. Shake my hand."

"Okay," and the man extended his hand.

Myron took it and they shook.

"So?" the dealer asked after he let go.

"You just shook the hand that shook the hand of Teddy Roosevelt."

"Are you kidding?" He turned to Carmen. "Teddy Roosevelt?"

"So he says."

"It was the summer of 1904," explained Myron. "He was campaigning for his second term and came to Butte, which had a hundred thousand people then."

"You're from Montana?" asked the assistant.

"Butte," Myron corrected. "It's different."

The man shrugged.

"Anyway, my father took me to the lobby of the Thornton Hotel where Teddy was meeting the public."

"How old were you?" asked Carmen.

"Four months shy of eight." He waited for more questions.

There were none so he went on. "There we were, waiting in line, and when we got to the president he shook my father's hand, then turned to me, bent down, hesitated, then shook my hand too. You know what he said?"

"What?" asked the assistant.

"Deee-lighted!" Myron tried to sound like the actor in *Arsenic and Old Lace*. But his voice was much too dry.

"That's a wonderful story," said the art dealer. "You must've been thrilled."

"Naw," said Myron, shaking his head. "I was disappointed."

"Why?"

"I thought he was going to kiss me like he did the other little kids." Myron couldn't remember when he began telling it this way. All he really remembered about TR was his teeth. He'd never seen teeth so big. "Just think of it, if Teddy had kissed me then instead of shaking my hand, you'd be kissing me now."

"Ugh," said Carmen.

"That's a wonderful story," repeated the art dealer. "Bob," he said, turning to his assistant, "shake this man's hand."

"But don't kiss him," warned Carmen.

Myron reached over and squeezed Bob's hand.

"Hey, listen to this," said the dealer, who had found something else of interest in the book. "'Myron Brinig, a Jewish novelist born in 1896, grew up in Butte, Montana and wrote realistic fiction about the miners, labor organizers, farmers, and businessmen who populated communities not far from the pioneering stage.'"

"Is that true?" asked Carmen.

Myron nodded. The art dealer went on.

"'When he first visited Taos, in the early 1930s, he was living in New York City and was spoken of by critics as one of America's leading young writers.'"

"Wow!" said Carmen. "I'm gonna treat you with new respect."

"I don't remember any old respect," snapped Myron.

"'Brinig was one of the several homosexual artists whom Mabel attracted—he might have said trapped—into her coterie.'" He looked up. "How'd she trap you?"

"She didn't. The whole thing's bullshit."

"You weren't trapped?"

"No." Myron wondered if he should explain further. But what business was it of theirs? Then he noticed that the art dealer was reading on. And he wanted the book back.

"Listen to this," said the man. "'Mabel Dodge Luhan has been imagined dead in a greater variety of ways than any other woman in American literary history. She has been disposed of by gang rape and suicide, had her heart torn out in an Indian sacrificial ritual, been squeezed to death by a snake and blinded by a vulture. None of these deaths, however, matches her apocalyptic finale in Myron Brinig's *All of Their Lives*, in which she is struck dead by a stroke of heaven-sent lightning as she gallops furiously across the most precipitous mountain peak in New Mexico.'" The art dealer looked up. "You really wrote such a novel?"

"Yeah."

"Was it a bestseller?"

"Yeah."

"Was it good?"

"No."

The art dealer nodded at Myron's honesty and began reading again. "In an unpublished short story called 'Derision Is Easy,' Mabel presents Brinig as a Hawthorne-esque Paul Pry who delights in a voyeuristic penetration of the hidden corners of people's lives."

"Who's Paul Pry?" asked Carmen.

"A character in a story by Nathaniel Hawthorne," Myron explained and saw the puzzled look on the bartender's face. "*The Scarlet Letter*? *The House of Seven Gables*?"

"So, were you?" asked Bob, the assistant.

"Was I what?"

"Like this guy, Paul Pry."

"Nobody's like him. He didn't exist. Besides, the woman only wrote that because she thought I was dead."

"Why'd she think that?" asked Carmen.

"Because everyone else in the book is dead."

"Yeah. I can see that. You're pretty old."

"But I'm not dead and she had no right to say that. I told her so. I called her and told her." Then it began, the same anger he'd felt when he first read the words. Lois Rudnick had invaded his privacy. "What right has she to say that?" he asked as if he were talking to himself.

"Say what?" asked Carmen.

"That I'm a homosexual! How does she know? Was she there? Did she watch?"

"But you are," Carmen pointed out.

"But I didn't give her permission to tell the world."

"She doesn't need your permission," the dealer said. "It's not considered a bad thing anymore." He closed the book and pushed it at Myron.

"Isn't it time you came out of the closet?" asked the assistant.

"We're in The Closet," snapped Myron and turned away from them. The two men went back to their three o'clock spot, Carmen standing before them. Myron was sorry for losing his temper. Someone's remembering you, he thought, and he touched the book. The trouble was that at this late stage of his life he wasn't sure he wanted to be remembered. The woman hadn't even known he was alive. Nobody did. If the world thinks you're dead, you're dead. It's better that way. If you're in your eighties you want to go gently, quietly. Myron stood, went to the jukebox behind him, and put in two quarters. On came Russ Columbo singing "Prisoner Of Love." Myron loved the old tunes in The Closet's jukebox.

"Want to dance?" he asked when he caught Bob's eye.

"Don't start, Myron," warned Carmen.

Bob looked at the art dealer, who nodded.

"Sure," said Bob.

"No dancing," said Carmen. "I'll lose my license."

They were in the space in front of the jukebox, Myron leading. "Prisoner of Love" was a slow fox-trot. He loved that name. Fox-trot. It reminded him of England and some two-step ceremony with horses and hounds. After a few twirls he dipped Bob. Myron kept a roll of quarters in his right-hand pants pocket and pulled the man's crotch against it.

"Wow," said Bob. "You sure know how to dip a guy."

Myron smiled broadly.

"No dancing, dammit!" snarled Carmen, and like a magician, he lifted a section of the bar. The lachrymose baritone of the crooner swelled, then went suddenly silent. The bartender had the jukebox plug in his right hand. The men stopped dancing and stood for a moment like confused children. Then Bob turned and went back to the art dealer, Carmen back behind the bar, and Myron to his twelve o'clock spot to sip his drink. After a while he opened the book to look at the smiling young man on horseback. The caption said the photo was taken in 1934. That was wrong. The year was 1933. It was his first summer in Taos.

"'One of America's leading young writers,'" he read silently.

Then how did it happen? He wasn't a flash in the pan. He'd gone on to publish twenty-one novels, his last in 1958 when he was sixty-one. At the time he would have said the odds for his being remembered were pretty good. But he'd lived long enough to see himself forgotten, his books out of print, first the mediocre ones, then even the good ones. That's what he never understood. At least seven of those twenty-one were very good. But by the end of the sixties even they were gone from library shelves. He and Steve used to go to the book cemeteries down on Fourth Avenue and buy them off the tables there. After a while they were gone, too. By the seventies it was as if he'd never written a word.

"You owe me fifty cents," he said to Carmen when he looked up. "You shouldn't stop an old man from dancing."

"Why not?"

"The urge doesn't come that often." He smiled. "You wanna dance?"

"No thanks. I've felt your quarters."

"Then get me another."

Another gin and tonic was in front of him.

"On the house," Carmen said. "We're even. But that's the last for you. It's quinine water after this."

Myron raised the drink in mock homage, then sipped. He put the glass down beside the closed book and was again facing Nicolai Fechin's portrait of Mabel. A fine painter, he thought, his portraits flattering, yet revealing. He studied the face of the middle-aged woman. The dowager empress, he thought. Turandot with no more suitors. There was cruelty, anger, little-girl hurt, and little-girl petulance. And there was bravery and toughness and pride that would brook no insult. What a woman, he thought. What a human being!

But the book-jacket picture was a poor facsimile of the painting. He remembered the original, the heavy line under the chin, the small, perfect mouth that could broaden to shark-like ferocity. Fechin got her. The Russian émigré had been painting portraits of New York millionaires, making lots of money and hating it. She heard about him, invited him and his family to visit, and that was it. Back then Taos was full of fine painters.

Myron opened the book to another group of photos. There they were: Mabel, Dorothy Brett, and Frieda Lawrence, three middle-aged ladies sitting side by side on the steps of Frieda's ranch house, the ranch that Mabel gave to the Lawrences. Mabel's the one in the white dress with the wide shoulders, the one with a big bright girlish smile. Brett's in the baggy pants with the bandanna around her head and lace-up boots on her feet. Between them, Frieda, in the flowered print dress, a cigarette dangling from her lips and smoke curling upward into her face, sits on a lower step closer to the camera. She's laughing. There's no date but Myron remembered it was taken in late September of 1935 at the second dedication of Lawrence's tomb. There was no photo credit either but he knew who took it, the same person who snapped the photo of him on horseback. And once again it occurred to him that none of it would have happened if he hadn't met Cady Wells. Best time of my life, thought the old man.

The Truth Game

One

"We made a date last night. I asked you if you wanted to drive up to Taos to see the pueblo and you said you did."

Myron didn't remember. What on earth had happened last night?

"Could you wait outside so I can get dressed?"

The young man nodded. Myron closed the door, glanced at the bed, thought to get back in, then went into the bathroom, peed, and tried to remember. The dude ranch had turned out to be more distillery than ranch. With Repeal soon to be enacted, the owners seemed to be giving their moonshine away. Last night he'd gotten drunk on something called Taos Lightning. He remembered having a great time dancing to fiddle music. But that's all he remembered. Who the devil is this guy? he asked the sleep-swollen face in the mirror. The face had no answer so Myron brushed his teeth, thought about shaving, threw water on his cheeks, and got dressed.

"I've read *Singermann* and *Wide Open Town*," announced the young man when they were side by side in his station wagon. "You're a fine writer, Myron Brinig."

"Who are you?" Myron asked bluntly.

"Why I'm Cady—Cady Wells."

"Sounds like an oasis," said Myron, trying to make light of it. Obviously he was supposed to know him.

But Cady Wells didn't take offense. He just laughed and started his car. At the highway they turned left and headed north on the same road Myron and his friends had driven down yesterday. In a while the road began to climb, and at a place Cady called Embudo, Myron saw the Rio Grande, not the muddy stream he'd always imagined but a clear mountain torrent. He didn't remember seeing it yesterday, but by then he was so sick of being in a car he wasn't seeing much. Now the road began to steepen and wind with canyon walls towering over them, not exactly rock, more like great piles of sand with some rocks in them. About a half hour of this and they came out of a hairpin turn onto a plain. Ahead were snow-capped mountains. Not Montana, Myron thought, but not Kansas either. As sparse as it was there seemed enough vegetation, creosote bushes and piñon pines, to hold down the dust.

"Nice," said Myron.

"Yes," Cady Wells agreed. Soon they were passing through a village. "Ranchos de Taos," Cady called out. Myron saw an adobe church that looked interesting, but they didn't stop. "There's Taos up ahead." They were on another straightaway. "The pueblo's on the other side."

A horizontal slum, Myron thought as they got to Taos. It was what he'd thought yesterday when they passed the town on the way down. He thought most mountain towns were fly-by-night things. Either you fled them or they fled you. The pueblo, however, was something else. Its clean geometry appealed to Myron's sense of order. They got out of the car and walked to the plaza, a wide spot between the north and south adobe apartment houses, where the dancing was already underway. It was different from Butte, where Crow and Blackfeet were brought in for the Fourth of July parades to dance on flatbed wagons, sometimes slowly, other times frenetically, but always in circles like the Indians in the movies.

"Those are reservation Indians," Cady said when Myron mentioned this. "Reservations are the creation of the government. The pueblos existed before Christ. This one's seven hundred years old."

He's trying to impress me, thought Myron. Why? What happened last night? He racked his brain but couldn't come up with anything. In the car Cady had told him that he was a painter and that he'd been in New Mexico less than a year. Maybe he needs a friend, at least someone to show the place off to. One thing Myron had promised himself was not to get involved with anyone. He couldn't afford it. Not if he wanted to free himself from Farrar & Rinehart. Oh well, let's see what happens, he thought and he listened as the young man explained the dancing, how it was part of a ceremony that included visits to shrines in the mountains and days of secret rituals in the kiva. Then he had to explain what a kiva was.

"Who are they?" Myron nodded toward a small group of nearly naked men in loincloths, their bodies painted white.

"They're called Koshare. They're the comedians. They make fun of the people who they think need to be taken down a peg."

Myron watched two of the white-bodied men circle an impressive looking man, a white shawl draped over his head and long black braids falling down his chest. They were standing on either side of him, pounding their chests as if arguing who was more important.

"He's really getting it," said Myron.

"Yeah," Cady agreed.

"What's this ceremony for?"

"I think it's a rain dance."

"Well, who isn't praying for rain?" Myron again thought of Kansas and Colorado and the blinding dust they'd just spent a week driving through.

"Dancing is a form of prayer for them."

The echelons of dancers dipped and dove in and out of figure eights, the drums guiding them, the singers around the drums commenting on the conversation the dancers' feet seemed to be having with the earth. Myron had to admit it was different from what he knew. Still, it left him cold.

"Every bone in my body says no to tribal life," he explained when they were back in the station wagon. "You read *Singermann*. It's tribal life I'm escaping."

It was good to have written a novel about your growing up. If they read it you didn't have to explain yourself. If they didn't you referred them to it and maybe sold another book.

"I don't mean we should be like them," Cady Wells was saying. "It's impossible. They're at a different time and place." They were on the road back to Taos. "But I think they've got something to tell us. I think we have to understand them to understand ourselves."

"Well, it's interesting," said Myron, "even beautiful. But I feel it's got nothing to do with me. It's . . . a side show."

And almost before the words left his mouth, Cady pulled his station wagon over onto the shoulder and cut the engine.

"That's Mabel over there," he said, nodding at a vehicle parked on the opposite shoulder. "Let's go over. I'll introduce you."

Myron knew who Mabel was. Everyone had heard of Mabel Dodge Luhan, the lady who'd married an Indian and brought D. H. Lawrence to Taos. And Myron had just read *Lorenzo in Taos*, her book on the Lawrences. Yet he was essentially shy, and his first reaction when called upon to meet new people, particularly famous ones, was to say no. Also it seemed to him Cady was acting out of character. He hadn't seemed the type to chase celebrities. But before Myron could protest that he didn't want to meet the woman, Cady was out of the car, and there was nothing to do but follow. Then, as he approached the other car, Myron's confusion was compounded when he saw not one but two women in the front seat. Which was Mabel? He guessed wrong. Mabel was the other one, the smaller one with bangs that squared off her face and made him think of a middle-aged Betty Boop. Cady introduced the driver as Muriel Draper, a name Myron thought he recognized. Then he realized the women weren't being at all friendly and when he was introduced to Mabel he wasn't sure she heard his name correctly or cared if she had.

"We've just been snubbed," he said when they were back in the Ford.

"Muriel's a snob," Cady said. "If our names were Rubinstein or Heifetz she'd be falling all over us."

"Didn't she write something about herself?"

"*Music at Midnight*," answered Cady. "It's about her love affairs with some of the famous artists of our time."

"And Mabel? Is she a snob?"

"Mabel? Oh no. You'll be hearing from her. You'll see. She'll be after you."

After me? What does that mean? How can she be after me? I'll be gone in a few days. Still, the thought of his own celebrity made Myron smile. Cady started the car and pulled onto the road. But not for long. He took the next right and after a few yards the street opened onto a plaza. Here was the center of Taos. It was a poor place with several empty lots, which Cady explained were due to a fire the previous winter that destroyed almost half the buildings. Better if they'd all burned, Myron thought.

"Where are we going?" he asked.

"I want to show you my work."

"Your etchings?"

"My watercolors," said Cady, acknowledging the joke with a smile. They'd pulled up in front of a small gallery.

"I thought you'd take me to your studio," Myron said.

"Only if you want to drive back thirty miles."

And again he was wondering what happened last night. Had he made a pass at Cady? Or Cady at him? Had they danced together? If dancing was prayer, had theirs been answered? He's attractive, Myron judged. But not my type. Too small and energetic. I like long, languid men. Then he wondered if people had seen them. After all, this was a new place and Myron liked to be discreet. All this while he was following Cady into the small building. A pleasant surprise. No, it was more. It was impressive. Cady Wells was not your usual Western artist. For one thing, these were watercolor landscapes with lots of unpainted space on the paper, and the brush strokes were singular and so much like writing they seemed full of meaning. Myron had never seen anything like it, mountains rising like messages from the earth, paintings like pages in a book. He pointed to an unpainted patch.

"Missed a spot," he said. But when he saw the look on Cady's face, he took back his joke. "They're wonderful," he said.

In fact they were so good that Myron tried to transfer the technique to the overwhelming mountains that surrounded Butte. If Cady had painted them, the huge granite outcroppings atop Pipestone Pass would be clenched fists, the earth around his hometown as tough as a bare-knuckled fighter.

"I'm so glad you like them!" Cady gushed as he examined

his own work. "I'm just a beginner, so I need all the encouragement I can get."

Myron heard the feminine in the young man's enthusiastic modesty and decided he liked it. The man was not ashamed to be himself.

"I know you plan to leave in a few days." Cady was looking at him. "But could you put it off? I want to invite you down to Española. I've got a little guesthouse on a friend's ranch there."

Myron was taken aback. They'd known each other only a few hours. What happened last night? Then he was startled again. In a sudden, sweeping motion Cady removed the wide-brimmed straw hat that kept the sun from his fair skin. He's bald, Myron noted, and had all he could do not to laugh. And why take it off now? Was he trying to be honest? Here I am, pate and all. But it was more than honesty. With his small size and feminine speech, Cady had transformed himself into a creature from another world. A Martian. Why do I find that attractive? Myron wondered. Is it some kind of perversion? Love with a different species?

"Well . . . " and again he remembered that he didn't want to get involved. He had to get to LA and find movie work so he could pay back Farrar & Rinehart's advances and be free of them. "Well . . . " He thought of Hans and Janet. Could he desert them? They were younger than he. He'd been taking care of them. But the Martian was smiling at him. "I'll have to talk it over with the people I'm traveling with. You must have met them last night. Janet? Hans?"

Janet Goldstein was a friend from New York, and the trip had been her idea. She said she wanted to show Hans the real America. Then why take me? Myron asked. I don't even drive. She said she wanted him along to share expenses and read maps and just be good company. I'm being cautious, she confided. Who knows how this thing with the Kraut will turn out? C'mon. It'll be fun. We'll take our time, get a feel for how the country's doing under Roosevelt. She touched his arm and Myron knew she was also doing it for him, that she wanted to get him out of New York.

He'd been very depressed lately. For one thing there was his last novel, *The Flutter of an Eyelid*. Someone, claiming to have been slandered by the novel, had gotten a court order suppressing it. Myron hadn't even known the person making the charge, but Farrar & Rinehart refused to fight it. After only a week the book was gone from the bookstores. He never thought it could happen to him. With six novels in four years, he was one of America's rising literary stars. Yet it had happened and there was nothing he could do about it.

Nor was there anything he could do about his love life. Despite the fact that Frank Fenton was married and had two children, he and Myron were lovers. When it was working, it was wonderful. When it wasn't . . . it wasn't the fact that they were both writers. It was Frank's terrible bouts of guilt and the drinking they would cause. Still, Myron had loved him and dedicated *The Flutter of an Eyelid* to him. The novel was about, among other things, the glorious six months they had lived together in Malibu. Frank had shown his appreciation by taking off for Hollywood and a screenwriter's job. And that's where he was now and that's where Janet was proposing they go. She's right, he thought, I can stay around here and mope or I can go somewhere fresh. But LA? Wouldn't that be like chasing him? On the other hand, a screenwriting job wouldn't be bad. If Frank could do it, so could he. And then I can buy my freedom from Farrar & Rinehart.

In Pittsburgh they stopped outside a mill by the Allegheny River to listen to labor speeches. Myron had heard it all before in Butte. He'd grown up with it. *Wide Open Town* was about the famous copper strike of 1917. One of its heroes was the IWW organizer Frank Little, who was lynched by the Anaconda Copper Company's goons. It was one of the great scenes in the novel. Hans, who called himself a Communist, loved the book. Here was another reason Janet wanted him along, to keep Hans happy. Who knows? Myron asked as they listened to speaker after speaker in city after city; comes the revolution, maybe we'll all eat strawberries and cream. One thing he did know was that even the most just cause expounded by the most righteously angry men, if repeated often enough, becomes boring. So by the time they got to Kansas City they were ready to choose jazz over labor,

Count Basie over John L. Lewis, who was in town organizing the stockyards.

But they weren't prepared for Kansas. They'd come out west to witness an economic disaster. What they got was a natural one that was turning the land into what was being called a dust bowl, no rain and constant wind. Janet, usually unflappable, kept saying she didn't understand, and Hans, who thought he had an answer for everything, kept asking what were they going to do? Only Myron, who'd grown up in a place where temperatures reached forty below and the wind blew fifty miles an hour for days on end, had a plan. We'll travel when we can, he explained. We'll drive at night and get off the road when it starts. He was looking at a map. We've been taking Highway 40. Let's cut south to Wichita and see if things get better. From there we can head west to Colorado, then south into New Mexico. It'll be like tacking, noted Janet of the zigzag course. Her family had owned a yacht in the twenties. We'll sail the rest of the way, she said. We'll discover the Southwest Passage.

So Myron felt responsible for them. It wasn't easy leaving people with whom you'd just spent three desperate weeks. Yet he made up his mind. Cady drove him back down to the ranch and left. Myron found his friends on the porch of their cabin.

"I met this man and I think I'd like to stay here for a while," he announced.

Janet looked at Hans, who burst out laughing.

"How'd you know we wanted to be alone?" she asked.

Myron hesitated, then laughed too. It was a relief. It seemed he'd done his job and was no longer needed.

"What do you think of Shangri-la now?" Janet asked. He had scoffed at *Lost Horizon* after she'd made him read it. And again when they were driving through Taos, which she likened to Hilton's Tibetan utopia.

"Maybe there's something to it," he admitted.

"Don't give in to romance, Myron," warned Hans. "Love is the death of all great cynics."

Myron smiled. He liked being considered a great cynic.

The next morning, after eating bacon and eggs with them, he said goodbye.

"You sure you have enough money?" Janet asked.

"Yes," he said. "Don't worry." He hugged her and kissed her cheek, then turned to Hans.

"Shake hands with Hans," the German said, but instead of shaking hands they hugged. It should have been a moment of sadness and maybe a little frightening for all of them. It wasn't. It was exciting. They were off, Janet and Hans down to Los Angeles and Myron to a nearby ranch.

The place Cady took him to turned out to be even less of a ranch than the one where Myron had been staying. It may have been a ranch once but now it was an estate called Swan Lake with formal gardens, fountains, stables, and garages full of cars. In the center of all this was a large, flat-roofed, brick-trimmed adobe hacienda. Myron asked about the source of all this wealth.

"Marie's husbands were very rich," Cady explained. "When the last one died he left her even more money than she had to begin with."

They went in and Myron met his hostess. Marie Garland, well into middle age, had clear blue eyes, a long straight nose, and a high flat forehead. Though she must have been a great beauty once, the way she wore her white hair, drawn back and caught behind with a ribbon, made Myron think of George Washington. Yet her clothes—a long black skirt, a turquoise shirt, a silver concha belt and a squash-blossom necklace—said she had gone native. She offered further proof of this by serving them a supper of the hottest food Myron had ever eaten: green chile stew, tortillas in cornhusks, and peppery beans. The best was the flan, its honeyed sweetness easing the fire in his mouth and allowing time for the sweat on his forehead to dry.

"I'd like to show you my bedroom, Myron," said Marie after dinner.

He looked at Cady, who looked away. Myron felt a sudden distrust of his new friend, as if he had been lured to this place to do something Cady was incapable of doing. In an instant Marie Garland had gone from a rich, kindly, older woman to a middle-aged sex shark. Oh well, Myron decided, I'll think of something, and he followed her up some steps, then down a long hall that seemed to end directly at her bed.

"It's from an old Spanish house," she said reverently as if the baroquely carved headboard had once been an altar in a medieval cathedral. Myron thought she might even cross herself but she turned away and walked over a large Navajo rug to her desk, which was also decorated with carved angels. There, like an actress finding her mark, she faced the room.

"Every morning when I wake up," she announced, nodding toward the bed, "I feel as if I'd just been born."

Myron wanted to ask why she thought just being born was such a great feeling. But the time for humor had passed. She seemed to be suggesting that the same experience could be his if only he would join her in it. Cady had mentioned that Marie was between husbands. Now Myron watched her sit down at her desk, open a side drawer, and take out a book.

"You're a writer," she said, "so I know you'll be interested in reading a volume of my poems."

Myron sighed. The danger was past. She was a poet. She'd written poems and gotten them published. He'd never heard of the publisher but that didn't matter. He watched her inscribe her name on the title page.

"Take this to your room," she ordered, "and read it at your leisure."

"I'll be happy to," Myron said gallantly and took the book. But as he turned to go, she raised a hand.

"Stay a moment. I'd like to read you some poems I've written since that book was published."

She reached into another drawer and brought out a folder bulging with papers. So that's it, and he was amazed at how deftly she'd sprung her trap. Some people have to sing for their supper. He would have to listen for his. So he did. For the next two hours he sat in the room's other chair and tried to look attentive. It wasn't easy. Her hot cuisine kept coming up, encores of chile and piñon nuts against a background of corn, beans, and spicy meat. And when his heartburn began to wane, he developed stomach cramps, which is why he didn't at all mind the difficulty he had finding his way back to the guesthouse. Each faltering step was marked by a gaseous explosion, his contribution to the erupting universe that was the star-filled New Mexican night.

"Excuse me," he said when he finally entered the cabin. Cady, already in one of the twin beds, a book resting on his chest, was waiting up. Myron rushed past the beds and into the bathroom where he deposited a good deal of the fiery meal. It must have been at least twenty minutes before he came out. He had needed a shower.

"You all right?" Cady asked.

"I'm better," said Myron.

"What happened?"

"She read me her poetry."

"I knew she'd do that."

"You could've warned me."

"I'm sorry."

"And there was an added complication." Could he discuss such things with his new friend? "I was in no condition to listen to poetry, not after so much hot food."

"You'll get used to the food," Cady said. Then he was looking worried. "What did you do?"

"What do you mean what did I do? I was polite. I made myself listen, or at least I tried to. But after a while, I realized I wasn't." Myron felt a lot better. He could see the humor of it. "I was watching her breasts."

"Her breasts?"

"The way their movement punctuated her poetry."

"What do you mean?"

Myron picked up some sheaves, chose a page, and began to read.

"I love you my darling with passion sublime, not only this night but endless in time." He looked up. "When she read a line like that, up they would come, a waxing of twin moons seeking caresses and kisses from the night."

"That's terrible."

"Awful," Myron agreed. "But then came," and he found another page: "The rain fell stark, the sky was gray, that day in May when you went away." He looked up. "When she read a line like that her breasts collapsed, disappeared. I was fascinated. How'd she do it?" He put the pages back and turned to Cady. "But after a while even they couldn't hold my interest. I couldn't help myself."

"What did you do?" Cady asked again. It was obvious he was afraid Myron had offended their host.

"I . . . I broke wind," Myron mumbled.

"What?"

"I farted!"

Cady burst out laughing.

"What did she do?"

"Nothing. She finished the poem she was reading, looked me in the face, pronounced me tired, and asked if I wouldn't rather read her poems tomorrow." Myron shook his head. "I mean a woman who seems to have known so many men in her life had finally noticed I was on the verge of exploding. Only I'm not sure she did notice. She never gave any sign. All she did was press these poems on me, and made me promise I'd take good care of them."

"It's a huge amount of stuff." Cady nodded at the pile on Myron's bed. "Are you going to spend the rest of the night reading?"

"No," Myron said. "I know what they're about."

"You do? What?"

"Well, there are the bed poems about men and how much she loves them and they love her. And there are the weather poems." Myron definitely felt better. His stomach had quieted and he had an appreciative audience. "In the love poems nothing comes out right. Either he leaves her or she leaves him. Someone's always getting out of bed and going away. Then there are the weather poems."

"I don't get it," said Cady.

"Well, after her lover leaves she goes to a window, looks out, and it's raining."

"In New Mexico?"

"No, Paris. It's always Paris. And it's not a heavy rain, just sort of a sad gray misty rain. She does the rain parts pretty well. Like, maybe he'll come back, but if he doesn't to hell with it, there's always the rain."

"You're not making much sense."

"If you had to spend two hours listening to a hundred lousy

poems, your throat full of acid, your stomach bursting, your asshole so angry it's trying to strangle you, you wouldn't make much sense either."

There was a long silence and Myron wondered if he'd gone too far with this description. He really didn't know how his new friend felt about their host. So he just stood there, hesitant.

"I guess you don't feel like . . . " said Cady and threw back the covers.

Myron gasped. In its rust-colored nest lay the bright pink chick.

"I didn't say that," Myron said, and like an eagle, swooped down on it.

They slept late and when they finally made it up to the main house for lunch, Marie was waiting for them.

"I've had a call from Mabel," she announced. "She'll be down here tomorrow to spend a few days and wants me to ask you two to dinner." Marie turned to Myron. "She probably wants to meet you, Myron."

"But they've already met," said Cady. "We passed her on the road a few days ago and I introduced them."

"And she was very rude," added Myron.

"That may be," said their host. "But Mabel isn't coming down here just to be with me. She must've heard I had a great author staying here."

A great author! Myron felt suddenly excited. The famous Mabel Dodge Luhan, who a few days ago would not give him the time of day, was now going out of her way to meet him! She must've asked about me, he decided. She must've heard good things about me. Who knows? Maybe she's reading something of mine right now.

"I told you she'd be after you," said Cady when they were alone.

"How'd you know?" Myron asked.

"You're a young, good-looking writer," he explained. "She does things like that." He paused. "I think she must get very bored up there in Taos. She always has guests staying with her."

"What about her husband?"

"Well, from all I've heard, and I've only been here a year, Tony's often away at some pueblo or another. There's a lot going on now what with the New Deal for Indians and John Collier being appointed the head of Indian Affairs. Collier's an old friend of Mabel's from her salon on Fifth Avenue." Cady was suddenly annoyed. "You know I don't really like her."

"Why?"

"I think she's up to no good," he said. Then he smiled. "But you can take care of yourself. You're a big boy."

So two days later at a table set with silver and gold flatware, water, wine and champagne glasses, and gold-rimmed white china plates, Myron found himself seated next to Mabel Dodge Luhan.

"Does she have to make everything so formal?" were her first words to him. "I wanted to talk to you alone." And she jerked her square head petulantly toward the rest of the table. "All these people . . . what a bore!"

Myron realized her remark was meant to ally him with her against the "boring" others and he was put off. It was such obvious flattery, such a blatant tactic, he was cautious and decided to say as little as possible to her, which turned out to be easy because everyone else at the table seemed anxious to talk to her. It was Cady, at Myron's left hand, who explained who everyone was. It turned out most of the dinner guests were painters, many of whom had come to New Mexico at the turn of the century and were the real founders of the Taos artist colony. There was an older man named Blumenschein and his wife and daughter, and another named Phillips and his wife, and there was a younger Englishman, John Young-Hunter, and his wife. But the only one Cady seemed excited about was Andrew Dasburg.

"Andrew's my teacher," Cady whispered. "You must see his work."

Myron asked who the woman was next to him.

"That's his new wife, Marina. She's the daughter of Owen Wister."

Myron nodded and for the first time was impressed. *The Virginian* had been one of his favorite boyhood novels.

Then the food, served by young Mexican girls, came, and once again there was too much, though this time it was ranch food: T-bone steaks, mashed potatoes, Brussels sprouts. And this time Myron managed to restrain himself. So he felt good when they adjourned to the couches at the other end of the huge room where there were floor-to-ceiling bookcases filled with leather-bound books. Myron sat down opposite Mabel and was served Grand Marnier in a tiny crystal goblet. But before he took a sip she jumped up, stood before the walk-in fireplace, and asked the room if they wanted to play a game of Truth. Then she was looking at him. Was she doing it for him? Did she see him as a seeker of truth? Just a month ago he'd seen an Ivor Novello comedy called *The Truth Game* with Novello himself playing opposite Billie Burke. It was about social climbing and secrets only the English would find embarrassing.

"How do you play?" someone asked.

"You ask the one who's 'it' a personal question," Mabel explained, "to which they must give a truthful answer no matter how embarrassing."

Marie Garland, with the dignity of General Washington declining the American throne, refused to play. But others agreed if Mabel would go first. She nodded. Then someone asked for a trial run and she turned to Andrew Dasburg.

"I think he's one of her old lovers," Cady whispered.

"Andrew, why do you walk with a cane?"

Myron looked at Cady, who was suddenly squirming in his chair.

"You know very well, Mabel," said the embarrassed man.

She didn't say anything, just waited.

"When I was growing up in Manhattan," he began, "we lived in a tough neighborhood called Hell's Kitchen and I ran with a gang." His face twisted in real pain. "On weekends we'd break into construction sites looking for building materials to steal and sell." He paused again. Obviously he was embarrassed to admit this. "One time the police showed up. I was on a girder, and misstepped, and fell two floors onto the concrete foundation." He paused again, closing his eyes. When he opened them, he spoke. "I couldn't move," he said. "My hip was broken. The police brought me to

Bellevue. It never healed right. My right leg's been shorter than my left ever since, and seems as I get older to be getting shorter." He looked up. "That's why I use a cane."

"You're lucky to be alive," said Mabel.

"You knew the story," Dasburg said. "Why did you ask?"

"I heard someone say you used a cane to make people think you had a war wound. I wanted people to know the truth."

What a good person, Myron thought. That's why she suggested the game, to halt the slander. But the game had not yet begun. Mabel awaited the first question.

"Did you have a sexual relationship with D. H. Lawrence?" a man with a Russian accent asked. Cady identified him as Leon Gaspard, a painter and Russian émigré. The question was not as impertinent as it sounded. In *Lorenzo in Taos* Mabel claimed she'd had an intimate relationship with Lawrence, though she never made clear what form that intimacy took. It seemed to Myron that whatever it was, it wasn't sexual. On the other hand, her writing left a lot to the imagination.

"Oh, honestly!" she answered now as if she were tired of hearing the question. "Of course I did!"

There were meaningful glances from the men; sighs, even giggles, from the women. Everyone leaned forward waiting for some detail they could get their imaginations around.

"But then," she went on, "aren't most close relationships sexual? I mean when you love someone, don't you love everything about them, sex included?"

She's weaseling out, Myron judged, and found he was disappointed. Let me rephrase the question, he wanted to say and thought of jumping in. Did you or did you not have sex with D. H. Lawrence? Did he penetrate you? How many times? Did you have an orgasm? Did he? On the other hand, he thought, I don't care. And everyone else seemed too respectful or confused to press on. Then Leon Gaspard was asked whether or not he'd really studied with Matisse as he claimed and the game passed into the hands of the painters.

"Oh, she's so evil!" Cady exclaimed when they were back in the guesthouse. "Wasn't the Truth game awful?"

Myron looked at him. She'd done such a nice thing for Andrew

Dasburg. Cady had been so afraid for his teacher. What have you learned from him? Myron had asked. How to work, Cady answered after a long pause. He's taught me how to work. It sounded as if the word *work* could be replaced with something more basic like *see*. He's taught me how to see.

"Now, really!" Cady was going on. "Implying she had sex with Lawrence! If you read his letters, you know how much he detested the woman! He thought she was a willful, overbearing bitch!"

"Well," Myron said, "I didn't think I would like her but I do. She's very smart, very quick."

The most important thing to come out of Mabel's visit was that just before she left, she asked them to spend next weekend in Taos as her houseguests. Knowing Cady's feelings about her, Myron hesitated. But to his surprise, his new friend jumped right in and accepted for both of them. Later, when they were alone and Cady was still finding fault with her, Myron offered to call the whole thing off.

"Oh, no," said Cady. "No one refuses an invitation from Mabel, not even D. H. Lawrence."

She put them in an adobe she called the Santa Teresa House. There were three large rooms whose floors were covered with red saltillo tiles and whose ceilings were made of exposed, stripped logs that supported the roof. Between these logs, which were called *vigas*, were hundreds of sticks in a tight herringbone pattern. Outside, on the house's north end, was an enclosed patio whose east wall was decorated with a plaque made of several tiles depicting the stylized, haloed face of Santa Teresa. But the best thing about the house was the second-floor bedroom, whose single large window faced a meadow full of wildflowers. Yet, as beautiful as the place was, on their first night they had an uneasy feeling.

"I don't know whether it's her or Taos, or you putting ideas in my head," Myron said, "but I feel something . . . sinister up here. I can't explain it. It's as if she's out there at this very moment weaving some spell."

"Well, I wouldn't put it past her," said Cady, going to the door and jerking it open as though to surprise their hostess in mid-conjure.

There was only blackness and the sighing of the wind in the trees. They joked that if she had indeed been out there, a spider spinning a web, she had swiftly turned herself into something else, the toad they heard croaking or the hooting owl. So they went upstairs to the bedroom, blew out their oil lamp, and got into bed. Of course they weren't sleepy. So, lying side by side in darkness, Myron asked Cady about that first night at the Clark ranch when he'd gotten so drunk.

"You don't remember?"

"No."

"Do you remember me?"

"Er . . . not really."

Cady laughed.

"What did I do?"

"You danced."

"I remember that."

"You danced with me."

"With you?"

"Yes. We tangoed."

"To fiddle music?"

"Yes." Cady paused, then went on. "You sure know how to dip a guy."

They burst out laughing and when it was quiet, Myron moved his hand slowly down Cady's body and once again marveled at how small the man was, how close together everything was.

Next morning Mabel joined them in her dining room for coffee. They were surprised, for she had told them that she always took her breakfast in bed. In a white dress she seemed as innocent as a girl at her First Communion.

"Did you sleep well?" she asked.

"Quite well," Myron said.

"The air here is so pure and it's so quiet. I've never known anyone not able to sleep." She paused thoughtfully. "Oh, sometimes, when Tony isn't here, I worry he's been in an accident." Then she mentioned that she'd just finished reading *Singermann*. "Lawrence was from a mining town too," she reminded him.

Myron didn't know what to say so he asked after Tony.

She told them he was off attending to some political business in Arizona and wouldn't be back for their stay. Cady had wanted Myron to meet Tony. You'll like him, he said. He's not exactly salt of the earth, but close to it. Now Myron wondered what the couple saw in each other. And later that day when he and Cady were alone sitting at the picnic table beneath the tree in the center of the patio, Myron again asked if he thought Mabel loved her husband.

"I'm sure she did at the beginning," the painter said.

"But?"

"Well, I wonder if she isn't having regrets." Cady shrugged. "Of course that's just a hunch." He hesitated. "What about you two?" he asked. "She grabbed you after breakfast. What were you talking about?"

"Nothing really," said Myron. "She said something about me helping her with her memoir."

"You going to do it?"

"I told her I was leaving in a few days for Los Angeles."

"A few days?" Cady seemed stunned. "I didn't know it'd be that soon. I thought you'd come back to Marie's with me."

"I've got to make a living, Cady. My family doesn't own The American Optical Company." He paused and shrugged. "It seems to me only rich people can afford to live in Shangri-la."

"I thought your books made money."

"They do, a little, at least until *The Flutter of an Eyelid*." Myron had told Cady the fate of his last novel and how angry he was with Farrar & Rinehart. "Like most writers, I live on advances. That means I always owe my publisher money." Even before *The Flutter of an Eyelid*, Myron had hated the rut he'd gotten into. Unless he could come up with a bestseller and pay them back, he was their slave. "Anyway," he went on, "I told her I could stay if I had a place to live and work."

"What did she say?"

"She said I could stay here as long as I wanted."

"Here?"

"Yes. In this house." Myron paused. "I asked her if you could stay too and she said of course." He looked at Cady. "What do you say, Cady? Would you like to spend the summer with me?"

Cady's face brightened and Myron realized once again how much he liked the Martian's smile, the way his ears moved back and his eyes got narrow and catlike. Love from another planet, he thought.

"Well," Cady said, "I could do some work at the pueblo." He paused. "And, besides, if she's concentrating on you, she won't have much time for me." He paused again. "You know how I feel about her. She's in the same room with you, but when she leaves she's still there." He paused a third time. "We'll be like man and wife," he said, perking up. "But who will be whom?"

"Oh," said Myron, surprised Cady might think otherwise, "you'll be the woman, of course."

"No," Cady said and thrust out his lower lip in a pout. "That's not fair. I don't want to always be the woman. It's too much work."

"Okay," said Myron. "We'll take turns."

Cady nodded. "Monday, Wednesday, and Friday, I'll be the man. You can have Tuesdays, Thursdays, and Saturdays. We'll take Sundays off."

"It's a deal." Then Myron was serious. "I have to play the Truth game with you, Cady."

"What do you mean?"

"I mean there's something I have to tell you." He paused. "I'm not like you. I'm not a homosexual in the same way you are."

"What are you then?"

"I'm bisexual."

"I don't believe you."

"Well, you, who are sure of what you are, may find it hard to imagine but I sleep with women."

"You do?" asked Cady, amazed. "Do you enjoy it?"

"Not really. I mean it's not the same thing." He paused. "How can I explain it?" He paused again. "I like women. Sometimes I just need their company." He hesitated. He wanted to tell his new friend the truth. But it was hard when you didn't know what the truth was. "I'm not brave like you, Cady. I can't stand being singled out by society as a depraved human being." He shook his head. He wasn't saying it right. "I want to keep my options with women open," he said. "If the going ever gets too rough for men like us, I tell myself I can hide with them, that they'll take me in."

"Is that fair to them?"

"No," Myron admitted. "And it got me into all kinds of trouble when I was young and just beginning to realize what I was." Myron looked up. What do I want, he wondered. His approval?

"I've never denied who or what I am," said Cady thoughtfully. "I've had affairs and relationships. Some didn't last very long, but they were always more than . . . " Cady went silent as if mulling over what he'd gotten into.

"You know," said Myron, still trying to explain, "I used to tell myself I was exploring new sexual frontiers. At times I believed it. I used to tell myself if I got bored with one sex I could always escape on the spaceship between my legs and go looking for new planets to conquer. I even took to calling myself Buck Rogers. Let's go, Buck, I'd urge whenever I got into bed with a woman. This is the way love will be in the twenty-fifth century." He looked up. Cady seemed sad. I'm ruining it, Myron thought. But he couldn't seem to stop. "And for the first few days it . . . "

"How do you feel about me?" Cady interrupted.

"About you?"

"Yes."

"I think I'm falling for you and I'm doing my best not to." Myron paused and shook his head. Should he tell him about Frank Fenton? "I mean it's all happening so fast. I was just passing through on my way to LA and you showed up. Even at Marie's I thought it was only going to be for a few days. Even here it was only going to be a weekend. I was going to be on my way to Los Angeles. But now . . . "

"Let's go inside," Cady suggested.

"Mabel's asked if we want to go riding."

"I don't know how." Despite growing up in Montana, Myron

had never been on a horse. Butte wasn't really Montana anyway. In the Butte of his childhood horses drew trolley cars, vegetable wagons, and ore cars.

"Oh, c'mon, Mike." Cady had taken to calling him Mike. "It's nothing to be afraid of and it frees you up around here. With a horse you can go anywhere."

Still Myron hesitated. Not that he was afraid. He was just embarrassed that he might make an ass of himself or his horse might make a fool of him, or worse, he might be thrown and injured, if not killed. By god, he was afraid.

"Oh, come now," said Mabel a little later when they met beneath the *portal* outside her front door. "I'll give you a nice old mare. You won't have any trouble. But you must ride. It'll shake up your biliousness and sharpen your faculties. You'll see. You'll come alive."

Biliousness! Only she could use a word like that. Was it a judgment? Did she see bile as his governing humor? And so disarmed was he by her medieval psychology he went back to the Santa Teresa house, put on the denim dungarees and cowboy boots he'd bought in a Taos dry-goods store, and went back out to them. The horses were already in front of the house, saddled and ready to go. Cady and Mabel, both in jodhpurs and English riding boots, showed him how to mount from the left side. Once in the saddle Cady snapped his photo with the little camera he always carried. Then he too mounted and they were off, Myron's horse following the others, their shod hooves clicking on the stones of Mabel's plaza, then going quiet when they reached the dirt road that took them passed the *morada*, the tiny chapel that served the local Penitentes, where they turned left onto the county road, and walked east toward the mountain.

After a few hundred yards Cady dismounted to open a barbed-wire gate. Myron's horse followed Mabel's into a dry field dotted with piñon pine. The field, she said, belonged to the pueblo. Cady closed the gate, remounted, and he and Mabel kicked their horses into a trot. Myron's horse trotted also, and he found himself bouncing in the saddle, each quick equine step a spanking. So they waited for him and showed him how to post. He tried it and felt instantly more comfortable. But he could only do it for a while—

put his weight on the stirrups, lift himself out of the saddle, and miss the bone-jarring horse's hips. For his legs quickly grew tired and he had to stay down in the saddle and take his punishment.

And he marveled at their ability. That Cady rode well was no surprise. But Mabel! A woman associated with salons, villas, and famous names! She was galloping away, her short stiff hair bouncing from side to side, Cady after her, his wide-brimmed hat jammed down so hard his Martian ears stuck out. Soon they were aiming their mounts at creosote bushes and clumps of sage and jumping them at full gallop. So to keep them in sight, Myron kicked his mare as they had told him. She jumped into a gallop, a gait he instantly found more comfortable, as if his horse had no hips at all. He dashed after them, caught up, gave a loud whoop, and aimed his horse at a bush. The mare jumped and Myron instinctively shifted his weight forward.

"You all right?"

He was hanging on to the saddle horn that just a moment before had punched him in the solar plexis.

"Uuuuugh," he groaned.

They were on either side of him, Cady holding the reins and supporting him and Mabel lecturing him on the differences between English and Western saddles and what each was good for. Then they left him to catch his breath. He caught up with them at the top of the hill where they'd stopped to look down at Taos. Mabel was telling Cady about the houses—who lived where and who had built what.

"There's my house," she said, pointing, "and due west almost to the main road is the house Nicolai Fechin built. You'll have to see it. It's a showplace." She pointed again. "There's the Kit Carson cemetery. And on the corner there, near the plaza, is the Kit Carson house." She shook her head. "A terrible man," she said, turning to them, "an Indian killer." She turned back. "There, just a little to the north, is the Manby House. That's where I lived when I first came to Taos." She shook her head again. "We rented from Manby. He was a crazy Englishman who thought he was Cecil Rhodes."

"What do you mean?" asked Myron.

"He wanted to own everything. He almost succeeded. At one time he managed to get hold of the old Spanish land grant. He had the deed to the pueblo, the town of Taos, and the entire valley north to the junction of the rivers and west to the Grand Canyon of the Rio Grande."

"What happened to him?" asked Cady

"He ran out of money and lost it all." She shrugged and shook her head. "Men like that make too many enemies. In the end he was murdered, and his murderers were never found."

"That's a great story," said Myron.

"We'll have to go to Manby's Hot Springs," she said. "I usually go once a week. They're a delight." She paused. "But let's go back. It's time for lunch."

At lunch Mabel was once again fresh and dainty in a white dress, her hair bound with a pale blue ribbon. Again she was a girl just home from school.

"You did very well, Myron," she was saying. "You're going to like riding, only you mustn't hold the reins so tight, and you must never show you're frightened. If you do, they'll take advantage of you. You must show them you're the master."

"Even when you're almost unconscious?" Myron asked.

"Especially then," said Cady and laughed. Then he turned to Mabel. "But you're such a good rider," he said. "Did you learn out here?"

"No." She was shaking her head. "I've been riding since I was a girl. When I visited my grandmother, I would ride nearly every day in Central Park. New York was so lovely then." She paused, a frown coming over her face. "It's different now, so dirty and overcrowded."

"What made you come out here?" Myron asked.

"I wanted to get out of New York. I was tired of all that artificiality. I'd had it." She paused and furrowed her brow. "I used to sit in that house on Fifth Avenue and on those evenings when people came to sprawl about and discuss the state of the world, mostly to hear themselves talk, there were moments when I wanted to scream! Sometimes I'd order everybody out. Out!" she shouted now.

Myron glanced at Cady. Then she was calm again.

"Most often, I'd just get up and go to my room. I'd leave them talking about all those stale things: art, music, and politics and, of course, all the while they were eating the food I set out for them."

She paused, suddenly sympathetic. "Some of the poor things used to come just to eat. I knew they were on the edge of starvation, scraping along in some dismal furnished room in the Village."

"But that's the way I lived, Mabel," noted Myron. "I loved it. I came to New York in 1914 to attend NYU and lived in a different furnished room every year. I wish I had known about your parties. I could've used a good meal."

"I'm surprised you didn't hear," she said and laughed.

They thought she was done and began to eat. But she wasn't.

"To tell the truth," she went on, "I did enjoy some of the young people: Van Vechten, John Reed, the radicals, Emma Goldman and Bill Haywood. Now there was a man. No show about him, nothing theatrical, not a bit like the usual labor leader. He once took me to a meeting of the striking silk workers. They were talking about a child who'd been hurt when the police were clearing the street of picketers. Bill told them how one of the policemen struck down the boy's mother. He spoke just the bare facts without comment or color and without raising his voice. When he was done there was silence until someone asked the policeman's name. Edward Duffy, said Bill, badge 72. That was all he said but you knew Edward Duffy, badge 72, would be dealt with."

Myron was amazed. Bill Haywood had been one of the gods of his youth, and she'd been at his side when he was in his heyday.

"Bill spurned eloquence and soapbox platitudes," she went on. "He never gibbered about the brotherhood of man, the socialist commonwealth rising on the ruins of the capitalist system, death to the exploiters, and all the other clichés of ordinary labor agitators." She smiled at them. "Workers want simple, homely facts, and that's what he gave them."

"But how did you get out here?" Cady asked.

"Oh, one day, I was married to Maurice Sterne at the time, I said to him, 'Let's get out of all this. I'm choking on words. Let's go somewhere where we can see the sky!' So he found New Mexico and I followed and bought land and started building a house." She paused thoughtfully. "You know Maurice designed the house you're in."

"It's lovely," said Myron. Cady had told him about Maurice Sterne, a painter of some reputation and a Jew also.

"How many houses are there?" Cady asked.

"Oh, there's this house. Tony built this. And the Santa Teresa, and across the meadow the Pink House, where the Lawrences stayed when they came, and down the hill the Two Story House and the Tony House and the studio, and across town, the Placita house. There are five or six of them."

"And you've stayed here all this time?" Myron asked.

"Well, I go to California occasionally, Carmel, and back to New York. But I like them less and less. This is my home. I never want to live anywhere else again."

"Not even Europe?" Cady asked.

"Europe? Europe's finished!"

Myron had the impression she thought Europe was finished the moment she left.

"I've noticed in your bathrooms, your towels have the monogram: MDS," said Cady and smiled his best Martian mischief smile.

"Oh, there are lots of them," she said. "MDS, MD, MGS." She was smiling too, the same smile she'd smiled in Marie Garland's library when the painter had asked her if she had sex with D. H. Lawrence. Behind the sweetness was pride and defiance. "The other day I came across one with the initials ME," she added.

"ME?" asked Cady.

"Evans was my first husband's name. You haven't read *Background*, Cady?" *Background* was the first volume of her four-volume memoir. It had come out in March.

"Not yet." admitted Cady. "I mean to."

"I'll give him the copy you gave me," said Myron and smiled at Cady as if to say, you talked yourself into that one.

"I loved *Lorenzo in Taos*," Cady said, trying to make amends. "Was he really as powerful a personality as you describe?"

"Powerful? I guess so. Beautiful is a better word. He was the most beautiful person I ever knew." Now a look of girlish sweetness came over her face. "I don't mean beautiful in the usual sense. He was like a flame." She paused. "You know he wasn't at all good-looking. But he photographed well." She pushed back her chair and stood. "I'm done," she said. "And when I finish eating, I like to get up."

And they saw that though she'd been doing most of the talking, her plate was empty. Somehow she'd managed to eat her salad without them noticing. Their plates were still full.

"So many times I've been trapped at someone's house after a meal, and people continue to sit endlessly talking. It drives me mad. When I sit down to eat, I eat. When I've finished, I get up." She smiled and turned, then turned back. "I'll see you both at six for drinks. We'll have dinner at seven. Promptly. I always have a nap at three. I suggest you do the same."

They watched her hurry up the steps that led out of the dining room, a child rushing off. No longer young, she was youthful. Spud Johnson, her secretary and main help with her memoir, had warned them about her moods and how quickly they changed. Youth, he said, is the worst because it's the fastest. Spud had been at Mabel's table last night. After she went to bed they'd invited him over to the Santa Teresa for a drink. A poet, he was known more for his humor magazine, *The Laughing Horse*, than for his verse. Myron had met him once in the mid-twenties at a publisher's party when Spud was working for a then-new magazine called *The New Yorker*. Though he didn't remember the meeting, Spud said he'd read *Singermann* and *This Man Is My Brother* and loved them. Good enough, Myron thought, and decided he liked the man. At the end of the evening Spud suggested they drive down to Santa Fe on Saturday afternoon for drinks at Hal Bynner's. He wants to meet you, Spud explained. Myron asked if that was the poet, Witter Bynner. Yes, said Spud, but everybody calls him Hal. Oh let's, said Cady. You'll like him.

Two

"HOLA!" SHOUTED SPUD TO THE TALL MAN in the bright blue Chinese robe advancing toward them.

"Hola!" answered the man, and when he reached Spud they wrapped their arms around each other. Then the tall man turned to Cady and engulfed him in blue silk. "Long time no Cady," he said. "Good of you to come."

"This is Myron Brinig," said Spud. "Myron, this is Hal Bynner."

"Glad to meet you, Mr. Brinig." Hal extended his hand. "I've read so much of your work I feel I know you."

"Then call me Myron," said Myron and they shook hands.

"C'mon up," Hal said, and he led them single file up the path through the prickly pear and under the trellises full of sweet-smelling roses. Inside Myron and Cady were introduced to the man waiting there. Bob Hunt, Hal's new secretary, extremely handsome and at least twenty years younger than Hal, was handing out whiskey and soda.

"Myron, before I forget," said the poet, "I want you to sign something for me." And he led Myron to a table on which lay a copy of *The Flutter of an Eyelid*.

"Where'd you get this?" asked Myron, picking the book up.

"I had the Villagra save it for me."

"You read it?" Myron asked in spite of himself. The question always sounded like begging.

"Yes and I loved it," said Hal. "It's *South Wind* set in Malibu. And some of it's about people like us."

"It's all about people like us," said Myron.

"So what happened?"

"A woman in LA thought she saw herself in it and brought suit."

"Farrar & Rinehart wouldn't go to bat for you?"

"No."

"Was it her?"

"The person I took the character from was a man. It was Farrar & Rinehart who asked me to change the gender."

"So they knew who the character was and still wouldn't defend you?"

"That's right. They'd rather take the loss than admit they had published a novel about homosexuals."

"Would you sign it?" Hal asked, offering a silver Waterman fountain pen.

"I signed my first contract with one of these." Myron smiled, opened his book to the title page, wrote on it, and handed it and the pen back to Hal.

"'To a toiler in the field,'" Hal read. "'May the time come when words are not crimes.'" Hal looked up. "Thank you, Myron."

"C'mon, Hal," said Bob Hunt, coming up behind them. "Don't keep him all to yourself."

"Coming," Hal said, and Myron felt tension between Hal and Bob. Had they come at a bad time? Might be interesting.

"You know, Myron," Hal was saying, "I read your very first story." They were all sitting now, Cady on the couch with Myron, Hal in an armchair, Spud in the other armchair, and Bob on the floor,

"You read 'The Synagogue?'" Myron's first published story appeared in 1924 in *Munsey's Magazine.*

Hal nodded.

"How'd you get hold of that?"

"Bob Davis told me to read it," Hal said.

"What's it about?" asked Cady.

"The battle between a father and a son over what religion really is," Hal said. "It's the forerunner of *Singermann.*"

"How do you know Bob Davis?" asked Myron.

"Back in 1902, when I was fresh out of college, I was hired as poetry editor at *McClure's*. Bob Davis was at *Munsey's*."

"I love Bob. He was much more than an editor to me," said Myron, happy to give his old friend some credit. "He literally kept me alive. In 1921 he got me my first New York job. I was a reader at the Selznick Fort Lee studio. And in 1927 he introduced me to John Farrar and Stanley Rinehart when they were still at Doubleday."

"Never heard of him," said Bob Hunt. In the car, Spud had described Bob as being not only pretty but also a talented poet, and very outspoken. He's a handful, warned Spud. He doesn't let Hal get away with anything.

"Among other things," Hal explained to his secretary, "Bob Davis was O. Henry's editor. In fact, he picked O. Henry out of the gutter. William Porter was an ex-con, a drunk." Hal turned back to Myron. "Did you know that Bob Davis was also a lyricist and collaborated with Paul Dresser on some of his best songs?"

"No," said Myron, amazed he didn't know this about his mentor.

"Who's Paul Dresser?" asked Bob Hunt.

"Theodore Dreiser's brother," said Hal, "and Tin Pan Alley's first great songwriter."

"Never heard of him. What's he done lately?"

"He's dead," Hal said with almost mock sadness. Then he stood and walked out of the room. Myron looked at Bob, who shrugged. Then they heard a piano arpeggio, then Hal's voice. "They call her frivolous Sal." He strummed a chord. "A peculiar sort of a gal." He strummed another.

"With a heart that was mellow," sang Myron even before he reached the doorway through which Hal had disappeared. It turned out to be a dining room with an alcove big enough to contain a six-foot Steinway. "An all round good fellow." In another moment all the guests were around the piano singing. "Was my gal, Sal."

"Did Bob really write the words to that?" asked Myron after a second chorus.

"No," Hal admitted and laughed, "but it's the only Dresser song I know."

"How about this?" Myron sat down beside the poet. "Oh, the

moonlight shines tonight upon the Wabash." He struck a C Major chord, the only key he could play in. "From the fields there comes a breath of new mown hay." He played chords in his left hand and octaved the melody with his right. They were all singing again, Hal harmonizing. "On the banks of the Wabash far away."

"Do you know who wrote the words to that?" asked Myron when it was over.

No one answered.

"His brother," said Myron.

"Really?" asked Spud. "Theodore Dreiser?"

"That's right," said Hal. "I forgot." Then he changed the subject. "How's Bob's sister?" Bob Davis had an invalid sister he lived with.

"Gone almost two years," said Myron.

"Sorry to hear that. But what's he doing now?"

"He took it hard. He quit editing and dropped his *Sun* column. I don't know what he's doing. Traveling, I think."

Hal shook his head, then stood and raised his glass: "To Bob Davis!" he toasted. "Unsung hero of American literature!" And he downed his remaining whiskey and soda.

So they all raised their glasses. "To Bob Davis!" they toasted and downed their drinks. Then, without warning, Bob Hunt threw his glass into the kiva. So they all did, except Hal.

"Gee Bob," he said obviously regretting the loss of his property, "he wasn't that good a friend."

Then they were laughing and Myron was telling Hal how much he loved his work, particularly his *Spectra* poems.

"Are you serious?"

"Absolutely. I fell for it hook, line, and meter."

"Fell for what?" asked Cady.

"*Spectra*," answered Myron and explained. "It was supposed to be a spoof of all the stupid poetry schools that came along before the war: Vorticists, Imagists, Futurists." He turned to Hal. "Who was the other poet with you?"

"Arthur Ficke," said Hal. "He wrote our manifesto announcing a new kind of writing dictated to us in our sleep by poets from the spirit world. We used false names. I was Emanuel Morgan. He was Anne Knish."

"What happened?" asked Cady.

"The worst."

"You were found out?"

"No. We were taken seriously."

"You were by me," said Myron.

"Are you kidding?" asked Hal, still not sure Myron was serious.

"I loved 'em. When was *Spectra* published, 1916? In 1917 I went into the army and took your book with me. In my spare time, I memorized a bunch. I can still recite 'em."

Myron used to memorize poetry all the time. Someone once told him that Karl Marx had memorized the entire Bible just for mental exercise. Myron couldn't do that kind of intellectual weight lifting. He had to love a poem to memorize it. But that was years ago and he wouldn't have made such a claim now if he hadn't come across *Spectra* in Mabel's library and refreshed his memory. Now like a chanteuse, he stood in the bend of the piano. "Opus 40," he announced.

Two cocktails round a smile,
A grapefruit after grace,
Flowers in an aisle
. . . Were your face.

There was applause and pleas for more.

A strap in a street car,
A sea-fan on the sand,
A beer on a bar,
. . . Were your hand.

"More! More!"

The pillar of a porch,
The tapering of an egg,
The pine of a torch,
. . . Were your leg.

"No more! No more!"

Sun on the Hellespont
White swimmers in the bowl

Of the baptismal font
. . . Were your soul.

"Are your soul!" Hal corrected, then laughed. Cady went to the piano and began playing the George M. Cohan rouser "Over There." Myron had no idea Cady could play. Then the little Martian began to sing. "Were your haaaand! Were your leeeeg! Were your face! O the Spectrists are coming! The Spectrists are coming! The Spectrists are coming everywhere!"

Then Cady, Hal, and Myron, in his by-ear octave-and-chord way, were taking turns at the piano playing and singing popular songs. And when that flagged, Cady began playing a Brahms sonata. Myron was amazed. It was so unexpected and beautiful he felt near tears. They were all sitting around the empty dining room table listening. When Cady stopped, Hal took over and played Chopin. Only after Bob Hunt insisted that dinner was getting ruined did the music stop. They filed into the kitchen for bowls of Bob's chile while from the oven Hal took tortillas and from the icebox, sour cream, chives, and tomatoes. They brought the food out to the dining room table. The last course was sopaipillas with honey and coffee. Then they were sitting and smoking.

"It's beauty that saves the world," said Hal, apropos of nothing.

"Even for people like us?" Myron asked.

"You means homos?" asked Bob.

"I hate that word," said Spud. "It's supposed to make us feel ashamed."

"We are ashamed," said Bob. "That's what the closet we're in is all about: lies, denials, disguises, and double entendres that allow us to express our sexuality by pretending it doesn't exist." He paused, thoughtful, then went on. "We do it because we don't have any rights. What we do to show affection and love is against the law."

"Good point," said Myron. "And the only way to change the law is to change the minds of the people who make it. And the only way to do that is to make them look at us and see that what we do is normal and human. It's what I tried to do in *This Man Is My Brother* and *The Flutter of an Eyelid.*"

For the first time a smile crossed Bob's face. It must have

seemed to him he had an ally in Myron. But none of them would have disagreed.

"You said you wanted to try a poem on us," said Hal in the silence that followed the seriousness.

Bob nodded, got up from the table, went out, and came back with a manuscript.

"Don't worry. I'm just going to read one," he said. "It's called 'Lesson Before Love.'"

Myron expected the worst. Men this pretty were not meant to write poetry. And he remembered his recent experience with Marie Garland. Bob began.

Oh, let the long flame fly upon your years
Or let it die!

Myron hated poems that began with *Oh* and he always filled in the word *shit* before the next word was spoken. But he wasn't quick enough tonight so he jumped on the end of the line instead. Okay, he thought, let it die.

It was not meant to last within these limits
Of lean love—
Or tears now suckled by quick hope.

Now that's not bad.

So let the cold
creep between the flame and crave the war
This is the mind's desire—
There is no light in any lovely name
The sun cannot darken
Or the night make fire.

"So let the cold creep between the flame and crave the war," Myron repeated aloud. "This is the mind's desire—There is no light in any lovely name the sun cannot darken or the night make fire."

"You really can memorize fast," noted Cady.

"When it's that beautiful." He turned to Bob. "Would you read us more?"

Obviously pleased by Myron's praise, Bob was smiling broadly. "I promised I'd only do one."

"Oh c'mon," urged Hal harshly. "One more won't kill you."

"No!" Bob snapped.

"Anybody home?" called a voice from the living room.

"Lynn!" Hal shouted and jumped up. "We're back here!"

A thin man in jeans, a flannel shirt, and neckerchief appeared in the doorway carrying a guitar. In another moment Myron was shaking hands with the playwright Lynn Riggs, whom he'd met once in the Village. Myron had seen *Green Grow the Lilacs* a few months before and thought it beautiful. When he told Lynn Riggs this, the party began again with Lynn singing Oklahoma cowboy songs. Then some of Lynn's friends came by. They were dressed as cowboys and in a while they were all square-dancing in the middle of Hal's living room, Hal doing the calling in an English accent.

Then things got muddled. Myron knew that at the end he must have gotten out of hand because he remembered Cady and Spud hustling him out to the station wagon. It had to do with, of all things, his third novel, *Anthony in the Nude*. Someone brought up the fact that its main female character was an older woman who ran a literary salon in her New York apartment. He asked Myron if he'd modeled her on Mabel. It was an honest question. But it was asked in an accusatory way, as if the man had found Myron out, as if Myron had done something underhanded. *Anthony in the Nude* was published in 1930, he answered. I only met Mabel Dodge Luhan last week. But he saw the smirk on the man's face. If I had modeled her on Mabel, he went on, she might have been a better character. Actually he loved the character and loved *Anthony in the Nude*, the story of an affair between a silly older woman and a vain young man. The critics had universally damned it as being at best in bad taste. You don't like my novel, he said some time later to the questioner. No, I don't, the man said. You're entitled to your opinion, Myron conceded, but then he added that in his opinion there was nothing worse than a prudish, cock-sucking fag.

∽

Yet he had a good time. For one thing, he'd discovered Cady's hidden talent. Now whenever they went up to the Big House, he asked his friend to play Mabel's Steinway. It turned out Cady had once thought seriously of being a concert pianist.

"What made you choose painting?"

"I love to make things. I hope I made the right choice. I play now just for myself and my friends. There's no pressure."

"You made the right choice," Myron assured him. "I love your playing, but I love your painting more. It's so different. It's modern, yet very old—as old as some kind of ancient writing. But it's hard to talk about. What kind of an artist do you think you are?"

"I'm not sure," Cady admitted, "but I know what I want to be."

"What?"

"A truly Western artist."

"What do you mean?"

"Well, I don't want to be just another European painting Western subjects. That's why I'm interested in the Orient. To me the natives here are still somehow tied to their oriental ancestors. I want to paint this land their way."

"You know, I watched you painting the other day," Myron said. He'd taken time off from his new novel and gone with Cady into the Rio Grande gorge. "Your lines were so meaningful, I felt you writing. I remember looking away to what you were painting and when my eyes came back you'd painted a curve much softer than the others. I didn't see you paint it and I felt I'd missed something. I wanted to ask how you did it."

"I know which line you mean," said Cady, obviously pleased Myron had noticed something so minute about his work. Then he paused and looked serious. "Point your index finger," he said after a moment.

Myron pointed his right index finger.

"Now close your eyes and imagine you're stroking the neck of a goose."

Myron closed his eyes, stroked the downy curve in his mind and felt the line his finger made in the air.

"That's the way it feels to paint that line," Cady said.

God, Myron thought, if only writing could be taught that way, and once again he had cause to admire his new friend. Then somehow they got onto the subject of feminine and masculine lines, and that led to the subject of Cady's own femininity, which Myron admitted he sometimes found embarrassing.

"The swish factor," Cady said and laughed. "It's been a problem all my life." He paused. "Not for me," he added, "but for other people, like my father. One time one of my aunts told him that she thought I behaved like a sissy so he took me out back to the garage and acted as if he'd give me a whipping. But even then I was taller than him and I think he thought better of it. All he ended up doing was slapping my face and telling me to act like a man."

Martians are very short, Myron noted.

"I didn't cry or anything. I just said I'd try, but I kept thinking I didn't want to be like him or any of the men in my family." Cady's smiled broadened. "I wanted to be like Gypsy Rose Lee and pretend I was stripping when I wasn't."

"You couldn't have thought that," said Myron. "Gypsy Rose Lee was a little girl when you were a little boy."

Cady shrugged.

"So what happened then?" asked Myron.

"I was sent off to a school in Arizona where boys live outdoor lives and learn to shoot, play football, and are yanked out of bed at six in the morning to do calisthenics. But nothing helped. Whatever my father hoped for, I was what I was, though I learned to ride and shoot and could outrun anyone else in the school."

"You are a great athlete," Myron noted and licked his lips.

"I remember one day in a race I ran so fast I lost my trunks. Afterward, the coach told me I had the prettiest ass he'd ever seen."

"A perceptive man," said Myron.

"A pervert," Cady said. "He was very masculine, but he had a way of looking at you as if he were sizing you up. One day I was passing the bungalow where he lived, and I happened to look through a window. There he was naked in front of a mirror shaving his pubic hair."

"What!"

"He was shaving his pubic hair. Anyway, he must've seen me in the mirror because he turned around. I ran away as fast as I could. A few days later I was expelled as a peeping Tom. Can you imagine? They expelled the best horseman, best shot, and fastest runner because he'd seen a real man shaving his pubic hair."

"Why was he doing that?"

"I don't know. It had something to do with sex, I'm sure. I know it made an impression on me. The first time I ever picked up a paintbrush I thought of that track coach and his razor. Sometimes it still pops into my mind when I paint."

"Is that what painting's like for you?" and Myron couldn't help smiling, "shaving pubic hair? I think I like stroking the neck of a goose better."

"Don't laugh. Think of it. You have this instrument in your hand and it's very sharp and intimate and you're going to change the way things look with it."

"What happened when you got home?"

"There was hell to pay from my father, but this time he didn't haul me back to the garage. He simply sent me off to Milton Academy near Boston. It was co-ed. He had some idea that with girls around, I'd change. Of course I didn't. I fell in love with a boy on the same floor of our dorm and we were discovered in bed together by some snoop and I was expelled again. I dreaded going home so I took a train to New York and applied for a job as a chorus boy in a musical."

"Did you get it?"

"Nah. Aside from the fact that I couldn't dance, I was much too young. And my father found out where I was and brought me home. I'll never forget what he said. He held up the letter he'd gotten from the headmaster and said that if he ever heard of me doing anything like that again, he'd kill me."

"How'd your mother feel about it? Did she defend you?"

"Oh, my mother's not much of a fighter," Cady answered, then added, "though who knows what was said when I wasn't around. But she's always been understanding. We adore each other." He paused and looked thoughtful. "Maybe too much. Even when we're not together, we're terribly close. It's impossible to describe the feeling, but I seem to know what she's thinking even when we're thousands of miles apart. It's amazing. I know when she's ill or when she's unhappy. I'll be painting or at a party and, out of the blue, I'll know she wants to talk to me, so I stop whatever I'm doing and rush off to get her on the phone. It's as if we've got the same heart and brain. That's frightening, too, because I wonder how I'll feel when she dies. I see myself in a baggage car, riding beside her coffin. Somehow that's the saddest thing I can think of, a baggage car with a coffin inside."

"That is sad," Myron agreed. "Is she a sad person?"

"Not at all. After I left New England I lived in New York and studied to be a set designer with Norman Bel Geddes. I was lousy but I gave good parties, and if my mom happened to be visiting, she'd join in and laugh and dance and camp with us. I think she was telling me it was my life and she loved me whatever I did." He paused. "When did you first know what you were?"

"Well, when I was a boy about ten I had a sexual experience with one of my brothers. I'm the youngest of six brothers and two sisters, and that meant we had to double up in our sleeping arrangements. One night when I was about nine I woke up and found Ike on top of me, pushing up against me and moaning. I didn't understand what was going on and tried to get away but he was too big. Then I realized he was still asleep. I was frightened. I'd never seen such need. He was moaning and pushing. But I didn't cry out. I think I wanted to see what would happen."

"What happened?"

"He came all over my stomach, then rolled off me still fast asleep."

"What did you do?"

"What could I do? I wiped myself with the sheets, turned over, and went back to sleep."

"That's a great scene."

"It was in one of my first stories."

"But when did you first realize what you were?"

"Not until I got to college. Not until New York."

"That late?"

"I was very repressed. But I had this friend, Rodney Ivers, a tall skinny guy from upstate New York. We called him Rod. Anyway, we were two hick misfits and found each other right away. We had a good time together. Once we took a trolley all the way to Philadelphia and back. You could do that then. And we went all over the city. But after a while I noticed that whenever there were girls around, Rod could hardly contain himself. 'Isn't she something?' or 'Look at the legs on that one.' You know the type. Another thing about him was that he was very poor and never had enough to eat. One day we were coming back from the Bronx Zoo and he fainted on the subway. When he came to I asked him if he'd had anything to eat and he said he'd forgotten. So I asked if he wanted to get something and that I'd treat and he said he couldn't, that he had an appointment. Turned out his appointment was at a whorehouse in Chelsea. Then he got the idea of taking me along. He said he had a girl for me who was smart and loved to read. I was flabbergasted. I used to sell newspapers in Butte's red-light district so I knew about whores. But I never thought of going to one. So there I was in a little room covered with red wallpaper in bed with a prostitute."

"Really?"

"Yep. She was a skinny thing, sick with TB, smoking and coughing. But Rod was right. She was smart and picked me out right away as not interested. Instead of having sex we talked, first about books, then about Rod. She said he was the sexiest guy she'd ever met, that he'd rather screw than eat, and that he had the largest member she'd ever encountered. You could tell how much she liked him. Here was a whore who'd seen it all, and she still could get excited over just the thought of him. In fact, she was so good at describing her excitement that without realizing it, I began to lust after him too. I was so repressed, so locked up, that that was the first time I ever consciously lusted after a man. It got so bad I couldn't bear to be around him."

"What happened?" asked Cady.

"Nothing. After Christmas he didn't come back to school."

"Did you ever see him again?"

"No. But I got a card from him saying he'd shipped out. He'd told me he wanted to do that. He wanted to write about the sea. He made me read Joseph Conrad. Two years later when the *Lusitania* was torpedoed, someone said he went down with it, but that may not be true. We wanted everyone to be heroes then."

"That's a great story," said Cady.

~

During the last weekend in May, Mabel gave a dinner for her only child, John Evans, who was visiting from Maine. The product of

Mabel's first marriage, he'd recently had his first novel come out to good reviews. But that wasn't the occasion. The year before John had divorced Alice Henderson, whom he'd married when she was only sixteen. Now he'd brought his future wife, the novelist Claire Spencer, home to meet his mother. Along with her usual dinner guests, Myron, Cady, and Spud, Mabel had invited Tinka Fechin and Marie Garland, and Marie had brought her new suitor, a small man in his sixties named Alan. Once again Tony was away. Yet he was there in spirit, or at least in the flesh of the delicious venison steaks that Mabel said he'd shot the week before. After dinner they adjourned to the living room, where Mabel suggested they play Truth. Myron glanced at Cady. It was an odd suggestion for the occasion.

"How's John in bed?" Mabel asked her prospective daughter-in-law, who had volunteered to go first.

Born in Scotland, Claire Spencer seemed reserved, even prudish. But Myron had read her first novel, *Gallows Orchard*, about a spunky girl from a small village who is eventually lynched by the villagers for acting on her ideas of sexual freedom. If Claire was shocked by the question, she didn't show it.

"Kind, considerate, and very exciting," she answered.

"Just like he is as a son," said Mabel and everyone laughed, trying to ignore and at the same time acknowledge the incestuous double entendre. Myron remembered that in *European Experiences* Mabel admitted to not being a loving parent. But she rationalized her coldness toward her son by suggesting John had an Oedipal passion for her. Being a good parent, she said, meant pushing him away.

"Does that answer your question, Mabel?" Claire asked.

Mabel hesitated, then nodded and released her future daughter-in-law. So it was Claire's turn. But she passed, pleading lack of any personal knowledge of the people in the room.

"I'd like to make a suggestion," said Myron. "Instead of playing the game as if we're in a courtroom cross-examining each other, why don't we write our observations on paper? Just pick out someone and write down what you think about them." He saw that if the game continued in this good-natured way, nothing would come of it, and he would have to take over. The last time they played, people had complained about his questions. "In a paragraph we'll describe as truthfully as we can what we think of some other person in the room."

"That's a wonderful idea," Mabel said and broke into a big smile. "There are paper and pencils in my study." She was out of the room before anyone had time to disagree, and, in another instant, was back handing out sheets of typing paper and pencils. Then she resumed her place on the chaise and looked at Myron. "Are there any rules?" she asked.

"No," Myron said. "Just pick a person in the room, tell what you think of them and do it as wittily and as truthfully as you can."

"The truth?" asked Marie Garland doubtfully.

"The truth," Myron answered. "But with wit."

"I don't know," said Marie and looked at her date.

"Oh c'mon, Marie," Mabel urged. "It might be the beginning of a group novel." At dinner she'd remarked on how many writers were at the table and seemed as pleased as punch.

"Does it have to be someone here?" asked Claire.

"If you don't do someone here," answered Mabel, "there's no risk in it."

"And you've got to read them aloud," Myron added.

"C'mon," urged Mabel, "let's go."

One by one they began to write. Of course Mabel was done first. She'd jumped right into it and scribbled like crazy. Myron, though he hated writing longhand, was also done quickly. Claire and John took a little longer, Cady, a calligrapher, longer still, and Marie even longer. Her beau, however, wasn't writing at all. When Mabel chided him he took a paper from his jacket pocket and said he'd already written something. Sitting at Spud's feet, Tinka Fechin scrawled in Cyrillic what everyone assumed would be a declaration of love for Spud. Spud, trapped in his chair, wrote quickly also. Would it be a plea for her to leave him alone? Did he have nerve enough to do that in front of all these people?

"Who wants to go first?" Mabel asked.

"I do," said Alan. "I never thought I'd get to read this aloud." He put on reading glasses and began. "Marie has crystallized." He paused, letting the observation sink in, then went on. "Holding her head up firmly for so long has stopped the circulation of her spinal fluid. She couldn't unbend now if she wanted to. But this doesn't matter for she has long since forgotten the pleasure of unbending." He paused again, looked at his subject, and continued. "Frozen on her face is an expression of kindness and tolerance, which, however, is belied by the watchful, suspicious child inside her, who from time to time rises and looks out of Marie's faded eyes. The child is dying in her prison. But Marie won't release her."

Again Alan looked at Marie. The mistress of her country was nodding grandly as if approving everything he was saying about her. He went on.

"Marie, studiously mature, more queenly and more stupid than any queen that ever lived, is sometimes taken unawares by scary thoughts that the malicious child is going to kill her. Marie's brain looks like last year's wasp's nest, dry and untenanted, and when unwelcome thoughts happen to fly into it, they rattle around its empty chambers until they die of exhaustion. Something is lacking in her life, these dying thoughts tell her. But what? She has pewter, curly maple, two pianos, three Victrolas, records, gardens, patios, beasts of burden, cars, trucks, and small boats. Yet her mind, ever counting, wonders how, with all this, it could still feel something was lacking. What was it? And the vengeful little girl answers. Not enough husbands! Not enough husbands."

Alan looked up and smiled impishly. He was done.

"Very good," said Mabel.

Hell, thought Myron. It was wonderful, He looked at Marie. Her face revealed nothing. A mask on the dollar bill.

"Do you want to go next, Marie?" he asked.

Marie nodded, her back as straight as Alan described it, her breasts, whose ups and downs Myron had found so amusing, now at mid-height, a kind of mournful half-mast. She removed the glasses she was wearing, found another pair draped about her neck, and put them on. Myron had never seen anyone with one pair of glasses for writing, another for reading.

"Alan quivered," she began. "His whole life was just one long quiver. Whenever he spoke, no matter if it was only about the price of beans, his voice trembled and his eyes filled with tears. He was 'sensitive.' Not sensitive about people or ideas or life or anything, but just sensitive, like an old peach or plum that's ready to burst and run all over your hand, an old piece of fruit that must not be dropped, a plum that's too far gone to be eaten!"

Marie looked up and removed her glasses. Obviously these two had had some kind of argument before they arrived and Myron was about to say that was very good and ask who wanted to go next when Marie put her first pair of glasses on while on her half-mast bosom, she laid the pair she had just used.

"Alan tries to keep himself together with many small pleasures. Corona after corona is destroyed for the perfume that is forever rising from his blurred mouth. His short fingers continually wrap around a glass of liquor he thinks renews him. He babbles lyrically about foreign food in confidential undertones, a hint of passionate excitement in his voice. And when he's talking to you he likes to repeat your name. His voice reaches out and holds you by your lapels while a gentle polish exudes upon his face, the faint phosphorescence of decay. He struggles feebly in a net he's been weaving about himself. In a few years, when he's faded away, he'll leave a mildly unpleasant odor."

Where had this come from? Myron wondered. It was by far Marie's best writing. He looked at Alan. Like Marie moments before, Alan was nodding in masochistic agreement. He seemed to be saying, yes my dear, we know each other. Myron turned to Mabel. She was beaming, her eyes darting with excitement. Once again something was happening in her house. It was a miracle. People she thought long dead were coming to life. And they hadn't even gotten to the professional writers yet.

"Claire," asked Myron, "would you like to go again?"

Claire nodded. She could have demurred. She'd already gone. But Myron had caught something out of the corner of his eye, her head coming forward, and guessed she wanted to go. She'd written quickly. Now she spoke quickly.

"John wondered when they could leave," she began, "but he knew it would not be soon. The big hot log was still almost whole and they could not go until it burned out and fell. That was the rule, so he turned to his new wife. Claire is so fine, sensitive, and beautiful, he thought, I must protect her from this harsh company. He believed this and didn't know that his need to believe he protected her came from his own need of protection. He would never admit this, though he felt vaguely something else, that somewhere in him there was fineness and sensitiveness and beauty that he'd buried long ago and that he longed to get at now."

She paused but didn't look up. She seemed to be mulling over what she'd just read and Myron thought she might start rewriting. Or perhaps she was reading ahead, doing some last-minute editing, for he could see there was more on her page. Whatever she was doing, they waited. It wasn't long.

"It seemed to John that what he needed was just out of reach, over there near Mother. But until he could secure this possession of himself, protection was the game he must play. Yet the question remained: How would he find the quiet spot in the vortex of his life, the spot where peace resided? It was his tragic mistake to assume quietude was some place, and only he was missing it, that others had it and were keeping it from him. Now he clung with his eyes to the mythical girl beside him and imbued her with the qualities he needed to discover in himself while the great whir and fluster of life dizzied him and made him weak."

She looked up. The room seemed to be waiting for more, but there wasn't more. Then, without being called on, John began to read.

"Claire smiles ironically. She wishes her nose were straighter and that she could deal with things. But something always stops her when she wants to move. Ice flowing in the climate of her northern soul hedges her round and only John's small fire warms her. She doesn't want to be cruel. It's so hard and tiresome to be cruel. But she has no choice. Surging contempt rises like gall in her throat as she sits pensive in velvet and controls the expression of her eyes. My soul hurts, she tells herself. My soul is an ache and a loss and deadly to me. Where shall I lay the burden of this wound I call my soul?"

John was said to look like his father, who'd died in a hunting accident just before John was born. When Myron had remarked on her son looking like an Indian, Mabel said that many people in Buffalo did, that there was a lot of Indian blood in the settlers there. But Myron found his articulateness surprising. Have to read his book, he thought.

"Then Claire remembers that she'll write three thousand words in the morning and paint three dark panels of memory on her boudoir doors. This remembrance brings patience and she knows she'll be able to endure these people, though she envies Mabel, who seems to be having fun, whatever that is. Claire has heard of fun. She turns to John, her future husband, as if to ask what it is."

There was a momentary silence, then laughter and then applause. Mabel was smiling broadly, even proudly. Her son and the woman he had brought had handled both her and each other with wit and kindness. She turned to Myron.

"You next," he said to her before she could call on him. She nodded back, took up her paper, put on reading glasses, and began.

"Myron thought well of this Truth game idea. He took an almost professional interest in Truth, not so much for its own sake, as for the sake of some book, for Myron wrote books with all the earnestness other people wrote checks. In fact, writing books was a kind of check-writing for Myron. He spent himself that way. Literature was his Stock Exchange and he had a Seat on it. He had a secret feeling that God might be able to make a tree, but only Myron could make a book, and he was so busy making them, he never had time for trees and such like. He left all that to God and women and the dogs while he refueled himself every night with hard drink."

She looked up.

"Is that it?" asked Myron.

Mabel nodded.

"No wonder you were done first."

"But she's got you, Mike," said Cady and giggled.

Myron smiled and nodded. Then it was silent and it was obvious they expected him to go next.

"We haven't heard from Spud," he said.

"I'm a professional," said Spud. "I'm not sure I want to give my stuff away." As he spoke he moved his feet, accidentally kicking Tinka's elbow. She moaned. Was it pain or pleasure? Whatever it was, he didn't apologize.

"Oh come on, Spud," urged Myron. "We're all professionals."

"I'm not," said Alan. "I want to keep my amateur status. I'm going to enter the writer's Olympics. Long distance meanness."

"You're certainly mean enough," said Marie. "So far yours was the worst."

"That's it," said Spud. "You sure know how to make a writer read, Marie. I've got to beat your boyfriend." He lifted his paper and began.

"Oh, Gosh! Cady's thinking, I suppose this is life and everything, but why can't these women keep their eyes still. Cady feels fretted but significant, as though borne on strong wings which turn out to be his own, for his face is like a little angel's, though drink makes his innocent eyes into crushed flowers."

"Crushed flowers?" asked Cady. "Don't you mean crossed flowers?" He crossed his eyes. There was laughter. When it died, Spud went on.

"Yet he has a hidden strain of steel in him that provides a framework for his friend, the protean Myron, who really has no form of his own to hold him up and has never bothered to get one from Heaven or make one for himself, being so busy writing books. So Cady holds him up. The little angel has a fine, strong structure for Myron to lean on, an open cage to run up and down in, and that's what keeps him from leaking away as he might so easily do after so many pages a day." Spud paused and looked up. "Should I go on?"

"Oh, do," said Mabel, glancing at Myron.

"Cady has a great talent for embodying the quality of an evening. He visibly takes on the tone and tempo of the unseen mood generated by a group. And at the end of an evening he will be a little undertaker, gently picking up the pieces of shattered egos and throwing them into the fire. He likes to tidy up a room after people have smoked each other and their butts lie dead, for he has order in his soul. Sometimes it irks Myron to have life tidied up. He likes it thick, natural, wrapping him round in a fog of happenchance where he doesn't have to do anything but lap it up and pour it out on paper afterward. Sometimes Cady will throw pieces into the fire before Myron has got all the good out of them. That makes Myron pout."

Spud looked up. There was a silence. Myron was mulling over this picture of Cady and him. Both Mabel and Spud had accused him of being a writing machine. They must have talked with each other about him. But there was something else, and Myron tried to remember what happened at Hal's party.

"Cady?" asked Mabel. "You ready?"

"As I'll ever be." He looked down at his paper. "Every once in a while," he began, "in company, Myron will start something just so he can watch the movements souls make. He'll raise his voice and say something strong and blunt and hurtful. He likes to see the wheels go round. As they do he turns his black eyes here and there and notes the pain he's causing. At the end of the evening he'll be standing before a dying fire, balancing on his feet, chin up, lower lip thrust out and thinking 'good job.'"

Cady stopped. Myron was standing before the fire in exactly the position just described. Everyone took note.

"He'll be looking at the gyrations his remarks have called forth, taking stock of the shadowy room and the agonized shapes born from his passion for material. Fertile Myron, creating characters out of the people around him! The question is, When will he create his own character?"

There were sighs and sidelong glances, and Myron wondered what to make of his lover's observations. They seemed a lot like Spud's. Were they saying he wrote as a way of hiding from himself? Myron shrugged, and took his turn.

"Mine's about Mabel," he said and began. "She's proud of her achievement along the literary line for unlike Myron and other writers she knew, she's always busy with herself. But not in a mere masturbatory way, for that will not satisfy her as it might the literary types for whom it seems a practical outlet. No, she is busy making Mabel. Obversely from Myron, who always faces the world when he writes, she writes so she can live deeper and understand herself better. By so doing, she thinks she will amount to something. She will be great!"

Myron looked up. Mabel was smiling. He went on.

"'This is the planet of achievement,' she tells herself. 'If I don't make something of myself, who will?' And resolutely she strips herself of illusion after illusion in her effort to find the real fact of her. Her world becomes an onion to her industrious observation and she doesn't realize that, like the onion, her world has no final core of reality. She hasn't learned this little bit of truth yet, and goes on undoing and undoing the small daily growths of her soul. No sooner does she grow a new skin than she tears it off to look for herself in it, not knowing that these frail coverings each bear a tiny fraction of her being. The ancient Egyptians believed the onion represented the infinity of the universe. It's the pharaoh's curse on the artist, Myron wants to tell her, that we must forever peel our own skin."

The following morning they were in her bedroom, Myron sitting on the edge of her bed, Mabel half reclining, half sitting on her chaise lounge. He'd been helping her edit some of her chapters for *Cosmopolitan.* She'd sent for tea and there was a fire in the kiva, though it wasn't cold. They were talking about last night.

"Yours was wonderful," she said.

"I thought Marie's was the most surprising," added Myron. He was about to say the best but thought better of it. "Who would have thought? You know she's an awful poet." He nodded at his own judgment. "But they were all wonderful: John's, Claire's, Spud's, Cady's, even Tinka's Russian oration. Now that's the way the Truth game should be played."

"It hasn't been this delicious in years." She looked at him. "Was it writing them down that did it?"

"I don't know."

"What made you think to do it that way?"

"It was an exercise in a class I took at NYU. The course was taught by Joyce Kilmer."

There was a silence.

"You know you wrote wicked things about me," she said.

"And you about me."

"But true things."

"Probably." There was another pause. "Should we apologize?"

"It wouldn't do any good," and she laughed. "We'd still think them."

"I supposed you want us to leave."

"Oh no," she said, and her soft brown eyes held his. There was a long silence and Myron had to look away. "What did you and Cady have to talk about when you went home last night?"

"You mean, did we have it out?"

"Did you?"

"Yes and no. I thought his description of me was very good. I do act like that. It must be obvious to you I love to stir things up. But I thought he attributed the wrong motives to me. I don't do it to get material. Material doesn't come that way. It's much more unconscious."

"Then why do you do it?"

"Because it's fun. You think you invented Truth when you were a kid, Mabel?" She'd made this claim in *Backgrounds*. "Everybody in Butte plays it. It's a low-class thing. You go into any bar and people are telling each other what they think. The same thing goes on in their houses. They say the most hurtful things, things you'd think would destroy a family, and they don't."

"Did you tell Cady this?"

"Sure. I told him you and he were alike, that you came from the same kind of Victorian households that won't even think about these things. Freud invented himself for you people. I think that's why you married a Jew."

"Maurice?"

"Didn't you tell me he picked on your weaknesses?"

"Maurice was even less of a Jew than you."

They were silent for a moment, Myron waiting for something more about her ex-husband. But nothing came.

"Did you see Marie and Alan exchange theirs?" he asked.

"No." She smiled. "Did they?"

"They did. Love notes from the elderly."

"Do you think I'm elderly, Myron?" she asked, rising from the chaise.

"Oh no," he said. "Age isn't your problem."

"What is?" She was standing over him.

"Youth." He would have stood but she was too close.

"What's the matter, Myron? Do I frighten you?"

"No," he said. "But I think you're playing games now."

He could see the mischievous glint in her eye. Was this going to be the payback for his telling her the truth?

"What kind of games?" she asked.

"You know what I am."

"Then why do I feel this way?" she asked.

"What way?"

"Like we're drawn to each other."

"I don't know," he answered. "Perhaps it's wishful thinking."

"Are you sure that's what it is? That I'm the only one feeling it?"

"I'm sure," Myron lied.

"I've talked about you with Dr. Brill," she said. Dr. Brill was her famous New York psychiatrist.

"What did he have to say?" She had suggested several times that he see the man.

"That you're probably not a true invert."

"He could say that just from your description of me?"

"He's read your books. You ought to speak to him yourself."

"Maybe," said Myron and, forcing her to take a step back, he stood just as Rosita arrived with the tea.

At the end of July Cady's parents arrived from Massachusetts for a visit. They stayed at La Fonda on the plaza. When Mabel heard they were in town, she invited them to the Big House for drinks and dinner. Cady was happy and told Myron that his father in particular was interested in meeting Mabel. Like many Americans, Channing Wells had heard about this woman who'd married an Indian. A marriage between a white woman and an Indian was rare, especially in the case of so celebrated a figure as Mabel. In her library Myron even found a clipping of a 1917 report in *The New York Times* quoting her as saying she was "tired of white men who'd lost their core and become dehumanized creatures interested only in money-making. She'd found a man of the earth, a man of the red race with blood in his veins." It was Mabel using Tony to challenge the respectability of her background. Myron thought that if he were Tony he wouldn't have liked the role assigned to him.

Cady brought his parents and Mabel seemed on her best behavior. Vivacious and energetic, she talked about New Mexico and Taos, smiling often at her husband, who looked back at her if not lovingly, then with interest. Though they'd been there over three months this was one of just a half dozen times that Myron and Cady had been at table with Tony. Myron had to admit he was a handsome man, and his presence added to the significance of the occasion. Yet it was his presence that caused the mood of the evening to change for the worse. Before they ever got to dinner, while still sipping cocktails in the living room, in response to a question of Myron's, Channing Wells had begun talking about a philanthropic enterprise he and his brothers had undertaken. It seemed that near their hometown, Southbridge, where they had their factory, they were creating a replica of a Puritan village, a kind of living museum where they could display their collections of seventeenth-century artifacts. Myron sensed Mabel's mood changing.

"It's what the Rockefellers are doing in Williamsburg," the president of the American Optical Company enthused. "Sturbridge, that's what we're calling it," and he glanced at his wife as if the name might have been her idea, then back at Mabel, "will be a lot like a Williamsburg but also the opposite in the same way that the Puritans who settled Massachusetts and the Cavaliers who settled Virginia were opposite kinds of Englishmen."

Myron was impressed. He was associating with people as rich as Rockefeller.

"Well," said Mabel, "you know the Puritans and the Cavaliers had something else in common."

"What's that?" asked Channing Wells.

"They both murdered the natives."

And that was the end of Mabel's affability. At dinner she even managed to maneuver the conversation onto the subject of homosexuality. She was playing the Truth game with the Wellses, who uncomfortably poked at their lamb chops and nodded sadly as Mabel spoke.

"The sickness is not in homosexuality," she was saying, "but in the shame many people attach to it. Provided homosexuality is deeply implanted in a man or a woman, anyone seeking to be 'cured' of it is seeking only an alleviation of shame." It was an excellent observation but Myron knew she was making it for the wrong reasons. She was looking at Cady's dad. "Don't you think so, Channing?"

"I . . . "

"I agree," said Cady, on the one hand rescuing his father from having to answer, on the other, finally having his say to the man who had dragged him into the garage and slapped his face.

"I'm being preachy," said Mabel.

Bitchy's more like it, Myron thought.

"It's my New England ancestors."

"I thought you were from Buffalo," said Irene Wells.

"I am," said Mabel. "But everyone from upstate New York is originally from New England. They just kept walking." She paused as if waiting for a laugh. All she got were uncomfortable nods. So she introduced a new subject. "I've just received a letter from Margaret." There were puzzled looks. "Margaret Sanger," she explained. "She's having trouble opening her Boston clinic. And there's such a need for it. Is there anything you can do, Irene?"

"Not much," answered Cady's mother. "Of course I agree with Mrs. Sanger. But I have very little clout in Boston. It's the Catholic Church you have to deal with there. They run the place."

"What about you, Channing?" asked Mabel. "How do you feel on the subject of birth control?"

"I'm for it," said Cady's father.

"Then perhaps you can use some of your . . . " and she turned back to Cady's mom and touched her arm intimately. "How did you phrase it, dear, 'clout?'"

So it went, one accusatory question after another. Myron wasn't surprised. He was really getting to know Mabel. Despite the evening's seemingly friendly beginning, he'd had the feeling that as soon as Cady's parents entered the room she wanted to run away. She'd been unwilling to be photographed by Channing Wells. I look a fright, she pleaded though she wore a startling gown made for her by her friend the Hollywood designer Adrian. It was Tony who saved the situation. Jodhpurs tucked into his boots, long black braids falling to his chest, a white sheet over his head, he stood like a king while Mr. Wells snapped him.

The Wellses didn't stay long after dinner. Cady went with them back to the hotel. Myron stayed. Now he, Mabel, and Tony were having coffee in the Rainbow Room.

"Well, they do explain poor Cady, don't they?" Mabel started right in. "The mother with her tea-table manners and secondhand culture gotten from books on the bestseller list, subscribing to all the must concerts, staying at the right hotels, and with charge accounts at all the best stores."

Myron was staring at the painted ceiling and wondering, why poor Cady? And why does she think she can say these things in front of me? Does she think so little of me? Am I nothing?

"Of course, the mother's not really too bad. One can understand Cady adoring her, considering the awful father. Did you notice the American flag in his lapel? I know him. He's the kind of man who belongs to all the right organizations, a little machine of a man who would die for his country not because he's truly patriotic but because defeat would wreck the economy."

"What do you mean they explain poor Cady?" Myron asked.

"I mean Cady's nothing more than a dabbler." She had turned a bright smile on him. "I've spoken to Andrew about him. A little talent, yes, but not serious, just another American millionaire's ne'er-do-well son sent out west to be gotten out of his parent's hair, an artistic remittance. . . . "

"I can't believe you're saying these things, Mabel," Myron interrupted. "You're reducing people to clichés. And there's no one in the world more vulnerable to such a reduction than you."

"What do you mean?" she asked haughtily.

"I mean the art patron who runs a self-flattering salon, the millionairess who buys meaning for her life from the peddlers of easy visions, the rich bitch who . . . "

"Mabel," Tony interrupted. "They're nice people." He was sitting across the room in a chair beside Mabel's statue of the Buddha. "You shouldn't talk like that, Mabel. You talk too much."

"And you know," Myron was saying, full of admiration, "after he spoke she didn't say another word about your parents. Not one goddamned word."

"But she's right about my father," said Cady. "He was showing off, one millionaire to another."

"Okay," agreed Myron, "and she was having none of it. On the one hand she hates hypocrisy, on the other she's so used to being the richest kid on the block, she can't admit her own hypocrisy."

"Where does her money come from?" asked Cady.

"In town they say that every drop of water that goes over Niagara Falls puts a penny in her pocket."

"What does that mean?"

"I'm not sure. Maybe that she owns stock in Niagara Light and Power."

"I like the image," said Cady.

"Mabel turning water into money? Yeah. A capitalist miracle."

"But I really do despise her," Cady admitted.

Myron looked up. If he despised Mabel why did he defend her? Did he despise his father more?

"Don't you want to hear what my parents thought of you?" asked Cady.

"Sure."

"Well, my mother thought you were very nice, very handsome and smart. When I first told her I was seeing you, she got *Singermann* from the Southbridge Library and read it. She said she was quite moved."

"Why didn't she buy it?" Myron asked. "I could have autographed it." He might have added that he didn't make anything from lending libraries.

"Of course my father had to bring up the fact that you're Jewish," said Cady, ignoring the question.

"All right, I'll bite. What did he say?"

"He said your face is a map of Israel."

"Israel, eh? What does that mean?"

"I guess that you look Jewish? I don't know."

Then they began undressing and when they were naked Cady turned out the light as if nothing was going to happen. Oh well,

Myron thought as he got into bed, maybe the presence of my folks would inhibit me. Especially since pop's been dead over twenty years. So he turned away to the window and saw from the glow that the moon was about to come up over Taos Mountain. He closed his eyes and was almost asleep when he felt Cady's lips brush his cheek.

"Here's Jerusalem," and Myron felt a gentle bite on his earlobe. "Here's Haifa." Haifa was Myron's left eye. Cady pointed it out with his tongue, then slid down the bed.

"Where're you going?" Myron asked breathlessly.

"Elat. By the Red Sea."

"Never heard of it," Myron said, then groaned with pleasure as Cady's mouth covered the old seaport. So Mabel and the tense evening were forgotten. And after, when Cady was breathing evenly in sleep, Myron lay facing the newly risen moon. In its glowing silence he was thinking a miracle had happened. Somehow, in a matter of months, he'd gone from one world to another, left behind his personal problems and those of the bread lines of New York, passed through angry crowds of out-of-work mill hands and factory workers and hundreds of miles of choking, wind-blown dust, and come out on the other side. Janet had called it Shangri-la. Mabel talked about special places where marvelous things happened. Myron thought he was immune to such nonsense. Yet here he was, his new lover asleep beside him, living happily ever after.

Where am I? he asked.

Just where you want to be, the Taos moon replied.

Three

At the end of September, Cady and Myron moved down to the Clark ranch. Though each had his own cabin, they slept in one bed. After breakfast Cady would go out to paint, while Myron continued working on *Out of Life,* his new novel about a single momentous day in a man's life. At first the arrangement was good. But after a while Myron found it hard living in the country. He didn't drive and depended on Cady to take him everywhere: Taos for dinner at Mabel's, Santa Fe for a party at Hal's, Española for a drink. So he was looking forward to summer. Mabel had offered the Pink House. But when it came time Cady didn't want to go. She doesn't like me, he argued. She puts up with me because of you. So Myron went up alone and was miserable. It wasn't just Cady's absence. It was Mabel as well. Though there were no more sexual encounters or suggestions that he talk to Dr. Brill, she insisted on lecturing him on the significance of everything that happened at the pueblo, cosmic footraces, and mystic pole climbing. After a while he got so angry he threatened to leave. Don't go, she pleaded. I need you. Tony's away so much. You're the only one I can talk to. So he stayed, and in a few days she'd start again: earth currents, sacred places, life forces, until he wanted to scream.

Then one day toward the end of August, she began working on the senatorial campaign of the incumbent, Bronson Cutting, and that was a relief. Because Senator Cutting was a Republican and she a New Deal Democrat, she couldn't come right out and back him. Instead she got the Dasburgs to head the Taos committee to re-elect the senator, and they got Cady involved. Myron didn't mind. He thought he would get to see more of his friend. And he liked Cutting. A Progressive in the LaFollette mold, he was liberal to the point of radicalism. But that wasn't the senator's most interesting facet. At Mabel's first dinner party, Myron realized, after meeting the senator's secretary, a beautiful young man named Clifford McCarthy, that Cutting was a homosexual. Later, Spud told him that Cliff McCarthy had once been Hal's secretary but in 1930 left Hal for Bronson. There'd been bad feelings between the two men until Bob Hunt came on the scene. Now Hal was a supporter.

In September Myron moved back down to the dude ranch and Cady tried to get him to go door to door in Española to get out the vote. Myron refused. I've got to work, he pleaded. Cutting won without him, and there was a party at Mabel's and another at Hal's, who'd headed the Santa Fe committee. But it was a close vote, and the Democrats, charging fraud, demanded a recount. Then the Southern Democrats who ran the U.S. Senate refused to seat Cutting until the case was resolved.

"It's not fair," said Cady. "Bron was the winner."

"He still is," said Myron, trying to comfort his friend. He'd never seen Cady take anything so hard. "They're just calling for a canvas. This happens in Butte all the time. You'll see. He'll be declared the winner."

But the battle went into December, and Cady and the Dasburgs had to go all over the state to witness recounts. Then the Dasburgs bought a house in Talpa, and Cady, who had spent so much time with them, felt shut out. Right after Christmas he announced to Myron that he was leaving New Mexico for a while.

"Why?"

"Because I got all wound up in this election and haven't worked. I've got to get away." He looked at Myron. "It's not you," he said. "I still love you."

"Where will you go?"

"China," said Cady. "I studied there once. I'd like to see my old teacher."

"For how long?"

"I don't know. A few months."

They drove west together and arrived in San Francisco at the beginning of February. Cady was delivering a painting bought by the California Palace of the Legion of Honor. Then it was time for him to leave. What could Myron do? This was how he and Frank Fenton had parted. Frank went to Hollywood for a month and never came back. Myron knew how these things went. It made him angry, and they had an argument their last night together. Cady cried but he didn't change his mind, and they parted. No one said a word about a breakup or what each expected from the other, but it felt like the end. Though Myron was devastated, he had a novel to write. It was another one about Butte that Farrar & Rinehart had asked for. That's what the public wants from you, they said. Though the critics had liked *Out of Life*, it hadn't sold at all. Oh well, he thought as he set to work in his new rooms on Taylor Street, it'll be like ten years ago in New York when I lived alone. But it wasn't. He needed people, and after a few weeks, he was walking the streets of this strange, exciting city.

One foggy night when Market Street flowed like a slow river so that Myron was only faintly aware of passing figures, he decided he was lost in hell. The mist was a cold cloth over his face and he stood a moment trying to get his bearings until he realized he was in front of a cigar store. He went in. As soon as the smell of tobacco hit, he wanted a cigarette. He bought a pack, lit one, and the smoke in his lungs was relaxing and dry. Then he went out and allowed himself once again to drift downhill in the slow fog. After a while he thought he heard music coming from a saloon. Through its window he could make out a combo playing hillbilly songs on an improvised stage behind the bar. It was quick tempo, fiddles and banjos streaking their sound out to the wet pavement. He went inside. For a moment the harsh light made him he sorry he'd left the street, but he went up to the bar and ordered a whiskey and soda.

From where he stood he had only to lift his eyes to watch the band, four men in blue jeans and checked flannel shirts with red and blue bandannas about their throats. There was a nervous intensity about the men, and they seemed to Myron more related to stage doors and nightclubs than cowboy camps and roundups. There was a resemblance to folk tunes in what they were playing and singing, but Myron thought that if they had ever lived under high pines or by starlit streams, it had been a long time ago. Now they were comrades in dirty hotel lobbies and dismal rooms, not campfires and cattle round-ups.

He drank his whiskey slowly, and despite his cynicism, found it pleasant just to be close to people. That's what he told himself. He was there just to be with people. It had been three weeks since Cady had sailed. Myron thought of the argument they'd had the last night. It's Mabel, Myron had said. She's gotten to you. No, Cady contradicted. It's me. It's us. Then he tried to explain. I can't stand the way you flirt with women. I don't know why. I know how you really feel. But still it bothers me. It's such a lie. It's demeaning to us, as if you're saying you're so weak that you're afraid to admit what you are. Think about how it makes me feel. It is Mabel, Myron insisted. He'd never told Cady about that time in her bedroom. Maybe, Cady conceded. I don't like her and she doesn't like me. She doesn't respect me. But you and I: Where are we going? What do you want me to do, Myron blurted out, marry you? Yes, Cady said quietly, I think that's exactly what I want.

Myron was on his second whiskey and soda. It was a good feeling, as if he were dancing though he hadn't moved from the barstool. And by the time his third whiskey was in front of him he felt as light as air. The strident tunes above him had begun to sound less professional, more impromptu, fiddles running through him in quick flashes of color and rhythm. He watched the players. Their fingernails gleamed like pearls on the strings of their banjos and guitars. He was softening toward the men on the stage behind the bar. The Back-Bar Boys, he dubbed them. And he was liking the place better if for no other reason than that it was beginning to fill with people, mostly men alone, but a few with women who had the look of having been here many times, neighborhood old-timers who greeted one another in low, confidential voices as if they were sharing great secrets.

Myron tried to imagine the lives of these women living in small hotel rooms or tiny furnished flats in old-fashioned wooden houses tucked away on San Francisco's hilly streets. What did they do for a living? They couldn't all be whores. He turned away. When the door opened he saw that outside the bar's entrance, the fog still lurked. But it was warm inside, and the customers brought in a cheap cheerfulness that made him think of Pickwick holding forth. Yet it wasn't the same. Pickwick had friends, an audience. So did Dickens. I should be home with a good book, Myron thought. Then it occurred to him that because no one knew him here, he could do as he pleased. He felt an unacknowledged tension going out of him, and allowed himself to drift away on the stream of music.

Polkas, square dances. He remembered dancing in barns under lanterns strung along beams, the dust coming loose from the boards under their kicking feet. He would do that, go with friends to some small town outside of Butte. He remembered cows lowing their protests, and horses whinnying and chickens clucking and scurrying away, a feathered frenzy to escape their dancing feet.

Change your partners
Back and forth
Roads go south!
Roads go north!

Myron had sprung his joints then, leaping up and floating down, changing partners and changing hands, dancing under wide prairie moons and by old mill streams, the dusty snuff odors of hay and yellow straw lingering in the air, drifting across the lantern-lighted barn. Through the sycamores the candlelight is gleaming, from the fields there comes a breath. . . .

And the evening might have played out in the snatch of remembered songs and dances if Myron's elbow, under pressure from his chin in the hand that bore the weight of his head, hadn't begun sliding along the bar until the angle became too great.

When it let go his face was saved from the slippery wood only by the elbow of another.

"Sorry," he said to his neighbor. "Clumsy of me.

Then man turned to him and Myron was astonished. For it seemed he was looking at himself. The man had jet-black hair, jet-black eyes, olive skin, and a wide nose. Is it possible, he wondered, that there are two people in the world who look exactly alike and are not twins, not even related? And even if it were possible, out of the thousands of public places in this city, how could he have accidentally entered a place to find this person? Was it the fog? He looked at the man again. It was definitely his own face, his own thin body. The effect was magical though for a few minutes he did not dare believe such a thing possible. He must say something to the man—or boy rather, because his twin was very young. He was Myron fifteen years ago, which was how Myron always saw himself when he'd had a few.

"Do we look alike or am I drunk?"

"I hadn't thought of it," said the other. He studied Myron. "Now that you mention it, I think we do. Yes, we do. Very much alike." He held out his hand. "My name is Abel Birmingham. What's yours?"

"Myron Brinig."

Myron immediately regretted giving his real name. But when they shook hands he felt as if he were shaking hands with himself. The man had the same expressions and gestures. Even his voice was identical. If you can't trust yourself, who can you trust?

"What brings you here tonight?" Myron asked.

"Let's call it the love that is known but rarely mentioned." The young man smiled. "And you?" he asked.

"Love of the unknown," answered Myron and smiled also.

Abel Birmingham nodded, slipped off his barstool and went to the door. Myron became alarmed and made as if to follow but the bartender called him back. He hadn't paid for his last drink. Shivering with apprehension lest he lose his twin, Myron pulled out a dollar bill, and then, without waiting for change, hurried to the door. What had he said? Had he offended the young man? He thought they'd reached some kind of agreement. Now the whole world was under the fog and he couldn't see a foot in front of him.

He groped through the swirling vapor. Stricken with the thought that he had lost the other, and in that losing had lost himself as well, he walked this way and that. Then he found himself once again in front of the saloon. He was looking inside when something touched his shoulder.

"Were you looking for me?"

"Where did you go?"

"I was waiting here all the time. I thought you wanted to be rid of me."

"God, I'm glad I found you," Myron said and without hesitation they embraced. Their lips, moist with fog, met and they moved through the swimming grayness to a lamppost and held each other up, pasted together by the mist.

"You're what I want," said Myron. "I mustn't lose you."

A taxi appeared like a goldfish, its carbuncle eyes weeping. They got in. Abel Birmingham gave the driver an address, and the cab jerked forward. Myron caught his breath and, realizing he was dizzy, snatched at his companion, held on, and felt better.

"Don't fall asleep," warned Abel.

"I won't."

"Sleep will spoil everything."

But he must have dozed, if only for a few minutes, because in no time at all the cab had stopped and they were on a silent street in front of a dark house. The fog was still thick and it was impossible for Myron to make out what kind of place he was going into. There was a hall, a living room, a bedroom. Then he was taking off his clothes, careless of where they fell, and he was in the bed warmly clasped by the other. He was nearly unconscious, yet there was the feeling of being loved, someone caring for him deeply and passionately. In the dark he was a naked swimmer. Arms outstretched, he was far out under the stars and moon, an ocean, a sea of mystery and delight. And, not wishing to return, not wanting to go back, he was picked up in watery arms and borne shoreward where he did not want to go. Where no one wants to go, what no one wants to do, where no one wants to be. I shouldn't, he kept thinking as he swam hard against it, I shouldn't.

"N-N-Noel Sullivan," said the man looming in the doorway.

"Myron Brinig," said Myron and shook the cavernous hand.

"Sh-sh-shall we go?"

Without taking a step inside, Noel Sullivan reached down and lifted the valise and Myron found himself following the man down the steps. As usual it was raining. He stood while Noel Sullivan opened his car's trunk, threw the valise in, and pushed the door down. It slammed loudly.

"P-P-Please excuse my car," he said. "Ordinarily I'd b-b-be driving a newer model but because of the D-D-Depression I lack the funds."

Myron looked at the car. It was a Cadillac and nothing to be ashamed of.

"It's been a b-b-bad year for me," Noel Sullivan went on. "I had to p-p-put the other one away. I can't afford t-t-t-to drive it."

The other one? The Packard? The Rolls? Did he put the chauffeur away too? Myron got in. It was as big and as beautiful a car as he'd ever been in.

"And I have t-t-to apologize beforehand for the p-p-p-plainness of your lodgings." They were pulling away from the curb. "I'm strapped for c-c-cash and have a very modest house. I hope you'll b-b-be happy there."

Myron was becoming uncomfortable. Why was this obviously well-off man crying poverty? Does he think I want a loan? Had he met other writers who'd asked him for a handout? Janet had described Noel Sullivan as a man of inherited wealth derived from blocks of San Francisco real estate. His father had been one of the original settlers of the city and its mayor too. No doubt the Depression had hurt him, but did he really expect Myron to feel sorry for him?

"And I w-w-want to apologize for my t-t-tardiness," he added after a long silence. They were leaving the city by way of Pacific Heights. "One of my d-d-dogs just died. When w-w-we arrive in C-C-Carmel, I hope you won't mind if I leave you for a time to b-b-bury the p-p-poor animal."

"I'm sorry," said Myron, joining the apology game though he felt no real sympathy. This meeting was Janet's idea. He'd called her desperate after his night out and she had suggested a new romance.

"G-G-Greta was very sick during the night," Noel Sullivan explained. "This morning I brought her to a v-v-vet up here. But she was very old. There was nothing he could do. The end was p-p-peaceful."

"And where," Myron asked in as solemn a voice as his lack of real concern could muster, "is Greta now?

"In the trunk."

Next to my valise, thought Myron. Shit! "A dog is a man's best friend," he said and almost laughed at the cliché.

"G-G-Greta was more than a friend," Noel Sullivan corrected. "She w-w-was irreplaceable in a w-w-way no human being could be."

"Under the circumstances," said Myron, "I appreciate your inviting me for the weekend." But he was annoyed. He'd just been told that he wasn't as important as a dog. Cady, you son-of-a-bitch. What am I doing here?

"I'm only sorry we couldn't have m-met under more cheerful circumstances. You m-m-must tell me about yourself. Janet wrote that y-y-you are a very distinguished novelist. I'm sorry not to have read any of your work. B-B-But I hope soon to remedy that situation."

There was a long silence and Myron decided Noel Sullivan was not so much saintly, as Janet had described him, as sanctimonious. There was something in his manner. It was as if, while still alive, he had already been granted absolution. What could you say to such a man? But Myron tried. He brought up the new bridge being built in the bay, which Noel pronounced a waste of money. He tried the longshoremen's strike that the mayor had turned into a war where people were getting killed every day. Noel dismissed the strike as Communist led. So Myron quit trying, and they rode in silence. And the nearer they got to Carmel, the harder it rained and the less inviting the weekend became. So Myron was trying to think of an excuse for getting away as quickly as possible and returning to the city by bus. Why didn't homosexuals have lasting relationships, he wondered. Why after finding such a lover as Cady was he adrift once again?

At that moment the clouds lifted, allowing him his first glimpse of the landscape, and he thought he'd never seen hills and trees so beautiful. A few minutes later they were entering Carmel, with its shimmering evergreens. The spicy fragrance of pine and cedar mixed with the salt freshness of the sea. They passed a rocky beach, rode up a hill into the trees, and stopped. The house was not far from the road, yet, because of the trees and shrubs, there was seclusion. They got out and went to the car's trunk. Noel opened it and lifted Myron's suitcase.

"I-I-I wouldn't think of burdening a guest with l-l-luggage."

Empty-handed, Myron followed to a Gothic-arched front door. Fixed onto the wood was a ceramic plaque on which were printed two lines of verse.

"I will arise and go now to Innisfree / And a small cabin build there of clay and wattles made."

"Oh," said Myron, "Yeats! That's a lovely poem."

"I-I-It's one of my favorites. I-I-I'm building a new house and I'm going to take this plaque there. I'll c-c-call the new house Innisfree also."

So that's where his money's going. Why all the bullshit about the Depression?

They went in. This old Innisfree, though small, was comfortable and pleasantly warm. After hanging his coat in the hall closet Myron followed Noel down a hallway into a living room decorated with religious pictures featuring bloody hearts and hands. Over the couch was a crucifix large enough for a church altar, and on shelves and tables were marble statuettes of the Holy Family. There were some secular prints and etchings, and, here and there, watercolors Noel said were by local artists whose names Myron didn't know. There were also autographed photos of famous writers: Robinson Jeffers, whom Myron had met at Mabel's, and two Negroes, Arna Bontemps and Langston Hughes. When they reached the guest room, Noel laid Myron's suitcase on a stand in front of the bed, showed him the bathroom, and led him back to the living room.

"M-M-mix yourself a drink. I have to g-g-get going."

"Can I help you?"

"N-N-no. Y-Y-You stay here."

A few minutes later through the window, Myron saw the man carrying the blanketed carcass into the rear garden where he deposited it on the wet grass, making sure it was covered. Then he disappeared but came back a few moments later with a shovel and began to dig. He must own this place too, Myron decided. Or why would he bury the dog here? Myron sat down on the sofa and sipped the scotch. After a while he put the drink down, watched the mournful scene, and dozed.

"I-I-I'm so glad you helped yourself." Noel was standing over him soaking wet. "I-I-I'm afraid I-I-I've been neglectful. You must excuse m-m-me."

"You ought to get out of those wet things," said Myron, now alert.

"Y-Y-You're right," and he sighed. "I seem t-t-to be getting a cold. Excuse me while I change. M-M-Meanwhile help yourself to another. I'm s-s-s-sorry. Eulah, the woman who t-t-t-takes care of me, hasn't come in yet. I'd like to offer you something hot. You must be starving."

Then Noel was gone. Myron poured himself another drink and sat down again. But he didn't have to wait long for company. He heard the front door and down the hall came a stout black woman in a shiny yellow slicker and hat she held high so as not to wet anything. She went through a door. It must have led to the kitchen.

"I'm Eulah Farr, Mr. Sullivan's housekeeper," she said when she came out. She was wearing an apron. "You must be the young man he told me about. I'm glad you could come." She was walking toward him. "It's a rather sad occasion, what with the dog dying. She was such a dear. I cried so when I heard about it."

"He's buried her out in the garden," Myron said and was about to add that he hadn't minded the sadness of the occasion but caught himself.

"I knew he would," said the woman, who sounded a lot like Noel but without the stutter. Noel had called her the woman who took care of him. But she was definitely not a servant. She behaved like a blood relative, an aunt keeping house for a favorite nephew.

"I offered to help him dig but . . . "

"Oh, he wouldn't have wanted you to do that," said Eulah. "It was between himself and Greta. You know, he was part of that dog's soul."

"You think dogs have souls?" asked Myron.

"Oh, yes!" she said with such a nod that her gold spectacles slid down her nose. "We're all children of God, you know, even the insects of the air. He created us all. Greta knew that. Oh, my dear, yes. When Mr. Sullivan prayed, you saw that the dog understood. She would just sit there quietly by his side, praying too."

Dear God, thought Myron.

Then Noel was back, preceded by two succulently shaped dachshunds, hysterically scurrying about and barking shrilly. One of them jumped into Myron's lap, and Noel admonished the dog.

"Hansie, dear, sit, sit baby." And then, turning to Myron, he said, "I hope you don't m-m-mind. They're young and still n-n-n-naughty." Then he smiled at Eulah.

"You two have m-m-met?" he asked.

"Oh, yes," Eulah said. "I was just telling the young gentleman how much we will miss Greta."

"You know, Eulah, Mr. Brinig is a distinguished n-n-novelist."

"How interesting," said Eulah. "I love to read. But so much of what is written today is trash. I prefer classics: Hawthorne, Emerson, Dickens."

"Don't you like any of the modern writers?" asked Myron.

"Some," she said, realizing she could be insulting him.

"Who?" Myron persisted.

"Galsworthy," she said after a moment. "I love him. He's so patrician."

"To be sure," said Noel, then turned to Myron. "Eulah is much m-m-m-more of a reader than I."

"Oh, I wouldn't say that, Mr. Sullivan. I know you read every night in bed."

"But not much," confessed Noel. "I-I-I fall asleep."

Whatever Eulah Farr's taste in literature, Myron enjoyed her dinner: rare roast beef, string beans fresh from her garden, and her homemade vanilla ice cream flavored with rum and coffee. But his host dined sparingly, and Myron remembered again what Janet had told him. He was dining with a saint and saints don't gorge.

"If I didn't know Mr. Sullivan was such a small eater," said Eulah as she cleared the plates, "I'd be offended."

"Eulah," he said, "I know what a trial I am t-t-to you. I want to apologize, but you know I am not unmindful of your culinary t-t-t-talents.

"Oh, Mr. Sullivan, I was only joking, and anyway there are other things in the world besides food."

"Music," Noel said and smiled, "the food of l-l-l-love."

Until now nothing the man had said could have been taken any way but literally. Yet here was a double entendre. Myron glanced at Eulah Farr but she seemed not to have noticed.

"Isn't sh-sh-she a lovely person," Noel said after she left the room. "You know I'm especially f-f-f-fond of her as I am of so many of her r-r-r-race." He seemed to have retreated from his observation about love. "They h-h-have gotten such a raw deal in our society. In my small way, I try to m-m-make it up to them."

Myron nodded and they talked about the problem of race in America and the egalitarian nature of Catholicism and Judaism and all right-thinking religions.

"Have you read the p-p-p-poet Langston Hughes?"

Myron shook his head no.

Noel got up and went to a bookshelf. They were in the library, Myron in a wingback chair facing the fire, smoking the Havana cigar Noel had offered. Now Myron took the book. It was entitled *The Weary Blues* and Myron was reminded of that night with Marie Garland and her book of poems. Read for your supper. Again he'd eaten too much and, though he was not uncomfortable in the same way, he was having trouble keeping his eyes open. This time he came right out and asked to be excused. Noel jumped up and they said good night.

Myron awoke in the middle of the night, aware of a presence beside the bed. The rain was over and the moon was out and he could see that it was Noel looking down on him, his demeanor mournful as if he were looking into a coffin. Myron had to remind himself that one of the man's saintly qualities was homosexuality. Not that he felt any desire. He was hoping Noel would go away, hoping the man would be not be too hurt at his inability to receive him into his arms. Myron had made up his mind on the trip down that there would be nothing between them, that even touching the man would be distasteful. But Noel just stood there. Does he know I'm awake? Then, after a while, Myron wasn't and the next morning when he awoke, he wondered if he'd been dreaming. He got dressed and went to the dining room. But he ate alone. Eulah Farr, who'd come early to serve him, explained that Mr. Sullivan had gone out on another of his errands of mercy.

"In the rain?" Myron asked, looking out the window at the downpour and thinking of the moonlight last night. Had he been dreaming?

"Rain or shine, Mr. Sullivan would never forget a sick friend," said Eulah. "He thinks of everybody. He has the kindest heart."

Myron was still eating when Noel returned. He greeted Myron as if nothing had happened last night. If I wasn't dreaming, Myron thought, why didn't I invite him in? It's not every day you get a chance to make love to a saint. But he knew why. It wasn't just that he wasn't attracted to Noel. It was Cady too. Then is it honest of me to stay here if he expects something I can't deliver? But why can't I? Haven't I already had sex with someone else?

Myron thought of saying something to Noel about the night but never got the chance. The weather cleared and there were more missions of mercy. So he spent the day walking around Carmel, discovering its windswept cliffs and hidden beaches. Like Taos, it was an art colony and Myron thought it might be a good place to stay for a while. He knew the Jefferses and, though he'd never met Lincoln Steffens, who had a house here, they'd corresponded. For the time being, however, he just walked, taking a lunch of fried clams on the pier, then walking some more. At dinner Noel reappeared but they both were tired and went to bed early. That night Myron awoke again with the big man hovering beside his bed. This time Myron called out to him. Noel? But all this did was cause the apparition to melt into the blackness. Myron had thought of Noel as a gray man: gray hair, gray eyes, gray clothing, gray shoes. But at night he was black. The next day on the trip back they hardly spoke. Myron kept thinking he should say something. But they'd never see each other again. What difference did it make?

"Thank you for your delightful hospitality," he said as politely and insincerely as he could. They were parked on Taylor Street in front of Myron's lodgings, and he wanted to get out.

"I'm s-s-sorry we didn't get to spend more time t-t-t-together," said Noel.

Myron heard a change in tone.

"I w-w-w-wanted to talk to you."

"About what?"

There was a long pause, then Noel blurted it out:

"I'm in l-l-love with another—I thought I c-c-c-could—"

"Is that why you came and stood by the bed?"

"Y-Y-Yes."

"Is that why you invited me?"

"Yes."

"I'm in love with someone else, too," said Myron.

Noel smiled and they began talking about their situations. Noel said he'd heard of Cady Wells from Una Jeffers and would like to meet him, and Myron said he'd like to meet Langston Hughes, who, it turned out, was the man Noel loved. They sat for an hour telling each other of their loves, and at the end when Myron said he liked Carmel and thought he might rent a place there and come on weekends, Noel said he'd scout around. When he was finally gone Myron decided that despite his sanctimonious ways, once he let his hair down, Noel was human. So the next weekend they drove down together. This time there were no nocturnal visits, and during the day Noel showed him around; vineyards, galleries, and the Carmelite Convent where Noel's sister was a nun. A week later he took Myron to a small cottage in town. It was really just a one-room tourist cabin but it wasn't far from the water and was perfect for weekends. So Myron rented it and they began driving down together on a regular basis.

It was several weekends before Myron got up the nerve to call on Lincoln Steffens. Steffens, who'd been a kind of god for Myron in the same way Big Bill Haywood had been, lived in a wood frame Victorian facing the bay. Myron had passed the house many times on his walks. Now he knocked. An attractive woman opened the door. He had phoned ahead. She let him in and led him to a side parlor that had been turned into a bedroom.

"I'm Myron Brinig," he said as he crossed to the bed. "We've corresponded."

"I recognize you from your jacket photo." In 1931, Myron had sent Steffens an autographed copy of *Wide Open Town* with a note saying he'd been the book's intellectual father. "It's a marvelous novel."

"Thanks," said Myron, shaking the man's hand. "When I first heard of you, you were known as a muckraker," Myron said as he sat down in the bedside chair. "Growing up in Butte I knew lots of muckers, but never a muckraker."

"Did you know Mucky McDonald?" Steffens asked brightly.

"Sure!" Myron was surprised. Mucky McDonald had been the first president of the Butte Mine Workers Union. "How do you know him?"

"I don't. But Bill Haywood used to talk about him and how tough he was. Mucky was a Wobbly legend."

"He used to come into our store," said Myron. "I once sold him a pair of overalls. My father was a Republican but he loved Mucky."

"Write something on this, would you?" From beneath the covers Steffens pulled the copy of *Wide Open Town* Myron had sent.

"Warm," noted Myron. "Where you been keeping it?"

Steffens laughed and Myron wrote something beneath his first autograph, then handed it back to the man. Steffens read the inscription aloud.

"'To Lincoln Steffens who put into words the truths we didn't know we knew. With kindest regards, Myron.'" The old man looked up. There were tears in his eyes. "Thank you, Myron."

There was a long pause, and to get the conversation going again Myron was about to mention the book Mabel was writing about her New York salon. You're in it, he was going to say. You're one of her movers and shakers. That's the title. But Steffens spoke first.

"I love what you did with Frank Little," he said. "It's a great picture of what the bastards do to men who try to stand up to them. It's the best portrayal of a union organizer I've ever read. You got into his shoes. You understood him as a human being. Yet you managed to make him bigger than life."

"But he's fiction," Myron said. "That's why I called him Phil Whipple. The real Frank Little was actually a local half-breed who could hardly write his name." Myron had made the character a Stanford graduate full of the enlightened spirit of the American Revolution. "Part of him is Frank Little," Myron went on, "and part of him is me. But the best part of him is you. You're the man who taught me what was right and what was wrong in the moral chaos I grew up in. You taught me about courage, about facing the things that these men faced, about what they were really up against and how nobly they could act."

"Thank you, Myron," said Steffens, and again there were tears in his eyes. Then he went on. "What's best about your work is that you call for action."

Do I? Myron wondered. He thought he'd done the opposite, shown the fated hopelessness. Ah well, hope is in the eye of the beholder. And he might have said something like this, but Steffens was talking about the labor movement in America and how it was moving forward on the talent of writers like Myron and Dos Passos and Steinbeck and all the other good men who told the truth. Myron was elated by the compliments and by the company he was put in. But he also felt he didn't deserve it, that he was neither that dedicated nor that optimistic about change. Then Steffens asked him what he was doing now, so Myron told him how he'd spent the past several months working on another Butte novel of labor strife, only the time was now, the Great Depression, and how hard he was finding it to write about that subject yet again. These observations were met with silence. So to change what seemed to be a dead-end subject Myron asked the old man about the old days and Mabel and her salon in New York.

"Ah, Mabel," Steffens said. "That was the Village right before the war."

"Tell me about it. You talk about it some in your autobiography."

"What do you want to hear?"

"Well, whose idea was it to have a salon?"

"Jack Reed's. They were lovers and he saw she was getting bored so he arranged that one night a week we'd all go over there and talk. She managed the evenings, but no one felt managed. I remember going there and talking about the same strike you describe in your novel. All kinds of people were there: Max Eastman, Ida Raugh, Emma Goldman, Bill Haywood." He looked up. "If only you'd been there, Myron."

Myron was amazed. The old man was full of revolutionary energy. When he'd entered the room Myron had thought that beneath the covers with his pointed gray beard and small wire-rimmed glasses, he looked like Lenin in his tomb in Red Square. He still did, but he was Lenin come to life.

"In a way I was," said Myron. "I came to New York in 1914. I was seventeen and just beginning at NYU. I used to walk by 23 Fifth Avenue all the time. But I didn't know what was going on."

"You should've come in. People were always coming off the street to eat Mabel's food and throw their two cents in."

"That's what Mabel said."

"It was a revolutionary time," the old man reminisced. "It was everywhere. In Russia it was political, in France it was in the arts, in Germany, where conditions were the worst, it was sex. They turned to perversion and homosexuality."

Trying not to take offense, Myron said, "America turned to sex too."

"The best writers in Europe turned inward, Joyce, Pound, Stein," Steffens seemed not to have heard him. "Did you know that the two most important women of this century are Mabel Dodge and Gertrude Stein? They made things happen."

"Gertrude Stein? Why her?" Myron found most of Stein's work unreadable and her recent memoir cloyingly cute.

"Because she encouraged younger artists to break away, to rebel, to dare. She was a powerful revolutionary leader who at the same time did her own work and was content to be herself." The old man paused and Myron thought he was done but he went on. "I heard her read once." There was awe in his voice as if he said he heard one of Lenin's speeches. "'Portrait of Jo Davidson.' You know it?"

"No."

"It was in a bistro and I was far back but I could hear very well and it sounded just like Davidson himself monologizing while he worked. He did that, talked as he carved. It was to keep his subjects entertained. Though the words she used didn't make any sense, nevertheless they were the right words. She struck me as not only a genius but a very wise woman. When you were with her you felt contentment, you shared her composure." He was thoughtful again. "She gave you a glimpse of what can be seen by just sitting still and looking."

It was a formidable picture and Myron thought of Mabel and how unassuming she seemed when he first met her, yet how everyone was drawn to her. Did Gertrude Stein have that same ability? The trouble with people like that is that once you get to know them, they're not like that. Then the young woman came in. The visit was over.

The second visit with the old man also went well. It was the following weekend and Steffens talked about the beginnings of Carmel as an artist colony, how there was nothing here when the poets Jack Sterling and Mary Austin came and built their little shacks before the Great War, and how in the twenties the place fell into the hands of real estate developers. "It always happens that way," he said. "Artists recognize the beauty of a place, build there and make it desirable. Then someone comes along and makes money from it."

Myron agreed and pointed out that it had happened in the Village too and in Taos. "Not now though," he added. "Nothing's happening now."

But Myron didn't want to talk about real estate. He wanted to talk about homosexuality. It's not what you think, he wanted to say. What would Steffens think of that? Who knows? Maybe he knew already. Maybe that's why he'd made the remark about perversion in the first place. And before his third visit Myron made up his mind to tell Lincoln Steffens what he was. But as soon as he sat down the old man began ranting about politics, about the Depression and the capitalist bastards who caused it.

"I don't think there are any villains in the piece," Myron commented as much to calm him as to express his opinion.

"No villains?" Steffens turned to him, his face red with anger. "Who hung your Phil Whipple from a railroad trestle and left his body for the crows?"

"Men do villainous things," said Myron.

"But there are no villains."

"If the Wobblies had had the strength, what would they have done to the bosses?" Myron asked.

The old man looked at him as if he were not sure he'd heard correctly. Then he turned away. There was a long silence.

"Do you want me to go?" Myron asked after a while.

Steffens nodded his head.

"Should I come again?"

The head moved once, side to side.

Myron left but instead of going back to his cabin he walked out to the Flavins. Martin Flavin, a businessman, had retired early to write plays. He and his wife, Sarah, were down-to-earth people, who'd had Myron to dinner a couple of times.

"They're really up against it," Sarah was explaining.

"What do you mean?" Myron had just told them what happened. He didn't know what he wanted from them but he had to tell someone. He was very upset. He'd just been disowned by the man he considered his mentor.

"It's the vigilantes," said Martin.

"Vigilantes?" Myron thought of Virginia City and the men who had brought law and order to the Montana mining camp. They were revered as heroes and became the early political leaders of the new state. But Sarah and Martin Flavin meant a different kind of vigilante. The American Legion over in Monterey had taken it upon themselves to clean out the "Communists, nigger-lovers, and fags" that they said the Carmel artist colony catered to.

"It's the reason Langston Hughes left," said Sarah. "He didn't want to bring their wrath down on Noel."

"It's hard to believe," said Myron. Yet it shouldn't have been.

After all, he'd just received news from Farrar & Rinehart that *Der Singermann Roman*, the German translation of *Singermann*, had been burned by the Nazis at one of their nighttime celebrations. It was a Jew's worst nightmare, the seething mob anger that boils up in hard times.

"Hughes needed to leave," Martin added. "He told me he needed to be around his own people. Here there's only Eulah Farr and her husband."

"Langston was saving face," Sarah contradicted. "He didn't really want to go."

"What did the vigilantes do to the Steffenses?" Myron asked.

"They wrote letters calling Steff and Ella Communists and saying they should be run out of town," Martin explained. "They quoted the famous remark Steffens made in the twenties after he got back from Russia about seeing the future and how well it worked. Of course, they couldn't frighten a warrior like Steff nor a fanatic like Ella."

The woman Myron had thought was a housekeeper or nurse was Steffens's wife. When Myron had asked Noel about her, the gaunt man said he liked her but that she was a card-carrying Communist.

"Is that all?" asked Myron.

"No," Sarah went on. "Recently there was an anonymous letter in the *Chronicle* calling their son Peter a Communist."

"Is he?"

"A Communist? He's nine years old!"

"Steffens has a nine-year-old son?"

"Yes. Ella wanted a child."

Myron nodded. "So they attacked a nine-year-old kid?"

"It's the only way they could get to Steff."

"What happened?"

"Well, you can imagine," said Sarah. "At school the older boys beat him up and threatened to kill him. Steff wrote a letter to the *Chronicle* calling the vigilantes cowards. He put on a brave front. But they sent Peter to live with relatives in San Francisco." Then she added sympathetically, "It's taken a lot out of them. They were supporting Harry Bridges and his longshoremen and Helen Bell and the field laborers' union. Now they've backed off."

On the walk back to his cottage Myron decided that despite the party rhetoric, what Lincoln Steffens had been asking of him was to be a loyal friend, and he resolved that the very next day he would stop by the Steffens house to apologize and explain that he hadn't understood the problem. He would offer his services, if not for the Communist cause, then to Steffens and his family. So the next morning he left his cottage early, and walked north along Twelfth Street to the Steffens house. It was so early he was only afraid they would not be up yet. But Ella Winter came to the door looking just as she had each time before. She was at least thirty years younger than Steff and very handsome in a dark, Semitic way.

"What do you want?" she asked. She didn't let him in.

"I want to speak to Steff."

"That's not possible."

Myron knew it was Ella's job to screen her husband's visitors. Otherwise he'd never get a moment's peace. Besides, couldn't he say everything he had to say to Steffens to her also? After all, she was the boy's mother.

"I want to apologize to Steff," Myron began, "and to you."

"Oh?"

"I've just heard about the vigilantes and how they threatened your son. I want to say I support you and will do everything I can, write letters, carry petitions, anything to discredit these horrible people."

"Is that what you wanted to tell Steff?"

"Yes."

"Mr. Brinig," she said, "we have plenty of that kind of help. Most fair-minded people are behind us. The vigilante strategy of intimidation has to fail. What is wanted from you is something else. You are a writer who believes he owns his own work and won't acknowledge that his writing belongs to the people he writes about, miners and laborers. I've read your mining novel. Its roots are deeply implanted in the masses. But they are only roots. Where is the tree? Instead of writing about the mining disaster that killed a hundred and sixty men and caused the strike you describe, you have your hero leave Butte to work in a mine in another place. Why didn't you include the disaster? Why didn't you make your miner a survivor who becomes a union man? And when your union organizer is hung by the company goons, why didn't you have your hero pick up the pieces and take over the organizer's role to work for the union?"

Myron was dumbstruck. She was making the same criticisms of the novel that several left-wing critics had made. But she was going farther. She was rewriting it. And she wasn't done.

"Instead you end in a melodrama of jealous sexual desire. It would have been all right for a lesser character. But not for a hero."

"What do you want me to do?" Myron asked.

"It's you who has to be heroic now, Mr. Brinig. Your work must be understood and loved by the masses. It must elevate their feelings, their thoughts, and their will and stir them to activity. It must develop the socialist instincts in them, and cultivate their desire to help each other." She took a breath. "That's the way you can help us. Can you do that, Mr. Brinig?"

If Lincoln Steffens looked like the chemically treated effigy of Lenin lying under glass in his Red Square tomb, Ella Winter, perhaps because of her clipped English accent and too-strong jaw, sounded to Myron as he imagined the Communist revolutionary Bela Kun might have sounded when she harangued the Budapest mob after the war. But Bela Kun had been lynched, her face beaten to a pulp. Myron feared for Ella Winter.

"I can't rewrite an already published novel," he said.

"But you could write another."

"Don't you want my help?" he asked after a moment.

"On your terms, no." And she closed the door in his face.

Later, when Myron thought about this confrontation, he decided she couldn't have ad-libbed that speech. They had to have talked about it. So Steffens must feel the same way, he decided. That afternoon he wrote to Cady.

"They were telling me what I should write about. They didn't understand that I've been writing my way out of Butte nor that every man who ever pitched a shovelful of muck into an ore car was in a sense writing his way out of Butte, that is, working toward the grubstake that would allow him to buy some land or start a small business. Most miners hate mining, not just the awful danger, the cave-ins, the floods, the fires and poisonous fumes, but the day-to-day backbreaking work. A miner knows something that the Communists, flush with their victory in Russia, have either forgotten or, in their intellectual isolation, never learned. Backbreaking labor is backbreaking labor no matter who owns it."

Not that Myron was repudiating his labor novel. *Wide Open Town* was about capitalism at its worst, its most unfair, greedy, and murderous. But with capitalism you at least had some hope of escape. Writing *Singermann* or *Wide Open Town* in small rooms in Greenwich Village and Chelsea and Washington Heights was a Herculean labor, never as dangerous as what the miners did, but Herculean nevertheless. And Myron had only partially achieved his goal of escaping the kind of life he was describing. Ella Winter said his work belonged to the people he wrote about. She'd intimated he was taking advantage of them, using them, stealing from them. No, Myron thought. I loved them, and while I was writing, I was one of them. I did more than walk in their shoes. I gave them a voice. And that argument sufficed until he mailed the letter. Then it came to him that he could just be justifying his own selfishness. He wished Cady were here now. He needed someone to talk to.

But Cady wasn't there and Myron, though he had written to the address on Cady's last letter, wasn't really sure where his friend was. So he went back to Taylor Street to think. He didn't try to write. Instead he began rereading Arnold Bennett's *The Old Wives' Tale*, which had always been one of his favorite novels. He saw it as a model for a new novel. He used models a lot. You have a shapeless mass of material in your head and you're searching for some way to manage it. Models saved time. Of course he didn't do this with the novels based on his own family life like *Singermann* or *This Man Is My Brother*. But *Wide Open Town* took its plot of star-crossed lovers, jealousy, betrayal, and revenge from a play he'd seen at Butte's Broadway Theater when he was a boy, ushering there.

He already had a title for the new book. He'd call it *The*

Sisters. It would be about the Kelly girls, the three daughters of the druggist who lived two doors down from the Brinigs on West Granite Street. As well as plot, what he wanted from *The Old Wives' Tale* was scope, an omniscient author who could conquer time and space with a few kind words. He'd done scope before. It was easy. But not kind words. He'd been too angry. Now he'd go back to the Butte of his childhood, not to the miners but to their bosses, the men for whom the miners' daughters set their caps. With Louise, he'd go back to turn-of-the-century San Francisco, with Helen to New York, but with Grace he'd stay in Butte and go through the consolidation of Anaconda Copper. It would be an American novel; Americans traveling the world while moving up and down the class ladder. Fluid, optimistic, and disastrous, this would be his answer to both communism and capitalism, the American answer.

"Sounds g-g-g-grand." Myron had driven out with Noel to the land upon which he was building his new Innisfree. It was a ranch-sized piece of property with a brook and a lake. "I h-h-hope I didn't interrupt."

"No," said Myron. "I've hardly begun."

Usually he didn't like to discuss what he was working on. Many a slip and all that. But there was a moment right before you started when talking to someone helped break the surface tension of inertia. Now you have to do it, he'd tell himself. But he'd said enough, so he changed the subject.

"Martin and Sarah told me how you protected Langston Hughes. I always seem to underestimate you, Noel."

"W-W-What do you mean?"

"I knew you were kind and generous. But I didn't know how brave you are."

"B-B-Brave?"

"I'm talking about your facing down the vigilantes."

Noel looked at him with disbelief.

"M-M-My father was m-m-mayor of San Francisco," he began. "M-M-My uncle was three times a United States senator from C-C-California. D-D-Despite these bad times I'm a very w-w-wealthy man." He'd never admitted this before. "I'm not brave," he went on. "They can't r-r-really get to me. It's Langston who's brave. To be b-b-black in this country is t-t-to be b-b-born cursed with bravery."

Myron nodded.

"Come. I-I-I want to show you the h-h-house."

When they came over the hill Myron was surprised by its size. "You're almost done," he said.

"Everything's enclosed, b-b-but the plasterers are just b-b-beginning their work."

They walked inside. Myron recognized several of the workers as men he'd seen around town. He remarked on this to Noel.

"I'm the local W-W-Works Project," he said and laughed.

He has nothing to fear, Myron thought. Here are his protectors.

"I wish it were d-d-d-done though," he was saying. "I'm giving a dinner p-p-party for a v-v-very important person and I'm afraid it will have to be in m-m-my present m-m-modest surrounding." He was into his Victorian novel manner again. "Y-Y-You are invited, of course."

"Well, thank you, Noel." Myron had gone to several dinners at Noel's Hyde Street house. He'd met Lawrence Tibbett, Nelson Eddy, and Marian Anderson. Noel was a singer of local fame and wrote music reviews for *The Chronicle.*

"Who's the guest of honor?"

"G-G-Gertrude Stein."

Gertrude Stein!

"C-C-Can you make it?"

"Who else will be there?" Myron asked coyly.

"The Jefferses, the Flavins, and some young p-p-p-people from the university, of course."

"When is it?"

"Er, d-d-day after t-t-tomorrow."

"Oh?" Myron was deflated. He was being been asked at the last minute. Someone had backed out. He was still only a second-tier celebrity. Should he go? He didn't like Gertrude Stein's work. But there was the accolade Lincoln Steffens had given her and the stuff in Mabel's *European Experiences.* And she was constantly making headlines. Wasn't she writing a libretto for a new opera by Virgil Thomson? She'd certainly be an interesting person to meet.

"I'll be there," said Myron.

That night he fell asleep wondering what he would say to Gertrude Stein. So he might have been dreaming the perfect words when there was a knock on his door. Myron sat up. In his new explanatory dream vigilantes had burst in to drag him out and hang him from the Northern Pacific trestle. Fear penetrated his heart and his surroundings were strange.

"Myron," a voice called through the front door. "Let me in!"

It was familiar. Who was it? Cady? Suddenly excited, Myron jumped out of bed and crossed the small room.

"Let me in!" the voice insisted. "I must talk to you."

He opened the door.

"Mabel!"

She was standing in the faint glow of a street light, her face soaked, her cheeks shining so that she looked as if she were wrapped in cellophane.

"I must talk to you!" she repeated.

"Come in!"

As soon as she was in she was removing her rain gear, a sou'wester hat and yellow slicker. Water was dripping on the wood floor so he took the coat and hat to the bathroom, laid them in the tub, and came out with a towel. She was sitting in his desk chair, which she had turned to face the bed. He gave her the towel, and thought that with her wet bangs she looked more than ever like a middle-aged Betty Boop. What's this about? he wondered as she dried her face. They hadn't parted on good terms and he'd never expected to see her again. Yet after a few months, when she was back from New York and he ensconced out here, she'd sent him a check for a hundred dollars for work he'd done on her *Cosmopolitan* piece. Since then they'd corresponded sporadically, a kind of feeling each other out. Her showing up like this was a great surprise.

"What is it?" He sat on the edge of the mattress.

"I don't know where to begin."

Myron waited. Then, realizing he was cold, he went back to the bathroom for his bathrobe. He tied the belt, came out, sat back down on the bed.

"What are you doing here?" he asked.

"I came to see Gertrude," she answered.

"Well, that's not hard to do," said Myron. "She seems to be on display. I've been invited by Noel Sullivan to a dinner he's giving for her day after tomorrow. Why don't you come along with me?"

But Mabel was shaking her head. "I was invited to that dinner party," she said.

"Then what's the problem?"

"Yesterday I was uninvited."

"What!"

"I was uninvited! That's why I'm here. Noel Sullivan called me and said that he had just spoken to Miss Toklas, who told him that if I was at the dinner, Gertrude Stein would not be there."

"I don't believe it! What did you say?"

"I didn't say anything. I just stood there with the receiver to my ear and listened to this stuttering ass tell me what a difficult position he was in. 'M-M-Miss Toklas has m-m-m-made the terms absolute,' he said."

Myron smiled. She'd gotten Noel to a tee.

"He said there was nothing for him to do but withdraw his invitation. He hoped I would understand."

"What did you say?"

"I told him I'd heard of his reputation as a good man and had expected better of him. He stuttered some more. I hung up."

"He just invited me today." Myron paused. "I guess I'm your replacement."

"Yes."

"I won't go," Myron decided.

"Would you do that for me?" Mabel asked. Then she shook her head. "No. You go. I want you to."

"Why?"

"I want someone I can trust to tell me what they're like."

"The Jefferses will be there."

"No, they won't. They've already called Sullivan and canceled."

Myron shook his head. It seemed the lion hunters were shooting at each other.

"Mabel, why is it so important you see Gertrude Stein?"

"I want to be reconciled with her."

"I didn't know there was a need for reconciliation."

"There is," she said, and she related her attempts to get in touch with Miss Stein on this American tour and how she had been rebuffed.

"But why did you want to get in touch with her?"

"How can you ask that, Myron? You've read *European Experiences*."

Myron nodded.

"Couldn't you read between the lines?" Mabel asked, a softer, fonder tone in her voice. "She loved me as an equal, someone who matched her strength for strength. She loved me the way Lawrence said love had to be, a struggle of equal passions and equal intellects."

Myron remembered the scene Mabel was referring to. It was at the Villa Curonia in 1911. She's in her bedroom with her son John's tutor, who is trying to make love to her. Gertrude Stein is in the next room writing. It's very late at night and Mabel both hopes and dreads that Gertrude Stein will hear the sounds of frustrated sex she and the tutor are making.

"Instead she settled for that nonentity, that woman who made herself into a servant and seduced her with comfort, and worshipped her so that Gertrude began to believe she was some kind of goddess."

"Are you saying that you and Gertrude Stein were lovers?"

"Of course not," Mabel snapped.

"Then why are you comparing yourself to her lover? I'm sure Alice B. Toklas has had an entirely different role in Gertrude Stein's life than you. You're comparing apples and oranges."

"Then why can't she see that?" asked Mabel, picking up his argument. "We went through so much together. We were a part of each other's beginnings. We were friends. I don't understand why she's rebuked me."

"Well, at least you understand that it's her and not just Alice Toklas." Myron didn't know this but he couldn't imagine how a woman as strong willed and self-possessed as Gertrude Stein could be led by anyone.

Mabel nodded.

"You know," Myron said after a moment, "I have an explanation for her behavior that has nothing to do with the past."

"What?"

"I think it's *European Experiences*," he said.

"How could she have read it? It hasn't been released."

"You said you sent Carl Van Vechten an advance copy. I'd bet my bottom dollar he's shown it to her."

She nodded at the possibility.

"Now it's out there for the world to see." Myron paused. "I've discovered something from my own experience writing about real people." He wasn't thinking of *The Flutter of an Eyelid* but his own family's reaction to *Singermann*. "You can't do it. What you think is a beautiful portrait of someone's humanity is to them a humiliating invasion of their privacy. They don't want to be caught like that on paper."

"But I let her do my portrait. It was one of her first recognized pieces."

"You're an exception. Besides," and he couldn't resist, "except for the title, who can tell it's you?"

"But she let Picasso paint her portrait."

"Painting is different. It's not words. It can't be misinterpreted. Think of it. Who's more private than Gertrude Stein? She writes and writes and says nothing about anything, certainly not herself."

Mabel nodded.

"Do you still want me to go?" Myron asked.

"Yes," and she was vehement again. "I want you there."

"But why? What do you want me to do? "

"I don't want you to do anything," Mabel answered. "Don't even mention me. I just want you there."

She's only taking me back, he thought, because she has a use for me. Ah, these important personalities. Yet they did have a special aura, a sizzle. How do they do it? In Mabel's case it was money. After all, wasn't capitalism really a kind of industrial egotism? Wealth wasn't just an accumulation of other people's toil. It was an extension of personality. He looked at her. What was he going to do? Even now, even though she was soaking wet and acting like a jealous child, he felt something for her. Though she was putting it in the wrong terms, though the words she was using rang false, there was real feeling coming from her eyes. In her own way Mabel had loved someone and that someone had rejected her. He couldn't resist the sadness of it. It matched his own.

"All right," he said. "I'll go."

Four

THERE WERE CARS PARKED ALL AROUND Innisfree when Myron walked up to the Gothic door. He opened it and the firecracker sound of barking dogs reminded him that Noel had replaced Greta with not one but two animals. Sure enough, four dachshunds bounded toward him, ferocity and menace in their dark eyes. They would let him pass only after a vigorous petting for each of them. Then Myron was hanging his coat on the already full bar of the hall closet, piling his hat on the already full shelf above the coats, and going down the short hall to the already full living room. Yet the first thing he noticed were the candles and shrines Noel had placed here and there, tiny votives to his favorite saints though the bloodiest of the religious depictions had been removed. And there was Noel, in uncharacteristic white trousers and a blue blazer, coming forward to greet Myron, his face above his jaunty attire looking as melancholy as ever. But before they could shake hands a female guest stepped between them, threw her arms around her host's neck, and kissed his cadaverous cheek.

"Darling, everything's so lovely!" she gushed. "I wish I knew how you did it. It's a gift!"

"Thanks for c-c-coming," Noel said after the woman moved off. "I'm afraid this isn't going to be a very b-b-big party." Then he leaned over, picked up a marmalade cat, kissed its nose, and set it down again. It stared up at him reproachfully out of saffron-colored eyes.

"I love parties when you give them, old dear," said another woman coming up to them. She was limber and smart in her white skirt and strawberry-red jacket and Noel introduced her to Myron as Irene Alexander, a reporter for the *Monterey Peninsula Herald*. Then she noticed the ash at the end of her cigarette and began looking frantically for an ashtray. Too late. The accumulation fell on Noel's beautiful oriental rug, which he promptly stamped into the weave, smiling at her forgivingly.

"There are n-n-never enough ashtrays," he noted as if ashtrays were a metaphysical problem.

Myron excused himself and went to the bar that had been set up in one corner. People were either sitting on the sofas or wandering around with glasses in their hands. He thanked the white-jacketed Negro for his whiskey and soda and crossed to the wall of windows. Outside, beyond where Greta was buried, a terrace opened to the first garden. Below this first one were descending levels of gardens, all the way down to a lovely pond in which Noel had placed a fountain he had designed himself and said he was going to take to the new place. It contained two statues. Why, Myron once asked, did you put the Virgin on one side of the pool and the devil on the other? Because good can transform evil, Noel explained. Our Lady is purifying the water that spouts from the devil's mouth. But isn't the water already pure? asked Myron. Of course not, Noel answered incredulously. How can it be pure, dear boy, if it comes out of the devil's mouth? But you put the devil there, said Myron. I put the devil there? asked Noel. Certainly not. The devil is everywhere. We destroy him with God. It's a constant battle. I see, said Myron. But he didn't.

Now he turned back to the room. Almost directly behind him was Jaime de Angulo, the anthropologist and linguist who had a small ranch up in the hills. Jaime had been pointed out to Myron on Ocean Avenue some weeks before. But the big surprise was that he was talking to Ella Winter. Myron didn't know whether or not to go over to them. He remembered his last meeting with Ella. And Myron had been told that Jaime was supposed to be too depressed to see anyone. The year before he'd been in a terrible auto accident. The story was that he'd fallen asleep, driven over a cliff, and broken his back. He was lucky to be alive. His young son, however, had not been so lucky. Myron was about to turn away when Ella Winter waved him over and asked if he'd met Jaime. He said he hadn't and the two men shook hands.

"Where are the guests of honor?" Myron asked.

"Here they are now," said Ella, looking over his shoulder.

Myron turned. He had to look twice. Noel was so tall and the two women so tiny. Then Noel cleared his throat and everyone looked over.

"Our g-g-guests," he announced and the murmur of the room increased.

He led the women over to the far couch where he bade them sit while he got them wine. People rose from the couch to make room. Gertrude Stein and Alice Toklas sat and to their pleasure and surprise the dogs, as if on cue, joined them in a melee of face licking and tail wagging. Unlike the dogs, however, Myron took an immediate dislike to them. It wasn't just the way they had treated Mabel. It was more visceral. He didn't like Gertrude Stein's looks. Why? And immediately it came to him. She looked like his brother Jack: short and round, a tough Jewish type, and sly, too. The diamond ring on the middle finger of her right hand didn't help either. Jack had flaunted just such a stone after he drove their father out of business. Was this the wise Buddha Lincoln Steffens had described? And Alice Toklas was even worse. With her dark mustache, hooked nose, thick piles of black hair held in place by a broad-brimmed cloche hat, and dark, flitting, suspicious eyes that moved from one face to another, she seemed to Myron Iago in drag, keeping watch on her stocky little Othello lest some gorgeous Desdemona come too close.

"Sorry we're late," said Gertrude Stein to the room after Noel had delivered their wine. "But we got lost." There was laughter. "No, that's not quite true," and she glanced at Alice Toklas. "I got lost. And by insisting I wasn't, I refused Alice's advice." She turned to Alice. "There," she said. "I told them."

Alice nodded and smiled, revealing large gray teeth.

"But here we are," Miss Stein went on, "in your lovely little town." She paused, and added, "I think that if Carmel had existed when I lived here, I might never have left California." She again looked at her friend.

"Yes, lovey," Alice Toklas agreed.

Gertrude Stein faced the room. "How did the place come into being?" she asked.

Myron stood in the background, whiskey and soda in hand, listening as the locals gave a short history of the place, how the poets Jack Sterling and Mary Austin found it, and how cheap it had been for them to set themselves up. Whenever the story flagged Miss Stein would ask another question and Myron realized that the writer could, as they say, chat people up. But when she was asked something, she had several evasive conversational gambits to avoid a direct answer.

"How have you found America so far?" someone asked.

"Maps," Miss Stein said, then added with a twinkle, "It's really quite easy."

A great deal of nervous laughter.

"What do you think of America after so long an absence?"

"I'm shocked by the condition of the roads but I adore the dust storms."

Nervous laughter, again. Even Myron, taken by surprise, laughed. But he didn't think it was funny.

"How does Paris feel about the rise of the Nazis in Germany?" he asked and wondered if she could turn Hitler into a joke. I disagree with his ends but you have to admire the way he accomplishes them. Smirk, smirk.

"Ah, Mr. Brinig," said Gertrude Stein, looking him directly in the eye. "I heard about your book. I'm so sorry." She paused and turned to the room. "Needless to say book burning is a hateful form of censorship. No writer can condone it."

Myron was flattered to be recognized, and by name, too, for they had not been introduced. He realized that Noel must have explained to her who each guest was and what his or her claim to fame might be. It seemed that to have had a book burned by the Nazis was his claim.

"Have you had any books burned?" he asked.

"I haven't."

"But you're Jewish." He thought she might deny this.

"None of my work has been translated into German. I'm told I'm untranslatable, that I make no sense in a foreign language." She smiled. "Most people say that's true in English, also."

More laughter.

"Who do you think is the star of the Paris art scene?" Jaime de Angulo asked.

"Ah, you're the linguist. I've heard a lot about you."

Jaime had made his fame as a recorder of Indian dialects. The first to take down Tiwa, the language of the Taos Pueblo, he was a great friend of Tony's, and Mabel had given him several pages in *Lorenzo in Taos*. He was the young man with all the muscles who insisted on going around in front of Frieda without a shirt, thus infuriating Lawrence.

"Picasso, without doubt," Gertrude Stein answered. "He never ceases to amaze. The new ideas just keep coming. But I'm afraid that with the legally elected government of Spain about to be challenged by Franco and his Falangists, he'll return to his native country and join the Loyalists."

Everyone in the room knew Picasso was the great man of the Paris modern art world, and that a civil war was about to break out in Spain and what Picasso's political sympathies were. Yet they acted as if this horse's mouth was telling them something new. And Myron was still thinking of her answer to his question about escaping book burnings. Was she saying that it was his own fault his book had been burned, that if he'd been the right kind of writer, the untranslatable kind, it wouldn't have happened? There was something self-righteous in her sympathy. Was this her charm? Her ability to judge? Had the art world at last found something it didn't know it needed, a Jewish mother?

"Do you own a lot of Picassos?" he asked, glancing again at the huge diamond on her middle finger

"I do," she said, a smile of pleasure beginning on her broad face. But only beginning, for in the next moment she understood the veiled accusation, one Jew recognizing the wiles of another. After all, what was *The Autobiography of Alice B. Toklas* really about but how to buy cheap, hold, and, at the right time, sell dear? Didn't his brother Jack have the same smile on his face when he bought the stock of a bankrupt competitor for ten cents on the dollar?

"I wish we owned more," said Alice B. Toklas defiantly. Another Jew, she too had heard the accusation.

"I wish I owned one," said Ella Winter and giggled. What had happened? The Red was totally out of character. There was laughter but Miss Stein kept a straight face and it quickly died. Then someone asked what she thought she'd given Hemingway as a writer.

"Directly," she answered, "not much." Then she added, "but he's taken a lot without seeming to know it. That way he doesn't have to acknowledge his debt." Some laughter and she glanced at Myron, who had the satisfaction of knowing she was going to be more careful of what she said. "But he loved the painters," she added, "the Cubists particularly. I never understood that until a few years ago when I reread *A Farewell to Arms*."

"What do you mean?" asked Martin Flavin. The Flavins had come in late.

"I think Cubism said something to him about war. I'm not sure he knew what he was doing. As I said, he's not a conscious artist. But at the beginning of those chapters where Frederick Henry is riding toward the front in his ambulance, there are descriptions of the Caporetto countryside he sees before him. As he draws nearer the battlefield these descriptions become increasingly abstract and geometric. The scene becomes a field of literary cubism."

Everyone nodded thoughtfully. And Myron tried to remember. It had been so long since he'd read the novel.

"Along with natural detail," she went on, "you get a projection of Frederick Henry's fear expressed in angles and circles. His mind is distancing him from the horror of reality. He's already retreating into the tunnel inside his skull."

"I don't know," Myron piped up. "I agree that those descriptions convey fear and tension. But I don't remember there being any of the language of geometry or abstraction. They just seem to be long camera shots of the battlefield. Are you saying that all long views are geometric?" It was an interesting observation. "Distance does have a tendency to abstract."

"I-I-I have a copy of the novel," said Noel, smiling. The party was going very well, his guests having an intellectual discussion. "Why don't I f-f-fetch it."

"Don't bother," said Gertrude Stein. "It's not that important."

Myron felt he'd been dismissed and, after getting a refill, found himself commenting on nearly everything she said, not impolitely or aggressively, but to keep her talking. The trouble was she didn't want to keep talking. Though she had a reputation as a conversationalist, it seemed that in front of a large group like this, she preferred to deliver opinions quickly and ex cathedra, like a pope or the oracle at Delphi. And as she began to say less, the other people in the room began to grow uncomfortable, and Myron realized that because he was not the star of this dinner, his own behavior was being seen not so much as thought provoking but obnoxious. Fame's political, he thought. You don't have the votes. Shut up. In a while dinner was served: Dungeness crab salad, salmon smothered in capers, and Eulah's homemade cherry pie. There were too many for the dining room so most of the guests ate casually at folding tables set up in the living room. Myron sat at the bar.

After dinner someone asked Noel if he would sing. There was a murmur of agreement among the guests including the guests of honor. Noel sat down at the piano at the end of the living room, looked around, and warmed up with a few arpeggios. Then he announced he would sing the Prince's aria of lost love from Tchaikovsky's *The Queen of Spades*. With no sign of a stutter he began in Russian in a bass voice that was so at odds with his physical appearance that Myron felt Noel must have toiled over its production for years. His voice gave an impression of power and manliness that he actually did not possess. Or was it the other way around? Was the power part of the real Noel, and the soft man the pretender? Was Noel, for some saintly reason, ashamed of his strength? Be that as it might, when he was done there was long applause from everyone and pleas for an encore. Noel demurred. Then someone asked if she could read something of Miss Stein's to the group.

Myron didn't know this person but she appeared from her clothing—brown corduroy trousers, a blue button-down Brooks Brothers shirt, a striped tie, and a tweed sports jacket—to be a kind of Ivy League lesbian. Gertrude Stein looked at Alice B. Toklas, then turned to the woman, smiled, and nodded. Myron was disappointed that the author wouldn't read it herself. He remembered what Lincoln Steffens had said about her, that when she read she exuded peace and wisdom. Her reading might have changed his first impression of her.

"'Lifting Belly,'" the woman announced.

Thinking he'd heard incorrectly, Myron wanted to ask the woman to repeat what she said. But he'd asked too much already.

"How did you get that?" asked Gertrude Stein, who seemed suddenly anxious. "It hasn't been published. I didn't think it was in America at all."

Myron looked at what the woman held before her and saw that it wasn't actually a book but a brown folder with a ribbon holding the pages in.

"A mutual friend," said the smiling Ivy Leaguer. "It's already famous among us. A classic." These extravagant compliments seemed to calm the author. She and Alice B. Toklas sat back. "This," the Ivy-Leaguer announced to the rest of the room, "is an erotic poem about two women who love each other very much." She paused to let the import of this sink in. Myron hadn't realized that Gertrude Stein wrote erotic poetry. He looked around. But there was nothing to be learned from the other guests. And he was still trying to figure out the title.

"I'm going to read from the middle section."

Gertrude Stein nodded and the woman began.

"I say lifting belly and I say lifting belly and Caesars."

He'd heard right. "Lifting Belly" it was.

"I say lifting belly gently and Caesars gently," the woman crooned in a soft sing-song. She seemed to be doing her impression of a high-priestess. "I say lifting belly again and Caesars again. I say lifting belly and I say Caesars and cow come out." She paused briefly at the introduction of this new bovine element. "I say lifting belly and Caesars and cow come out."

Myron looked around. There was confusion on some faces, knowledgeable looks on others. He turned to Gertrude Stein and Alice B. Toklas, who were listening intently. He turned away and decided he liked it. For the first time Gertrude Stein was getting through to him. It was nonsense. It was repetitive. But it was also affectionate if you filled in the right body parts.

"Lifting belly say can you see the Caesars. I can see what I kiss. Of course you can. Lifting belly high. That is what I adore always more and more. Come out cow. Yes oh yes cow come out."

But if you didn't fill in the right body parts it was very funny. So in order to keep from laughing Myron kept trying to make sense out of it. The cow that came out could be a breast, or a clitoris licked by a rough bovine tongue. Yes, it was baby talk but erotic also. And this understanding might have kept it serious if he hadn't attached the writer's body to the words. For he suddenly saw Gertrude Stein's very own large round naked belly being held like a beach ball. He turned away, caught the eye of Jaime de Angulo, who turned away from him. Was he thinking the same thing? Then Myron thought he heard something from the kitchen. Was Eulah Farr listening, Eulah, who preferred John Masefield, good old nineteenth-century Eulah and some of the necessarily brave Hyde Street staff? Did they see it also? Myron looked at the guests of honor. They'd heard the laughter but were taking it well. The humor was intentional.

"Lifting belly can you say it. Lifting belly persuade me. Lifting belly has a dress. Lifting belly is a mess. Lifting belly persuade me."

Now there was definite giggling, and not only from the kitchen. Ella Winter, rabid Communist, target of the American Legion, was biting her lip, and tragic, filicide Jaime de Angulo was smiling. And the Flavins. Even Noel.

"Lifting belly, Chickens are rich . . . "

Chickens are rich?

There was a howl from the kitchen.

Then everyone in the living room was laughing, even the poor reader, who until that moment had been oblivious to her audience's reaction. Myron was one of the last to lose control. He tried to hold on. He bit his lip, pinched his thigh. No avail. He was seeing Gertrude Stein naked, her paunch in her hands like a colorful beach ball. She was walking toward Alice. He knew the poem was meant as playful, sensuous nonsense, a lover seen lovingly by a partner. But the nonsense far outweighed the sensuous, the cartoon vision of the skinny, mustachioed Alice catching the fleshy ball, then throwing it back. Myron had to let go. His laughter exploded and he turned from the reader and that's when he saw Gertrude Stein glaring at him. Then she was leaning toward the reader and whispering something. The woman closed her folder.

The laughter subsided, and Eulah and another member of Noel's now straight-faced, lip-biting Hyde Street staff brought in a tray of coffee. But the party had run out of steam. People hurried the hot liquid down their throats, and Gertrude Stein and Alice B. Toklas came round to shake everyone's hand. Myron, embarrassed by his behavior, was already in the hall getting his raincoat. When he turned he found himself facing the two tiny women in their coats. He turned back to get his hat but Miss Stein tapped him on the shoulder and he faced her.

"I hear Mabel's in Carmel," she said. "I know you're a friend of hers." There was accusation in this recognition. "When you see her, I hope you won't mention I'm here. I don't want to see her."

With that request Myron's remorse evaporated. He turned to Alice B. Toklas and her beady black eyes, then back to Gertrude Stein. They saw him as Mabel's lackey. Now they would make him their lackey. Suddenly he admired Mabel. Not only had she stood up to these two, she was also a much better writer than this charlatan so admired by the world. Mabel had put herself on paper for all to see while this woman hid behind her cute wordplay and tautologies. But tonight Miss Stein had been flushed out. All her life she'd hidden herself so she could laugh at others and here, for a few moments at least, she'd been recognized as silly and laughed at. And everyone knew that a celebrity with a bestselling book who lectured at universities and was interviewed by the press, the priestess who promised secret cabalistic meanings if only her readers concentrated harder, was not to be laughed at.

"What did she ever see in you?" Myron snarled.

The two women took a step back. Then they held their ground.

"Grow up, young man," hissed Gertrude Stein. And Myron thought she might strike him. But she turned and went out into the rain, followed by the mysterious, scheming, Byzantine Alice.

Myron smiled at their backs. I'm not that young, he thought.

The next day he called Noel ostensibly to thank him and to apologize if anything he said had seemed out of line.

"I may have had a bit too much to drink. I'm told that I get pretty disagreeable when I've had too much."

"N-N-No," said Noel. "Y-Y-You were the life of the p-p-party. W-W-Wasn't that poem or whatever it was ghastly?"

"If a fat, homely, middle-aged, Jewish woman is your dish, it was quite pornographic," noted Myron.

Then he told Noel that Mabel was in Carmel.

"Oh n-n-no," the man cried. "Had I known I w-w-w-would have asked her to my dinner. It w-w-w-would have been exciting h-h-having them b-b-b-both there."

Liar, Myron thought, and repeated what Gertrude Stein had said to him at the end about not wanting to see Mabel. He was giving Noel yet another chance to come clean.

But Noel would not own up.

"What g-g-gives between them?" he asked in all innocence.

"Do you know Mabel?" Myron asked.

"Oh, y-y-yes. Sh-Sh-She used to own property here. M-M-Maybe she still does. I m-m-met her at the Jefferses' house. I admire her enormously, and you m-m-must tell her how sorry I am not to have known she was in town. I certainly would have asked her t-t-to m-m-my dinner."

So he's sticking to his story, even knowing that I'll hear the truth from Mabel. But he doesn't care if I know the truth. That's how little he thinks of me. What can you do with rich people like Noel and Mabel? Is that what Cady's really like too? Does he make the world into what he wants it to be?

"Noel," Myron said, interrupting the man's stuttered musings about what great conversation there would have been if only he had known Mabel was there. "I'm going to level with you. The night before your party Mabel came by my cottage and told me she'd been invited to your party by you and then uninvited by you at the request of the guest of honor. I realized then that I was invited to fill her place. You knew I was a friend of hers and yet you were prepared to have me, albeit inadvertently, risk that friendship. You put me in a bad position, Noel, and one I would never have known about if Mabel hadn't told me."

It was delicious, this irony of who knows what, of who is doing what to whom. It certainly can take the wind out of one's sails, something that was at that moment happening to Noel. Myron waited but there was nothing from the other end, not even a hesitation. He remembered that first night when Noel stood in the gloom beside the bed, unable to make up his mind, unable to speak.

"I think you'd better mend some fences, Noel," Myron prompted. "Gertrude Stein's going back to Paris never again to be seen in these parts. Mabel's about to come out with two very good books." Myron was pointing out that in his effort to bag one trophy, Noel had given up another, possibly of greater value. "Lincoln Steffens thinks these two women are the most important contributors to the ideas that have created our century. And you've managed to alienate one of them."

"Wh-wh-what do you mean?"

"I'm saying they're a matched set." Myron was making this up on the spot. "You've got to have both."

"I g-g-get your drift. W-W-What should I do?"

"Be honest. Mabel's nobody's fool," and, he added silently, nor am I. But after he hung up he felt terrible. What am I doing with these people? he wondered. Why am I playing these stupid games?

Myron opened his eyes. He wasn't sure where he was. A thin slab of light appeared at one side of the bed and for a moment he felt he was back in his own room in Butte; but it wasn't his room. Then he moved his leg and felt the warmth of a human body. His heart accelerated. Obscure pictures appeared before his eyes. He remembered going into the hillbilly bar to find his look-alike friend. But he wasn't there and he remembered going to two other bars to ask for the man with the same name as the capital of Alabama. Myron knew all the state capitals by heart, some of the first things he'd ever memorized. Now he lifted himself slightly. His head felt like stone, but stone that felt pain. He could see that the other man was lying on his back, breathing heavily through his open mouth. His face was pale and thin, the skull of a man just dead, still unclean from living.

Myron was fascinated. Thin, sickly pale hairs were growing out of the chin and throat, and the arms over the quilt were pale, limp, and long without muscle, strength, or force, the hands long and thin, crab fingers. From the mouth came pointed puffs of sound that stank of whiskey and ill-digested food. Who is he? Myron wondered. Then he looked at his own body. Thin and without stamina it lay there in a state of sickness beside another body already stinking of death. Where am I? he wondered and slipped out of bed, picked up his clothes and dressed as quickly as he could, not daring to look again. He didn't want to wake the man. He couldn't bear those eyes opening to look at him, nor words spoken, questions and replies. His skin felt dirty and there was a movement through his hair like lice, but it may have been only his own nerves wriggling under his scalp. Dressed, he went softly to the door, opened it, stepped into the hall, opened another door, and found the morning.

But the cool, fresh air buckled his knees. He got to the curb and looked up and down the street. Not a sound, not a movement, and all the houses identical, impersonal as slabs in some potter's field. He started walking to the corner, wavering from side to side, his body trembling, feverish and hungover. At the corner he looked for a cab, but there was none, and he began walking again. After a few blocks he lost the sense of urgency. A few stray wisps of life, men going to work or on their way home from night jobs, brought him around enough to think about what happened. He had spent the night with a crate of bones, imagining pleasure and love. But instead of finding love he'd been measured by the inchworms of disgust. He was being measured now. They were crawling over his skin, under his clothes. He arrived at a wide boulevard, saw a taxi, lifted his arm. When the cab pulled up he opened the door, got in, and told the driver to take him to Taylor Street.

The cool wind that blew across his face felt fresh. He leaned back and closed his eyes, but felt his garments stinking over his body. Another man's sweat and pollution was soiling his pores. In his room he undressed, went into his tiny bathroom, and stood under a hot shower for ten minutes. Would it have been any different with Abel Birmingham? No. He'd felt just as terrible that morning, too. He threw himself onto the bed and instantly fell asleep.

When he awoke things weren't any better. What was causing this? It seemed to him to have begun with Gertrude Stein. All his brashness had done was point out to him his own failure. Why was she so certain of her fame, which had nothing to do with her art? As far as he could tell her art was nonexistent. A charlatan was being rewarded by the world while he was failing. The blunt apparition of failure had been growing in him. None of his recent writing had found readers. Was it his fault or the fault of the world? Was the world so confused that all they wanted from an artist was ego, someone who would lead them? Didn't the work matter at all?

Myron couldn't write. *The Sisters* wasn't going well. It wasn't going at all. So he decided to read. Sometimes reading helped. If you read something really good that had been well received by the world, it was encouraging. It meant the world wasn't in such bad shape. It meant it might like your stuff, too. So he bought *Of Time and the River,* Thomas Wolfe's new book, read it, and was bowled over. It was Wolfe's heartfelt love of a place and people. And Wolfe was the writer with whom, after *Singermann*'s release, Myron had been compared. The reviewer in the *London Times* had called them the rising stars of the American literary scene and the future of the novel in America. But Wolfe seemed to be getting better and better. All Myron was doing was marking time. So instead of making him feel better, Wolfe's novel only exacerbated his despair. It's not Gertrude Stein's fault, he told himself. You've no one to blame but yourself.

The day after he finished *Of Time and the River* there was a letter from Mabel asking him to tell her all about what happened at the dinner as if they were the best of friends. She wanted gossip. God-sib. God sister. Is that what he was? All right. You want us to be close? You want us to be friends. Then you have to listen to me as I listened to you.

May 2, '35.

Dear Mabel:

I finished "The Sun Sets In The West" and sent it to Farrar. I suppose there are good pages in it. But it's not what I feel I should be doing. But what should I be doing? I've finished Thomas Wolfe's "Of Time And The

River," a magnificent novel which I commend to you. Perhaps there's such a novel in me—But it hasn't come yet.

"Singermann" and "Wide Open Town" were written out of an overwhelming youthful memory; but nothing has happened since and I seem to have tapped the source dry. Perhaps if I quit seeing people altogether, I can recapture that old enthusiasm. I'm so oppressed with the sadness of people around me that nothing I do comes to life.

It may be a physical thing. Perhaps I drink too much. But I'm drifting. I'm beginning to doubt whether I have anything more to say. Five years ago I was deep into something very moving and poetic. Now there's a flatness and thinness in everything. I'm no Jeffers living in a world of his own. The world overwhelms me and knocks me down.

Have you ever known anyone in this state? It isn't that the will isn't there. I work as hard as ever. But the thing just doesn't come off. I can't seem to feel it as I should. My resources are limited, something I didn't realize a few years ago. I thought I'd go on to new things with little trouble. There was a tremendous upsurge in me then. But I've lost something powerful and don't know if I'll find it again.

And it isn't only my writing. The people I know leave me cold. There's something rotten about them. I used to dream of real people and now I find they're mean and petty. Worst of all, I find I'm mean and petty. What can I do about it? The adjectives, the descriptions, the full-bodied sentences are missing. I struggle over words. I feel that I've said it all before.

You live in your successes and die in your failures. I'm with it now, failure. It stares me in the face and it's abominably ugly. And you can't put your head under the covers. It's there all about you in the dark. But maybe it's best to look at it full-face rather than make a Gertrude Stein show of it. She does a vaudeville act and persuades herself that she's the real thing. I can't dismiss my situation that easily.

Sorry to bore you with this drivel.

As always, Myron

At first he thought to tear it up or send it to Cady. But he hadn't heard from Cady in weeks. Then he remembered the night just a few weeks ago when she came to him and cried because Gertrude Stein wouldn't see her. He'd felt so much for her then. There's something between us, he thought now. So he sent the letter and spent the next few days walking around the city. There was fog all around. Fog wasn't hell. It was limbo. Then one morning there was a letter from Mabel.

May 12, 1935

Dear Myron,

It was good to hear from you though I'm sorry about the circumstance of your writing. I don't know what to say that would make you feel better but to tell you the truth. This is the way it is for people like us. Not that I mean that you are a true manic-depressive. But you are an artist and artists certainly have their ups and downs of mood. Usually our ups are controlled by our work, that is, we work out our manic energy in our creations. This is one of the joys of being an artist and I'm sure one of the reasons we do what we do.

But sometimes we are caught between creations and drop into despair. Beauty will never happen again, or it never did happen. All the work we did, as beautiful as it was, is nothing. I think this is one of the reasons artists keep working, to find it again. What am I saying, Myron? I guess it's that you must get to work, but not the kind of work that your disciplined nature lets you do, but that other kind of work, that inspired work that destroys the bad stuff in you and makes you begin again to fight your way through to what you know is true.

Now to change the subject. I don't know if you have heard but we've had a terrible shock here. Bronson Cutting is dead. He was killed a few days ago when the plane taking him back to Washington went down in a storm. I still can't believe it. He was such a good man. On the other hand these things happen. Of course our wonderful Governor Tingley has appointed the loser of the election to his seat. Politics is such a dirty game. So here I am off to a funeral where I will see the Dasburgs and Cliff McCarthy who are taking it very hard. I am too. We had such high hopes.

Feel better, my darling man

Mabel

Surprisingly, after he read it, despite the terrible news or perhaps because of it, Myron did feel better. Not that he wasn't shocked and saddened by Cutting's death. The man had been so alive, so intelligent and kind. He wondered if Cady knew and if he should write him about it. How would he take it? The next day Myron got a letter from John Farrar praising *The Sun Sets in the West* and with it a check for five hundred dollars, an advance on *The Sisters*, which John said sounded like a fine book. Myron knew that if he cashed the check it was tantamount to signing a contract. He hesitated a day, then deposited it, and just like that his depression was gone. Is that's all it takes, praise and money in the bank? Am I that easy?

When he told Noel that he had decided to return to Taos, the man offered to drive him. Myron knew what Noel was doing, making a pilgrimage, mending social fences as he had advised. It was a pleasant drive, Noel's new sixteen-cylinder Cadillac moving quickly from the cold dampness of the coast to the warm California wine region, then down into the Arizona desert where each blooming saguaro wore a single flower like a cheap hat.

"I-I-I hope you'll tell Mabel how much I look forward to seeing her."

"But you'll tell her yourself when you call her," Myron said.

"N-N-No!" said Noel. "You speak for me. I-I-I've given her a terrible affront."

Myron nodded, though he had the same feeling as when Gertrude Stein tried to use him as a messenger—which was odd because he'd planned on his own to speak up for Noel. When they got to Taos, Myron directed Noel to the Pink House, where Mabel said he was staying. After they pulled up, he made a suggestion.

"We could walk over to the Big House right now," he said.

But the tall man demurred, saying he wanted to get a room first. Of course! Casually dropping in isn't the same thing as being asked to come by. Myron said there was room enough here in the Pink House if he wanted to stay with him. But even that would be imposing on Mabel's hospitality. So Noel went off to La Fonda, and as soon as Myron was unpacked, he called Mabel to say he had arrived and to mention that Noel Sullivan had driven him down and would be staying in Taos for a few days. All she said was that he should come over as soon as he could. When he got there she was in the Rainbow Room on her chaise, a turban on her head, a gown around her like a comforter, sipping a cocktail and looking like—well, like Mabel.

"Noel Sullivan drove me from Carmel," Myron said again. "You know, he admires you so much and he told me how much he's looking forward to seeing you again. I know he wants to apologize." He paused. "He's leaving tomorrow or the next day." She didn't say anything. "He wants to tell you how sorry he was about the way he handled the Gertrude Stein dinner."

"I'm glad I didn't go." She was suddenly pouting. "She was always jealous of me—why, I haven't the faintest idea. Was it because I sided with Leo?" She paused. "They were always squabbling about who owned what paintings and they haven't spoken for years. You know, it was Leo who first put her onto art. Now she takes all the credit for that."

Myron had forgotten Gertrude Stein's brother was a friend of Mabel's.

"Really," she went on, "I have nothing against her." As if to make this point she jumped up from the chaise-lounge and went to her statue of the Buddha. Lifting Belly, Myron thought. "She begged me to let her come stay at the villa, and I introduced her to quite a number of important people."

This was Mabel's latest revision of history. In *European Experiences* she had written that the Steins had a salon back in 1906 when she was still a depressed Buffalo matron. Not until she arrived in Paris and saw the Stein salon at work did she realize its value. For entertainment alone a salon was priceless, not to mention the power it gave you. In *European Experiences* she acknowledged this debt with a brilliant description of the Steins' famous apartment full of Matisses, Cézannes, and Picassos. But Miss Stein, not so generous in *The Autobiography of Alice B. Toklas*, never once mentioned Mabel, never once acknowledged what she owed her one-time friend. It was Mabel who had done the first article on Stein's writing telling the world why it was so good and original, and it was Mabel who, at her own expense, had four hundred copies of the *Portrait of Mabel Dodge* published.

"It's all Alice's fault," Mabel went on. "She's getting revenge for what happened at the Villa Curonia when Gertrude showed special interest in me."

"I agree," said Myron though in his mind he still believed it was Gertrude's doing. His agreement seemed to please her. He turned the conversation back to where it had started. "You know, you could ask Noel what he thinks. It turns out he didn't like them at all. Won't you see him?"

"Oh, well," she said. "Tell him to stop by tomorrow. But not before three in the afternoon, after I've had my nap."

There. It was done. Myron felt better, relieved. None of it had been his fault but somehow he felt responsible.

"I'm glad to be back," he said, now that was out of the way.

Mabel left Buddha's side and came over to him. "I'm glad you're back too, Myron." Her face brightened into a beautiful smile and she wrapped her arms around him. "I've missed you," she said, then stepped back. "Now tell me what happened. I heard you were magnificent."

Myron relayed the message, and at three o'clock the following day, Noel drove his new washed Cadillac up to the lower lot, where Myron had told him to park. He got out, walked slowly up the wooden walk over the *acequia madre*, the irrigation ditch just west of the house, crossed the stone plaza to the portal, and, using the brass whiskers of the Florentine lion door-knocker, rapped on Mabel's front door. Nothing happened. Myron watched from his window and thought to go over but didn't. After a few more minutes of knocking and waiting and looking around, Noel left. When Myron saw him a few hours later at La Fonda, he was still white with rage. It was not the same Noel who when discussing death said he was resigned to living an eternity in the bosom of Christ, his Lord. No, this was the Noel who, impressed by reputation, desperately wanted some claim to worldly fame.

"She's a third-rate w-w-woman! I always s-s-suspected it. Look at the way she pursued L-L-Lawrence and all the others, and her b-b-b-books are stupid."

"I like her books."

"They're so. . . . " He stopped. "I hope you w-w-won't repeat what I've just said." He seemed suddenly aware that he was acting in a very uncharacteristic way and that it would get back to Mabel. "It's all s-s-so unimportant and I'm n-n-not unhappy about n-n-not having seen her."

Of course they both knew he'd been punished. If Mabel couldn't get at the person who actually insulted her, she could strike at an underling who had aided in that insult.

After all, what were underlings for?

"I w-w-wanted to make amends," Noel said.

"But you have," Myron said. "You've driven over a thousand miles and not seen the person you specifically came to see. Furthermore you allowed that person to do to you exactly what you did to her. Think of this trip as an act of contrition. You've offered the other cheek and it's been slapped."

"I c-c-couldn't help myself," Noel protested weakly after mulling over what Myron had said. "Gertrude Stein m-m-made me do it!"

"Yes," said Myron and realized that he was taking satisfaction in Mabel's snub of Noel. "You couldn't help it."

So Noel left without seeing Mabel. And Myron was invited to dinner, where he once again brought Noel up by reminding her she had agreed to see him and telling her how the man had shown up as she had told him to do and how distraught, angry, and hurt he was. Though he was couching the story in terms of a reprimand, he knew this news would give her pleasure.

"I must've forgotten," she said, though she was a woman

who never forgot anything, "because every Thursday, as you know, Tony and I drive to Manby's Hot Springs to take the baths. We feel much better afterward. You must come with us next week. It'll do wonders for your circulation."

"He wanted so much to see you," Myron persisted. "He wanted to apologize. He was terribly disappointed."

"I don't believe that," she said, not about to take any blame. "He seems to me a very superficial man with all those sodden, religious mannerisms as if he were a martyr about to be thrown to the lions. Then he can go ahead and do something like that to me." She paused thoughtfully. "I know the Jefferses think highly of him and I suppose that's to his credit but you know how Una has a habit of latching onto people with influence and money who she feels may benefit Robin's career. I've always found the man absurd, that too-solemn air of his. He hasn't a real idea in his head. He's peripheral." She faced him. "Don't tell me you find a man like that interesting. He's so false, so bogus."

"He was kind to me."

"Let's change the subject," she said. "I've just finished *Of Time and the River*. It's everything you said. A magnificent work."

"I'm so glad you liked it."

"What a powerhouse the man must be! I'd love to meet him."

"I hear he's difficult."

"As difficult as you?" This was her first reference to her anger at him last summer over the sacred Taos crap. Would they talk about it?

"Oh, I'm a pussycat," he said smiling broadly. He felt complimented. Great artists should be difficult.

"Well, I'm glad you're back," she said.

For the next two months *The Sisters* just seemed to pour out of him. There was no sign of Cady, though they were writing letters again. It had been almost six months and Myron was getting resigned to the fact it was over. It wasn't so bad. Then one day in mid-August, Mabel called.

"Guess what?" she asked.

"What?"

"Thomas Wolfe just phoned from Santa Fe. He's on his way from New York to the West Coast, and asked if he might spend the night up here. I said of course, so he's coming."

Thomas Wolfe! Myron knew at once that of all Mabel's famous guests, here was one he really wanted to meet. After he hung up he got out *Of Time and the River* and read its opening. He loved how Wolfe maintained the energy of his sentences. Who cared that he repeated himself? Each repetition was from a slightly different angle. You read one sentence into the next into the next. Only after you'd finished a paragraph could you sense the grandness of the movement. It was Keats walking around the urn, or a Hollywood close-up camera moving around a star's face. Myron put the book down and hurried up to the Big House.

"Why are you here?" Mabel asked as soon as she saw him. She was directing her servants in a massive cleanup. "I didn't call to invite you. I think one writer at a time is enough. I'll tell you all about it."

Myron turned and walked back to the Pink House. Only after he got over his initial shock and anger at her bluntness did he realize how disappointed he was. What had happened to the woman who'd written him a wonderfully consoling letter and welcomed him back? She knew how much he admired Wolfe. Why would she keep him away? Then it came to Myron that, like Noel, he too was being punished. It made no difference that she had pleaded with him to go. He'd been there and that made him part of her humiliation. And so angry was he at this injustice that he barely slept that night. But he vowed not to say anything.

"How did you get along with Wolfe?" he asked the next morning.

"I didn't see him," Mabel said. "He didn't arrive at my dinner time and I waited and waited. Then I ate. When he still didn't show up I went to bed. He arrived around midnight, dead drunk and with two women. He frightened poor Beatrice to death." Beatrice was Mabel's housekeeper.

"Oh? Where did he spend the night?"

"At La Fonda," she said. "Why don't you go down there. I know how much you wanted to meet him. If he's feeling any better, bring him up here to lunch."

Myron couldn't believe it. A second chance. Of course, she wasn't doing it for him but to save the situation. She needed him again. But he didn't care why she was doing it, and he rushed down to the hotel. He looked around the small lobby but saw no one resembling the elephantine Wolfe. Myron had heard different things from people who'd met him. The general opinion was that Wolfe was a genius with a bad temper and a bad drinking problem. In New York, one woman told Myron that Wolfe had chased her around a dinner table with a kitchen knife. Perhaps Mabel was lucky the genius hadn't stayed. Myron asked at the desk. Mrs. Karavas, the owner's wife, said Mr. Wolfe was in the dining room having breakfast. A darkly pretty, petite woman, Mrs. Karavas didn't seem frightened at all. You can't miss him, she said, smiling. She was right. Even seated, he was unmistakable. As Myron approached the table, Wolfe held out his empty glass.

"I'm not a waiter," Myron said and introduced himself.

Wolfe laughed and asked him to sit down. Then a real waiter came over. Myron ordered coffee and Wolfe got his refill of bourbon and water.

"You never got to see Mabel," he said.

"Would you believe it?" Wolfe asked with innocent incredulity. "By the time I got there she'd gone to bed."

"I just spoke to her. She wants you to come up for lunch."

"Hell no," Wolfe said. "I'm told there'll be a bus out front in a half-hour and I'm getting on it. To hell with Taos. I'm on my way to the coast."

"Well, it's too bad you didn't get to see her."

Myron didn't know what else to say. In a way he couldn't believe his good luck. Here he was sitting with Thomas Wolfe, the one author in all of America he admired the most. Here was a chance to really talk to him. So why did he keep bringing up Mabel? Gertrude Stein had tried to treat him like a messenger boy and he hadn't put up with it.

Now he was treating himself like one.

"Oh, I don't know," Wolfe was saying. "Maybe it's for the

best. This way she'll never get around to writing about me." He smiled. "She's probably a nice enough old woman." He took a swig of his just-delivered bourbon. "You want a drink?"

"No thanks." Myron paused, sipped coffee, then plunged ahead. "I'm a great admirer of yours, Mr. Wolfe," he said. "I love your work."

"Call me Tom," said Wolfe, then added, "I'm just a country boy who's learning how to write."

A country boy learning to write? Come off it. Who does he think I am, a critic? Wolfe had been hurt by critics who said his prose was sloppy and prolix, that he went on about himself too long, and worst of all, that he couldn't write without the help of his editor, Maxwell Perkins.

"Some people think I overwrite," Wolfe said.

"I think," said Myron, remembering how some critics attacked his style, "a writer is sometimes all the greater for his so-called defects. A writer lives in his style," and he paused, trying to get it right. "I think a writer's style is part of his integrity."

"What's your name again?" asked Wolfe, seeming to perk up. "I know you said it but I'm not good with names."

"Brinig. Myron Brinig."

"Myron Brinig? Don't I know that name?"

"You might. Like you I'm a writer. My second novel, *Singermann*, came out in September of 1929, two weeks after *Look Homeward Angel*. We got reviewed together in England. *The London Times* said you and I were the two best young writers in America."

"I saw that!" Wolfe said excitedly, his soft brown eyes aglow. "Max showed it to me. You know he read your book and passed it on to me." Wolfe reached across the table and shook Myron's hand. "I'm proud to meet you, Mister Brinig," he said, then looked away. "But I'm sorry to admit I haven't read your novel yet." He shrugged. "I'm too wrapped up in my own work."

"It's all right," said Myron, thrilled that an editor like Maxwell Perkins had read him. He wanted to tell Wolfe what *Of Time and the River* had done to him, how its lush beauty had depressed him and filled him with despair. But did he need to know that? "I never have enough time to read either," he said instead.

"You know," said Wolfe, his face lighting up as if he'd just found something he'd lost. "I was supposed to look you up."

"You were?"

"You write for the movies sometimes, don't you?"

"Not really, but I used to read for studios so I know lots of people who do."

"Look at this, would you?" and he pulled a letter from the inside pocket of his jacket and shoved it at Myron. It was from Sam Marx, MGM's story editor. Marx said he was writing on behalf of Irving Thalberg, and asked that Wolfe stop by the studio when he was in Hollywood so they could talk.

"What do you think?" Wolfe asked.

"I think they'll offer you work."

"And money?"

"Anywhere from thirty to fifty thousand a year." Myron let the numbers sink in, then delivered the next bunch. "Or you can work by the week and make a thousand to fifteen hundred." He paused again. "It's a lot of money in these bad times."

"It's a lot of money any time." Wolfe was wide-eyed at the prospect. "What do you think I should do?"

"Take it by the week. It gives you more flexibility."

"No, I mean what do you think I should do about working in Hollywood?"

"You really want to know?"

"Yes."

"Don't do it."

"Why?"

"Because you'll hate it. It's a waste of time." Myron had heard all this from Frank Fenton when they shared the house at Malibu. "They write by committee. Then the director changes everything and the producer changes that."

"Sounds like writer's hell."

"It is." Just then the waiter came over and Myron let Wolfe order two bourbons and water. "Here's what you should do," he said after the waiter was gone. "Sell them a novel and forget it. As my brother Jack used to say, take the money and run."

"But my novels are so long. How could they do them?"

"Size makes no difference," Myron explained. Usually he

hated thinking like this, hated the idea that the best of himself was for sale. Wasn't it why he he'd written about his family and their money-grubbing ways? He was above that. Or was he? The waiter was back with their drinks. "Plot, character, style make no difference," Myron went on after the first sip. "Hell, they'll invent most of it. All they want is your name and your book's title, and if you're offended by that, don't be."

"Offended?" Wolfe shook his head. "You know I've spoken to writers who shudder at the mention of Hollywood. They ask me if I could possibly submit my artistic conscience to prostitution by allowing something of mine to be made into a movie." He broke into a big grin. "My answer is always a fervent yes. If Hollywood wants to make me a prostitute by buying my books, I'm not only willing," and he broke into a huge grin, "I'm eager for these seducers to make their first dastardly proposal."

"That's it," said Myron. "Your position in the matter is very much like that of the Belgian virgin the night the Germans marched into her village." This was a joke he'd heard in the army. "She had only one question."

"What?" asked Wolfe.

"When do the atrocities begin?"

"That's it!" said the laughing giant and raised his glass in a mock salute. "Let the atrocities begin!"

Myron was laughing, too. And realized that he wouldn't have missed this for the world. Here were two of America's leading writers drinking and laughing together and talking shop. This is what he'd wanted from Mabel, and despite her, he'd gotten it. But as soon as he thought this, he was struck by a wave of self-pity over the suppression of *The Flutter of an Eyelid*. He hadn't thought about it in ages. Old business, he told himself. Forget it.

"Did you ever have a novel suppressed by a lawsuit?"

"No," said Wolfe. "I've made a lot of people in my hometown angry. I've been threatened, but nobody's ever actually gone to court, not yet anyway." Wolfe paused. "Why do you ask? Somebody threatening you?"

"Threatening, hell. It happened." And Myron told the story of *The Flutter of an Eyelid*.

"Now that you mention, I heard about that. It's terrible," said Wolfe, pulling out an address book. "Who you with?"

"Farrar & Rinehart."

"I'm surprised they didn't go to bat for you. That's supposed to be a good house. You should try Max Perkins at Scribner's." He tore out a page, took the pencil from the book's spine, and wrote the name and address of his publisher. Then he shoved it across the table at Myron. "And what about an agent?" asked Wolfe.

Myron said he'd never had one.

"Get one." He reached across the table, took back the paper, and wrote another name down. "He's left-wing as hell but he's good. Publishers will screw you on all kinds of things. Foreign rights and deals with Hollywood."

Myron nodded and took back the paper. Then he looked around. People were paying their bills and getting up.

"I think your bus is about to be called."

"It can wait."

"Where you going?" asked Myron.

"Today?"

"Yeah."

"Flagstaff. Gonna see the Grand Canyon." Wolfe picked up his glass and downed the remaining bourbon. "Ever done that?"

Myron shook his head no.

"After that California, then up to Oregon and Washington. I have relatives in Seattle. I wanna see this country. I envy you growing up in a place like Butte." Wolfe's eyes were glowing again. There seemed to be a demon inside of this soft man. "That's the real America," he said.

"It's just a glorified mining camp." Myron was elated. Wolfe had remembered the *London Times* review where they said Butte was his hometown.

"It's America," Wolfe said. "I want to write about America, all of it."

"Well," said Myron, nodding. "I'm not so ambitious. I can only write about what I know. And I thought I'd exhausted Butte."

"Have you?"

"No." He shook his head emphatically. "I'm writing about it again and I'm not repeating myself. You see it one way one time and when you do it again, it comes out different." Then he was telling Wolfe about his last visit with Lincoln Steffens and how angry Steffens had been because Myron didn't fit his idea of him.

Wolfe kept nodding. "I never met the man," he said when Myron was finished, "but I wanted to stop by Carmel and see him. Maybe I'll skip it." He was looking at his empty glass. "I've been hit by those kinds of critics. Granville Hicks at *The Saturday Review of Lit-tra-ture.*"

"Another?" asked Myron. "Let me buy."

They waited in silence. Wolfe seemed to be thinking. Then their bourbon and water came and they raised their glasses to literature and their place in it.

"Ah lit-tra-ture," said Myron after the first sip. "I used to think all I had to do was sell that first novel and my life would be different, that I'd move into some kind of new realm, the writer's world. But you know, there's no such place."

"You know, it's true," said Wolfe after his first sip. "I had this idea when I began writing that I could keep on growing as I'd started to grow, I mean grow in the same way, a kind of happy establishment of myself for the rest of my life, a business of me that I could go to everyday and have lunch with, and later in the afternoon, a drink with, and later still, come home with."

Myron nodded enthusiastically. It was exactly the way he'd felt.

"I'd be this writer," Wolfe went on, "and that would be a noble vocation. But I've found something out about writing. Every sentence has to be earned and the earning's hard because with each new effort comes new, what? . . . desperation. I thought I'd learn some magic formula for doing it. But I haven't learned anything, not one goddamned thing. I seem to be reinventing the wheel every time I write a word. That's why they take my style to task. I'm always starting over. I'm always a beginner. Every book is the first book."

"That's it!" said Myron and remembered Wolfe's remark about being a country boy just learning how to write. As well as pose there was truth in it.

"Yeah," said Wolfe, then leaned back. But Myron kept going.

"That's the real honesty," he said. "You have to learn how to write every time out so your style's always fresh. And you know what? In fifty years your style will be the model for the best prose. Take Dreiser, for instance. So many people think of him as a sloppy writer, but it's that very sloppiness and moralizing that makes him Dreiser. It's all part of his greatness." Myron paused and decided he liked what he'd just said. So he went on. "If he'd written like Flaubert, he wouldn't be Dreiser, would he? In some strange, magical way, his deficiencies are his integrity."

Myron was really talking about himself. They had complained about his style. One reviewer had used the word *hortatory*. Myron had to look it up. It meant *urging to action*. If that was bad, then so be it. In *Wide Open Town* his hortatory style worked because it implied there were actions to be taken that could change the situations described. His style said that fated as they were, his characters were also full of the author's hope. Then Myron remembered his conversation with Lincoln Steffens. This was what Steffens had meant when he said the novel left him with the feeling there was something to be done.

"I never thought of it that way," Wolfe said, obviously thinking of his own work. "But you're right. Unless you believe in yourself, you'll collapse under the doubts and reservations other people have about you. Your whole life, everything you hope, want, and dream of, everything that gives life any value . . . "

Someone was calling Wolfe's name. It was Mrs. Karavas. She'd come into the dining room to say that she was holding the bus for him and that he must get on it. Gulping the rest of his bourbon, Wolfe rose and for the first time Myron saw him full length. Well over six foot six with a body narrow at the top, widening to a soft middle, then sloping precipitously to his feet, he was an erect oval. Myron also stood and Wolfe said good meeting you and shook his hand. Then Mrs. Karavas, like a circus lady with a trained elephant, led him outside.

"He wouldn't come?" Mabel asked.

"No," said Myron. "He was catching the ten o'clock Trailways to Flagstaff."

"Did you get to talk to him?

"We had a couple of drinks together."

"What did he have to say?"

"Well, we discussed our lives as writers, what writing does to us. I told him how much I loved his last book and how reading it almost did me in. I was so jealous of its beauty." Myron didn't know why he was making this up. What was actually said was more than good enough. Or was it? He was drunk now, expansive and trying to make her jealous. "You know, Mabel, it's ironic. This wouldn't have happened if you had invited me to dinner." He looked at her. He was definitely gloating.

"Well, it all worked out for the best." She looked up. "I'm sure that in some way I meant it to happen when I sent you down there. I'm glad you got to talk to him. I felt bad about not inviting you last night. I remembered you saying in your letter how much you liked his work. I was thinking of calling you over to wait up for him. Who knows what might have happened if you had confronted him." A smile came across her face. "Think of it. Two of America's leading novelists squaring off in my front parlor." She paused, and added, "I like him. I kept my door open and listened to him rant and rave. He has the spirit of real genius."

Myron burst out laughing. The idea that he'd fight a giant, albeit a soft one, was funny. Yet he also knew from experience that with Mabel words said in jest had to be examined carefully. Was this her idea of what should have happened? She wouldn't have him over so they could meet and talk. Not enough drama. Fighting, on the other hand, would have been a different story.

"Can I offer you some coffee?" she asked.

"No," he said. "My writing day's shot. I need to sleep off the bourbon." He paused and smiled. "Wolfe's asleep already," he said, "mouth open, head against the window. He won't remember either of us."

"Not true," said Mabel and broke into a grin so big her gums showed. It was a facial expression she guarded against. "He'll remember me."

Five

"We made a date last night."

Myron opened his eyes. The room was empty.

"I asked you if you wanted to drive up to the pueblo."

"Cady!" He jumped out of bed, ran through the front room, threw open the door, and wrapped his arms around his friend. "I thought you'd never get back!"

"Don't you remember?" Cady closed the door behind him, pulled his polo shirt over his head, and threw it on the floor. "We made a date."

Myron laughed. He'd been thinking about this meeting. He thought he would be angry at the cavalier way Cady had treated him, that he would demand an apology, do something to show his hurt feelings. But that wasn't the way he felt. Just the sight of the little Martian was enough to quiet his anger. They were in the bedroom.

"I haven't brushed my teeth."

They fell onto the bed.

"God, I missed you, Myron," said Cady.

"And I you, Cady."

Then they were all hands, mouths, tongues, and orgasms, and then they were asleep in each other's arms. When they awoke it was hot and they were hungry so they washed and dressed and walked down to the plaza for *huevos rancheros*.

"How was the trip?" Myron asked as they ate.

"I wrote you everything in my letters," Cady said.

"But you didn't say anything about what was happening to you personally. It was all about your art."

"That's all I was interested in. That's why I went. I began in Kyoto where I started lessons in Japanese brush painting from a Zen master. But I gave it up after a couple of weeks."

"Why?"

"I don't know if it was me or them, if I felt I knew too much or if I just wasn't interested in what they knew. But Kyoto's a beautiful city, so I stayed there and studied bonsai and flower arranging."

"But what happened to your teacher in China?" Myron asked. "You were going especially to see him."

"I didn't go," said Cady, looking down. "When I had the chance I realized I didn't want to."

"Why?"

"You know I wasn't quite truthful with you when I told you about him." He was looking up now. "When I knew him before we were lovers. When he contacted me this time I knew he wanted to start again."

Myron was astonished. He couldn't imagine Cady lying. "And you were going to take him up on it?" he asked, feeling suddenly hurt.

"I thought about it. Maybe I was." He sat for a moment. "But I didn't. When it came right down to it, I couldn't."

"Oh, Cady," and Myron reached across the table to take his hand. They held each other's hands a moment. Then Cady withdrew his.

"How was San Francisco?" he asked.

"Wonderful. Great eating. I went out every night for dinner, Italian, Chinese, and real cheap."

"What did you do for entertainment?"

A dangerous question. Was Cady asking if he had been true?

"I went to Carmel on weekends."

"Why there?"

"Well, I met the strangest man. His name is Noel Sullivan. He's very rich and has a house in San Francisco and two in Carmel."

Myron saw the look of concern on Cady's face. The look told him what he wanted to know, that his friend would be hurt if he told him all that had really happened, how he had really acted. Truth was always the best. He would have to tell him of his despair and what he had done with that despair. But it would have to be later. Not now. "We never made love, no sex at all." What had he felt about Noel? It still confused him. "I liked him. No, that's not quite true. At times I did. But in many ways he was a lot like Mabel, really exasperating"

"What do you mean?"

"Well—he was a celebrity hound. He flattered himself with other people. I met Nelson Eddy and Lawrence Tibbett and lots of Negroes for whom he has an especial love. I met Marian Anderson and Paul Robeson. I even had dinner with Gertrude Stein at his house in Carmel."

"Gertrude Stein!" Cady was obviously impressed.

"Yes, and Alice B. Toklas." So he told Cady about the dinner and "Lifting Belly" and what Gertrude Stein had said to him after.

Cady laughed in all the right places. But when the story was over he was serious again. Myron knew he couldn't evade it that easily.

"So what are you saying about this man?" he asked.

It was a legitimate question. What about Noel Sullivan? Desire alone should have made them try sex at least once.

"Well, I'll be truthful, Cady." No, Myron thought, I'll throw a sop at the truth. "I wanted to have an affair. I was so angry at you for taking off like that out of the blue, particularly after you told me that you were going to see a man who I sensed had once meant something to you. I thought it was over between us. I guess I was looking for someone else."

Cady nodded.

"You know the old saying that any sex is better than none?"

Cady nodded again.

"Well, it's not true. Sometimes no sex is better."

"What do you mean?"

"I mean I knew that Noel wasn't for me the moment he opened his mouth. It wasn't just that he stuttered. It was him. Somehow I knew sex with him would be like making love through a toilet partition. Have you ever heard of that? They're called glory holes. It would be like that. I wouldn't see him, nor he me. At first I thought it was because we were so different, a godless Jew and a devout Catholic. But such differences can be attractive. So it had to be something else." And he told the story of Noel standing by the bed in the middle of the night.

"Why did he do that?"

"Well, he told me a few days later that he was in love with another man but that they'd been forced to separate. He said he found he had to be true to him." Myron thought of mentioning Langston Hughes by name. He'd read *The Weary Blues* and loved it. But he decided not to. "So I told him I was in love, too." Myron paused. "But you know, even if there wasn't you, I don't think it would have happened."

"Really?"

"We were too different. He doesn't see the world the same way as you or I. There's a wall of abstraction around him, a wall of dogma, metaphysics and ceremony that tells him the rest of us aren't real, that he's dreaming us. I think that's why he likes Negroes so much. They fit his metaphysic. Because of their suffering they're like angels to him, closer to God. I wonder if he thought a Jew might be similar. I'm sure he sensed right away I was much too worldly."

There was a long silence.

"That was your affair?" Cady asked at last.

Here was the chance, the place to tell him what else had happened, what he had really done. But he knew it would hurt him and Myron didn't want to spoil the moment. He remembered those times with Frank Fenton and how angry Frank had made him when he confessed he was still sleeping with his wife. How can you do that? Myron screamed. It's not like it's another man, Frank countered.

"That was my affair." Myron shrugged. "I got a lot of work done. I finished *The Sun Sets in the West* and started a new book."

"You're always starting a new book."

"What about you? What really made you say no to China?"

"You."

"Really?"

"As soon as I left you, I realized I missed you, that it wasn't you I was getting away from but all that had been going on here. I can't stay here anymore." He nodded. "Mabel wears me out. And I'm tired of throwing money away on renting. So I'd like to build us a house."

"You've always wanted to do that."

"Yes. But now I want you to live there with me."

As soon as the words were out of Cady's mouth, Myron felt constrained. Again, it was as if Cady were talking about marriage.

"What do you say?" he asked.

"I don't know." Myron looked up. "Would it hurt you very much if I said no, at least for the time being?"

"No," said Cady. "I guess not. But I'm disappointed." He paused. "How do you want to live, Mike?"

This was a legitimate question. He would be thirty-nine this December. How did he want to live?

"I think I'd like to have my own house."

"I could build a guesthouse and you could live in it."

"But I'd still be miles from town."

"You've got to learn to drive."

Myron nodded. There was a silence.

"Did you get to Butte to see your mother?" asked Cady at last.

"Yeah. I took a trip over and stayed a week."

"How was it?"

"Freezing. And the conditions of the miners are terrible. They're a beaten lot. The Anaconda Copper Company isn't much better. There's always that danger with mining. When the price of copper goes low enough, you're out of work. If the miners don't work, the whole town suffers. You either leave or starve. A lot of my family's moved to California." Then Myron brightened. "I finally got down into a mine. The Speculator." It was the very mine that Ella Winter had wanted him to portray in *Wide Open Town*.

"The Speculator? Wasn't there a great disaster down there?"

"Yes." Myron was surprised Cady had heard of it. In 1917 he couldn't have been more than thirteen. "Over a hundred and sixty men died."

"Was it safe?"

"I'm sure it was. It's open to the public. I went with a tour."

"What made you do it?"

"Because one of the criticisms of *Wide Open Town* was that I never showed my miner hero at work in the mines. That hurt because it was true. I got the same kind of criticism from Ella Winter, Lincoln Steffens's wife." And he told Cady what Ella Winter had said to him.

"I hate that," said Cady. "They just want you to write propaganda."

"Yeah. But there's some truth to her argument. Writers do owe something to the people they write about."

"So you went down."

"Yeah." Myron paused a moment. "The weirdest thing was that even though I was with a tour I felt like I was alone, just me and the dead men. I listened to the guide give his spiel and all the while he talked I heard voices."

"Sounds like Dante."

"When I told my brother Jack what I did he said many of the men who died had worn gear from our store, and that I had probably sold some of it to them." Myron paused. "You've got to go down there, Cady. It's eerie. There are shafts going every which way, up, down, across. You need a three-dimensional map. The bodies are long out but you still feel them there and the whole city above them. You could paint it."

"But there's no light."

"But there is. That's the weirdest part. They give you a miner's helmet with a carbide lamp. It's like the light comes out of your own eyes, like you're creating what you're seeing. You get a sense of power and feel vulnerable at the same time."

"That used to be the theory of light in the Middle Ages," said Cady, "that it came from your own eyes." He paused. "I have that feeling when I'm painting. Maybe every painter does."

"Maybe. But it's a weird way of seeing. If the dead can see I think it has to be that way."

"Yeah," Cady agreed, but he seemed lost in thought.

"We're pretty lucky," Myron said, trying to bring him back. "You decided you loved me and were faithful. I decided I loved you, tried to be unfaithful and didn't succeed." Myron was pushing his luck. Did he really want to talk about it? "You know what I thought? That our separation was my fault and that my punishment would be making love to a man I didn't care for. I was going to come back to you and tell you I loved you so much that if you didn't want to make love to me anymore, you didn't have to, that I'd be happy just to be your friend."

Myron had thought this several times. Is this what he wanted to say to Cady? Or was it something else? For as he spoke he was hit with the overwhelming desire to tell the truth. How can you love someone and not tell them the truth? It's just cowardice and ego, my attempt to look better in his eyes. I have to be honest with him and let the chips fall where they may.

"Cady," he began, "I'm not telling you the whole truth."

"What?"

"There were . . . a few . . . one-night stands."

Cady looked like he'd been slapped, his head turning suddenly and sharply. And Myron was surprised that in a strange way it felt good to do that to him. That's for leaving me, he thought. But in the next instant, he was feeling Cady's pain. Again it was just like with Frank Fenton. They were always hurting each other. He'd told Cady about Frank during their first weeks together. But Myron had made light of it. It's over, he said. It's lovers under the bridge. Now he wondered if such painful things were ever really over.

"Were there many?" Cady asked, turning to face Myron.

"No. Just a few. Guys I met in bars." Myron paused. Don't go into detail. That's where the real pain was.

"Did you enjoy it?"

"I hated it." That was true. He did hate it. After it was over. But he enjoyed it before. He always enjoyed pickups. And he thought of the boys in Washington Square. They were wonderful, the way they would take you to their pitiful rooms and kneel down in front of you as if you were some kind of a saint, and there was always a picture of their mother in a gilt frame. Why do you have that picture of your mother there? he always wanted to ask. But the question would get lost in ecstasy and by the time he thought of it again he would be back outside going to class. Then he thought of Cady's mother in the baggage car. Then he thought of his own. He'd gone back to Butte with the idea that he would tell her about himself. But he couldn't do it. Was that one of the things that led up to his depression?

"You know, I think that too sometimes," said Cady.

"What?" Myron looked at him questioningly.

"That some day we might stop being lovers but we'll never stop being friends."

"But not yet."

"No," said Cady, squeezing Myron's hand. "Not yet."

A few days later Mabel asked them to dinner. Dorothy Brett, the painter who'd come to Taos with the Lawrences, was there, as was Tinka Fechin. But the conversation was all about Frieda Lawrence. It seemed Frieda's husband, Angelo Ravagli, had brought Lawrence's ashes back from Italy and there was to be some kind of interment ceremony at the ranch. None of this was new. Myron and Cady had heard the plan that very first summer. At one of Mabel's garden parties, Frieda announced her idea for building a shrine to Lawrence. She would have him exhumed from his Vence grave, cremate his remains, and Angelo would bring them back to Taos. It was obvious that she made the announcement to enlist Mabel's aid or at least deflect her disapproval. It didn't work. Though Mabel said nothing at the time, Myron knew she was against it if for no other reason than the attention it would bring to Frieda. Now, after dinner, they were all sitting in the living room, the women telling them the story.

"It was two months ago," Brett began, her ear trumpet in her lap. "She got a telegram from Angelo saying he couldn't get Lawrence through customs. She called me in a panic and asked for help. So I called Stieglitz. If anybody could help, he could." Brett nodded at her own action, her weak chin receding into her neck, then emerging again. "I didn't give a hoot about the wop, but I wanted respect for Lawrence."

Myron was surprised by her use of American slang. She was the daughter of an English aristocrat who'd come to Taos with the Lawrences in 1924 as the only member of his utopian community,

Rananim. Unlike Lawrence, however, she stayed. "Stieglitz got them through."

"A week later," Tinka Fechin chimed in from the other end of the sofa, "Frieda ask her neighbor, Mr. Hawk, to driff her to Lamee." Tinka wore a white peasant blouse embroidered with tiny Xs and Os, a long shapeless black skirt, and dull brown peasant boots. It was her uniform. "They pick me up on way and I think we are all there is but when we get there, Hal Bynner and Bob Hunt are on platform. While we wait, Hal ask us to tea. He say because Lawrence spend his first night in New Mexico with him, he should spend his first day back with him also."

"I'm sorry I ever brought Lawrence to that man," commented Mabel, who was reclining on the chaise lounge.

"Tell them the rest," Brett urged.

"The train come and there is Angelo, all smiling, suitcase in one hand, package wrapped in noospaper in other. He put them down, take her in his arms and kiss her on mouth."

"Disgusting," said Brett, who now held the trumpet to her left ear.

"They're married, for God's sake!" protested Myron.

"Myron," said Mabel patiently. "Let them finish." And, as if directing traffic, she waved Tinka on.

"There's to-do about lougatch, then we are off to Santa Fe. After a while I haff stranch feeling and ask where are ashes and Frieda shout stop and Hawk jam on brakes. Then we turn and go back to station. There, waiting on platform, is Lawrence still wrapped in noospaper."

"They left him as if he was yesterday's fish," snarled Brett.

"What happened next?" asked Cady.

"We go to Hal's house," answered Tinka. "We stay too long and start late."

"Did they remember the urn this time?" asked Myron.

"I take charge," said Tinka. "I haff it on floor between my boots."

"Good," said Cady.

Myron and Cady were being disingenuous, for they'd already heard the story of the tea party from Hal and Bob and there was more to it than these ladies knew. For one thing, Hal told them he'd laced the oolong with vodka and they were a lot drunker than they would admit. For another, he said that for safekeeping and with everyone's knowledge, he moved the urn out to the kitchen where Bob was warming the chile. Unfortunately Bob somehow knocked it over and some of Lawrence spilled into the pot. Bob said he tried to put the ashes back but couldn't without getting too much chile into the urn. So he topped the urn off with ashes from the stove, then stirred what he spilled into the chile and served it. It seems we all ate some of the great man, Hal told them and roared with laughter. Now Myron bit his lip to keep from laughing. The whole Lawrence thing was absurd.

"When we get to my house I ask them in." Tinka's house was to the north and west of Mabel's. "It's dark and they still haff hour more to get to ranch so I ask them to stay and go in morning. But Hawk say he must get back. So they go." She paused, then said, "I was cleaning when I see it."

"What?" asked Myron, having a good idea.

"The urn. They haff leaf it again."

"Hah!" Brett exclaimed and ear trumpet nodded.

"Talk about Freudian slips," noted Mabel.

"I know what I must do," said Tinka.

"What?" asked Cady.

"I make little altar under Fechin's icon of Peter and Paul and put Lawrence there with candles all around."

Nicolai Fechin, Tinka's former husband, had literally carved his house out of wood: fireplaces, doors, jambs, lintels, sills, stairs. Though built in the adobe style, the place was considered a wonder of the Russian woodcarver's art, and Fechin was said to have been heartbroken to give it up. To add to this loss, Tinka had also kept all of his paintings that were in the house. Periodically the artist, now living in Los Angeles, would show up in Taos and hire a lawyer. They are not part of the divorce, he would say to anyone who would listen. I have papers! But to no avail. It seemed possession really was nine-tenths of the law.

"When I do that," said Tinka, her eyes looking off into the distance, "peace come offer me. I feel radiance coming from urn."

Might have been Bob's chile, Myron thought.

"It was three days before they came for him," noted Mabel.

"Three days?" asked Tinka. "But I give him to you next day."

Here's news, thought Myron. Mabel had the urn to herself for a couple of days, plenty of time for her to do what she wanted with its contents.

"Do you know what they were doing that was so important?" Brett bubbled up angrily from her end of the couch, the trumpet in her lap again. "Screwing their bloody heads off! That's what they were doing!" She shook her head. "That was two months ago," she said. "Well, I was up there yesterday and finally told her what I thought. I told her that if she wanted to pay homage to Lawrence she should bury his ashes beside the great pine tree by the old ranch house. He loved that tree. I told her to make the tree an altar to him. But the Hun said nein. So I said she could at least put something beautiful in that thing they call a chapel."

"What did you have in mind?" asked Mabel after the trumpet was up.

"I wrote Brancusi to see if he would make a sculpture of a phoenix and what he would charge." She shook her head. "But they won't spend any money on him," and she added emphatically, "and it's his money."

"She won't take any money from me," noted Mabel.

Myron was surprised again. Had she offered Frieda money?

"There's still a third way," said Brett, lowering her voice.

"What?" asked Tinka.

"Steal the ashes!"

"It needn't come to that," said Mabel, sounding deceptively reasonable. And again Myron wondered if she had them. He looked around the room. There were several urn-like receptacles.

"Did you see the notice posted in the Plaza?" asked Cady. "There's to be a formal dedication of the tomb next Sunday and everyone's invited."

"To exploit that lovely man," Brett moaned. "To make a carnival attraction, to put him in a showplace with a visitors' book!"

"Perhaps it'll be a greater punishment for her," said Mabel, "for everyone to know her vulgarity."

"And that Italian!" Brett went on as if Mabel hadn't spoken. "He's a common gigolo. He's only after her money. And it's Lawrence's money. I've told him this! I told him he isn't fit to make a monument to a monkey! I told him I hoped to live long enough to bury his ashes in a drain pipe!"

"Calm yourself," said Mabel but she was loving it. It seemed these two old rivals for Lawrence's affection were now allies.

"To be the adoring widow of a great man, how easy that is!" snarled Brett. "To be the wife of a great man, how difficult that was and how bad she was at it."

Angry tears rolled down her puffed cheeks and her two protruding upper teeth gnawed her lower lip. She's nobody's idea of British nobility, thought Myron.

"But even she must realize that ashes need respect," Brett went on. "They need remembrance and tenderness. A tomb that looks like a railroad station toilet! Is that a fitting resting place? That old whore! A mattress is all she needs!"

"Calm yourself," urged Tinka.

But Brett would not be calmed. "I know what they'll say, that I'm green-eyed with jealousy and that a bit more four-postering on my part would have done me a lot of good. But they don't know." She was hinting at something. It's what she did when she got hot on the subject of Lawrence. "They don't know."

∽

"Gimme a DEEEEEE!" Cady's hands were megaphoned around his mouth.

"DEEEEEE!" Myron screamed as he ran from casement to casement, twisting the handles to close the metal windows. You could hear everything on these quiet Taos nights.

"Gimme an AAAAAAITCH!" Small, effeminate, and balding, Cady had camped cheerleaders for Myron before.

"AAAAAAITCH!" Myron yelled and ran to the kitchen to make sure the back door was closed. Though he didn't want Cady to stop, he wasn't so drunk that he didn't care who heard.

"Gimme an ELLLLLLL!"

"ELLLLLLL!" shouted Myron. Satisfied he'd done all he could to keep their voices in the house, he was in the bedroom again.

"WHAT HAVE YOU GOT?"

"LAAAWRRRRENNNCCE!" they screamed as they leaped into the air and fell backward onto the bed.

"I've been thinking," said Cady after a moment. "A gallery owner I know says Stieglitz is a compulsive collector, that he can't let go of anything he thinks valuable." He turned to Myron. "He had those ashes over a weekend. He could've emptied them into something and replaced them with ashes from his gallery's ash trays." He sat up. "I wouldn't put it past him."

"That's funny," said Myron, also sitting up. "Because you know what I think?"

"What?"

"Mabel had them for a few days, right? I think she took them riding with her and sprinkled them over pueblo land. That was always her idea of what should be done with Lawrence. She could've taken them out back with no one seeing her. So the joke's on her if Stieglitz got to them first."

"On Bob and Hal, too. They think they ate Lawrence."

"Wishful thinking." Then Myron broke into a big grin. "What about this? What if Angelo never did what he was supposed to? If he's as bad as Brett makes him out to be, then why wouldn't he keep the money Frieda gave him for the exhumation and fill the urn with ashes from his house in Italy?" Myron knew it was a terribly unfair portrait of the man, that he seemed to be nothing like that. "I can see him giving his ex-wife and kids that money. Why not? He must be feeling guilty as hell for leaving them like he did."

"Then the joke's on Stieglitz as well."

"On all of them," Myron agreed.

"Poor Lawrence," said Cady.

"He doesn't give a damn," said Myron. "And none of it makes any difference. As far as the world's concerned, Frieda has his ashes."

They got undressed and made love but Myron didn't sleep. He couldn't get Lawrence out of his head. What had he done to these women? Brett and Mabel were both strong and independent. Yet when it came to Lawrence, they were obsessed. So they attacked Frieda. But was it really Frieda they were after? Wasn't it rather Lawrence himself? Hadn't he led them on with the idea that he was the man to take them up in his arms and love them? What about him? If I had written *The Rainbow* and *Women in Love,* Myron thought, it would've been enough. But not for Lawrence. Is that the difference between genius and talent? A genius is never satisfied. After *War and Peace* Tolstoy turned to religion. After their great work Melville and Twain became cynics. After his great novels Lawrence tried to become a leader of men. Only at the end did he return to the novel and produce *Lady Chatterley's Lover.* Myron thought of the first time he met Frieda. He'd wanted to meet her ever since he heard she was back at the ranch. So when Mabel asked if he wanted to go, he said yes for himself and Cady. He'd noticed this about his new friend. Though he often complained about not having enough time to paint, he hated to be left out of anything.

"It's about an hour's drive," said Mabel. "I hope the road up there isn't too bad. With these rains, it could be washed out."

"That makes it all the more exciting," said Cady from the back.

"It's always exciting to go up there," noted Mabel.

It was. Imagine it! They were going to a place where Lawrence had lived and worked. And they were going to meet the famous Frieda von Richtofen, the woman who was the model for Ursula in *Women in Love,* one of Myron's favorite novels. Was she really as honest and passionate as Ursula? Was anyone? Myron tried to think of questions, not prying ones, but questions about the writer's intensity and vision. Did he really live as passionately as he seemed to? Was it the fever of his disease that drove him, the tubercular's life burning up a degree or two faster than our normal 98.6? Or was it some unique wisdom or talent? Didn't it take courage to be unique? I'll not go to war. I'll not be quiet about sex. I'll show the world the battle waged in the bedroom is as dangerous as any front-line encounter in France. Of course, Myron could have asked Mabel these questions. But he knew her answers. He'd read *Lorenzo in Taos* and they'd already had conversations about Lawrence's inner fire, his all-devouring passion

"This is the Hawk ranch," she said as she turned off the main road. It had taken three quarters of an hour. "They're a nice family who take care of the place for Frieda when she's not here."

They passed a house, then a barn and corral. "Mr. Hawk!" Mabel shouted after she'd stopped the car. A man in faded overalls came over. "Is the road passable?"

"You got two pushers, Mabel," he noted. "You can make it."

She nodded and shifted into low. The old Ford lurched forward. Just like Montana, thought Myron as they entered a pine forest, water running everywhere including the middle of the road. The car straddled it, and they kept bumping along for about twenty minutes. Then they came to a faded wooden sign full of bullet holes. Myron could just make it out: "LYING ART RANCH—ALF MILE."

"The Lying Art Ranch," he read. "What critic put that up?"

"The eff's missing," explained Mabel.

"The Flying Fart Ranch?" asked Myron.

"One f," said Mabel.

"Ah, the Lying Fart Ranch."

"Don't be crude, Myron."

Cady was giggling in the back.

"It was once called The Flying Heart Ranch," she explained as they moved into a thickly forested area. "Lawrence renamed it the Kiowa Ranch. To honor the real owners, he said."

"Are there Kiowa around here?" asked Cady from the back.

The engine answered with a cough and died. Mabel pulled the floor lever that set the emergency brake.

"We seem to be out of gas." She was looking at the dashboard. "The gauge is broken. It always says empty. I was sure Tony had filled it."

"Maybe it's the altitude," Cady suggested.

"We could always get out and walk," added Myron. "The sign said it was only a half mile."

"We'll just let it rest," said Mabel. "I've had this happen before. A bubble of air in the gas line. If we can make the next steep grade we'll be there. When we come back we'll coast down to the Hawks place. Just to be sure we'll get gas there."

Myron formed a mental picture of their descent at full speed around the curves they'd so slowly traveled up. An old Mack Sennett bit. She'd do it too. She was a good driver, better than Tony. And he remembered her on horseback, short hair bouncing.

He took out a pack of Luckies and offered cigarettes. And there they sat, in the middle of a wet pine forest, smoking. When they were done, Mabel tried the car again and, in spite of what the gauge said, it started right in. A bubble of air, she repeated, and they were off. Soon they turned off the road and drew up behind a small half log, half board-and-batten house, its splintery wood weathered black. They got out, walked around to the front of the house, and were met by a blast of wind.

"There's some game," shouted Mabel over the blast. She was pointing to three deer in the field on the other side of the split rail fence. "Tony still keeps his horses up here." They turned their backs to the wind. "There's the bull Lawrence painted on that little cabin down there."

So this is Lawrence's beloved ranch, Myron thought, and a feeling of cynicism came over him. Tobacco Road West, he dubbed it. Though Mabel had never asked for payment, Frieda had insisted on handing over a manuscript copy of *Sons and Lovers*. Much too high a price to pay for this dump, Myron thought now. He knew lots of places like this in Montana, whole mountainsides full of squatting miners and their sad families. He turned into the wind again and looked west beyond the huge pine tree and the cleared field to the high desert plateau where the unseen Rio Grande had cut its canyon, and forty miles beyond to the faint Jemez Mountains, blue shadows in the white afternoon haze. The landscape seemed to roll like the waves of a vast stone ocean. This is what he loved, Myron decided. Unfortunately the wind was blowing so hard you couldn't look for long before your eyes filled with water.

"They're home," said Mabel. "The car's here." An old car was parked beside the cabin. But there was no one about. "Wait here. I'll go see." She climbed three wooden steps onto the porch but the door opened before she reached it and a man who looked like a laborer intercepted her. He had on faded blue denim overalls, a khaki shirt, and a handkerchief knotted in each corner to fit snugly on his head. He stood barring Mabel's way. She said something to him.

"Frieda, she no feel good," the man answered so loud they could hear. And Myron realized this was Angelo Ravagli, the model for Mellors, Lady Chatterley's gamekeeper.

"This is Angelino," shouted Mabel, and Myron and Cady waved at him just as she slipped inside. Angelo Ravagli came down and shook their hands and they said they were glad to meet him. Myron thought he should have been thrilled, but it was hard to imagine this man as Mellors. He was handsome enough, but very Italian.

"Come in," Mabel called from the house. "Frieda will see you!"

They climbed the rickety steps, opened the door, and immediately papers began to blow around the room. They pulled the door shut and dropped to their hands and knees to gather sheets. Myron saw a title page, *Not I, But the Wind*. There's my alibi, he thought. Then he remembered Mabel saying Frieda was writing a memoir. This was it, and he tried to read a page. But it was handwritten and he couldn't. When the pages were back on the table, he looked for a paperweight. But there was nothing to use so they stepped across to where Mabel stood by the bed. On it was a heap of what appeared to be soiled laundry. Mabel called Frieda's name and the heap moved. They could see an eye peeking out. Then some words emerged, English with a soft German and English accent. Their names were being repeated. Then a hand rose from the pile, which first Cady, then Myron touched.

"Abscess in my ear," Frieda whispered from under the sheets. "Such a bother and we are so far from doctors up here. I use hot water and clean cloths. Ach! Such a thing to have in this wonderful clear air."

"Did you swim in the pool on board your ship?" asked Cady.

"Ya."

"That must be where you picked up the microbe."

Frieda made the sheets nod. She seemed grateful for this explanation. The infection was the ship's fault, not hers or these mountains'. There seemed nothing more to say, and Myron was about to suggest they leave when the door opened again and the papers blew around. It was Angelo with an armload of books. Somehow Mabel had communicated to him that there were books in her car. Cady rushed to help him and Myron was on his hands and knees again gathering paper.

"I've brought more books," Mabel said to Frieda and went to

the pile Angelo had just put down. "Here's the one by Myron I told you about."

She took *Singermann* from the pile and brought it to the bed. Frieda exposed the end of her nose and nodded at Myron. He said she should use it as a paperweight. Frieda laughed and Mabel stooped to pull books that she must have brought on a previous visit from under the bed. Myron thought of the questions he'd wanted to ask Frieda, but it was the wrong time. Cady produced from one of the big pockets of his hiking shorts a little camera he often carried. He wondered aloud if there was enough light, decided there wasn't and put the camera away. Then Frieda said she was tired and Mabel said it was time to go. But Frieda said she wanted to talk to Mabel for a moment so Cady, Myron, and Angelo, opening the door just a crack, slipped out sideways.

On the trip up Mabel had told them how the ranch had depressed Angelo when he first saw it but she didn't say why. Now Myron understood. Like most Italians, he must have had a mental picture of America as full of modern comforts. But here were conditions the ex-policeman wouldn't have tolerated in a barracks. Mabel had described Angelo's reaction as if there was something wrong with the man though she herself would never have put up with such a place. So Angelo had decided to build a house fit to live in. Mabel said he'd chosen a site below the old house, chopped down trees, leveled the ground, and excavated for the foundation. I'll say this for him, she conceded, he knows how to build. Now he was leading them down to the site. There was a small cement-encrusted mixer and a big metal hod also coated with dried cement, and there were piles of cement blocks, the same kind that had been used for the partially finished foundation. It wasn't going to be a large house but it was easily three times the size of the old one. Angelo jumped down into the open basement.

"Looka," he said. He was standing in one corner of the rectangle holding up a piece of granite. "*Pietra*."

They nodded. It was stone all right.

The Italian put the stone down, reached into one of the cement blocks on the top course, and pulled out a bottle full of purple liquid from which he tugged the cork. He offered the bottle to Myron, who took it.

"*Vino*," he explained.

"*Salud*," said Myron and lifted the bottle to his lips. It tasted something like Chianti. He took a second swallow and handed it to Cady.

"I maka," said Angelo proudly.

"It's good," said Myron. "Thanks."

From his Butte days Myron was used to drinking homemade Italian wine. When you went to an Italian's house it's what you got first. They called it homesickness in a bottle.

"Good," said Cady but Myron could tell he didn't like it. And he hardly took a second swig when the bottle came around again. Then Mabel was calling them and they handed the wine back to Angelo, said goodbye, again shook hands, then walked back up to the old house. They went up the steps and were about to open the door but thought better of it and just yelled to Frieda that they hoped to see her when she felt better. They heard an English "goo-bye" and went to the car, which started right up. When they got down to the Hawk ranch, Mr. Hawk stuck the gas tank with a gauge stick. It was empty. Mabel paid him to fill it from his farm tank and soon they were on the road to Taos.

"I'm sorry she wasn't feeling better," said Mabel.

"Yes," said Cady, who now sat beside Mabel. "Who wants to be seen like that?"

"You know," Myron said from the back, "as I leaned over her bed, I realized the latent, healthy life-force that had been temporarily subdued by the abscess. I felt the attraction of the woman. And when she pushed up her bandage to get a look at me with one keen eye, I saw a resemblance to a photo of Lawrence's mother. It gave me a clue to understanding the great man's work."

Mabel shot a glance in the rearview mirror.

"All I saw was a sick woman," said Cady.

"No, there was more than that," Myron went on. "Frieda's eye had a childlike squint to it. I'm sure it was the same way she looked at Lawrence, the wistful lonely look of those who never grow old, the look of the ever-seeking. She will believe in what she sees until the end of her days."

Again Mabel glanced at Myron in the rearview mirror.

"Sounds like you're preparing an article, Mike," noted Cady.

"I am," said Myron, who'd never written an article in his life. But he went on. "She's an untrammeled, free individual who, having lived her life intensely and having paid for it at every step, has made up her mind to return to the stark reality of her ranch and draw whatever she may need from its eternal strength."

"You saw all that?" asked Cady.

"Yes, and more."

"Myron's doing a word portrait," said Mabel.

No, Myron thought. I'm making fun of you and your incessant over-reading.

"How about you Cady?" Mabel asked. "How would you paint Frieda?"

"I don't do portraits," answered Cady. "And besides I didn't really see her."

"Then do Lawrence," she suggested.

"You've seen enough photos of him," urged Myron, liking the idea of his friend joining in. "How would you do him? He's mostly beard."

"I don't know," said Cady. He obviously did not want to play. "I'm not good with words the way you two are."

They all knew from the night of the Truth game that that wasn't true, that Cady was very good with words. Still, thought Myron, if he doesn't want to, and he stepped in for his friend.

"I think you'd do him as landscape. You'd put in all the majestic beauty of these distant mountains," and Myron waved his arm west toward the Jemez Mountains, whose view was blocked by the local hills, "and the opalescent desert colors that spread out in that eternity beyond the ranch," and he waved his arm again at the gravel-filled marl. "You'd do him listening to silence as if some newborn loveliness had cast a spell over life. You'd do the tenderness of spring filling the evening air, the ineffable beauty of the light."

"And that's just his beard," said Cady.

"Horse manure," said Mabel.

"You'd do that, too," said Myron and they were laughing.

The dedication of the Lawrence Shrine was set for the afternoon of Sunday, September 15. There were handbills pasted all over Taos Plaza and in the galleries and cantinas promising food and drink, music by a mariachi band and a display of native dancing. Mabel was unable to hide her scorn, and to get away from her Myron went down to stay with Cady in his cabin on the Clark ranch. They'd get up at dawn, eat breakfast with the Clarks in the main house, then walk over to where Cady was finally building his studio. Myron thought it was a dumb idea to build on someone else's property, particularly when you were about to move. You can't take it with you, he said. But Cady insisted he needed it now. So they'd begin before it got hot and quit about noon. Mostly they mixed mud, straw, and water for the brick mold, their work supervised by Juan, the twelve-year-old son of the contractor. The boy showed them how to lift the wet bricks without breaking them and how to set them out to dry.

It was a wonderfully efficient way to build. When Myron first saw adobes he dubbed them earth blisters. Now he knew from Mabel's houses how comfortable they were, perfect for the climate here, dark and cool during the glaring heat of day, yet ventilated to pick up night breezes, and, with a fire in the kiva, warm and cozy in the winter. When the time came, he thought, I'll buy one. But I'll leave the countryside to Cady. I need to be able to walk to the plaza, to restaurants, cantinas, and bookshops. Cady will be out here. We'll have parties in each other's houses and stay the night. The secret of living like the rich was having two places. You have to be able to get away. Unfortunately, it turned out the dude ranch wasn't far enough. Three days before the interment ceremony Cady got a call from Frieda. When he came back from the main house, he rolled his eyes.

"What is it?" Myron asked.

"Mabel mischief."

"What?"

"It seems Tony's been telling the Taos dancers there's a curse on the ashes, that they're the remains of a great man whose grave has been disturbed. So the Taos dancers won't dance."

"So what does Frieda want?"

"She wants me to find some other dancers."

"Can you?"

"I'm gonna try."

"Where?"

"San Ildefonso."

"You know if you get them, you're making an enemy out of Mabel."

"I've already made an enemy out of her. She puts up with me because of you. So you've got more to lose than I." He paused. "You coming?"

"I wouldn't miss it."

They headed west on the state road. It wasn't a long drive, and the road, which eventually led to a place called Los Alamos where there was a boys' prep school, wasn't bad. For most of the ten miles it followed the usually dry Pojoaque River, which lately, because of all the rain, had been running. They had to cross it, and Cady warned that it was dangerous to be caught in more than six inches. But they made it easily. When they got to the pueblo, Myron saw that it was very different from its Taos counterpart. For one thing, the buildings were only one story high. And though there was a north and a south section, the two halves were divided not by a stream but a wall. Cady said it had to do with a tribal argument. Myron thought of the two synagogues in Butte, Reformed and Orthodox. Then Cady, who seemed to know his way around, pulled up in front of a door and got out. Myron followed. He remembered Cady talking about certain Indians and their artistic skills. So this place was a part of his friend's life that Myron didn't know, which made it even more interesting. Cady knocked and immediately, as if they were expected, the door opened.

"Mr. Wells," said an old man. "Come in."

"This is Myron Brinig, the writer I told you about," Cady said when they were inside. "Myron, this Abel Sanchez. He's a painter too."

"Glad to meet you," said the old man and extended his hand. Myron shook it. It felt soft, like good leather.

"Good to meet you," said Myron.

"What brings you here?" said Abel, turning to Cady.

"I need your help."

"What can I do?" asked Abel Sanchez and directed them to sit at the table in the center of the room. They sat and Myron noted that the room was full of paintings, some finished, some in progress. Animals on stretched skins.

"What do you think of this curse?" asked the old man at the end of Cady's story.

"I think Mabel made it up to frighten the dancers."

The old man nodded.

"The ashes are the remains of a very great artist," Cady explained. "When he was alive he loved the place where his wife wants to put him."

Abel Sanchez nodded again.

"I need four dancers," Cady went on. "Tell them the occasion and let them choose what they dance. It'll be this Sunday. You and I can take them and their stuff in our cars but they'll have to find rides back." Abel Sanchez nodded. "There'll be plenty of food, lots of tourists to sell things to, and Frieda says she can give each man ten dollars."

That's very generous, Myron thought. It was at least twice what native dancers usually got.

"Your wife and family are invited as are all the San Ildefonso artists and their families." Cady paused. "I know it's only three days' notice. But can you do it, Abel?"

Abel nodded and they all shook hands again.

∽

"The fat's in the fire," said Myron when they were back at Cady's cabin.

"I guess so." Cady seemed thoughtful.

"Are you excited?"

"About going against Mabel? No." He hesitated a moment. "I'm thinking of you—about what I did to you leaving you like that. I think it's one of my big faults. When I'm upset, I take off. I've always done that."

"I understand," said Myron though he was surprised by his friend's change of subject and mood. "I guess it's a natural thing if you can afford to do it."

"But I want to make it up to you, Myron," he said, a new urgency in his voice. "I want to give you something that will show you how much you mean to me."

"Oh, Cady, you don't have to do that."

"But I do," said the little man. "I've been thinking about it for a while. I mean what kind of a gift to give you."

"Now you're making me uncomfortable."

Myron thought Cady was going to give him something valuable. All that would do was show the difference in their financial states. Maybe he'll even offer money. Was this a way of getting him down here to live with him? A bribe? Will I have to refuse him yet again?

"C'mon," said Cady.

He headed out the door. Myron could do nothing but follow. They walked down to another cabin, the one Myron stayed in that first winter. It seemed Cady was renting it now. He unlocked and opened the door and nodded for Myron to go in. He did but it wasn't familiar. Cady seemed to be using it for storage. There were boxes piled everywhere, and all kinds of equipment, skis and snowshoes, as well as art supplies, cartons of paper, and sketch pads. Not that it was messy. Cady was never messy. Every box was labeled and he watched his friend go right to a large one, open it, and take out a smaller one, a shoe box.

"Here," he said.

Myron took it, thought for a second it held shoes, and lifted the lid. He looked at Cady, then down at the box's contents. Then he put the box down on top of another bigger one and lifted the thing out. It was a carving of a man. Myron held it at arm's length and examined it. With its black, wide-brimmed hat, black beard, black eyes, and heavy black eyebrows, it looked like the Jewish peddler from his childhood, the one who walked the streets of Butte singing I—Cash—Clothes! I—Cash—Clothes! The real I-Cash-Clothes man had looked like a rabbi with a pile of rags on his back. That's what religion was then, the transmigration of cotton and wool. Now Myron looked at this carved rabbi. He knew Cady collected them. They were the first things he'd shown him on Myron's first visit to his studio, not his etchings, not even his own paintings, but his budding collection of *santos*, *bultos*, and *retablos*, primitive paintings and carvings done in the last century by anonymous craftsmen and artists.

"Who is it?" Myron asked.

"San Isidro de Labrador," said Cady. "The patron saint of farmers. It was carved some time in the 1890s by someone who worked near Mora."

Cady dipped his hand into the shoebox and came out with a tiny pair of yoked oxen and a little angel. Then he pulled something else from the box, a thick wooden base into whose slots he set the angel, then the oxen, and then a small plow. Myron thought of Spud's description of Cady that night in the Truth game. He collects things. Now the collector took the carved saint from Myron and put the pegs that came out of the soles of his boots into holes in the wooden slab. San Isidro looked like a giant holding the handle of a toy plow and driving oxen that looked like dogs. Myron looked at Cady. It always surprised him that his rich friend could live as primitively as he did. These figures helped explain it. There was something ascetic about him, something sparse and self-punishing.

"I want you to have this," said Cady again, turning to the statue. "Look at the boots. Real leather. And how small the angel and oxen are. That's to show how important Saint Isidore is."

Myron remembered saying to Cady once when he was going on about them that they weren't real statues, that they were really just dolls. But that's it, Cady had said. They're like any good religious art, abstract enough so that no one's represented.

"You sure you want to part with this?" he asked now.

"I'm sure." Cady touched Myron's arm. "I want you to have him." He picked up the slab with the saint and the angel and the oxen and held them out.

"Cady, you love it so much," said Myron, still hesitant.

"That's why I want you to have it."

"But I have nowhere to keep it," he protested. And he felt near tears. For the first time in his life someone was giving him a gift that held deep personal value. His family never gave gifts. Not for birthdays or anything. "You know how I live. I rent a place, write a novel, and move on."

"But you won't always live like that," said Cady. "You said

you wanted to buy a house someday. Someday you'll have the money to do it. I'm sure of that. This is for your house."

Still Myron didn't take it. Where would he keep such a thing? Not that these santos were considered valuable, though they did mean a great deal to the locals. And they were fragile. Myron wasn't used to taking care of possessions. What if he broke it or lost it?

"I'll tell you what," said Cady as if reading his mind. "I'll keep it for you. When you get your own place, I'll bring it to you then. It'll be my housewarming gift." Then he was looking at Myron. "But you've got to put it in a place of honor. There's got to be a niche for it."

"There will be," said Myron, tears in his eyes. Then the two men went to each other and hugged and kissed.

I'm getting in over my head, Myron thought later when he was back in the Pink House. I'm more in love with him now than that first summer at Mabel's. Be careful, he warned himself, and tried to remember the pain he'd felt in San Francisco, tried to use it as a check, a brake on his feelings. But the remembered pain only seemed to add to the depth of his present pleasure. I lost him and then I found him. There's so much more between us now. They'd had a rough past, but all that did was suggest a future. Myron thought of the San Isidro and his entourage of small things, and he thought of the I-Cash-Clothes man he once followed on the cobbled streets of Butte. Cady was wrong. The saint wasn't abstract at all. I knew him when I was a kid. Yes, it was all there from the beginning, all connected, a pattern of cause and effect that was as clear as a buyer of old clothes shouting to the windows. I—cash—clothes! I—cash—clothes! An old Jewish man with rags on his back, the patron saint of farmers who once walked the streets of Butte. How could Mabel say cities were corrupt, when such people lived in them?

Six

Waiting by the pueblo gate were four dancers and two singers, young Indian men in jeans, cowboy hats, and boots. Cady and Myron shook their hands, then asked about Abel. He's coming, they said. Cady opened the station wagon's back door and the young men loaded the big drum and the eight leather bags full of costumes. Cady had removed the back seat to make room. When Abel drove up in his ancient Packard, the young men got into it, and, with Cady leading the way, the two cars headed east to the main road, then turned north. It was slow going through the gorge but once they reached the high plain they were speeding toward Taos. Yet they never got to it. Cady took a left onto the Placita Road that skirted the town's west side and came out on the highway north of the pueblo. Abel asked me to do this, he explained as they continued north. He didn't want to be seen. Not borrow trouble, he said. They were passing the road to the WPA bridge being built over the Rio Grande Canyon. They talked about it and in another three miles they passed the Arroyo Hondo gas station. They rode five more miles to the cluster of adobes called San Cristobal and turned east there. They passed the Hawk ranch and climbed. The whole trip took almost three hours.

They parked side by side just off the dirt road, got out, and thought about unloading. Then Frieda was before them in a faded calico housedress and green rubber gardening boots. Cady introduced her to Abel Sanchez, who introduced her to the dancers and singers. She shook their hands and thanked them for coming on such short notice. Abel asked where they could dress and she directed them to the old ranch house, then left saying she had to get dressed, too. Myron looked at her as she waddled away. Though undoubtedly once a great beauty, she was middle aged now and definitely not the siren of Brett's heated imagination. He turned back to the station wagon. The two singers already had the bass drum between them and Abel was warning the dancers who were pulling out the leather bags to be careful. In a moment they were all standing in the board-and-batten ranch house where Myron and Cady had first met Frieda. It was dusty and empty, and they left quickly.

"Let's get a look at the chapel," Myron suggested.

It was just a few hundred feet east of the old house, and tourists were coming out of it, complaining how bad the road was, implying the trip wasn't worth it. As far as the chapel went Myron and Cady had to agree. The sculpture of a phoenix that straddled the roof beam over the doorway looked like a chicken whose neck was being wrung, and the "Rose" window that Brett had painted, which was supposed to not only make the edifice look more sacred but also to let in light, didn't let in enough. The chapel faced south and was whitewashed. With no trees to shade it, there was an awful glare so that when you stepped in you were blinded for several minutes. After your eyes adjusted you saw only a concrete altar whose front was decorated with an L and upon which rested a guest book. Myron and Cady signed it, then left and went down to the huge pine tree by the old house, the very tree near which Brett had suggested Lawrence be buried. That's where they were when Frieda, in a flower print dress, looking not beautiful but authoritative, came at them again, this time accompanied by an entourage.

"I want you to meet my daughter," she said, turning to the young woman trailing her. "Barby, this is Cady Wells, who has paid for the dancers. He's a very fine painter." Frieda nodded emphatically.

Cady shook hands with Barby.

"And this is the novelist Myron Brinig."

"I've read one of your books," said Barby, brightening.

"Oh? Which one?" asked Myron as they shook hands.

"*Copper City.*"

"*Copper City*?" asked Cady, looking at Myron.

"It's the English edition of *Wide Open Town*," Myron explained.

"I loved it," said Barby.

"And this is my son-in-law, Stuart Barr," said Frieda of the young man in the dark suit who was standing beside Barby. They shook his hand and said they were glad to meet him. Stuart Barr mumbled something British. He seemed to be ashamed of his teeth, which could not be seen.

"He's a journalist," Barby said proudly.

"And he has consented to read the dedication speech," added Frieda.

"What happened to Judge Kiker?" asked Myron. The famous local lawyer had presided at Mabel's marriage to Tony, and more recently Frieda's to Angelo. The judge had a reputation for making everything that happened in Taos legal.

"Mabel got to him," Frieda explained. "He called last night." She shrugged. "It will be better if Stuart does it. More family."

A trumpet made them all turn. A man in a mariachi outfit was blowing a bullfight fanfare while Angelo pulled at the ropes of the flagpole. In the next instant the breeze caught the fabric and there was the green, white, and orange flag with the crest of King Victor Emanuel.

"You know Miriam Golden, don't you?" asked Frieda, returning to the business of introductions.

"Of course," said Myron. She was an actress of some note, and Myron had seen her in New York as Lady Macbeth. He shook her hand and introduced Cady.

"Miriam has consented to read a Lawrence poem at the ceremony," said Frieda.

"Where's the dancing going to be?" Barby asked her mother, then turned to Myron. "They've hired a mariachi band."

"Out there," said Frieda, pointing south at the field beyond the ditch. "Food and drink is by the new house. Hotdogs and Angelo's red wine."

"Very American," said Myron.

"I think so," said Frieda. "But I have to go and see to the food."

"Hotdogs and homemade wine," said Cady after the entourage had walked away. "Mabel's going to love that."

"Yeah," Myron agreed. "But I didn't know you were paying for the dancing." Not that Cady couldn't afford it. Myron had decided that that was one of the things Mabel disliked most about Cady, that he was richer than she. "I thought you were just going to arrange it."

"I asked if I could pay," he admitted. "Not many people can say they paid for part of D. H. Lawrence's funeral."

Gimme a Dee! Myron was about to shout when someone touched his shoulder. He turned.

"May I speak to you, Mr. Brinig?" It was Barby. She had somehow doubled back and come up behind them.

"Call me Myron, please. And certainly you can speak to me."

He thought she wanted to talk about *Copper City*. But she stood there looking at Cady, who took the hint and excused himself.

"What is it?" he asked when Cady was off a ways.

"It's my mother. I think she's in danger."

"Danger? What kind of danger?"

"You see how tired she looks. I think Angelo is poisoning her."

"What! What makes you think that?"

"He's having an affair with a woman in town. I don't know her name but I've seen them together. I thought it was just a flirtation. Then I met Mabel in the post office and she told me that she'd heard that there was a plan by Angelo to poison my mother."

"That's ridiculous," Myron snapped. He was looking at the young woman. She was straight featured but not beautiful or even pretty. It was her coloring. It was so bland. She must resemble her father. "Why would he do that?"

"For another woman. For the rights to Lawrence's books. I don't know."

"Don't you think Mabel told you that just to make trouble for your mother? You know Mabel's not happy about this at all."

"I know. But the idea's in my head now. I don't like Angelo. He thinks Mussolini's the greatest Italian since Garabaldi."

"I don't really know him," Myron admitted. The only time he'd ever had anything like a conversation with the man was that first time when Angelo had shown them the house he was building for Frieda. But Lawrence had liked him enough to use him as the model for Mellors.

"From what I've seen of them," Myron added, "I think they love each other."

"I don't," snapped Barby. "My mother's such a fool, such a romantic fool."

"She may be romantic," said Myron, "but she's no fool."

"You won't help me?" asked Barby.

"What do you want me to do?"

"Speak to her."

"Have you spoken to her?"

"Not yet."

"So you want me to spread gossip." He shook his head. "You should speak to her."

"She'll say I'm meddling."

"What will she say to me?"

Barby shrugged angrily, turned, and walked away. That's what you get, Myron thought, when you desert your children as Frieda did when she ran off with Lawrence. Very angry children.

"What was that all about?" Cady was back.

"I'm not sure." And he repeated the rumor.

"Mabel can pick out a weak link a mile away." Cady was looking over Myron's shoulder. "Turn around slowly and look up past the chapel."

Myron turned. Somebody was behind a tree, peeking out. At first he thought it was a cowboy. But no. It was Brett. She was in her western outfit: a ten-gallon hat whose crown was so high it made her look like a pinhead, baggy men's denims so long they had to be tucked into her boots, and boots so over-tooled with spurs, saddles, and lariats that they shouted dude to anyone looking. Why was she here? She was supposed to be boycotting the ceremony.

"This is going to be fun," said Cady and they both started

toward her. But as soon as they moved, she disappeared into the trees.

☙

The native dancing would take place in the field where Tony Luhan once pastured his horses. That was one of the reasons Tony was so angry when Mabel gave the ranch to the Lawrences. He didn't understand the value of the manuscript of *Sons and Lovers* that Frieda had insisted Mabel take as payment. Paper for land? Even to the local people who could read, it seemed like a bad deal.

"What dance are they going to do?" Myron asked as they waited.

"The eagle dance," said Cady.

"Why that one?"

"Because I told them that Lawrence's personal symbol was the phoenix. They never heard of a phoenix. But after I explained what it was they decided that such a marvelous bird had to be an eagle."

Myron smiled. Then the dancers in doeskin leggings and black tunics were coming out of the old ranch house carrying their leather bags. It seemed they would finish dressing in the field. Myron and Cady followed them over the dry irrigation ditch all the way out to the huge pile of wood Angelo had gathered for the bonfire. Behind the pile they began whitening each other's faces with what Myron guessed was zinc oxide. Then they were tying belts of bells around their waists and smaller garter belts of bells just below their knees. Bells were standard equipment for the native dancers Myron had seen in Montana. But the five-foot lengths of brown and white eagle feathers the men were now carefully pulling from the leather bags were not. They ran them along their shoulders and down their arms, then tied them in place for each other. Then they were flapping to make sure their movements were comfortable.

"It's a wonderful illusion," noted Myron. "They really look like birds."

When they were satisfied with the way their wings worked

they went back to dressing. Over their heads they slipped white surplices that covered their necks. Then came white cotton hoods painted with yellow eyes between which rose an attached hooked beak carved from yellow pine. These vicious-looking beaks stood up like rhino horns, and there were cutouts so you could still see their faces. Not until they tucked their chins into their necks and looked at the ground as they flapped did their white faces become part of the eagles' necks, their yellow beaks, moving forward and down, their most dangerous weapon.

Then the drumming began. The two singers had set up the drum out in the field halfway between the irrigation ditch and the piled wood. Peeking out from behind the wood, Myron could see a crowd gathering around them. When he turned back to the dancers, they were already lined up. Then they were walking out. When they neared the crowd, the circle opened and allowed them to enter. Myron, Cady, and Abel Sanchez followed them and joined the onlookers.

"What are they singing?" Myron asked Cady. It was always hard for him to imagine the falsetto chants of Indians had any meaning. Cady said he didn't know and asked Abel.

"It's the Song of the Sky Loom," Abel said.

"Can you translate?" asked Myron, who knew a sky loom was what the natives called rain falling in the distance.

The old man nodded. "Weave for us a garment of brightness," he began. He had a round Mexican face and a body thicker than wide. "May the warp be the white light of morning. May the weft be the red light of evening."

Myron listened as if he could understand the singers.

"May the fringes be the falling rain. May the border be the standing rainbow. Weave for us a garment of brightness that we may walk where birds sing, that we may walk where grass is green."

Cady and Myron nodded. But before they could say anything the dancers began. First they flew as far from each other as they could get. After a while, however, they were flying at each other, then folding their wings and moving backward to show they were diving, all the while keeping their feet to the earth, taking short steps, toes first once, then heels down three times.

"There's a story," said Abel Sanchez without taking his eyes from them, "about two young men chosen to perform the dance who were told not to look upon two women with strange eyes that lived close to the base of Black Mesa."

Myron had hiked Black Mesa with Cady. Unlike most of the terrain around here, which was stratified, Black Mesa looked like a single substance, what geologists called a batholith. It wasn't really, but when he first saw it, the mesa made Myron think of what Butte might have looked like before the miners came.

"Of course," Abel Sanchez went on, "the young men were overcome with curiosity. So they crept quietly out of the kiva and went to see what manner of women were these two who lived apart. They were welcomed and fed and entertained not only until the moon went down but until the stars faded."

Yours 'til the stars lose their glory, Myron sang to himself.

"Silently they stole back to the kiva and when they came out for the dance they looked at the cloud-filled sky and knew the gods were not happy. But the young men did not confess their disobedience. When the drums called from across the plaza, wearing their headdresses and wings, they began to dance. And you know, no one had ever seen the Eagle Dance done more beautifully." The old man paused and nodded at the real dancers who were circling each other. "Then the drummers stopped, for the feet of the dancers had left the ground and they were dancing higher and higher into the morning air. Looking up, the people saw two female eagles circling, and soon the young men joined them and flew away over Black Mesa and never returned."

Myron squinted up. The sky was an empty, cloudless glare. He looked down and tried to think of something to ask. Why are there four dancers now? Are two there to keep the other two from flying away? But just as he was about to ask, he saw Brett scampering away from them, and he found he wanted to shout at her to stop being a fool, to come join them, that this was too important. But Cady did more. He took off after her and caught her. Myron watched their heated conversation until she pulled away and fled into the trees.

"I asked her to join us," Cady said when he came back. "I told her she was being stupid, that she'd helped create this monument, and that she was Lawrence's best friend and should be a part of this dedication. But she refused." Cady looked at them. "Did you see her? She stamped her feet like a little girl. I can't believe it. She's so childish. Did you see her?""

"We saw," said Myron.

"Give her time," said Abel Sanchez, who knew Brett as a fellow artist. Pueblo dances were one of her favorite subjects. "She was standing right behind us. I told my story for her too. She needs stories."

But Brett never did join them. All she did was lurk.

It made no difference. Everyone was having too good a time. After the Eagle Dance was over, the mariachi band started to play by the old ranch house where there were trees and it was much cooler. People coming in from the field began to dance there in the western way, and Myron noticed a few of the men had grown Lawrencian beards. A couple of them even wore what looked like laurel wreathes on their heads. Myron and Cady watched for a while, then, deciding it was a little early for dancing, wandered down the hill toward the new house.

"Caddy! Marone!" shouted Angelo from the pavilion tent. "You help!"

So Caddy and Marone put on white aprons and got behind the picnic table beside which Angelo had set a giant vat of boiling water on a cast-iron wood stove. Beside it was a huge barrel of the Italian's homemade red wine, which he served in pint mason jars. So they began pinching tubes of bobbing red meat with metal tongs, putting them in long buns, smearing them with mustard and piccalilli, and handing them to friends and strangers on the other side of the table. It seemed all the Taoseños were there. The painters: the Blumenscheins, Bisttrams, Ila MacAfee and Elmer Turner, the Ward Lockwoods, Bert Phillips, the Andrew Dasburgs. And the gamblers: Long John Dunne, Doughbelly Price, Mace Machorse, Curly Murray and Mike Cunico and their wives. Bertha Gusdorf was there, a tiny Jewish lady who had just been made president of the First State Bank of Taos that her late husband, Gerson, had founded thirty years before. She introduced

Myron and Cady to her two married daughters, who'd come down from Colorado Springs, and then to Jim MaCarthy and his wife, who'd been partners with Mr. Gusdorf in the dry-goods store that was now the Taos Variety Store.

Spud was there too in his suit of lights, the toreador costume he'd worn when Nicolai Fechin painted his portrait and Tinka fell in love with him and broke up her marriage. Spud must have heard she would not be here. He would have come anyway, of course, but not in the toreador suit. Hal and Bob were there too with several women from Santa Fe, and Jimmy Karavas and his wife, Noula, were there with their teenage son, Saki. Noula was the lady who had directed Myron to Thomas Wolfe. Now I'm serving you, Myron said, and the Karavases talked about their plans to enlarge the hotel by adding a second story and a new bar and restaurant. Then there were the lean men who'd grown the Lawrencian beards and the women they'd brought, and there were the general tourists: the southern drawls, Midwestern twangs, and the broad New York and Boston vowels. And there were strangers who'd come for the food. After all, a Depression was still going on. Myron, Cady, and Angelo fed them all and poured wine though Myron thought boiling hot-dogs was wrong.

"Ever have a Nathan's Hot Dog?" he asked when there was a lull.

"Oh, yes," said Cady. "We'd go out to Coney Island just for that."

"Ever try the potato knishes from the street vendors?"

"Oh God!" said Cady. "I love them. The onion ones in particular!"

"We gotta go to New York."

"It'd be fun," said Cady. "Should we taste one of these?"

"Wouldn't be the same. They're boiled, for god's sake."

"I'm curious," Cady insisted and made one up but without mustard and relish. They each took a bite.

"Wow," said Cady and fanned his mouth.

"Yeah," said Myron, "that'll butter your necktie," and he went to the piccalilli jar and spooned its sweetness on the rest of the dog.

"Chorizo," said Cady, who'd made himself another.

"Too hot for me," said Myron but he finished the one he had

and, as the afternoon wore on and the lulls came and went, had two more.

About four o'clock the music stopped. Angelo had gone into the house to change out of his chef's clothes. Now he appeared in the full dress uniform of an Italian policeman, which was what he had once been.

"*Attencione!*" he called. "*Attencione!*"

Frieda had come up to stand beside him, a cigarette dangling from her mouth, smoke rolling into her eyes.

"Lawrence would've loved that," Cady whispered. Spud had told them how much Lawrence hated Frieda's smoking.

"Please," Angelo went on, "to follow to the chapel so the proceeding can . . . "

Frieda whispered something to him.

"Proceeeed," he said and shrugged, then laughed. Then he began slowly walking up the hill, Frieda on his arm, and close behind, Barby and her husband and the actress Miriam Golden.

Cady and Myron undid their aprons and followed the throng. When they reached the chapel area, they stopped at the outer edge of the crowd and would have stayed there if Frieda hadn't motioned for them to come up to the front. They did but still she held up the proceedings. She seemed to be looking for someone, perhaps Brett, whom Myron saw up the hill peeking at them from behind a ponderosa. What's she doing, he wondered? And he thought of the cockeyed silent film comedian, Ben Turpin, who was always spying. That made him smile.

"We are gathered here this evening," Stuart Barr began at last, "to dedicate this chapel to the memory of David Herbert Lawrence, a genius of our time. First, I would like to introduce Miriam Golden, who has kindly consented to read one of Lawrence's poems to us."

He stepped back, and Miriam Golden stepped forward.

"When Frieda asked me if I would recite something of Lawrence's at this ceremony, I was thrilled. And when she said I could choose what I wanted, I was humbled. In a sense I was being allowed to speak for Lawrence. But as I reread the poetry, a new problem presented itself. An abundance of riches. I could do no wrong."

Until *Lorenzo in Taos*, Myron hadn't even known Lawrence wrote poetry. There was only the fiction writer. Poetry seemed a contradiction, and the fiction writer was contradictory enough. There was the angry crackpot enraged by society who dreamed of Utopias and wrote bad novels like *The Plumed Serpent*, and there was the equally angry pacifist under house arrest during the war who wrote *The Rainbow* and *Women in Love*, two of the best novels in the English language. The crackpot, he decided, belonged to acolytes like Brett and Mabel, the great writer to Frieda.

"The poem I've chosen," Miriam Golden went on, "is called 'Snake.'" She put on the glasses she held in her hand and began.

A snake came to my water trough
On a hot, hot day, and I in my pyjamas for the heat,
To drink there.

Myron realized again why Miriam had been chosen. She could still project her voice without shouting or straining.

In the deep, strange-scented shade of the
great dark carob tree
I came down the steps with my pitcher
And must wait, must stand and wait,
for there he was at
the trough before me.

Abel Sanchez joined them with the four dancers and two singers who were once again in their clothes. Myron glanced around at the other Indians who'd come, maybe a dozen of them. They seemed to be listening. Or if they weren't, at least they were being respectful of this voice from the dead.

He reached down from a fissure in the
earth-wall in the gloom
And trailed his yellow-brown slackness
soft-bellied down,
over the edge of the stone trough
And rested his throat upon the stone bottom,
And where the water had dripped from the tap,
in a small clearness,

He sipped with his straight mouth,
Soft drank through his straight gums,
into his long slack body,
Silently.

Myron found himself looking at the earth. He loved poetry. Though he'd no longer admit it, he still believed beauty could save the world, that complexity and paradox were wrapped up in the word, that truth was there also, and that people would be better if they could see it. He thought of his old writing teacher, Joyce Kilmer. It was he who had advised Myron to write. He would read Myron's stories to the class, Yiddish accents and all. In 1916 Kilmer went off to Canada to enlist. Six months later he was dead. In some ways Myron never got over that. Now when he wrote he sometimes heard Kilmer's voice reading his words.

Someone was before me at my water-trough
and I, like a second comer, waiting.
He lifted his head from his drinking as cattle do,
And looked at me vaguely, as drinking cattle do,
And flicked his two-forked tongue from his lips,
and mused a moment,
And stopped and drank a little more,
Being earth-brown, earth-golden
from the burning bowels
of the earth
On the day of Sicilian July, with Etna smoking.

Myron didn't write poetry. Poets were brave men, heroes. Myron was brave enough but not heroic. Writing poetry was dangerous, deadly work. It was like looking at a god. It almost always was fatal.

The voice of my education said to me
He must be killed,
For in Sicily the black, black snakes are innocent, the gold are venomous.
And voices in me said, If you were a man
You would take a stick and break him now, and finish him off.

Miriam Golden looked up for a moment. Myron tried to remember her as Lady Macbeth. Out, out, damned . . .

But I must confess how I liked him,
How glad I was he had come like a guest in quiet,
to drink
at my water-trough
And depart peaceful, pacified, and thankless
Into the burning bowels of this earth.

And yet those voices:
If you were not afraid you would kill him!

And truly I was afraid, I was most afraid,
But even so, honoured still more
That he should seek my hospitality
From out the dark door of the
Secret earth.

"I thought Mabel would show up at the last minute," Myron whispered to Cady. He had to take the edge off Lawrence's words.

"She sent flowers," Cady whispered back.

"She did? How do you know?"

"Frieda told me." Myron remembered Cady talking to Frieda while they were working behind the table. He'd wondered what they were saying.

"Well, that's something," Myron said.

"No, it's not," said Cady. "Frieda showed me the note. It said the roses were out of respect for Lawrence. As far as the ashes were concerned, Mabel said she would get them after Frieda was dead."

"What did Frieda say?"

"That she wasn't worried, that when Angelo mixed the concrete for the altar, she had him dump Lawrence's ashes into the mix."

He drank enough
And lifted his head, dreamily, as one who has drunk
And flicked his tongue like a forked night on the air,
so black,
Seeming to lick his lips,

And looked around like a god, unseeing, into the air,
And slowly turned his head,
And slowly, very slowly, as if thrice a dream,
Proceeded to draw his slow length curving round
And climb again the broken bank of my wall face.

Myron peered into the chapel. It was black. You couldn't see anything.

And as he put his head into that dreadful hole,
And as he slowly drew up, snake-easing his shoulders,
and entered farther,
A sort of horror, a sort of protest against his
withdrawing into that horrid black hole
Deliberately going into the blackness,
and slowly drawing himself after,
Overcame me now his back was turned.

He's not in there, Myron thought, and turned away. He's out here.

I looked around, I put down my pitcher,
I picked up a clumsy log
And threw it at the water-trough
With a clatter.

I think I did not hit him,
But suddenly that part of him that was left behind
convulsed in undignified haste,
Writhed like lightning and was gone
Into the black hole, the earth-lipped
fissure in the wall front.
At which, in the intense still noon,
I stared with fascination.

Myron glanced at Cady who had touched his hand.

And immediately I regretted it.
I thought how paltry, how vulgar, what a mean act!
I despised myself and the voices of my
accursed human education.
And I thought of the albatross,

And I wished he would come back, my snake.
For he seemed to me again like a king,
Like a king in exile, uncrowned in the underworld,
Now due to be crowned again.

They were holding hands. It was the first time in public.

And so, I missed my chance with one of the lords
Of life.
And I have something to expiate;
A pettiness.

After the ceremony the mariachi band led the crowd away from the chapel and back into the field. The sun was low and there were clouds in the west. There was nothing to do now but dance. Rebecca Salisbury, who Cady said was a very talented painter, asked Myron to dance. Cady danced with Nina Otero, one of the three Santa Fe women Hal and Bob had brought. The two other women, according to Spud, were the lady friends of Thomas Wolfe who had last month accompanied that author to Mabel's house. Wolfe had dubbed them Miss Sage and Miss Brush. The ladies had liked the names so much they began using them.

"I'm Imogene Sage," said the shorter one.

"And I'm Bonny Brush," said the taller.

Myron and Cady danced with them. The music was mostly rumbas with a few fox-trots and tangos.

"Have you noticed," Nina Otero asked Myron when they were dancing again, "Dorothy Brett is here?"

"Yes," he said and laughed. "We've been trying to coax her out of the woods all afternoon. But she's stubborn as a mule."

"Why won't she join us?"

"Aesthetic principles. She thinks the chapel's ugly."

"It is," Nina Otero agreed.

Then he was dancing with Imogene Sage, who was bouncy and aggressive and had breasts as hard as wood.

"Where's Mabel?" she asked.

"She doesn't approve," said Myron.

"She's just jealous."

Then he was dancing with the taller, softer Bonny Brush. Myron asked her what really happened with Wolfe at Mabel's.

"It was our job to get him there," she said. "He kept wanting to stop at cantinas: Pojoaque, Española, even Taos. I tell you he's a party boy. He wouldn't have got there at all if it hadn't been for us." Then she pulled Myron to the edge of the circle of dancers, opened her purse, and took out a pint of something that Myron realized at first taste was sloe gin. He took a second swig and she finished what was left.

"Don't worry," she assured him. "There's more in the car."

Then he was dancing with Rebecca Salisbury again, who Myron now remembered was the daughter of the manager of the Buffalo Bill Wild West show. He wanted to ask her about the show. He'd seen it when he was a kid in Butte and loved it. But just then Spud danced by with Miss Sage.

"You look like Manolete," Myron shouted and Spud, without missing a beat, spun a perfect veronica with an imaginary cape. Then he was dragged off by the powerful Miss Sage.

"Who are all these Lawrence lookalikes?" Rebecca asked. "It's eerie to see them floating by."

"I don't know," said Myron. "Why don't you dance with one and find out?"

Then the sun was gone and everyone was gathering around the woodpile to watch as Angelo soaked it with kerosene. When he was satisfied there was enough, he struck a match and threw it onto the wood.

"I rise in flame," shouted one of the bearded Lawrences. Then everyone was shouting, "I rise in flame! I rise in flame!"

As the fire grew in intensity it seemed to steal the last of the day's light. Part of the effect was the thunderheads coming in from the west. But they didn't deter the mariachis, who called themselves the San Cristobal Orchestra. They struck up La Paloma, and people locked arms and began to move sideways in an Indian circle dance of friendship. But after a while some of the dancers were drawing closer to the fire until they were so hot they had to back away, which made the circle undulate like a snake. Not since Myron was a kid had he partaken in anything like this, a mad Maypole dance at Butte's Columbia Gardens where all the schoolchildren had been taken. Then he and Cady broke out of the circle, and there was Frieda dancing with Angelo.

Then she was dancing with Cady, then Myron, while all around them whirled Lawrence lookalikes, hirsute salamanders wriggling out of the very center of the fire. Then someone cut in and took Frieda off, and Myron pushed his way out of the circle and found Cady just as lightning began to crackle the black sky to the west.

"Isn't this crazy?" Cady asked.

"It's wonderful!"

They began dancing with each other, side by side, hands held in front in the chaste Indian way, like skaters. Others joined them and after a while this group was circling the flames, too, and getting too close. So Myron and Cady moved away again. Abandoning the dancing they walking east to the field's edge where the ground began to rise steeply. They stopped to look back. Lightning flashed in the west, and the field glowed with firelight. They entered the woods. Though they could still hear the music, in a few minutes, trees blocked the fire's light. But they kept moving up the slope and somehow, instead of it getting darker, the young night seemed to be growing brighter. And there was no hint of the approaching storm so they kept moving up. It wasn't a hard climb. It fact it felt as if they were being pulled. Then Myron saw the moon just beginning to show itself through the trees ahead. Cady stopped. He was looking at something ahead and Myron thought of bears. In Montana bears were the usual nocturnal marauders. Were there any here? Then he saw there was a clearing just ahead and something was in it. It wasn't a bear.

It was Brett. Her back was to them, her face tilted toward the full orange moon, her arms seeming to reach for it, her legs pushing the ground as if climbing toward it. In the moon's soft light she looked young again and Myron was just about to say something to Cady when she half turned. He was startled and didn't understand, and when he did, he couldn't believe his eyes. Though she still had on her ten-gallon hat, her white shirt was around her waist. Myron looked away and thought they should leave, but Cady held his ground. She hadn't seen them. Her eyes were on the moon. So Myron kept looking. Her breasts were low hanging, yet full and perfect, youthful with aureoles like medallions. Myron couldn't remember the last time he'd seen a woman's breasts. They didn't interest him. But for some reason Brett's did. He couldn't take his eyes off them. Why? Was it the surprise of them or the craziness of the situation? Or was it just that what she was doing seemed so out of character for a middle-aged English noblewoman, even one as eccentric as Brett?

Or was it her breasts themselves? They were so young, so perfect. Who would have thought? But no, not quite perfect. For he noticed now that her nipples were too long, too aggressive upon the night air, too dark and hard. They seemed engorged, as if something was exciting them, as if something had hold of them and was giving them pleasure. Myron turned away to the moon, whose yellow immensity now showed itself above the trees. Behind them, to the west, the rumble of thunder was getting closer. He noticed the music had stopped. Was it raining down there? If it was, in a few minutes it would be up here.

"It's going to rain," he said, and took Cady's hand. "Let's go." They turned from the clearing and started down.

"Do you think we should tell her?" asked Cady after they'd gone a little ways. "I don't think she can hear the thunder."

"No," Myron said. "It'll be too embarrassing for her." Then he added more practically. "If she can't hear it, she can certainly see it. Besides, she has a cabin down on the Hawk ranch. She'll be home in a few minutes. We've got a long way to go."

When they reached the ranch everything was chaos. The rain hadn't actually started but the cold wind had hit and people were rushing for their cars. Once in them, they were trying to get out onto the road. Cady, thinking it might blow over, waited until most of the cars had cleared out. That was a mistake for it really opened up and gave no sign of stopping. So after a half hour they decided to try it. They made it about halfway down before they slid off the road, which was now a stream. There they sat, up to their axles in muddy water. Caddy turned off the lights. Except for the flashes of lightning, it was pitch dark, the storm blotting out the moonlight. The temperature must have dropped twenty degrees. Cady had the heater on but after a while he turned the car off and quickly the air chilled.

"We may have to spend the night," he said.

"Could be worse," said Myron, looking into the back. "We'll have to get that drum out of the way."

"Let's move it up here."

That's what they did, small Cady wiggling over the seat into the back and Myron moving over to the driver's side and guiding the drum over, then climbing into the back to give the drum the whole bench. Then they were arranging the leather bags.

"I hope the old Packard makes it," said Cady.

"Yeah," Myron agreed. They were lying side by side, the store-bought bags full of leggings and shirts beneath their heads, the long, soft deerskin bags filled with eagle feathers over them like a down comforter.

"Don't you love the smell of their leather?" asked Cady. "They cure everything with piñon smoke."

"Smoke. It's the smell of Indians everywhere."

Then the car was rocked by a terrifically strong gust of wind and they lay listening to the rain pounding on the old Ford's roof. It seemed almost wrong to be so comfortable and cozy.

"Did you notice her nipples?" asked Cady in the darkness.

"I couldn't take my eyes off them," Myron admitted.

"Do all women have nipples like that?" Cady sounded as if he were asking about earthlings.

"No," said Myron. There was a silence.

"This is like a nest," said Cady of their new bed.

"Yeah. It's really comfortable."

"Did you see her face?" asked Cady.

"No," said Myron. "I didn't."

"I think she was coming. She had that look on her face."

"What look?"

"Pain. Her forehead was wrinkled and her eyes squeezed shut."

"How do you know about that look?"

"You told me."

There was a silence. Then Myron felt Cady moving closer. But who could make love in such conditions? Yet he had to ask. Cady said no—that he just wanted to be held. So they lay in each other's arms while the storm raged, while the wind roared, the lightning flashed and the thunder clapped, and they felt the car rock like a boat. But it wasn't until Myron was almost asleep that he remembered the two dancers who'd been seduced by eagles.

What had happened to them? Were they lost forever or had they found themselves, truly found themselves? Had they discovered that they were meant to fly? That was it, he decided. They were. But they had to come down somewhere. And here they were.

The living room of the Big House was a history of Mabel: the chaise from Florence, the damask curtains from 23 Fifth Avenue, the Duncan Phyfe sofas from her mother's Buffalo house. Every object was part of her persona. Of course there were mysterious things, like the bronze Buddha that stood on the mantle smiling down on whomever looked at it. Where had it come from and when had she acquired it? He'd have to ask. He did know about the Taos things, paintings mostly, a Max Ernst, a John Marin, an Andrew Dasburg, a Victor Higgins, as well as some early photographs by Stieglitz. But these artists were more like herself, that is, more or less transplanted to Taos. The only things that were uniquely from here were the flowers, many from her own garden, though she loved the wildflowers—red and blue lupine, daisies, buttercups and iris and Indian paintbrush—that grew on the mountain meadows just east of the house. They'd live for a day, then be discarded and replaced by fresh asparagus and plum blossom and the red and yellow roses that grew wild by the road. The Pueblo girls who cooked and cleaned would pick them on their way to work.

It seemed to Myron that Mabel did not so much arrange flowers as push them into convenient receptacles, drinking glasses, pottery jugs, and vases where they looked carelessly right. It seemed to him that everything in the living room was calculated to appear without calculation. And at least once a day she would light pine needles and wave them about until it seemed she would burn her fingers. Then she would throw them into the fireplace where their odor continued to sharpen the air. It's so stuffy in here! she would exclaim. When Myron first saw her do this he took exception. Is she saying I smell bad? So he complained to her. You don't smell bad, she said and laughed. And you're never boring.

So there they were in this carefully casual room, piñon logs burning in the fireplace. It was the Sunday after the Lawrence dedication and Mabel had decided to have a small party to celebrate the almost simultaneous publications of her *European Experiences* and his *The Sun Sets in the West*. But that was a contrivance. She'd heard what a success the Lawrence dedication had been. So now she invited many of the same people to what she called a review party. Who knows? Maybe it was to test their loyalty. If so, none of them knew it. They had seen the dedication up at the ranch as a remembrance of Lawrence, which is what it had been. But what Myron resented most about this review party was that without a by-your-leave he was being used as an excuse for the gathering. She'd gotten Spud to collect the reviews, then said it was natural that if they were any good they should read them aloud. So there he was. She began with the *New York Times*.

> The Sun Sets in the West *is not a cheerful or even hopeful story. It has less of the humor, less of the gusto, less of the high color that went to enhance the pleasure that many of us found in* Singermann *and* Wide Open Town . . . *But it is a fine, thoughtful, and deeply felt contemporary story or group of stories woven together—stories which Brinig tells as fascinatingly as ever.*

There was applause from the assembled: Spud and several of the artists, Victor Higgins, Andrew and Marina Dasburg, Tinka Fechin, and Judge Kiker and his wife, Florence. Now it was Myron's turn to read a review of *European Experiences*, the second volume of Mabel's memoir. He'd underlined what he wanted.

> *This much may be said without a chance of contradiction, about her latest book: It may infuriate you, it may make you sick in spots, but it will hold you. You cannot stop reading it. Moreover, it will be for various reasons, worth reading.*

"Oooh!" everyone sighed.

"Who's the reviewer?" asked Cady.

"M. L. Becker."

"Never heard of him."

"Where's it from?" asked Mabel.

"*Books,*" Myron said and held up the respected book review sheet.

"Praising with faint damnation," said Spud. "I like it."

"Does he name the spots that will make you sick?" asked Andrew Dasburg.

"Or does he mean you'll get spots if you read it?" asked Marina Dasburg, who always seemed a little drunk.

"Let me read another of Myron's," said Mabel, taking the copy of *Books* from him and turning to a marked page.

> *Myron Brinig contemplates his people with an understanding that is at least the beginning of wisdom. As a novelist he is speculative rather than didactic; thoughtful rather than dynamic; more puzzled than cocksure. His stories may lack force and conviction and may lose something thereby. But they are vital and alive even if they will not teach you right from wrong, separate sheep from goats, set the world afire or bring on revolution.*

"Ah, that's nice," said Spud. "Who's the reviewer?

"David Tilden," said Mabel, looking down at the paper.

"Lincoln Steffens won't like it," said Cady.

"The book or the review?" Myron asked.

"Both," said Mabel and laughed.

"Well, I would've liked him to like it." Myron looked at Mabel. "Don't you think it makes me sound wishy-washy?" he asked.

"No, it makes you sound wise," said Cady.

"You are wishy-washy," said Mabel, as if Cady hadn't spoken.

"Now it's your turn," said Spud to Myron.

Myron looked at Mabel a moment longer, then began leafing through the pile of newspapers until he found the one he wanted. It was one he hadn't planned to read.

"This is from yesterday's *Chicago Sun Times,*" he announced.

Mabel Dodge Luhan has done literature a service in recording with the enthusiasm of a participant, a period, and a social scene which have all the charm of the excitedly unimportant. She has also done it a service in recording a psychology rare but not unique: for whether wittingly or unwittingly, she has detailed a person, in herself, who has a passionate compulsion to minimize everyone else.

There was a silence, the guests looking at each other uncomfortably. Then Cady spoke up. "Who wrote that?" he asked.

"Fanny Butcher," answered Myron.

"Aptly named," said Spud.

"Are there any others?" asked Andrew Dasburg.

"No," said Mabel, though she had four more in front of her. "That's all."

Seeming relieved, Mabel's guests drifted outside with their drinks to enjoy the late afternoon light. Autumn was the beautiful time. The weather was growing cooler. But she asked Myron to stay.

"What's eating you?" she asked when they were alone.

"You," Myron answered. And he realized that he was once again a little drunk. Would he have to stop drinking altogether? It's one thing to dance at funerals and sleep in cars. It's quite another to bite the hand that's petting you.

"Don't you like the competition, Myron?"

"What competition?" he snarled.

"Other writers."

"This has nothing to do with writing or writers. No, that's not true. It's got to do with one writer."

"Who's that?"

"Lawrence."

"So you went up there."

"Of course I went. You knew I went, Mabel!"

"I did not!"

"You did! And now you're acting like a petulant child. But why does that not surprise me? Sending a bunch of flowers along with a spiteful note. Lawrence was a great artist, Mabel, and a great man. You've got to do something to show your love and respect!"

It was obvious she couldn't believe he was saying these things to her. Nor could he. Not that he had trouble being honest with Mabel. But he'd kept his mouth shut about this particular subject too long.

"Myron. I'll not have you defend that woman," she said. "Her daughter told me some of the things she did after Lawrence's death."

"Like what?"

"Like right after the funeral having sex with Middleton Murray, like . . . "

"So what!" Myron interrupted. "Mabel, you're going to regret what you're doing!" He wondered if she ever regretted anything she did. "You're turning your love for Lawrence and all the good feelings you put into *Lorenzo in Taos* to ashes. You'll end up choking on them."

". . . and how she tried to get her own daughter to have sex with some young Italian because she thought it was sexual frustration that was causing Barby's intense mourning. Can you imagine? Because she'd lost interest in Lawrence, she couldn't imagine anyone else caring."

"Mabel," Myron snarled angrily, "are your actions beyond reproach? Lusting after men like Lawrence and Jeffers while trying to palm your marriage off on the public as some kind of ideal." Stop, he told himself when he saw the anger in her eyes. You're going too far. But he couldn't seem to stop. "You're nothing but a spoiled rich bitch who fell for a fortune-hunting Indian and is regretting it!"

"You can't speak to me this way, Myron!" she shouted and rose from her chaise. "I won't stand for it!"

"You slander Angelo and set family member against family member! Did you know Frieda had to order Barby and her husband off the ranch because of what they were saying about Angelo?" As soon as he said it Myron knew this would be good news to her. How could he make her see how awful she was being? "Worse than the things you're saying are the reasons you're saying them! Your own destructive jealousy!"

"You can attack my motives," Mabel said righteously, "but you can't defend her actions."

Myron shrugged and almost gave up when he caught sight of *Lorenzo in Taos* on the bookshelf. He went to it and took it down.

"You said it yourself better than anyone has ever said it." He found the page. It was the beginning of the description of the day Mabel and Tony picked the Lawrences up at the Lamy station. The very first moments of their meeting. Her observations were perfect. "You want to read stuff aloud, then read this." And he handed her the open book. She looked at it a moment and began to read.

> *Lawrence and Frieda came hurrying along the platform, she tall and full fleshed in a suit of pale pongee, an eager look on her pink face, with green, unfocused eyes, and her half-opened mouth with the lower jaw pulled a little sideways. Frieda always had a mouth rather like a gunman.*

"That's not the passage I mean!" Myron snatched the book from her. "Here! Read this!" And he had his finger on the spot.

> *The Lawrences seemed intensely conscious of Tony and embarrassed by him. I made out in the twinkling of an eye that Frieda immediately saw Tony and me sexually, visualizing our relationship. I experienced her swift, female measurement of him and how the shock of acceptance made her blink.*

Mabel looked up.

"Keep reading," Myron directed.

> *In that first moment I saw how her encounters passed through her to Lawrence—how he was keyed to her so that he felt things through her and was obliged to receive life through her vicariously.*

"Stop!" ordered Myron.

"No. There's more!" said Mabel.

But he snatched the book. "I know what you say next. You take your greatest insight, Lawrence seeing the world through Frieda's eyes, and try to make it sound as if he's her sexual prisoner and that you're the angel who will free him. But it's your original insight that's the truth. He wasn't her prisoner. He believed in her and loved her and not you. He trusted her and you still can't admit that."

Mabel didn't say anything. She sat back down and Myron realized he could have called her names for the rest of the afternoon, repeated over and over how badly she was acting and it would have done no good. But her own words had gotten to her. She looked like a hurt animal and his anger left him. He was kneeling beside the chaise. Was this the first time she had admitted the truth? That there was nothing between her and Lawrence except her desire. Now she was crying. She never cried, and Myron felt terrible. So he began apologizing for his remarks about Tony, which he said he hadn't meant, nor what he'd said about her.

"You're a great artist," he said. "If I could love a woman, I would love you."

"What can I do?" she asked.

"It's simple." He and Cady had talked it over. "There could be another dedication. A small one. And this time you have to attend. "

She looked up. He thought she was going to say no. But she held her tongue.

"You'll have to call Frieda and apologize for your behavior and ask if you could pay your respects to Lawrence."

"What if she says no?"

"I don't think she will. But if she does, you'll have tried." Myron paused. "They went to a lot of trouble last Sunday. You'll have to tell them you don't want anything like that. You want just a few friends, and you'll handle the food and drink. You just want a small picnic outside the chapel."

"I can do that," she said. "Hotdogs and homemade wine. I can do better than that out of my kitchen right this moment."

"Mabel! You're not going there to show them up!"

"You're right," she said. "My pride. My overweening pride."

She was using the same words Lawrence had used to describe her mental makeup. It was all in *Lorenzo in Taos*.

The next day Myron talked to Brett. He looked at her now with new respect. In her strange Edwardian way, she was more a child of nature than any of them. He had already suggested to Cady that he paint her the way they had seen her in the moonlight. Cady gave it some thought but decided he couldn't do her justice. I'm not that kind of painter, he said. I could do the night and the moon. I could give her spirit a place to live. But I couldn't do her. Now Myron used the same argument on Brett he'd used on Mabel, that she was insulting Lawrence. But only after he told her Mabel had changed her mind and was going to the chapel did she relent. Then he couldn't resist and asked if she'd gotten caught in the storm. She said no, that she'd gone home before it hit. Then he and Cady drove up to Frieda's and suggested that she hold another ceremony that Mabel and Brett could attend. She wasn't hard to convince.

"The living have to stick together," she said laughing through a haze of cigarette smoke, "otherwise, you know, the dead will bury us."

Myron and Cady laughed, too, but when they were in the car they asked each other what the hell she meant. It wasn't important, and two days later, Thursday, September 26, 1935, Lawrence's tomb was rededicated, this time with hardly any ceremony at all, no native dancers, no mariachi band, no Lawrence lookalikes, no strangers to Lawrence at all except Myron and Cady. Brett was there, and Mabel, Frieda, Angelo, Spud, and several of the older painters who had been at the first dedication. Myron had even asked Hal and Bob to come and cleared it with Mabel. But Hal refused and blew up at the idea that Mabel should get a special ceremony of her own. No, he said angrily, I've been to the real dedication. Though Myron and Cady continued trying to talk him into it, they saw his point. Mabel had somehow gotten her way, a dedication of her own. There's no winning with these people, he thought.

"May I see the chapel?" Mabel asked.

"Of course," Frieda answered.

So she and Frieda, with Brett following, went into the structure that Brett had described as a railroad-station toilet, the one with the dying chicken over its doorway. Myron had told Mabel about Frieda having Angelo mix Lawrence's ashes into the cement that made the altar. Now he watched as she ran her hand over the rough surface. Is this the closest she'll ever get to his body? he wondered. Or had she already had her way with what she thought were his ashes? Was Lawrence a trophy in one of her living-room urns or was he blowing over Taos Mountain?

"He's here," said Mabel.

"Ya," said Frieda.

Then Myron recited, "Look! We Have Come Through!" a Lawrence poem he'd learned especially for the occasion, and Cady snapped photos. With all the excitement of getting the San Ildefonso dancers, he'd forgotten his camera at the first dedication. This time he clicked away. Like father, like son, Myron kidded him. And that was all the ceremony there was.

Myron forgot the photos. So he was surprised a couple of weeks later when Cady showed up with them. They looked at them together. There was Myron lying on a blanket with Mabel, the chapel in the background. And there were Angelo, Myron, and Spud on the same blanket. But the best was the one of Brett, Mabel, and Frieda sitting on the steps of Lawrence's old ranch house, laughing at something Cady had said: Frieda von Richtofen Lawrence, first cousin of the fabled Red Baron, cigarette dangling from her crooked mouth, smoke floating into her eyes, looking more like a frump than a gangster, and Mabel Dodge Luhan, the closest thing to American royalty there was, a millionaire married to an Indian, plump and youthful, hair cut in bangs, and a smile so wide you can see her gums, and silly, serious, slack-jawed, passionate Lady Dorothy Brett, daughter of Reginald Brett, Second Viscount Esher, chief advisor to Queen Victoria and then, to her son, Edward VII, in motorcycle boots laced up to her knees, a wallet in her left hand, a gypsy bandanna around her head.

"The Three Fates," Cady dubbed them as he looked through his viewfinder.

That's what made Frieda and Mabel laugh. Brett didn't hear him.

Seven

"I'm not staying here another moment!" Cady was throwing things into his suitcase. His easel and paints were already in the station wagon. "She called my dancers scabs." It was just a day after the second dedication. Not even a day. It was right after breakfast. Mabel had gotten Cady alone and lit into him.

"What did you say?"

"I told her that what she was saying was ridiculous, that my hiring dancers had nothing to do with labor problems and everything to do with how mean-spirited she was."

"What did she say?"

"She said I was a spoiled, rich brat trying to make up to Frieda." He snapped the suitcase locks closed.

"What are you going to do?"

"I'm going back down to the cabin. Tomorrow I'm going out and look for a place." He picked up the bag. "Coming with me?"

"Of course."

Myron threw a few things into his overnight bag and in ten minutes, without saying goodbye to anyone, they were on the road heading south.

"You know," said Myron as they passed Ranchos de Taos, "I was certain she'd changed. Think how well she behaved at Frieda's. I was sure I'd gotten to her." He'd told Cady about making Mabel read her own description of Frieda. "I guess it was just my ego thinking I could do something like that."

"You did get to her," said Cady. "For a day she changed. But she must've had second thoughts or maybe no thoughts. She's angry. At Frieda, at Lawrence, at life. It was like I was a trigger."

"How did it start? Did you say anything to her?"

"No. She just called me into her office and said she had something to talk to me about."

"Did she say anything about me?"

"No." He glanced at Myron. "She likes you, Mike. No, it's more than that. She's fixated on you. You can do no wrong."

"What an unhappy, restless spirit," Myron said. Then they agreed to stop talking about Mabel and began talking about what kind of place Cady would buy. An hour later, when they reached the cabin, there was a message on the door for Cady to call Hal. He went up to the main house. When he came back he told Myron that Hal had asked them to a party but that he'd said no.

"Maybe we should go," said Myron. "It'll clear the air, get us thinking about other things."

So Cady called Hal back and that night they drove down to Santa Fe.

This time it was Myron who got called aside. Hal said he had a bone to pick with him and Myron knew he was angry.

"You are an upstart," Hal began.

Myron wanted to laugh. He was kidding, right? An upstart. The insult was out of Elizabethan drama.

"When I first met you I thought better of you. You recited my poetry and I was flattered." Hal was doing his best to sound like an Ivy League professor. "But I see now you're nothing but a lackey, a lickspittle working for Mabel."

Again Myron wanted to smile. Why the archaic insults? And Spud, who in fact did work for Mabel, was there and could overhear. It was that inconsiderateness that made Myron realize Hal was serious and that what he was on about was the second ceremony at the ranch.

"I don't deserve this, Hal. I did what I thought was right. I tried to reconcile Frieda and Mabel and you, too. But you wouldn't join in."

"You think Mabel and Frieda are reconciled?" Hal turned and looked to the other end of the room. "Cady!" Cady came over. Now not only Spud and Bob Hunt, but several men Myron didn't know were looking at them. "Of course you know what she said to Cady."

"I know." Myron wondered for a moment how Hal knew, then realized that Cady must have mentioned it on the phone and that Hal must have decided then and there that it was Myron's fault in the same way Mabel had decided it was Cady's. Was that why Cady hadn't wanted to come?

"And you can still defend her?" asked Hal.

"I'm not defending her, Hal. I'm defending myself. I was trying to get all this backbiting crap to stop." Myron's temper was coming up. "You obviously don't want it to stop, Hal. It makes you happy to be self-righteously angry. So go on being angry. I don't mind being the object of your anger. Innocent as I am, you seem to need such objects. You create them."

"So it's all in my head, eh?"

"It's in both of your heads."

"Don't lump me with her, Myron."

"Why not? Aren't you both rich bitches playing king of the Sangre de Cristos? I think you're very alike."

"Alike? I would never have said to a guest what that woman said to Cady. I place too much importance on hospitality."

"Then why do you insult me?"

"I'm not insulting you. I'm telling you the truth about yourself!"

"This is a stupid argument," said Cady, perhaps sensing Hal was backing down. "Let's forget Mabel. She's not worth it. Think of the satisfaction it would give her to know we're talking about her this way."

"We're not arguing over Mabel," said Myron. "We're arguing over the kind of host Hal is." Then he turned back to the big man. Myron didn't want it to be over. "You know Hal, I see myself in the same position Robert Frost was in this past summer."

Myron hadn't been there but he'd heard. Hal had been furious at Frost for being late for the lunch he was giving in his honor. So when the poet finally arrived Hal began going on about Horatio

Colony's latest book. Horatio Colony was a Harvard classmate of Hal's and a homosexual, and his poetry was full of thinly veiled celebrations of homosexuality. Hal announced to all that it was the best book of verse he'd read in years thus discounting Frost's rising reputation. But Frost, no slouch in temper, pretended to like the poems and volunteered to read one aloud. Hal fell for it, passed the book, and Frost seemed to pick one at random. It turned out to be a vivid description of a sex act and there were several gasps from the women in the room. Realizing he'd been had, Hal had walked up to Frost and, towering over him, emptied his mug of beer over the poet's head. For weeks it was all Santa Fe talked about.

"That was a joke," said Hal.

"Bullshit!" snarled Myron. "You're jealous of his reputation, Hal. He's on the rise and you're sinking, and you know it."

"Myron!" shouted Cady.

"You are no gentleman," said Hal in as condescending a tone as he could muster.

"Nor am I a hypocrite," said Myron.

"I want you to leave my house, Myron, and never come back."

"Or you'll do what? Pour your drink over me?"

It never came to that. Myron allowed Cady to lead him out, and they were silent for a long time as they drove back to the cabin. It was Cady who finally spoke.

"I'm sorry," he said. "I should've warned you."

"You knew?"

"I knew he was angry with Mabel. I told him what she said to me. Maybe I shouldn't have. But I told him you had nothing to do with it."

"Well," said Myron, "it seems Taos and Santa Fe are out for us."

"That clinches it," Cady said, suddenly cheerful. "I'm going to have to find my own place."

"And while you do that, I'm going back to San Francisco and finish this novel."

"And when I have a new house and you have a great financial success we'll move in together and live happily ever after."

"You bet your sweet ass!" and Myron slid his hand up the driver's thigh.

"We'll be the two happiest queers in all America."

"You bet your rosy red rectum!"

But the night wasn't over. When they entered Cady's cabin, Myron's arm over Cady's shoulders, Cady's arm around Myron's waist, there on the bed was a note from the ranch owners, Marjorie and Allan Clark. It seemed Cady had already given them notice. But instead of being gracious and thanking him for renting from them for the past two years and being their meal ticket, the Clarks showed their gratitude by billing him not only for the next month's rent, but also for marring their property, that is, for building his just finished studio on it without their permission. The note said the need for such permission was in the rental agreement and they claimed the studio's demolition and cleanup would cost two hundred dollars, which was twice what it cost Cady to build it.

"But I got their permission. I told Allan he could have it when I left." Allan was a sculptor. "He thanked me."

"How come you gave notice already?" Myron asked.

"I've already bought a place," Cady said. "I wanted to surprise you and take you there tomorrow. It's on the Nambe River between Tesuque and San Ildefonso."

"That place you showed me last year? The one that looks at the Barrancas?"

"That's it. What did you think?"

"I told you then. It's a beautiful spot. But the house was a wreck."

"It still is."

"Where are you going to live?"

"I'm going to fix it up and add onto it."

"I mean now."

"Well," said Cady thoughtfully, "I guess I'll camp there while something's being built."

"I've got an idea. Why don't you get Juan to build you a studio there? If he'll do it, you and I can take off and you'll have something to come back to. Who knows? Maybe Judge Kiker can get Allan to remember giving you permission."

"Yeah!" said Cady, his smile pushing wrinkles all the way to the top of his head. "But where will we go?"

"How about Butte? I've never taken anyone home to meet

my mother. How'd you like to meet her and see the town? It's like no place you've ever been. We could even go down into The Speculator."

"Wow!" said Cady. "Then we could drive over and see my folks in Palm Springs."

"I could catch a bus to Frisco from there."

"And I could have Mason meet me and come back here and we could start to build in earnest. He wants to help and he's really good at it."

"What do you say? Should we do it?"

"You bet your sweet ass," said Cady tearing up the note.

"He's a rotten sculptor," Myron added. "Art deco nudes in Indian warbonnets. He might as well make bronze Kewpie dolls."

It took two days to get to Salt Lake City. They visited the Temple and Salt Air and bounced buoyantly in the awful water. It was two more days to Butte, and the closer they got, the more nervous Myron became. He was afraid to show his family what he was and he was afraid they might insult Cady. Where's he from? Jack asked after their first meal. Mars, Myron wanted to say. He's from Mars. But Jack knew what planet Cady was from. He's a millionaire, he said. Marry him. It was the first time any of them ever acknowledged what Myron was. So Myron showed Cady the family store now run by Ike. Did he really go three rounds with Ketchel? asked Cady, who seemed to know a lot about boxing. Yeah, Myron said. He's tough. Then he took his friend down into the store's basement and showed him the piles of overalls where he used to hide from his father. I read *Middlemarch* down here, he said. Then they went down into The Speculator. Hear them? Myron asked as they rode the horse drawn tramcar. But it was the tunnels themselves that seemed to impress Cady.

"They're like trenches," he said.

"That's because there was once a war down here," Myron explained, and he told Cady the story of Augustus Heinze and how his men would break into these tunnels and steal ore and the brawls that used to go on deep under the ground.

"A battlefield," noted Cady.

They stayed a week, and Myron never did know if his mother caught on. But he knew she liked Cady because when they left, as undemonstrative as she was, she hugged the Martian and kissed his cheek. Then they were back on the road south toward Palm Springs. Cady's parents were there and it was grand lying in the sun, and swimming in their pool, and when they finally went their separate ways, it seemed to Myron they were more in love than ever. He spent the winter and spring of 1936 in San Francisco in a sublet on Joice Street writing *The Sisters*. As soon as Mabel found out where he was, she began sending letters. Again it was as if nothing had happened. And that June, while Cady was busy building his house, Myron returned to Taos to stay in Mabel's Placita house. 1936 would be the first year since he'd begun publishing that he wouldn't have a novel out. He was taking his time, being careful. That September he went back to Joice Street and polished *The Sisters* before sending it off. In February 1937, it came out to rave reviews. In less than three weeks it was on the *Times* bestseller list, where it stayed for five months. Then his new Hollywood agent, Rosalind Schmidt, called to say she'd sold *The Sisters* to Warner Brothers for $25,000. It seemed Myron's time had come, and his publishers urged him to take advantage of his momentum.

So he spent the spring of 1937 in a rented LA house working on another novel he called *May Flavin*. Before he was anywhere near done, Rosalind phoned to tell him she'd sold it to MGM for $50,000. Myron couldn't believe it. *Gone with the Wind* hadn't gotten more! And all Rosalind had were the first hundred and fifty pages. So he never made it back to New Mexico. Cady would visit him in LA or they would meet in Death Valley where Cady liked to paint, or at Mason's place in San Diego. In June of 1938 *May Flavin* came out. The story of an Irish girl who marries the man she loves, and who, after he deserts her, is left to raise their children, was perfect for Myron's new audience. Not that it was written for them. Myron had known women in Butte like May Flavin, powerful women who used their love for undeserving men to raise themselves to heroic levels. He loved them and wanted to tell their stories. The trouble was he rushed it. After the first hundred and fifty pages, the novel was little better than a first draft—repetitive, and full of clichés. Somehow the money had caused him to lose focus. Though his new reputation brought *May Flavin* to the bestseller list, the terrible reviews and word of mouth quickly removed it. He knew he'd done a bad job.

So he decided to get out of LA and called Cady, but there was no answer. Cady seemed to be away. Myron had a bad feeling. They'd had their first real difference that winter. It was over Cady driving him. Myron was surprised. Cady always seemed to enjoy their trips. They were great traveling companions, Myron reading maps and navigating, and the two of them singing at the top of their lungs. Cady would pick him up and they'd head south to La Jolla and stay in a room overlooking the Pacific. Or they'd go all the way down to San Diego and stay with Mason, then cross the border and head for Ensenada, where there were motels on the beach, or farther south to Buffadora and rent a house for a week near the famous blowhole. But lately there seemed to be less time for trips. In fact the last time Myron suggested one, Cady blew up. I want you to drive for once! I'm tired of chauffeuring you! Though he apologized soon after, Myron remembered the Truth game they'd played that first summer and how Spud had described their relationship.

After a week of calling and getting no answer at Cady's, Myron called Mabel. They'd had lots of communication by letter and phone since he had begun making money. She'd even called him once and asked for a loan. When he asked how much, she laughed and said she was only joking. But he felt there wasn't the kind of closeness they'd had before his success. He thought that in a way she was afraid she'd lost control, that he didn't need her anymore. So he was glad to ask her for a favor, put himself in her debt once more. I need to get away for a while, he said. What about the Placita house? She said it was taken but that he could have the Pink House. He said he'd pay rent. She said that was good and to come on and she asked what train he was taking so Tony could pick him up. He said Tony didn't have to do that. He was a big boy now. He'd learned to drive and owned a car. Again she said good and to come on. So for the first time in his life Myron made a long road trip alone. At every stop along Route 66, places like Barstow, Kingman, and Gallop, he talked to people on their way to California. Just like *The Grapes of Wrath*, he thought. He always gave them money. It was amazing to him that, in these hard times, he was making so much.

When he finally got to Taos, Mabel was waiting for him. She hugged him and said it was good to see him, and he said it was good to see her and asked how long it had been. Two years? No! That long? Then she admired his almost new Chevy business coupe and helped him unload it, all the while asking about Hollywood. When would *The Sisters* be released? It had been delayed a year. It turned out Kay Francis, for whom the novel had been bought, was in Warner Brothers' doghouse. On the last year of her contract, she had asked for a raise. So the studio stopped production and refused to renew her contract. She finished her year in B movies, and *The Sisters* languished until Bette Davis, who, since her Academy Award for *Jezebel*, had also been in Warner Brothers' doghouse for refusing roles, accepted it.

"They're wrapping it up as we speak," Myron explained. "As for *May Flavin*, there's nothing on the horizon. No script. No casting. I think they're disappointed the novel didn't do better."

Mabel was very knowledgeable about Hollywood. As well as Adrian, the costume designer, another of her good friends was the screenwriter Sonya Levien, to whom a few years ago Mabel had written about getting him a job. Recently he'd been offered fifteen hundred a week from Warner Brothers and turned it down.

"What's with you?" he asked. "You look like a cat eating a canary." They were at the little dining table sipping the cold gin and lemonade she had prepared.

"It's my guests," she said.

"The Jefferses?"

"Yes. And Hildegarde."

"Hildegarde? Who's Hildegarde?"

"Hildegarde Donaldson. She's a friend from back east."

"So?"

"She's fallen in love with Robin."

"Really?"

"Yes. And he with her."

"Has anything actually happened? Any sordid details?"

"I don't think so. I'd say no."

"Then how do you know they're in love?"

"Una."

"Una told you they're in love?"

"No. But she's acting so crazy." She paused. "I think Hildegarde's in danger."

"You think Una is dangerous?" Myron almost laughed. It was all suddenly so melodramatic, like that night when she burst into his room in Carmel. He sat back and took a long swig of gin and lemonade.

"Listen to this." And she related a story that she said Una Jeffers had told her and Hildegarde while they were driving somewhere, a story about Una attacking Robin in the middle of the night on a deserted road somewhere in the wilderness of the Monterey Peninsula, about her trying to kill him because she thought he was going to kill her, and how she sprang at him and sank her teeth into his throat and how blood spurted all over and how he grabbed her by the hair and tried to pull her off him and how she hung on with her teeth until he'd pulled out a whole fistful of her hair.

"Good Lord." said Myron. "It's right out of one his poems." Then he thought a moment. "I can see her telling you this, Mabel, but why in front of a total stranger?"

"That's just it, Myron," answered Mabel. "She wasn't just telling me. In fact I don't think it really happened. I think she was making it up on the spot just for Hildegard's sake."

"But why? To tell a person you consider a possible rival that your marriage is in trouble doesn't seem smart."

"Maybe it's not smart," said Mabel, "but it's brilliant. Think of it! She was telling Hildegarde the Jefferses were not an ordinary couple, that theirs was a marriage to the death."

"Ah," and Myron nodded. "Did it work?"

"No. Hildegarde's no ordinary person either." Mabel's eyes were afire. Here was the Truth game at its best, at its most exciting, and he felt suddenly swept up in her world, as if he'd never left. "If anything I think it only made the situation more attractive to her."

"But if nothing's happened why does Una suspect this woman?"

"That may have been my fault." Mabel glanced down at her hands. "When I told Una we had a new guest coming, I told her everything about Hildegarde." Pride crept into her voice. "It was innocent on my part. I'm in the habit of confiding in Una, so I told her about Hildegarde's situation."

"Her situation?"

So Mabel began a second story. There once was a woman in her late thirties with a nice husband, a beautiful house, and a career as a concert violinist. But her husband had outlived his early attentiveness, her two children were off to college, her career as a violinist was going nowhere, and all of these things conspired to remind her that she was nearing middle age. So what did she do? She tossed her head, stuck out her chin, and defied time by willing herself on one of her husband's editorial interns in such a way that the young man was snared instantly.

"What happened?"

"It went on for five years, the passion of his youth and her experience. Then he fell in love with a girl younger than he and one day came to Hildegarde leading this girl by the hand. He asked her to accept his new wife, to be a friend to her and to wish them both well."

"The cad," said Myron, and thought of the Marschallin in *Der Rosenkavalier*.

"To add insult to injury, he insisted on keeping them both, only now he wanted his former lover to change into his young wife's mentor."

"And did she?"

"She told me, painful as it was, she welcomed the girl."

"What does all this have to do with Una and Robin?"

Mabel raised a hand as if to say be patient, that she had to tell this in her own way. She went on.

"Hildegarde said that at first she suffered terribly. But time heals everything, and after a while she realized that she had weathered the storm. And that's when it came to her that life, which had been so cruel might now bestow a reward on her as it sometimes does when one weathers its storms."

"You mean she began cruising?"

"Myron, you can be so crude."

"What happened?"

"I invited her here."

"And?"

"It was amazing. The first time Robin and she met at my dinner table they gazed across the board and in one flash plunged deep into each other's stream."

Room and board! thought Myron. Diving board! But if you're swimming in each other's stream aren't you still alone?

"What did Una do while all this plunging was going on?"

"She didn't do or say anything, at least not until her story last night."

"Mabel, I'm not sure what you're up to," said Myron, feeling suddenly fearful, "but I don't think I want to get mixed up in it."

"You don't have to," she said with a warm smile. "I just need someone to talk to." She came around the table, knelt beside him, and put her arm over his shoulder. "It's good to have you back," she said and kissed his cheek. She stood. "See you at dinner." Then she left.

Myron stood and went to the bookcase across the room. He had known of Mabel's feeling for Robinson Jeffers before he ever got to Taos. There it was. *Lorenzo in Taos*. A copy in every one of her houses. He took it down and opened to the part toward the end after Lawrence's death. She's addressing Jeffers. "Perhaps you are the one," he read, "who will do what I wanted him to do, give voice to this speechless land." Myron turned the page and there was a photo of the poet taken in 1929, looking lean and handsome and athletic. He closed the book. Jeffers had not given voice to this land. He'd been a great disappointment to Mabel. And Myron may have been the first to point it out. It was back in July of 1933, his very first summer here, when she asked him to read an article she'd written about the poet and his wife. It was supposed to acquaint Myron with the Jefferses before their visit and she wanted his opinion of it. After he read it, he was so upset he had to show it to Cady.

"Good, you're home," he said. "I need some advice."

"What is it?" Cady laid his knapsack full of brushes on the table.

"Mabel asked me to read something she's written."

"You've been doing that all summer."

"This is different."

"What is it?

"An article on the Jefferses and their marriage."

"They're not even here yet."

"It's about knowing them in Carmel."

"So?"

"It's a piece of flattery."

"What do you expect? She loves them."

"No, she doesn't."

"Really?"

"It's not that long, Cady. Read it."

Myron went for the pages, gave them to his friend, and took a bath. When he came out, Cady was done and Spud was there.

"I've read this," said Spud, waving at the article. "In fact I typed it. She wrote it last January in Carmel."

"What do you think?" Myron asked.

"It's gushy," Spud said, "but well-meaning."

"I disagree," said Myron. "It isn't well-meaning. She's describing two people in the process of devouring each other. One's passive and one's aggressive, but they're both awful in what they're doing to each other."

"I've never heard you so vehement," noted Cady.

"I just want Mabel to tell the truth. Nobody's like the people she describes."

"Have you met them?" asked Spud.

"No." The Jefferses would arrive in a week.

"Well," Spud explained, "I think Mabel's put a good face on them. She's saying that whatever you may think of the life they lead—and there are lots of people who adore them and lots who criticize them and think they're out of their minds—it has produced great poetry, and that's justification enough. Una's not your normal wife, nor Robin your normal husband. I think Mabel's saying that both of them would've been dead a long time ago without the other, that for better or worse, their marriage has helped them live."

"I don't know anything about their marriage," said Myron. "It's what Mabel's doing that I find so awful."

"What's that?" asked Cady.

"She's holding up their marriage as an ideal when in fact she hates it. If she publishes this as she wants to, she'll be exposing them to ridicule." He looked at Cady. "What did you think of it?"

"I don't know," said Cady. "I haven't had time to think." He paused. "It's gushy but I'm not sure of the harm in it."

Myron got up, took the manuscript, and thumbed through it until he found the part he wanted. It was toward the end.

"Listen. This is Mabel talking."

> *Women yearn to get a chance with Robin to see what they could do with him. Failing to get at him, they even hope some woman will come along who will succeed where they have failed. Una guards him from them all, not, as they believe, for her sake alone, so much as for them all.*

"What does she mean 'for them all'? Who does the 'them' refer to? Us? Is he a goddamned national park that we get to camp in?"

"More a national monument," said Spud.

"Listen to this."

> *Robin has no stubborn, resistant denial in him, and when Marcella, waiting for him to pass her door,called him in and gave him a drink, he went in smoothly and easily and drank and sat with her—a little self-conscious, perhaps, but not unwilling, exactly.*

"Who's Marcella and why is one drink so bad?" asked Cady.

"She's a Carmel neighbor," answered Spud.

"I think he has alcoholic tendencies," Myron added. "But listen."

> *Una went home to Tor House for a moment before she joined the Orages and the Steffens at Marcella's for tea after the lunch party at Steff's.*

"Who's Steff?" asked Cady.

"Lincoln Steffens. They're old friends," explained Spud. "They live in Carmel, too."

"Stop interrupting," Myron ordered, and went on.

Robin said: Marcella gave me a nice drink a little while ago. Where? demanded Una. At her house, said Robin. I was going by and she called me in.

"Why does he tell Una this?" Myron asked looking up. "Does he feel guilty for having taken a drink? Or is he trying to get a rise out of her? And why does Mabel choose to tell this story about them? It makes them both look like idiots."

"It does?"

Myron rolled his eyes and went on reading.

Una saw that whole small plot in a flash, for Marcella had left Steff's before them all. She knew Marcella just wanted to see if she could get Robin the way she got so many other men: she had felt that minx thing in her. In a flash, the compact rage mounted in Una and she ran all the way to the house nearby, in the door, through the easy-going, laughing group, to confront Marcella. She was as white as a sheet and her eyes simply blazed.

Myron skipped a few lines.

"Marcella! You leave Robin alone. I won't have you doing that. Robin isn't for that kind of thing!" She put such an intensity into it, her attack was like a violent explosion. She scared the usually intrepid Marcella, who burst into tears. Una didn't care. She turned and marched through the house and back to Robin. She didn't want Robin to get mixed up in the looser strands of living, after all her work upon her pattern for his life. She didn't want it spoiled.

Myron looked up. "Can you imagine a life with a husband

who would wander off with any woman who comes along and shows him the slightest interest? Mabel makes Una seem like a jailer to the village idiot."

"Idiot savant," Spud corrected.

"Whatever. Listen to what she has Una think of him."

Why should she let it be spoiled? She knew Robin was no more invulnerable than any man should be, not being neurotic nor impotent, not a god, nor yet a fool— but just a man.

"Just a man!" snapped Myron. "It sounds like all men are raging immoral pricks. Is that Una's judgment or is it Mabel's? And listen to this last summary of their marriage."

Knowing no one could take Robin's love away from her was not enough for her realistic knowledge of human nature. She knew and knows their structure has the fragility that requires daily, hourly creating. It is not something that, once made, will endure forever. At any moment it could change, be messed up, altered and spoiled—unless she watches over it. So she stands at the door with a sword. She likes that, too!

"Mabel wrote that because she wants to accept the Jefferses' marriage," said Spud. "Glorifying it makes it worthy of her acceptance."

"Do you really think this glorifies it?"

"It tries," said Cady, "but I agree that if they're like what Mabel's described, they've got problems. If they're not, then Mabel does."

"Then what should I tell her?" asked Myron.

"Tell her what you feel," advised Spud, "but put your criticism in terms of misreading. Tell her how the piece could be misread. That's what I do."

But when the time came Myron found he couldn't even do that. Mabel asked if he had a chance to read her article. He paused, then said he had and when she asked what he thought he told her.

"It sounds to me," he began, "like a marriage made in hell."

"What do you mean?" she asked surprised.

"The way you tell it, they're strangling each other. There's no space between them. You make Una Jeffers a paranoid and Robin a weakling. I don't know what they're really like, which is why I didn't want to say any of this. But that story you tell at the end, the one of him having a drink with another woman, sounds like you're reporting a true event." Myron paused. Mabel didn't say anything. He went on. "I guess the worst thing about the piece is that I want to argue with it." Myron looked up. "No, I think the worst thing is . . . "

"What?" asked Mabel when he didn't go on.

"I get the feeling you're really furious with them." Then Myron realized he'd said way too much and shut up. Mabel was looking out the window. "Do you want me to go?" he asked at last. He meant not only from her room but Taos itself.

"No," she said calmly. "I disagree with you. I think my motives for writing it were pure." Her voiced trailed off. "But if you can read it that way, it's a failure."

They never discussed the article again and he thought it was forgotten. Now, five years later, it seemed she'd taken his insights about her views of the Jefferses' marriage and was using them for her own ends. Well, she could have them. What did he want them for anyway? But he resolved to be on his guard and stay out of it. Besides, he had other worries. He still hadn't been able to get in touch with Cady. That was bothering him. It always did when they went too long without seeing each other. And he noticed that Mabel hadn't asked him about Cady. What did she know?

Myron met Hildegarde Donaldson at dinner that night. She was a tall woman with racehorse legs, a slim yet powerful figure, and glorious red hair. But it soon became apparent she was more than the sum of her parts. There was an allure about her that came from the way she carried her head, a possibly new, wistful femininity combined with what might have been, before she suffered the loss of her young lover, a hard and ruthless personality.

Strange, Myron thought, how people modify themselves by their own willful acts. He looked at Hildegarde again. If she'd done the things Mabel attributed to her, she had survived and seemed to be, if not a better person in a moral sense, then a warmer, more human person.

"I think she's a fine physical specimen, don't you?" Mabel asked when they were alone. "And you know she told me she's had a crush on Robin ever since she first read *Roan Stallion*. Can you imagine?"

"Do you believe that?" Myron asked.

"Oh, yes."

"Mabel, why did you ask this woman here now?" As soon as he asked this Myron wanted to bite his tongue. Such a question was an involvement.

"I've felt for some time that Robin needs a change from Una," she confessed. "I think it's bad for an artist to have the same woman on his neck day after day. I don't know how you feel about it, but I think Robin's poetry has become rather repetitious over the past years, as if the routine of domesticity has had an inhibiting effect on him. I know how much he enjoys being here in Taos after spending week after week in that stone mausoleum in Carmel."

So there it was, the side of Mabel that everyone disparaged, the woman bent on making mischief. Why does she do it? Myron wondered. Is it because she's so embittered within herself? He knew there were many occasions when she wanted to interfere with him. All that stuff about seeing Dr. Brill and becoming the man she wanted him to be. There's a fine line between shaking things up and destroying them. Did she really think that Robin, at this late date, needed a change from Una? Myron didn't know them very well but you didn't have to know them to see what they were like. Without Robin, Una's life would be a blank. If theirs wasn't a perfect marriage, it was, as Una pointed out in her story of their knock-down-drag-out fight and as Mabel herself had pointed out in her 1933 article, one that was for keeps. You can't separate people like that, Myron thought, not without tragedy.

And how could she jump to the conclusion that Robin's poetic malaise was the fault of his marriage? Maybe he'd just said all he had to say? Though he liked Robin, he wasn't a fan of his poetry. When they'd met that first summer, it seemed to Myron that the poet was as dour as his verse, and his twin sons, Garth and Donnan, not much better. Una, on the other hand, talked a blue streak, mostly about people from Carmel whom Myron didn't know. Then Mabel asked Cady and Myron if they would like to go on a horseback trip up to Blue Lake with Tony, Robin, and the twins while she and Una did some shopping in Santa Fe. So they went. And it was amazing. On horseback the Jeffers males became different human beings, the boys boisterous, rushing ahead, racing each other, coming back to challenge their father and he joining them.

"You follow," Tony said to the Jefferses, who kept racing ahead.

"'You follow,'" Myron murmured in his best Tony imitation. Ahead of him Robin laughed. Tony didn't turn around. It was a little after six, and the new day wasn't pretty. Gray clouds hung around Taos Mountain, and the air was damp, though off to the west the sky was blue. Cady kept telling Myron that the rainy season would begin any day now. Myron couldn't wait to see what they called the monsoon.

Now, single file, they entered a stand of ponderosa. The trail was taking them north. Though Myron had the same mare he'd ridden that first day and many times since, she'd recently given birth and a golden colt was walking beside them. Mabel and Tony hadn't bred her and had been surprised by the pregnancy. So they'd named the foal Surprise.

After a while, realizing how much ground they were covering, Myron decided once again that horses were the way to go, that if he ever owned a house here he'd get a horse. He could feel the energy the mare was putting out, much more than usual, for she was not only carrying him but also keeping an eye on her colt. This was probably Surprise's first trip into the mountains. Myron patted the mare's neck, promising her not to be too much of a burden. But as the monotony of the trees took over, his mind wandered, and he was surprised when they came into a clearing and stopped. Robin and the twins were looking down on Taos. They were much higher and farther north than when they first viewed the town with Mabel.

"It's like a map," Myron said to Cady, who was now beside him.

Tony came back to see why they'd stopped. Myron thought he'd get them moving again. But Tony turned his pinto so he could look down, too.

"There house we build for Mabel." He pointed south toward Los Gallos. "And there house I live in when we build." He pointed to a house in Placita behind Spud's house. "There plaza. A big fire last year." He waved an arm. "Whole west side." He turned to Robin and pointed to the large fields of alfalfa surrounding the Placita houses. "Next two summers those fields belong to my family." Myron knew the pueblo owned land in common. Now he understood that they took turns working it. "Water." Tony was pointing to the small stream that divided his fields. Then his finger moved across the landscape to the pueblo. It was the same stream that divided the pueblo and it came down from Blue Lake and would probably have run all the way to the Rio Grande if it hadn't been sucked dry by irrigation. "We go," said Tony, who wheeled his pinto around to face north and up the trail. "Close gates. Good season."

They were moving again, always gaining altitude, and Myron let the rhythm of his horse's hips push him easily from side to side. Mabel had told him how well he was built for riding, high-waisted and long-legged, which meant a low center of gravity in the saddle. So the motion felt good, fitting, and it seemed to Myron that he could keep it up forever. And he did for three hours until he almost fell off. The colt had nudged his right stirrup with its nose and he had to grab the saddle horn. Myron thought it was just coltishness, the bored animal wanting to play. But the third time it happened he realized his boot was in the way of lunch.

"Tony," Myron yelled. "Surprise wants to eat. Let's stop for a while."

The colt was already sucking when Tony came up. He looked at the animal, then around at the small clearing, and said it was a good spot for lunch. He rode ahead again and came back with Robin and the twins. Cady dismounted first. He was in charge of the packhorse that had the picnic hamper. They all dismounted, tied their mounts to trees, and helped Cady spread a tarp on the ground and unload the food. There were ham and Swiss cheese sandwiches on rye bread baked in Mabel's kitchen. They sat down around the tarp and ate, and Myron told Robin how much he liked a recent poem of his.

"Which one?" Robin asked.

"'Shakespeare's Grave,'" said Myron.

"Oh?" asked the poet noncommittally.

"Be careful," said Cady, "or he'll recite it."

Jeffers looked at Myron as if to say go ahead if you can. So Myron began. He spoke the words conversationally.

"'Doggerel,' they thought, 'will do for church-wardens. Poetry's precious enough not to be wasted.'"

Jeffers nodded and Myron proceeded to recite the whole eighteen lines. The poet sat looking at him after he was done. He didn't seem to know what to make of it. Was it a trick? A piece of blatant flattery? How do you take such a compliment? Myron grew uncomfortable, as if he'd made a social gaffe.

"He loves poetry," Cady explained, rescuing the moment. "He memorizes it all the time."

"I'm flattered," said Robin and smiled. "What do you like about my poem?"

"Well—the subject for one thing," answered Myron. "And the fact that it demands I accept Shakespeare as a human being."

"Really?" Robin's smile broadened. On such a thin face the creases cut by the happy expression went clear to his ears. "Do you know that I believe the real Bard had to be at least two people, possibly three? It's the only way to explain the extraordinary vocabulary and expertise on so many subjects."

"Really?" asked Myron. He'd never heard this idea before and they talked about it as they ate, or rather Robin talked and Myron listened until they realized no one else was interested. So they didn't mention Shakespeare again for the whole five-hour trip, nor when they were screwing down the wheels of the floodgates, nor much later when they were in the corral removing saddles, bridles, and headstalls, then watching the happy animals trot off in the last of the light and drop to their knees and roll over on their backs in the dust. In fact they held off until after dinner when they were in the Rainbow Room sipping brandy.

"Why," Myron asked, "if you believe Shakespeare was at least two people, didn't you use the plural pronoun in your poem?"

Myron recited the poem again, changing the pronouns. Jeffers listened with interest, then pointed out that that trick would change the poem's focus and make it a criticism of Shakespearean scholarship rather than an appreciation of the plays. Myron nodded. But he was still fascinated by the idea that Shakespeare didn't write the plays attributed to him, so his next question was who did write them. Jeffers offered Marlowe, and when Myron pointed out that Marlowe had been assassinated before most of the plays were written, Jeffers said the story of Marlowe's death might have been manufactured so the queen's favorite spy could go into hiding and escape his many enemies. It was much more likely, he said, that he'd been sent into exile in Italy, which would explain the Italian locales of so many of the plays.

"I like him," Myron said to Cady when they were alone that night. "His mind's so much livelier than he lets on."

That was 1933, their first summer. Things were so different then, the place a novelty. But Myron didn't feel he really belonged in Taos until the summer of 1936 when he stayed in the Placita house on the other side of town. Though there was no plumbing and the windows fit so badly they let dust pile on the floor beneath them, Myron loved it. Around four in the afternoon, after working on *The Sisters* all day, he'd step outside, cross the highway, and follow the Placita road to the post office behind the new WPA courthouse. More often than not he'd run into someone who lived on Dent Street: Bert Phillips or Becky Salisbury or Bertha Gusdorf, whose bank was nearby. Bertha wanted to find him a nice Jewish girl, particularly after he overdrew his checking account. The old lady felt a wife's most important duty was as accountant. Sometimes he'd see no one, just take his newly arrived galley proofs across the plaza to the restaurant in La Fonda where he'd sat with Thomas Wolfe. Sometimes people would come up to him and ask him to sign *Singermann* or *Wide Open Town*, which at the time were still his best-known books.

Sometimes Angelo Ravagli would come in without Frieda. Jim Karavas spoke Italian as well as Greek, and the two men would join Myron and have friendly arguments over Mussolini or cooking. Myron would go on reading proof and every once in a while they would translate something for him and he would nod. Myron preferred the cooking arguments because they often led to food, the two men going into the kitchen to prove a point and coming out a few minutes later with something for him to taste. Other times he'd go into the bar, walk to the back and through the curtained doorway to where the poker game was going on. Just like Butte, he'd think, even the same sign: LIQUOR IN THE FRONT. POKER IN THE REAR. Long John would ask him if he wanted in. He'd sit for a while, then get up. The only game he'd play for any length of time was blackjack. An instinctive card counter, he did well. Sometimes Spud would be in the bar and they'd talk about what was going on in publishing. Spud liked to set up a little stall and sell books outside the hotel. That summer he saw more of Spud there than he did in their houses though they weren't fifty yards apart.

But that was 1936. Now, two summers and a lot of money later, he was back in the Pink House. Had she done it purposely? She said that she had a young writer living in the Placita house, that he'd lived in it all spring and had fixed it up, put in new windows and sealed the roof, and because he had lots more to do, she didn't want him to leave. So there Myron was in the middle of her intrigue, which wasn't all that intriguing. For one thing, Mabel wasn't there at night. The Jefferses were staying in her bedroom, she in the new place she was building at Embudo. Hildegarde was in the first of the row of outside rooms whose doors opened to the portal. The twins were at the other end, the last room in the row, the one that had originally been a cabin.

Without Mabel they were a restless lot, Hildegarde pacing among the hollyhocks that grew between the flagstones, violin tucked beneath her chin, expertly playing her scales, and Robin, trying to write, pacing the floor of whatever room he happened to be in. The twins would leave early to tend the horses and Una would plant herself on the newly constructed bench beside the acequia madre, the irrigation ditch that watered Mabel's garden, her knitting needles clicking. Myron would see them when he went up to the big house. There he would call Cady and listen to the phone ring until the operator came on to tell him what he already knew. Nobody was answering. Then he'd go back to his typewriter. So he was surprised when one morning Mabel showed up a half hour before breakfast.

"It's happened," she said.

"What?"

"They got together."

"Really? How do you know?"

"She told me. She said she met Robin up on the mountain early this morning."

"Met?"

"Well, nothing was planned. She said for some reason she couldn't sleep. She said dawn was just starting and it was so wonderful and calm and fresh she got up, got dressed, and walked up the hillside. It seemed Robin had done the same and they met there." Mabel paused, mulled the coincidence, then brightened. "She said he told her that he loves her."

"Just like that?"

"Yes. I asked her if she was sure. She said she was and then she told me that Robin's so unhappy, that he can't stand his life as it is."

"Does Una know he went out?"

"I asked her that. She said Robin told her Una was asleep when he went." Mabel paused but not for long. "Oh Myron! It's so exciting. She said he told her how joyless his life is, how everything was dead. She said that when they walked back he told her he hadn't talked to anyone about himself for twenty-five years and that he must get away—that he was afraid something terrible would happen. He said that he has no life, that he's turned into a nothing."

"Hmmm," said Myron.

"You know," Mabel went on, "I remember Una telling me last year that Robin wanted to get away to the High Sierras—build a small house and get away from people. She said she discouraged him, that she just couldn't face starting over again, building another life in a new place. I told this to Hildegarde and I asked her if they talked about his work."

"Mabel, you may regret this. You're encouraging them."

"She said he told her he hates his work and couldn't write another line," she went on, ignoring his warning. "He told her he feels as though he's been under a witch's spell all these years, that he's been hypnotized."

"Is he blaming Una? Is she the witch?" Robin sounded to Myron like a middle-aged man full of regrets for the way his life had turned out. And he thought of Mabel's article and his reading of it.

"Yes, he's blaming her. It's exactly what Una has done, put a spell on him."

Mabel has met the enemy, Myron thought, and it's her best friend.

"Now I'm more worried than ever," she went on. "I asked Hildegarde if Una saw them coming back together and warned her that she better be careful. She said that they separated before they got back to the house and that Robin circled around and came back by way of the morada." She paused. "Hildegarde wants to help him. He needs my help, she kept saying. I told her I was terrified for them."

Again Myron thought of her article. She was taking his insights and running with them. But he'd meant her portrait of them, not the real couple. And he realized again that she was making him part of her conspiracy against Una. Was this punishment for his criticism? To make it his fault? And he became truly concerned. Something was going to happen. You could feel it at meals. Taciturn Robin began making wry comments, smiling, while Una went silent. The twins, taking their cue from their mother, were even quieter than usual, and Tony never spoke at all and seemed to absent himself from the house as often as he could. Myron asked Mabel if she'd told Tony what was going on. She said she had.

"What did he say?"

"Well, he shook his head and said poor Robin, what a life he has, not a man's life at all. But you know, though he's been fond of Robin from their first meeting in Carmel, he's never liked Una."

Myron looked at her. She was enlisting everyone against Una, and he remembered a dinner here two years ago. Back then he thought the dark mood at the table had been his fault. He was depressed over his career. More and more his lack of recognition was gnawing at him. And Stanley Rinehart was on him to do another labor novel. *The Sun Sets in the West* had come out the year before and been a failure and it was a labor novel. Why do another one? He was an artist and would not write to order. They want me to sell my artistic birthright for a mess of pottage, he thought. What's pottage anyway? Didn't we used to say porridge when we were kids?

"What's pottage?" he asked the silent table.

"A mixture of potatoes and porridge," Garth Jeffers volunteered without missing a beat. He was the burly, fair one. The twins had just finished their freshman year at Berkeley.

"No," countered Donnan, the dark dandy. "Pottage refers to the age of a pot."

"But the Bible refers to 'a mess of pottage,'" Garth countered.

"It's a misprint," said Donnan. "It's supposed to be a 'mass of pottage.' It refers to all the pots owned by the tribe. It was the way Jews measured wealth then, by how many pots they owned. They'd have big parties to show them off. They were called potlatkes."

"No," Garth contradicted. "Those parties are called potlatches and they're given by the Indians of the Northwest to show how many potatoes their pots can hold."

"That's knishes," said Donnan, "pot knishes."

"Knishes? Latkes? What are they teaching you at college?" asked Myron. It was the most he'd ever heard them talk. "Sorry I asked." But he was smiling. Blessed are the children who try to cheer up. Yet he also saw it was doing no good.

"I'm tired, "said Una. "I'm going to turn in."

"Me too," said Robin and they both stood.

Myron stood. That summer the Jefferses were in the Santa Teresa house. The twins stood and followed their parents out. Myron sat back down with Mabel and Tony.

"What's up?" he asked. "That was a very uncomfortable dinner."

"What are you up to?" Mabel asked right back.

"You're not Jewish," Myron snapped. "You're not allowed to answer a question with a question."

"They're having marital troubles," said Mabel bluntly. "Now what about you? You weren't great company either."

Myron paused and looked at her, then at Tony. Here was his chance to talk to her. He looked at Tony again. Not that he minded him being there and hearing what he had to say. They were a team. But Tony wasn't usually interested in Myron's world and would get up and leave when these kinds of talks began. Tonight, however, he just sat and it occurred to Myron that Mabel had asked him to stay. What did that mean?

"I want to buy a house here," he announced to them.

"Is that all?" asked Mabel.

"Yes. Will you sell me the place I'm in now? I don't have any money but I could pay a little at a time if you would give me a deed for contract." It's what they'd done for Spud when they sold him his little house.

"The Jefferses are going to divorce," said Mabel. "Robin isn't writing at all."

Myron didn't know what to say. Hadn't she heard him?

"I thought Robin was the man to succeed Lawrence," she went on. "Just to be near them, I spent my winters in Carmel, and each summer I've opened my house to them. I went out of my way for them in so many things."

"What did you want Robin to do?" Myron asked and thought, all right, if that's what you want to talk about, I'll play along.

"I felt he could be an intermediary between the truth of the land and the lies of its people. Like Lawrence, Robin sees the lies and he sees the truth. But he's too much Una's creation. He has to be free of her to do it. Now it's about to happen. His life is about to blow apart, his little family about to explode, the result of which will either set him free or destroy him."

"Mabel," asked Myron, "what happened to the Una and Robin you wrote about? You wanted the world to believe they were perfectly suited to each other."

She didn't answer.

"And what does any of this have to do with my buying a house from you?"

"Why did you come here, Myron?" she asked.

"To Taos?"

"Yes."

"I guess I came as a tourist."

"And why did you stay?"

Myron glanced at Tony. He must know. "Because of Cady," he admitted.

"Is that your only reason?"

"Not anymore. The place has long since taken me in. I feel I have friends here. I feel you're a friend and Tony, too. I want to stay because I need a home, a haven, a place to work. I think I've found it here."

"But I don't want you to stay," said Mabel.

"Huh?" He was stunned. "Is this about me or the Jefferses?" he asked.

"It's about you."

"I don't understand."

"Let me put it this way. I wouldn't like *Out of Life* or *The Sun Sets in the West* if you'd written them as well as you wrote *Singermann*."

"Why not?" She'd told him she loved *Out of Life* when she read it in manuscript. Obviously she was attacking now where she thought it would hurt most.

"They're not my kind of books. It's the subject and the setting."

Myron didn't know what to say.

"When you first came here, Myron, I thought there was something behind all that feeling you express in your novels, a consciousness of something other than the world you were writing about. But I see now it's nothing but forced sentiment. You're a sentimentalist, Myron. Your characters feel things they have no reason to feel. In fact, if they truly saw the world they were living in, they would feel only the darkest despair."

He was confused. She seemed to be attacking not so much the novels but where they took place. "You mean New York and Butte?" he asked.

"Yes." She paused. "Don't you understand, Myron? I don't want you as a neighbor. You're not good for this place. If you can't see what's wrong in those places, you can't see what's good here."

He thought of her lectures on place, her insistence that some places were sacred and that they elevated the people who lived there, and that other places were damned and destroyed their inhabitants. The last time they talked about this he had flown at her and said it was the *damned* places of the world that were the only real testing grounds for the noble soul, that the best thing that happened to him as a writer was being born in Butte, that places like Butte and Buffalo and New York City were what made for artistic growth. Then why don't you live in one of those places? she'd asked. I have and I will, he'd said. But I'll never fool myself into thinking that I live in utopia when all I'm really doing is raising the value of my own real estate. It was the same thing he'd done with Gertrude Stein and her collection of Picassos, a not-so-veiled accusation of greed masquerading as aesthetic idealism.

"Mabel, are you calling me a . . . liar?" he asked now.

"As a writer, yes. I think you're self-deceived." She paused and he thought she was done. She wasn't. "I once thought you a great artist, Myron, even a great man. I no longer think that."

"And that's the reason you're not going to sell me the house?"

"If you want to buy a house here I can't stop you." This wasn't true. Nobody else would give him credit. "But I won't be the one who sells it to you." She stood, went to the arched entry, stopped and turned. "I think Santa Fe would suit you better," she said, then turned again and left the room.

Myron was stunned. Santa Fe? Hal Bynner's town. Home of the evil homos. How long had she felt this way? What about her kind letter last year when he felt so low in San Francisco? Myron jumped to his feet. He wanted to throw that letter into her face. You're the liar, he wanted to say. He wanted to tell her that her letter hadn't meant anything, that she could show sympathy when it served her purpose. He heard her bedroom door close. She was gone.

"Mabel talk too much," said Tony, bent over the fireplace. He was poking the ends of the logs toward the middle so they would burn completely.

"We all do," said Myron.

Two weeks later he returned to San Francisco. One of the first things he did was look up Mabel's third husband, Maurice Sterne, the Jewish artist who'd gotten her to come out to New Mexico and who built the Santa Teresa House. Myron saw the man's name on an art gallery flier so he went to the show and introduced himself. It turned out Sterne was teaching at the San Francisco Art Institute and the next day they went for coffee. Naturally, they talked about Mabel. The artist kept saying how lucky he'd been to get away from her, and warning Myron not to get mixed up with her. He was a handsome man, but excitable and emotional. She'll turn on you, he kept saying. In fact he complained so much that Myron couldn't get his own complaints in. Yet the conversation was therapeutic. What Mabel had done to Sterne was much worse than any of the little insults she'd given him.

That's what Myron felt now, that nothing she'd done to him could compare with what she was doing to the Jefferses. I'm not going to get involved, he thought, and decided it was time to leave. He hadn't wanted to be there in the first place. If Cady had been home he would be down there. He could live with his rich friend now. He was able, if not to equal him, then at least to hold his own and pay his own way. And he had a car. He'd never liked the inequality of their relationship. That's what had held him back. It was important they get it right. This would be the closest either of them would come to marriage. I can drive now, he would say. I won't feel trapped out here nor be dependent on you for rides. And I have money, more than I ever dreamed of having.

So Myron called his friend one more time to tell him the good news. Once again he got no answer. Then he tried Spud down in Santa Fe at the Villagra Book Shop where he was working. Spud said he didn't know where Cady was, that he hadn't seen him in over a month. Then Myron thought of calling Hal and Bob but couldn't get himself to do it. What would he say to them? Do you know where my lover is? Is he safe? Is he all right? What would Hal do with that? Then he thought of Mason in San Diego and got the operator to dial the number. But there was no answer there either. So he got her to dial Palm Springs. An answering service picked up and gave him a Massachusetts number. Myron thought of calling it. No, he decided. Not yet.

Eight

Only once before had Myron felt anything like the intensity he felt for Cady. That was back in New York, and then Malibu with Frank Fenton. The affair started innocently enough, a writers' group reading each other's manuscripts, with Frank, who had published a novel and was freelancing scripts for movie studios, as its leader. The group was serious, but the affair began as a lark. Myron knew he was getting involved with a married man with two young children, that Frank had another life. In the beginning this limitation was part of the attraction. Writing was the important thing. But after a year it got out of hand, the logistics too difficult, Frank's guilt too great. So they broke it off. But not for long. The attraction was too much and breaking up became part of the romance, renunciation by Frank for the sake of his family and by Myron for the sake of his art. In fact, Frank was the reason Myron had gone out to Los Angeles that first time in 1930. He had to get away. But Frank followed him and they lived that amazing six months in a Malibu beach house. Myron thought it was forever. Frank told his wife he'd found movie work, that their separation was only temporary. Turned out it was.

Who knows? If Myron hadn't stopped in Taos that first summer, if he had gone on to LA with Janet and Hans, he and Frank might have started up again. But he doubted it. By that time Frank and his family were living in Culver City and Frank was playing the game with a different man. That's one of the reasons Cady was such a breath of fresh air. He was honest. He never thought of telling a lie. Perhaps it was the family money. Why would he lie? What was there to be afraid of? His father? Cady was never afraid of his father. Mabel never lied either. Lying wasn't so much beneath them as simply not necessary. Maybe that's why when Myron got drunk, truth would burst from him in angry intensity. But weren't such outbursts really an admission of weakness? Was it that hard for him to confront the truth when he was sober? And where was Cady? Here was another reason people marry, he thought, to keep track of each other. Then he remembered Frank Fenton and how he made it impossible for his wife and lover to keep track of him.

Myron wanted to ask Mabel if she knew where Cady was. She might. She kept her ear to the ground, kept track of the people around her, particularly those she didn't like. On the other hand, to ask her would be a betrayal. Whatever was going on, innocent though it might be, it would be a way for her to criticize Cady. Besides it would be just a matter of time before his distress would become apparent and she would ask him. Or maybe not. She had her hands full. Things were heating up in the Big House. He tried to stay away, take his meals at the hotel, slip out for walks to the post office. But every time he ventured up there something happened. So he stayed away until one day Mabel crossed the field and begged him to come to lunch. You'll ease the tension, she pleaded. So he had to witness an argument between Robin and his son. Donnan had grown sideburns for the summer, and Myron thought they lent a Bohemian charm to his face. The twins were entering their senior year at Berkeley and seemed more and more to be going their own ways.

"I think you'd improve your appearance if you shaved off those things," the poet remarked in a low, stern voice.

"I do not agree," replied Donnan in that stiff way the twins talked.

"Robin," Myron intervened, "I like them! They make him look like a character in a nineteenth-century novel."

"Does he have to look like a pimp to have character?" asked the poet.

"They are my own affair," the young man insisted. He had turned pale and his voice quivered. "At least it seems that way to me."

Robin stood, saying he was taking Haig, their English bulldog, for a walk, and left the room. Then Myron stood and climbed the steps out of the dining room just as Robin appeared with the frantic dog tugging at his leash. Myron followed them out. For a moment, Jeffers stood in the middle of the terrace looking west, the leash in his left hand, his pipe in his right. What's he thinking? Myron wondered. After all, wasn't he the real culprit in all this? Three women, each in her own way, were fighting over him while he looked off into space. Myron thought of Lawrence and his effect on women. But Lawrence stayed true to Frieda and probably never stared into space. He'd throw a fit, maybe, but never stare. Only Jeffers got lost in gaze. What was he doing? Evading the imperfections around him? Imagining some horror or majesty out there? Then the poet was walking away. Myron watched him and his fat dog disappear into the lane that divided Los Gallos from the Santa Teresa property.

That night, again at Mabel's request and against his better judgment, Myron had dinner at the Big House. It was tense but uneventful, and after the boys left for a movie, Mabel announced she was going to the hospital to visit one of her workers who'd been injured on the Embudo job. She looked around to see who'd offer to go with her. Surprisingly Una spoke up. But if Una went, Hildegarde would certainly not go. Robin said he would pass also. Mabel looked at Myron but he felt he had done enough just being there. So the two women left and were gone about an hour. When they came back Robin and Myron were as they had been, reading.

"Where's Hildegarde?" Una asked.

"She went to bed," Robin said, getting up and knocking out his pipe on the edge of the fireplace. "She said she was sleepy."

"Sleepy, was she?" asked Una.

Mabel shot Myron a look as if to ask what happened. He looked away. Then Mabel said it was late and that she had to drive to Embudo. Myron said he was turning in, too, that he had to get up early to drive down to Cady's, and again he resolved not to take any more meals up there. He stayed away from breakfast.

But there was Mabel knocking on the door with sweet rolls and a thermos of coffee.

"What brings you here?" he asked.

"You know very well."

"I do? I don't. What?"

"I got up very early and went looking for Hildegarde in her room."

"Did you find her there?"

"Yes. And I told her she'd better look out, that Una's very angry. Last night Una let me know that in no uncertain terms."

"What did Hildegarde say?"

"That it was too late."

"What does that mean?"

"That's what I asked. What do you mean? She said it was simple. She said that they'd had each other."

"Had each other?"

"Yes! She said the instant Una and I left last night she went out the front door to her room and in a little while Robin went through the back room and came to her. She said it happened without a word."

"It's true," Myron said. "They both left. I can be a witness in the proceedings. But he wasn't gone fifteen minutes. I never thought anything like that happened." It had seemed harmless to him. "It couldn't have been much fun," he added.

"Myron!"

They looked at each other. Was this the desired outcome, the jumping into each other's streams? Whoopee!

"What's going to happen now?" he asked.

"I don't know. Hildegarde said he told her he loves her and needs her and she said she loves him."

"What did you say?"

"Nothing. All I thought to do was go to my office and get my article. Maybe this will tell you about them, I said, and I gave it to her." She looked at him. "I know what you think of it. But it does tell something about them."

"Well, Mabel," said Myron, "you've stirred it up this time. Someone's going to get hurt." He stood. "But I'm not going to be around to see it. I'm going down to Cady's to stay awhile."

"Oh. Have you gotten in touch with him?"

"No," he said, and he realized from the way she asked that she knew something was amiss. "There's no answer. But I'll drive down anyway. I'm not getting much done here, and what's a car for?"

After she left he got dressed and did what he said he would, drove down to Jacona. The station wagon wasn't there and no one was home. I should've called, he thought. But he'd been calling every day since he'd gotten back. What was there to do? So he slipped a note under the door saying that he needed to get out of the Pink House, that he was being driven crazy by what was going and to *please* call him. Then, instead of going back, he drove down to Santa Fe and parked behind the cathedral. What was he going to do? Search the streets for Cady? He went into the cathedral and stood in its nave listening to a guide explain to a group of tourists who Archbishop Lamy was. Then he walked down to the Museum of Fine Art and bumped into Georgia O'Keeffe in the lobby. It was she who recognized him. To her he was Cady's friend. So Myron thought to ask her if she'd seen him. But she asked him first so Myron lied and said Cady was fine and was visiting his brother in San Diego. Then he left and returned to Taos. But not before stopping by Jacona once more. Nobody there.

"Hildegarde says he wants to get away." It was morning and Mabel had come over once again. "He told her he was finished if he didn't go. That's when Hildegarde got her idea."

Myron didn't say anything.

"She said that as soon as she gets home, she and her husband are leaving for Bermuda for a month. She wants Robin to stay in their house. She said he'd be alone in a new place where he could relax and think things out. Most importantly, he would get away from Una's eternal vigilance. So she made this proposal to him."

Myron thought Hildegarde's husband had to be either the most sophisticated man in America or a complete idiot.

"What did Robin say?"

"That he wouldn't know how to do such a thing!"

"What?" Myron smiled. It was such a stupid evasion it had to be true. "What did Hildegarde say to that?"

"She pointed out that he must have some money, that he had to pay his bills with something. He said they have a joint account but he'd never drawn on it. He said he'd never made out a check in his life."

Myron burst out laughing. There was an old joke about a little boy walking around and around the block where he lived. When a neighbor asked what he was doing, the boy said he's running away from home. So the neighbor asked if he's running away from home, why did he keep walking around the block? Because, the little boy replied, I'm not allowed to cross the street by myself.

If there was humor in an unworldly poet failing to reach the real world because he was unable to cross the street alone, Myron also could see the possible horror of it. Una, smoldering before, was now white hot. You could feel it at the table where she had gone dead silent. And Myron noticed that from his front window she would sit for hours in the bench on the platform over the acequia madre. From that vantage point behind a screen of willow branches she could watch Robin in the upstairs bedroom. If he paced back and forth he cast a shadow, or if he came downstairs with Haig for the usual walk, even if he went out the back way, he had to pass the window on the stairs and she could see him. Hildegarde could be observed, too, her door opening onto the portal. Myron wondered if he should call it to Mabel's attention. Then he decided that it wasn't his business, that his business was finding Cady. He crossed the field and passed Una with a grunted hello.

There was no answer from Una or Cady. So he made other calls. Spud, down in Santa Fe, still knew nothing. Marie Garland was in Europe, and Andrew Dasburg was annoyed at being bothered. I'm not his keeper, he snapped. Then Myron thought to call Beatrice Johnson. Beatrice, Mabel's former housekeeper, was now running Cady's new house, much to Mabel's chagrin. I should've thought of this sooner, Myron told himself hopefully. She'd know where he was. Beatrice lived in Santa Fe. Myron looked her up. But there was no answer. So he took down her address and jumped into his car. He was excited and optimistic, so optimistic in fact that as he approached the cutoff at Pojoaque, he decided to take yet another look and turned right. There, parked in front of Cady's studio, was the old Ford station wagon with the wooden body. Myron pulled up to it, got out, went to the studio door and knocked. No answer. He tried it. It was locked. That was unusual. When Cady was home he always left it open. Myron turned toward the dried riverbed. Maybe he went for a walk. But he saw no one out there and Myron turned back and knocked one more time. Then he heard footsteps.

"Who is it?" Cady's voice asked.

"We made a date," Myron said to the closed door. "Don't you remember?"

The door opened and there Cady was looking disheveled, as if he'd been asleep. He's just gotten back, Myron thought and stepped in. He gave him a hug and stepped back. Cady smiled and Myron relaxed. Hi, the smile said. I'm from Mars.

"You bought a car," Cady said looking over Myron's shoulder.

"And you're adding on again." There was a new pile of adobe bricks.

"I want you to drive me somewhere," said Cady.

"Where?"

"Anywhere. You owe me."

"You want to change?"

"No, I'm fine." He grabbed his wide-brimmed straw hat from the coat rack and closed the door behind them. Myron had never known him to go out looking so mussed up, not even when he was painting. Cady was fastidious and changed clothes several times a day. In a moment they were in Myron's Chevy heading toward the road.

"Nice car," said Cady.

"Thanks."

"About time, too."

"Cady, I'm sorry I made you drive so much. I thought you liked driving."

"When I first met you I thought you needed taking care of," Cady began in a voice that said I'm going to level with you. It was an alarming tone.

They had reached the main road. Myron turned right. He thought they could go into Santa Fe and have a beer.

"Not that you couldn't take care of yourself," Cady went on. "You're the most self-sufficient person I've ever met. But I knew you found everyday chores annoying and preferred not to do them. So I took over. I had so little respect for myself I thought making myself necessary was the only way I could hold on to you."

Myron glanced at him. Things had suddenly gotten too serious. It sounded like a game of Truth.

"I became, among other things, your chauffeur," Cady went on. "Then the same doubts that made me act that way crept back in and I began to think you didn't care for me at all, that you were only using me."

"Cady," Myron interrupted. "I don't know what to say. I suddenly feel I don't know you." There was a moment of silence, then Myron blurted out what he had come to say. "I came back to tell you I love you and want to live with you. I'm ready for it now. I'm independent. I have a car. More than that, I have money. I won't be dependent on you in any way. I was always afraid of that."

He waited for Cady to say something. Cady didn't. Myron saw that the man from the red planet had turned white.

"What's the matter?" Myron asked. "Are you sick?"

"I'm seeing another man," Cady blurted out.

Myron felt the air go out of his lungs and he pulled the car over onto the shoulder and stopped. At first he just saw the empty road ahead, the heat making the air waver above the pavement. Then he thought about the way Cady had greeted him and how he'd gotten him out of the house.

"He was there, wasn't he?"

Cady nodded.

"You were . . . " It explained his disheveled appearance. "You bastard!" he shouted and his right hand whipped off the wheel and backhanded across Cady's cheek. "How could you?" Myron felt tears rushing into his eyes. Cady, despite the blow, held onto the hand that had slapped him. Myron thought to pull it away but even in these circumstances he found Cady's touch comforting. They sat for a moment. Myron was sobbing. Then his anger came rushing back.

"Who is it?" he snarled.

Cady let go of his hand.

"Do I know him?"

"Yes.

"Who?"

"Maybe if I tell you, you'll understand."

"Who?"

"Cliff."

"Cliff?" Cady had said the name as if Myron would recognize it. But he didn't, not right away. Then it came to him. "McCarthy?" Myron hadn't known he was still around.

"Yes." Cady looked down at his hands. "He was so lonesome and lost after Bronson's death. We began palling around and . . . "

"Bronson died three years ago," said Myron in amazement. "How long has this been going on?"

"Not long. For a long time we were just pals."

"Is that all you are now? Just pals with a little sex?"

"No," said Cady and seemed to be pondering whether or not to go on. "I'm in love with him," he said at last, then added, "It's just this past month. I don't know if he's in love with me. He's such a wreck."

"Was I a wreck when you met me?" Myron snarled.

"Yes." Cady answered. "You cried to me that first night about a man you were in love with who had gone back to his wife."

So that's how I made a fool of myself, Myron thought.

"I still want to be your friend," Cady said. "You once said that no matter what, we should always be friends. I feel that way. I trust you, Myron. I trust you in ways I've never trusted anyone else."

"So you do this to me?"

There was a silence.

"I still can't believe it," said Myron at last. "You're such a fine artist. When I think of my writing as painting, compared to you I'm nothing more than an illustrator. You're a poet. You look at things, see what they are, then make them into a painting and I see what they are. I always thought you were doing it for me, to show me what was true." Myron was crying again. For the first time in his life he was saying what was in his heart: no wit, no bullshit, no sarcasm. He was telling Cady the truth. "I don't understand how someone I love could do this to me."

"I'm sorry," said Cady. "And I'm sorry you had to find out

like this." He was crying, too. "I never thought you'd drive up like that. I was going to tell you when we got together."

"When would that have been? For two weeks I've been trying to get hold of you, calling three or four times a day and stopping by and leaving notes. You could've told me as soon as you knew I was back."

"I couldn't," said Cady.

"Why?"

"Because of Cliff. He was so frightened of you. Every time I told him I had to see you, he would go to pieces."

The manipulative bastard, Myron thought.

"I was going to tell you right away."

But you didn't, Myron thought. You cared for his feelings more than you cared for mine. "Bastard!" he shouted and his right fist shot up just six inches as Ike had taught him. But he missed Cady's jaw, got his cheek instead, and Cady's hat flew out the window. "Get out!" Myron snarled. Cady looked amazed. Then he opened the door, got out, found his hat, put it on, and closed the door. He hesitated, then walked around the back of the car to the driver's side.

"I'm sorry, Mike," he said.

"Don't call me Mike."

"I want us to be friends."

"Do you want to have dinner with me tonight?"

"I can't."

"Then go to hell."

Myron pressed the starter. Cady stepped back and for the first time in his life Myron gunned a car. It jumped forward and he almost lost control on the soft shoulder. But he didn't and the car roared back onto the pavement. He went a few hundred yards, slowed, and U-turned, making the tires squeal. I'll run over the son-of-a-bitch, he thought. But Cady was already short-cutting across the field. And the sight of him hurrying back to his lover angered Myron even more. He thought of beating him to the house and confronting Cliff. He'd tell the asshole what he thought of him, maybe even bloody his nose. If he's afraid of me, I'll give him something to be afraid of. But when he reached the turnoff, Myron sped by. Cliff was such a pitiful case. And he wasn't what this was about. No, it was between him and Cady. So he kept going. Driving felt good. But when he pulled up in front of the Pink House, he saw his front door was open and someone was inside.

Was it Cady? And his heart raced with hope. Has he somehow beaten me home? Was he going to try to make up with me? Myron stepped in. Mabel and Hildegarde were sitting at the table. Mabel greeted him saying she had seen he was out and that they'd needed a place to talk and they'd be going soon. Myron wanted to scream at them to get out, that this was his place, that he'd paid for it. But he knew if he did that, they'd know how upset he was and it would all come out and he didn't want it to come out. The last thing he needed was Mabel saying she told him so. So he went into the kitchen for a glass of water, drank it down, then out to the toilet to pee. When he came back they were still there. Myron didn't know what to do to get them out so he stood listening. They didn't seem to mind.

"I'm leaving Sunday morning," Hildegarde announced. "That's only four days. I told Robin that Tony was going to drive me up to Raton to catch the train. Do you know—we thought—if Robin could drive over with us I'd put off going until—maybe—Wednesday—and we could stay somewhere together."

"Are you crazy?" asked Mabel. "Una would never let him."

"I don't see how she could help it if he told her he was just motoring over and coming back with Tony. He could send a note back saying he'd decided to walk over the Raton Pass or something and come back on the stage and let Una think I'd gotten on my train. Would Tony help? Would he invite Robin to go along?"

"I could ask him but I don't think he will," said Mabel.

"I hate to interrupt, ladies," said Myron, "but I have to get some sleep."

"Oh, I'm sorry, Myron," said Hildegarde. "It's thoughtless of us." She stood, as did Mabel.

"I was going to ask you to go to the hot springs with us," said Mabel. "But you seem too tired."

"I am," he said. "I couldn't sleep at all last night."

"Anything the matter?" She looked him in the eye.

"No," he said, "everything's fine."

After they left Myron lay down on his bed. But he was miles from sleep. He lay waiting for the sound of Mabel's Ford. When it left he got up and walked down to the plaza. In the new two-story La Fonda, he walked into the new bar. Except for the bartender it was empty. He ordered a whiskey and soda and for some reason thought of Ella Winter. Once again he was arguing with her over what she had called his melodramatic ending of *Wide Open Town*. Is confronting treachery with a gun false? he asked her now. Is killing the person who has betrayed you wrong? Don't you know anything about passion, Ella? Is that what comes of marrying a man thirty years older than you? It's the right ending. Such treachery has to be dealt with. I've got to kill him. It's there in my own novel. He downed his second drink and walked out. The bright New Mexican sun stopped him and he squinted around the plaza. To his right was old man McCarthy's Mercantile. How odd. The same names. A sign, Myron thought, and in a few strides he was inside the store walking to the back. In the case behind the counter stood the hunting rifles and shotguns: Rugers, Ithacas, Remingtons. Walnut stocks and blue steel barrels. He'd never noticed how beautiful they were. But where are the pistols? He wanted something to hold in his hand, something to point with. First of all a weapon must be an accusation.

"May I help you?" asked the clerk.

"Yes," said Myron, glad it wasn't old man McCarthy. "Where are your pistols?"

"We don't have any in stock," said the clerk.

"You don't?" Myron was confused. He hadn't expected this. This was the Wild West. All it took in Butte was a five-dollar bill.

"Mr. McCarthy's getting out of the firearms business," the clerk explained.

"Why?"

"No profit in it. Everybody's selling guns. Look in the paper. Try the pawn shop. Try Long John."

Myron thanked the man, went out, and walked back to the hotel. Long John would be at the poker table. But he stopped before he went in. John Dunne was a good friend of Mabel's. Myron had eaten with the Dunnes. Did he want everyone in Taos to know he was buying a gun? He should make some attempt to cover his tracks, at least before anything happened. Tomorrow he'd drive down to Santa Fe and hit the pawnshops. So he walked back up to the Pink House. Do I really want to do this? he asked himself. Maybe I just want to scare them, warn them I won't be taken lightly. But he'd need a gun even for that. Then he remembered Tony's gun cabinet in his bedroom. For years they'd had their own bedrooms. Not so romantic anymore. Myron walked up to the Big House. No one was about. He walked upstairs to the landing and knocked on Tony's door. There was no answer. He opened the door. There was the gun case. You could see everything in it. And there was a Colt .45 in a tooled leather holster. He reached for the dent in the glass door and pushed. It didn't move. It was locked.

When it was time for dinner, though he'd again resolved not to go, he found he didn't want to be alone. Who knows? Maybe nothing will happen, he told himself. Of course something did. Right after cocktails Una lost control. There was a little Italian ebony and silver box on the table beside her. About five inches long and shaped like a coffin with a skull and crossbones inlaid on the lid, it was a receptacle for tokens of revenge and went back to the days when outraged lovers, husbands, and wives appeased their anger by killing or castration. Three years ago Myron had looked for Lawrence's ashes in it. But it was too small. Now he thought of Cady. Could I do something like that to Cady? Kill Cliff, cut his cock off, and present it to Cady? No. Too gory. He wasn't that kind of person. You needed to be someone who got enjoyment out of someone else's pain. Myron didn't want to cause anyone pain. All he wanted to do was stop his own. And the only way he could that was to kill Cady and then himself. It would be their last act together.

"You see this?" asked Una. Just as they started for the dining room she grabbed the box and was shaking it in Hildegarde's face. "I wouldn't hesitate to use it. Not for a moment."

Hildegarde looked surprised and puzzled and Myron was sure she didn't know what the box was for. She turned to Robin for an explanation but all he did was smile his kindly, perpetually knowledgeable, and, in these circumstances, totally enraging smile.

"Come on! " said Mabel. "Let's go in to dinner," and she was sweeping them down the three steps into the dining room.

Una sat by Myron and glared at Hildegarde, who had seated herself at the other end of the table. "If I thought Robin was unfaithful to me I'd ruin him," she whispered to Myron so loudly everyone could hear. "I'd make it impossible for him to repeat it. I won't have my husband sowing his seed around. Robin's seed is precious to me. It's mine! I don't believe in all this. . . . "

At the mention of Jeffers's seed, Myron almost burst out laughing and had to turn away. He saw Robin looking embarrassed. But Hildegarde, who by now must have figured out what the box was for, was returning Una's look with such hatred and contempt that Myron thought Una might be further incited.

"The Italians are so expressive," Mabel was saying. "Imagine going to all the trouble of having that little box made!"

The box was on the table. Donnan had brought it in. Mabel picked it up.

"Do you suppose you could buy them in shops, picking out the one you liked from a number of styles?" Mabel was trying to make light of it. "Or did you have them made by artisans specializing in such things?"

"Would one's little concubine use it afterward for pins?" asked Donnan, also trying to turn it into a joke.

"Conversation rather broad tonight," Garth added.

Una subsided, but the meal was spoiled.

Myron found a pistol in Mora, a little village on the other side of the mountains. If he had known he was going there he could have driven east over the pass directly to it. It was a tough unpaved road open only in summer but he was familiar with it. He and Cady had used it several times on their trips to out-of-the-way villages looking for bultos and santos. But Myron was already on the main road south to Santa Fe when he thought of it. So he took the cutoff to the highway to Denver, which took him north. Mora had once been a rustlers' hangout, or at least that's what he'd been told by the Tinkers, who owned the old hotel and bar. When he got there, they asked after Cady. Myron told them he was fine and that he, Myron, had bought a house and felt he needed a gun to protect it. They directed him to the General Store and he came home with an ancient three-dollar Colt .45. The man who sold it to him was nice enough to load it and let him take some shots at a tree trunk out back. It made a terrible noise but Myron hit the tree three out of four times.

Back in the Pink House he took the pistol out of the newspaper the man had wrapped it in, stood in front of the mirror above his dresser, and pointed it at himself. He wanted to see how steady he could hold it. The dark eye of its muzzle stared unflinchingly back at him, and he could see the dull lead heads of the bullets in the wheel that held the chambers. He cocked the hammer, spun the wheel, and aimed again at his glass image. He knew he'd be killing himself. That went without saying. His work, ten novels, two movies, would be orphans. They'd have to stand by themselves. He used his thumb to uncock the hammer and let it come to rest gently against the firing pin. Then he put the gun down and began to cry. There was no anger in his tears, just self-pity. He was already in mourning for himself. He hadn't deserved this. He sat down on the edge of the bed, the revolver in his lap. Then he lay back, his feet still on the floor, the .45 now on his chest. He was thinking of his father and remembering the story about his father killing a man.

Myron had heard it from a cousin, a surgeon over in Helena. The doctor had invited him to lunch and they got on the subject of the name Brinig. All Myron's cousins, including the doctor, were named Fligelman so Myron asked the man why his father had taken the name Brinig. You don't know? His cousin asked. Myron shook his head. Your father killed a man back in the old country and had to flee. Myron was astounded. I wish I'd known that, he said, I would've put it in *Singermann*. What happened? So the doctor told the story. It seemed that as a young man, his father ran a tavern. One night there was a fight and he had to break a bottle over someone's head and the man, a gentile, had died. Romania's an anti-Semitic country, the doctor explained.

What chance did a Jew have? So he fled. When he got to Antwerp they asked him his name and he saw a sign that had the name Brinig on it so he took it. Myron was stunned. It wasn't simply that his father had killed someone and become a fugitive. It was the speed with which things like that happened. His father's life had been one thing one moment and something entirely different the next. Is that possible?

Of course it is, Myron thought now. The real question is how in the world did I not hear of it? Because it happened in Romania. Another world. People will hear of these murders, he thought. Our families, our friends. And what if I decide not to follow through on my own death? Would I be able to face the consequences? Just a bunch of queers in a love triangle, people would say. They're like that. Then Myron realized that the act itself would take him beyond humiliation, that there was an order of magnitude of things that had its own rules. Take something to a higher level and the sensations of the preceding lower one pale. As a Jew and a homosexual, he was always aware of the possibility of shame. Shame itself was never unbearable. What was unbearable was this pain that grew out of what was best in him, his love for another man. Once again he decided that the only way to stop it was to remove its cause. If this operation were to be successful both the doctor and the patient had to die.

He wrapped the gun in fresh newspaper, took it out to the car, and put it in the glove compartment. The gun compartment, he dubbed it. When he got to the main road he headed south. He took his time. He didn't want to get stopped for speeding, but he seemed to get there quicker than ever. Of course the station wagon was gone. But he could wait. It was almost dark and he parked around the side of the studio so he couldn't be seen from the road. Then he turned the car off and waited. Off in the distance the Barrancas became marching shadows. After a while there was lightning but no rain. Every so often car lights would appear on the road and he cocked the gun. But none of the lights turned in on Cady's road. He uncocked the gun and sat listening to crickets. When the sky cleared there was a moon, and he began seeing rabbits, roadrunners, and lizards that you wouldn't have imagined were there. Around five the moon set, and he started his car and left. Cady had slept in Cliff's bed. Around six Myron fell into his bed. He slept until noon.

"Tony's refused to lie for them."

It was Saturday morning. Tomorrow Hildegarde was leaving. This would be their last day. The morning passed. They all lunched together, and nothing happened. After lunch Myron took over Una's vantage point by the irrigation ditch. It turned out to be a nice place to smoke. There he thought of Cady, not as angrily as before, more sadly. So he was caught by surprise when they all came out of Hildegarde's room. He hadn't seen them go in. They strolled by him, said hello, and continued down to the cars. Robin and Hildegarde got into Mabel's Ford and drove away. Una came back up and Myron followed her into the house. She was telling Mabel in a calm voice that Hildegard and Robin had gone to the plaza to pick up photos and Mabel reminded them both that they'd promised to go to the Lockwoods' for mint juleps at five. The Jefferses would go in their own car and Mabel would take Myron and Hildegarde. Then they waited for the return of the happy couple. They were only gone a half hour. He's fast at things he should be slow at, Myron thought. At five they left for the party.

The Lockwoods' long living room was already crowded when they arrived. Mabel had whispered to him as they walked in that she couldn't wait for this day to be over, but the party seemed to Myron singularly light and easy after the mood at Los Gallos and after his own troubles. Mabel felt it, too, and seemed to relax, and Myron thought Una, Robin, and Hildegarde did as well. Then Judge Kiker's wife, Kathleen, arrived and exclaimed loudly while going up to Una: "Oh, I don't suppose I'll ever get a chance to talk to Mr. Jeffers!"

Every head turned to locate Robin at the other end of the room. He was talking happily with Ward Lockwood and Hildegarde, who held a book of the artist's drawings. It looked innocent but Una saw something that set her off.

"Robin!" she called sharply. "Come here by me."

He rose obediently and Kathleen Kiker made room for them

on the low carved chest. Myron looked at Mabel, who shrugged. But the tension was back, and he knew she wanted to flee. He did, too. So he wasn't surprised when, after they'd finished their drinks, Mabel rose and gathered her difficult flock. But Kathleen Kiker had already played a second inadvertent trick on them by inviting the twins to a picnic her children were having. The boys had left already in the Jefferses' car. They'd all have to go in Mabel's. I should have brought my car, Myron thought as he took the seat beside Mabel. Una sat between Robin and Hildegarde. And no sooner were they moving than in a low growl she began grinding out words.

"Whore!" she snarled. "Harlot!"

Myron didn't know what to do. He kept turning away and then back. So he saw the exact moment when Una, face white as milk, grabbed Hildegarde's forearm in her two hands and began twisting. Hildegarde reared back and tried to pull away. Robin, inert, did nothing.

"Whore! I'll teach you!" Una said, drawing her nails down Hildegarde's bare arm, leaving bloody scratches like narrow red ribbons. Hildegarde's arm seemed disembodied, a dead object, a piece of meat. But meat doesn't bleed. Myron looked away and saw that Mabel was driving at top speed, her eyes darting back and forth from the road to the rearview mirror. He turned to the back again and saw that Una had moved to a new level and was trying to bite her rival's arm, Hildegarde keeping her away with her free arm. But not until the car was parked in the field below the house did she manage to break entirely free and run to her room.

"Una! " Mabel shouted. "Stop it! You're a worldly woman—act like one!"

"The whore!"

"Come on," said Mabel, "and sit through one hour of dinner and then you and Hildegarde can have it out. There's no reason to involve other people in this."

"Why should I take this from her?" Una shouted. "She says I've ruined Robin! She told him so!"

"She did not!" exclaimed Robin, finally speaking up.

"She did! That vile harlot who deceives her husband, who neglects her children, thinks she can get my husband! Well, she won't. I'll ruin her." And she dashed toward the house, Robin following slowly, shaking his head. He looked like an old man. Mabel and Myron followed them.

"Oh thank goodness," said Mabel when they got inside. There was Tony looking large and serene. Soon they all went into dinner together, and Una, sitting beside Tony, was silent. Except that she refused to eat, no one would have suspected her tantrum.

"What's the matter?" Tony asked her kindly. "You not hungry?" She smiled with white lips and shook her head and took a sip of water. The meal came to an end at last, and Mabel, finally admitting that this Truth game had become too much even for her, suggested to Tony that they go to the pueblo. So they went out into the early evening, leaving Myron behind with the others.

He found he didn't mind at all. It had become interesting. Was it the writer in him? For he was still running the car scene through his mind. Would that be the end of it? And he found himself wishing he could get Una alone. That's not the way to do it, he would tell her. Let me help you. I have a gun. I'll lend it to you. But before he could say anything the Jefferses retired to their room. Only Myron and Hildegarde were left. They sat in Mabel's living room as if they were reading. But they were listening to the voices from upstairs rising in recrimination and accusation. It sounded as if Una was ripping Robin to pieces as she had in her story. Myron kept glancing at Hildegarde, who seemed at certain moments about to fly up there to protect her lover from the madwoman as he had not protected her. After a while it grew quiet and Myron heard the phone ring. Then Rosalie, who was just finishing in the kitchen, came in to tell him he had a call. Somehow Myron knew it would be Cady.

"I've got to talk to you," he said.

"Go ahead," said Myron.

"No, I mean face to face."

"Face to face?" He thought about how he'd waited for him last night.

"I've got to apologize to you for what a mess I made of things."

"I'll see you tomorrow at noon at your place," Myron said.

"Do you mind if . . . ?"

"No," he said, "have Cliff there, too."

"Okay. Tomorrow."

As soon as he hung up he began to pace. Could he wait for tomorrow? His steps led him into the Rainbow Room, Mabel's library, where he began looking at books. But he couldn't get his mind off Cady and Cliff. He wanted to get into his car right now and go down there. Take a lesson from Una, he thought. Listen to your rage. Let it be your guide. Take a . . . Pow!

What was that? Then he heard a second pow and ran out into the entry. There was Hildegarde lying at the bottom of the steps leading up to the bedrooms. He rushed to her. She seemed unconscious. Robin came running down.

"What happened?" the poet asked and kneeled over her.

"I think she's been shot," Myron said.

"Impossible." Robin looked up the steps, then down at Hildegarde and touched her forehead where there was a red dent. Then he looked up the stairs again. "She must have hit her head on the lintel."

Myron looked up at the wooden beam that supported the ceiling over the stairway's upper landing. Was Hildegarde that tall? "But I heard a shot," he insisted.

"That was Una. She's shot herself. I'm going for a doctor."

Robin stood and hurried out of the house, leaving Myron with the unconscious Hildegarde and who knows what upstairs. He hesitated, then began to climb. The door to Mabel's bedroom was open, but he couldn't see anyone. He stepped into the room. Nobody. But the bathroom door was open. He stepped forward and there was Una sitting upright in the bathtub, holding her nightgown above her torso, baring her low, flat breasts. And there it was, a dark hole above her left breast. When she saw him she smiled an angry smile.

"Did she smash her head? Is she dead? I hope so. I'll meet her in hell!"

"Una?" asked Myron, as if she hadn't spoken. "Are you all right?"

"I've killed myself," she said and dabbed at the wound with a bloody towel that was in the tub with her. He stepped forward. Blood was flowing out of her chest, down her stomach, and around her bare legs. She seemed to be trying to keep her nightgown from getting stained.

"The doctor's coming," Myron said. "Robin went for him."

"I don't need a doctor," said Una.

Myron saw the gun. It was a purse-sized automatic, a B movie prop. It was lying in the brass soap dish that was hooked over the far edge of the tub. He looked from the gun to her wound and back. His own anger seemed to be draining out of the hole in her chest. She's had a gun all along, he thought. She's shot herself in the heart. Then how could she still be sitting there talking to him? He stepped closer, looked into the dark, seeping wound. It seemed to be the same caliber as her pistol.

"Do you want me to stay with you?" he asked.

"No. You shouldn't see me like this, Myron."

He didn't know if she was referring to her nudity or her dying. But he stayed anyway. Though he couldn't help her, he thought she mustn't be alone. In a while he heard a noise downstairs. "I think they're back," he said. Una, her eyes still wide, seemed not to hear him. Suddenly embarrassed, Myron left her and went out onto the small landing. He was looking down on Mabel and Tony, who must have returned just as Robin and Dr. Pond got there. All four of them were kneeling over Hildegarde, the doctor waving smelling salts under her nose. Myron went down to them.

"What happened to her?" Mabel asked when he was beside them.

"I'm not sure," said Myron.

Just then Hildegarde opened her eyes. "Is Robin dead?" she asked.

"I'm here," said Robin.

But the question reminded them that there was someone upstairs more in need of their help and they all left Hildegarde, who was struggling to stand. In the bathroom, at the doctor's direction, Robin, Tony, and Myron lifted Una from the tub and laid her on the bed.

"She swallowed a bottle of sleeping tablets, then she got the gun," Robin said.

"We better get her to the hospital," said Dr. Pond.

"I'll call the undertaker," said Mabel.

Robin looked stricken.

"They've got the only stretcher in town," she explained.

"That little old thing," Tony said in a low, angry voice. "We can't invite her here ever again. She spoil our nice house." They were sitting in the Rainbow Room. "I don't want to go upstairs to our rooms ever again."

It was only half past ten but it seemed years since Una had been taken to the hospital.

"Maybe she'll die," Mabel speculated.

"She's a witch," Tony said. "She shoot herself in heart and live."

Incredibly, what Tony said was true. When Mabel called the hospital she was told by the sister on duty that the bullet had glanced off a rib, traveled around Una's rib cage, and exited her back. The next morning, Sunday, Myron and Mabel went to the hospital together. Tony was driving Hildegarde to Raton to catch a train. Myron had gone over to the Big House early to say goodbye to the woman. There was a black and blue lump on her forehead. As far as a punishment went, it was a light one, Myron thought. He had decided he liked Hildegarde. She was plucky. But she wasn't in Una's class. Not a creature out of Irish mythology. Not even in my class, he thought. There was never any danger of her killing anyone. And now there was no danger of him killing anyone. Somehow what Una had done was enough. She had taken him where he wanted to go. So the first thing he did this morning was call Cady and cancel their meeting. We shouldn't see each other anymore, he said.

Robin came downstairs to the hospital's lobby and they went outside to sit on the ditch bank under the cottonwoods. The poet looked almost dead.

"There was exploratory surgery," he explained. "But the worst is over and there seems little risk unless she tries something new."

"What are you going to do now?" asked Mabel.

He rubbed his forehead with long bony fingers, not sadly, not anything really. He's like water, Myron decided. Water can be ruffled by small winds or tossed high by hurricanes. Yet, left to itself, it's placid. He is what he is, cold and slow. But the man had made a philosophy of such an attitude, a credo, a truth to be passed on to others to live by. Myron sat silent looking at the worn face. Who knows? Maybe he's right. Maybe in the long run nothing matters. What if I had killed Cady and Cliff? I would've killed myself, too. If nothing matters, you're as good as dead anyway.

"Can you get away?" Mabel asked. "Find a change of scene?" She was still working Hildegarde's side of the street.

"I must," he said, looking even bleaker. Though his philosophy of indifference seems to be working, thought Myron, he's still under a great deal of stress. "I promised Hildegarde I'd let her know." He thought a moment. "I can write her, though of course she can't write to me."

This caveat brought them back to Una. He was taking his wife into account after all. Myron looked at Mabel and they all knew the game was over. They were seeing the same thing, years of care and nursing ahead for Robin. Una's and his roles would be reversed. Robin would learn to write checks. Una had won a pyrrhic victory. Medea-like, she had pulled her house down. But fate had intervened. Tragedy became comedy. She would get to witness her denouement. Things would be different, but not in a way either of them had intended.

"Her grandfather leaned over a washbowl and slit his throat with a knife when he was ninety," Robin said as if suicide was an inherited trait.

"What started her off last night?" Mabel asked.

"When we went upstairs she accused me of lying to her, which I admitted," he began. "She was on the bed with Haig beside her. She lay so quiet I began explaining to her why I had to lie. But before I got very far she told me to shut up. She was thinking."

"What was she thinking?" asked Myron.

"I don't know. I stood a while, then went to the bed and lifted the dog, saying that perhaps she'd think better without me there and that I'd take Haig for a walk. So, you would take the last thing from me, she said, and jumped up and ran into the bathroom.

I hesitated, not sure what she meant, then I went in and saw her swallowing all the pills from the bottle of Phenobarbital that had been prescribed for my back pain. I'm going for a doctor, I said, and left her there. That's when I heard a shot and ran back in. She was slumped in the tub, a bullet hole in her chest."

Myron thought it sounded implausible. Could he really have been that slow? And where had she gotten the gun? Did they keep it in the soap dish? He'd asked Mabel this and she told him it was Robin's, that he kept it against intruders. Still Myron felt doubt. Why? Was it Robin's lack of emotion? And if his story wasn't true, what was an alternative one? That he shot her? Myron again thought of Una's story of attacking her husband on their way home. Maybe that really did happen, and Robin's anger at his wife had simmered for this long? And what about Una in the car? I should ask these questions, he thought. In the name of justice I should play the Truth game with him. But do I really care? No. It's not that important.

"You know, Robin," Mabel was saying, "I don't feel the same toward Una now. Maybe I will again later on. I just feel nothing for her now."

Myron wasn't surprised by Mabel's honesty. He thought of her article again. Though she had tried to convince herself otherwise, she'd never felt anything for Una but hatred.

"Of course," Robin answered, nodding his head as if he were telling her there was room for this meanness in his philosophy too.

"The last straw was when you told me she didn't blame me for anything."

Myron hadn't heard this. They must have spoken on the phone.

"It was as if she was saying the whole thing was my fault."

But it is, thought Myron.

"Una always felt you were a very dangerous woman," Robin said and looked as though he wanted Mabel to understand his wife. "She always thought she had to defend herself against you."

So Una knew her Mabel, Myron thought. Yet to advance her husband's career, she had accepted Mabel's hospitality. Perhaps then she got what she deserved. Then he was thinking of Cady and himself. Have I also gotten what I deserve? Did I in some way use Cady? Is that all love really is, utility with feeling?

Una stayed in the hospital for five days. Then she lay convalescing in the first bedroom in the row of outside rooms along the portal. Far from ruining their house forever as Tony had feared, after a ceremony of purification that he insisted on, he and Mabel reclaimed their bedrooms before Una was back from the hospital. It's better that she's downstairs, Myron thought, but did they have to put her in Hildegarde's room? Yet he couldn't really blame Mabel for this thoughtlessness, if that's what it was. It was a hard time for her. Dr. Ruddleston, who'd been called in to assist in the surgical probe for the bullet, had picked up the whole story from Una's ravings and by twelve o'clock the next day, being a gossip and a lush, had told everyone in the Martin Hotel where he lived. Soon all of Taos was buzzing with versions of what had gone on at Los Gallos. For weeks Mabel had to go about the town looking as though the world had ceased to exist, unable to talk to anyone.

The worst of it was that Una wouldn't leave until the Wilders came. She said she wanted Thornton, whom the Jefferses seemed to know, to see that she was a nice woman. She was convinced that back in New Haven, also the Wilders' hometown, Hildegarde would "fill them with lies." Dr. Pond told her she should get psychiatric advice, but that only angered her. Young fool, she called him. And she was still having loud scenes with Robin. Myron would see the poet sitting alone on the bench by the ditch, leaning over, his head in one hand, his pipe in the other, as if he were weighing them. Myron also noticed that in the two weeks Una stayed on, when she and Mabel talked, neither mentioned what happened. There was nothing to say, though Mabel, in an effort to lessen the magnitude of it, portrayed Una as simply an inconsiderate guest. Una tried to downplay it, too, telling Myron once that she shot herself while cleaning the automatic, and another time that she hadn't shot herself at all but stabbed herself with Tony's cuticle scissors while trimming her nails.

Myron also noticed that Robin didn't seem to miss Hildegarde. It looked like a case of out of sight out of mind. This bothered Mabel, too, his seeming lack of responsibility to either woman. She was polite to him, attentive but withdrawn. Then Myron noticed that though she tried, she couldn't pretend life would go on as though nothing had happened, a little storm on the sea's surface. Myron had never seen Mabel dealing with real trauma. She'd had a shock that seemed to be working its way into her, not just the shock of blood, death, and disharmony, but of finding out, as she said, the truth of what Una had done to Robin, that is, what Robin really was.

"Pussy-whipped," Myron told her one day.

"What?" she asked.

"He's pussy-whipped," he repeated. It was a term Myron first heard as a boy in Butte. The miners would accuse each other of it when they were out drinking and one of them said they had to get home. Myron once accused Frank Fenton of it. But that was before he knew what Frank was really doing.

"I never heard that expression before," she said. "It's disgusting."

Myron nodded.

"But apt," she added after a moment.

As soon as she said that, Myron began to think it wasn't apt. What had Una done to Robin that Robin hadn't wanted done? What about all those books of poetry? Would he have written them without her? Hadn't she drawn them out of him? Hadn't she been the subject of them, the raging core of passion around which he could stretch his elastic numbness? Then he realized he was making the same argument Mabel had made in her original article on them.

"The truth is," he said, "if anybody's done any pussy-whipping around here, it's you, Mabel. You wanted Robin to be something he couldn't be. No one could be what you wanted. You almost killed them. How could you have interfered like that? More than anyone, you knew what she was capable of!"

He was about to say more when he saw the look on her face. She was admitting it to herself. It wasn't Jeffers's failure. The failure was hers and had been all along. It seemed the mold of her will, with which all her life she had tried to shape the world, had been cracked from the beginning. There was no shape it would hold. No matter how hard she pressed the clay, the world would leak out.

"Mabel, you should do yourself what you wanted Jeffers and

Lawrence to do. Forget about molding people and become truly creative yourself."

"What do you mean?" she asked.

"I mean you should write novels. Give a voice to this place. You're capable of it. You're a fine writer. Your observations about other people are wonderful, and you know more about yourself and why you do things than most authors, myself included."

"Dr. Brill once told me I should do that," she said sadly.

"Well," said Myron, "for once he's right."

When the Jefferses were gone there were the Wilders to deal with. They were nice people, though not nearly as interesting as the Jefferses, who, before Hildegarde, had been so dull. Did Mabel have anything planned for Thornton Wilder? No. Nice seemed to be what was needed. Not Wilder but tamer, though Wilder got more interesting when he remarked one evening that he had discussed Myron with Gertrude Stein and defended him against her charges of rudeness by giving her a copy of *Anthony in the Nude*. She wrote me, Wilder said. She said she read it and liked it though it wasn't her way of doing things. Then he took a copy of Stein's *Tender Buttons* down from Mabel's bookshelf and asked Myron to read it. Myron did and loved the wordplay: witty, quick, clever, even expressive of feeling. Of course we still don't have to like each other, he said to Wilder when they talked about it. Then the Wilders were gone. So one day in late September Myron saddled Surprise, rode down to the bottom of the Rio Grande gorge, and threw his Colt .45 into the rough mountain water. His family would have been annoyed. Sell it, they would have said. At least get your money back.

Mabel was getting ready for her annual check-up in Albuquerque. After that she'd be off to New York to see Dr. Brill. She'd asked Myron about Cady. He told her they'd broken up and that Cady and his new love were in California. She said good. That was all she said. Then she was gone, and Myron took a place in Santa Fe with Spud. There was nothing between them. Spud knew what had happened and, kind person that he was, didn't want Myron to be alone. Myron had thought of asking Mabel again about the Placita house, but he was no longer sure he wanted to live in New Mexico. He seemed to have reached the end of something. He had money now and a reputation as a bestselling author. Maybe he would go back to Carmel and buy a house there. He thought of Mabel. On her next birthday, which he remembered as being some time in February, she would be sixty. By Christmas he'd be forty-three. We're getting up there, he thought. Then he thought of Cady and Cliff. He was jealous of them. I want that, he decided. I want to be in love.

Nine

On Friday, October 14, 1938, *The Sisters* opened at the Strand Theater in Times Square, and, a week later, in Warner Brothers' movie houses all around the country. One of these was the Lensic Theater in Santa Fe. Spud, who handled publicity for the Lensic, had promised his boss and the *Santa Fe New Mexican*, for whom he did freelance work, that Myron Brinig would be there opening night. If Spud hadn't made that promise, Myron probably wouldn't have gone. Then Hal and Bob got hold of the idea and offered their house for an opening night party. That made Myron even more wary. Though he had long since made up with Hal, he still felt the man was unpredictable in his tempers. Malicious menopausal malice, he told Spud. He could be honoring me or having fun at my expense. Myron had heard from his Hollywood agent that last-minute changes had been made to the movie—not by the producer or the director but by the brothers Warner themselves. What did they do? Myron asked. Rosalind said she didn't know, but whatever it was they had a right to do it. They own it, she reminded him. It's their baby. Unfortunately Myron, forgetting the advice he'd once given Thomas Wolfe, considered it his baby, too.

So Spud went ahead and rented two searchlights from the National Guard, and the Santa Fe world premier was on. Left over from the Great War, when the state capital thought it needed protection from German bombers flying from airfields in Juárez, the searchlights in the plaza pierced the night with news of *The Sisters'* imminent arrival. Then Hal decided his party would be formal: tuxedos, evening gowns, and rented limos that were really old Harvey House tour buses. Regardless of sexual preference, everybody was to have a date of the opposite sex. Spud would interview "celebrities" for the local radio station as they entered the theater while two policemen and two sawhorses held back the throngs of adoring fans. The throngs consisted mostly of tourists and Indian jewelry sellers just closing their spots under the portal of the Palace of the Governors. Luckily the legislature was in session and mixed with the natives and the sightseers were politicians and their wives who, when it became apparent the Lensic would not fill, were offered tickets.

It was easy for Hal and Bob to find dates. Hal brought Nina Otero and Bob his own sister, Martha. Myron, on the other hand, had a more difficult time. Mabel was in New York and probably wouldn't have gone anyway. Hal suggested Tinka but Myron, knowing Tinka was the last person Spud wanted to see there, said no. What about Brett? Myron almost agreed until he thought about an evening shouting into her trumpet. Bob Hunt then suggested the two ladies who had accompanied Thomas Wolfe to Mabel's doorstep and with whom they had all danced at the dedication of Lawrence's tomb. Myron agreed. After all, Wolfe had just died. Weren't these women a living memorial to that author's only visit to New Mexico? And Myron decided that if he were called on to speak, he'd mention Wolfe's passing and ask for a moment of silence. Like everyone, he'd been shocked by the author's death the previous month. It happened so quickly. The man had been so strong, so vital. But when you thought about it, it wasn't so surprising. Wolfe was a tempter of fate.

"What do you think of all this, Mr. Brinig?" asked Spud. They were under the marquee. Instead of a tux Spud was wearing the suit of lights he'd worn to Lawrence's dedication, the same suit that had turned the head of Tinka Fechin and broken up a marriage of twenty years. If she could see him in it now, thought Myron. From beneath the gold bolero jacket bulged a paunch full of Myron's carne adovada.

"I'm overwhelmed," said Myron into the mike. "I never thought something like this would happen to me."

"I hear it's happening all over the country," noted Spud.

"Yes. *The Sisters* is opening right now in theaters all over America. I was invited to appear in Butte, Montana, for this very same ceremony." Myron was making this up.

"And you turned down Butte, Montana, to appear here with us."

"He's a very gracious man," Miss Sage chimed in.

"Won't you introduce these ladies, Myron?"

"Miss Sage," Myron said of the women holding each one of his arms, "and Miss Brush."

"Are those your real names, ladies?" asked Spud.

"Yes," said his right arm. "I'm Imogene Sage."

"I'm Bonnie Brush," said his left. "And we can't wait to see it."

So they went in and took three reserved tenth-row center seats in a now full house. Immediately the lights came down, and, after the credits and applause when Myron's name appeared, the movie began. In the novel Myron had gone to great lengths to describe the Elliotts' drugstore and their small apartment over it. Built at the thirty-degree junction of Granite and Crystal streets, the frame house formed a kind of prow that looked out over the beautiful Silver Bow Valley. The real sisters, whose family name was Kelly, would sit up in the second-floor windows of this ship and gaze out at Mount Haggin, the highest peak in the Pintlars and the only mountain in America named after a Turk, the millionaire mine investor from San Francisco, Ali Haggin. Myron was disappointed that the movie did nothing with the house's odd shape, and that they made the place so much larger than it or any house in that neighborhood dreamed of being. The highlight of the novel's first section, the ball to honor the election of Teddy Roosevelt, was overblown as well. It's after this ball that Bette Davis, playing Louise, the Elliotts' oldest daughter, elopes with the dashing newspaper reporter Frank Medlin, played by Errol Flynn.

If the sets were wrong, the actors were wonderful. Myron had worried about Bette Davis. He'd seen *Jezebel* and thought she'd be much too sharp and hard for Louise. But from the opening frame she was an even better Louise than he'd written. What if she wins another Oscar? he wondered. Then came the climax of Louise's section. When the earthquake hits, she's down on the San Francisco wharves looking for Frank, who's left her. By the time she gets back to her rooms the fires have begun, and she's getting sick. Flora, her neighbor played by Gail Patrick, rescues her and takes her to her mother's house across the bay in Oakland. Louise has typhus and is nursed back to health by Flora's mother, Laura Hope Crews, whose home, it turns out, is a whorehouse and she its madam. At this point Myron noticed the women beside him had tears running down their cheeks. Then came the parts about the other two sisters, and the failures of their marriages. In the last scene four years have passed and there is another ball, this time to celebrate the victory of William Howard Taft. The sisters are united again, a little older, a lot wiser.

"Author! Author!"

Hal was already on stage holding out his arm, and, as planned, Myron was being escorted down the aisle and up on stage by Spud. The house lights had been brought up and Myron climbed the steps at the end of the side aisle. Then he was standing in front of a microphone at center stage, looking down on some faces he knew, most he didn't. The applause died. They were expecting him to say something. He wanted to ask how many of them had read the novel. He wanted to tell those who hadn't, which surely would be most of them, that it didn't end like that. But as he looked out at their smiling faces, he realized that as far as they were concerned it didn't make any difference about the ending, that whatever it was, they loved the movie.

"I want to say," Myron began, "I had nothing to do with the making of this film. The Warner brothers simply bought the rights to my novel and had it adapted to the screen. So Milton Krim, the man who wrote the screenplay, should be standing here with me. He did a great job." Myron paused as they applauded Milton Krim, whoever he was. When the applause died down he went on.

"Credit certainly should go to the director, Anatole Litvak, for coaxing such fine performances from his cast." Myron meant this. It was Warner Brothers' stock company at its best: Ian Hunter, Donald Crisp, Beulah Bondi, Lee Patrick, Laura Hope

Crews, Henry Travers, Patrick Knowles, Alan Hale. He cited each one, and there was applause at the mention of each name.

"When I heard Bette Davis was going to play Louise, I had my doubts. I'd just seen her in *Jezebel*." Myron paused again as they applauded Bette Davis. "Perhaps we've just witnessed another Academy Award performance." More applause. "But it just may have been by Errol Flynn. Wasn't he wonderful?"

Tumultuous applause for the actor who had brought sympathy and intelligence to what might have been a villainous role. Then Myron thanked them all for coming and exited stage right. He had forgotten about Thomas Wolfe. When he remembered, it was too late. Oh well, he thought.

"That ending," Myron snarled in the car. "I can't believe it."

Imogene Sage and Bonnie Brush had just commented about how much they loved the movie. Their praise seemed to be the last straw. You dumb bitches, Myron wanted to shout. But he didn't. Instead he listed the many variations from his novel, which he said he forgave until he got to the ending. The bittersweet ending Myron had written, Louise accepting the demise of her marriage, had made his argument for the beauty of renunciation and should have ended the movie. Yet who had shown up in the very last frames, sent no doubt by Jack Warner himself, but a contrite Errol Flynn! Miss Davis looks at him once, they fall into each other's arms, and in the new The End is an implied consummation and salvation.

"It makes no sense!" Myron snapped. "The women aren't allowed to grow. They keep making the same mistakes. You've been divorced," he said to the Misses Sage and Brush, who had confessed this to him sometime during the Lawrence dancing. "Are you going to keep taking up with the same man and think this time it will be different, that this time he won't betray you?" By now Miss Sage and Miss Brush were agreeing with him and saying they hadn't meant it, that the movie really wasn't all that good, as if that would make him feel better. Then they were at Hal's and there was nowhere to park so he stopped in front and let the women out.

"Fucking idiots!" he exclaimed when they were gone.

"Lawsy me, Missa Brinig!" said the pot-bellied toreador from the back, "sometime I dasn't know what gets into you."

"This was Hal's doing," said Myron, refusing to see anything funny in what had happened. "He knew they'd turned it into a piece of crap. That's why he made such a big deal about it. He's trying to make a fool of me!"

"Myron," said Spud, now serious. "You're wrong."

Myron had parked a hundred yards past the house up Buena Vista, the unpaved street that marked the north edge of the property. But he didn't get out. He just sat.

"C'mon, Mike," urged Spud. He was standing beside the driver door. "You're the guest of honor."

"On All Fools Day Quasimodo was the guest of honor. Should I go in and get whipped?"

"Myron," Spud said, exasperation in his voice, "I liked the movie. I agree the ending was dumb. But most Hollywood endings are dumb. C'mon."

Myron got out of the car, and together they walked to the house. It's only a movie, he told himself. And he had nothing to do with the making of it. Why should he be upset? Bob greeted them at the door, handed them each a drink, and the crowd of booksellers, painters, and writers burst into applause. Myron smiled and acknowledged them with a wave, but he couldn't get over the feeling that someone was having fun at his expense. For one thing, no matter how conversations began, whether with questions about the movie or the novel, people always got around to asking him what had happened with the Jefferses and if Una was all right. So he kept telling one of the lies that Una herself had told, that it was a gun-cleaning accident and she was fine. But after an hour he cornered Hal in the kitchen and came out with it, first about the movie and its terrible ending, then about the festivities he thought were mocking him.

"You know," Hal admitted, "I think I was predisposed to do that. Ever since I heard about Una Jeffers, I've had it in for Mabel. You had an excuse. You had to deal with your breakup with Cady. But she . . . "

Myron was thunderstruck. Without coming out and saying

it in so many words, Hal was blaming him for what had happened to the Jefferses.

"But I couldn't use the movie if I wanted to," Hal went on. "In spite of the ending, which was obviously tacked on, it's very good. I read the novel. If the movie has a fault it's not giving the other two sisters their due. They made it a vehicle for Bette Davis."

"What did you say?"

"I said they should have made it longer and done the other two sisters better."

"No, I mean about Una Jeffers."

"That Mabel drove her to attempt suicide."

"And that I helped?" Hal looked up from the punch bowl. He was spiking its contents with a fifth of vodka. "Is that what people are saying?"

"Well—yes."

"Who? What people?" He was sure it was Hal himself.

"Isn't it true Una tried to kill herself?"

"We heard she shot herself in the heart and missed," said Bob Hunt, who'd just come into the kitchen. He was smiling. He thought that was funny.

"Who'd you hear that from?" asked Myron.

"Lots of people," said Bob more seriously. "For weeks it was all anyone down here talked about. We heard Mabel set Jeffers up with a woman and that Una got wind of it and tried to kill herself."

"Who's given herself more to her husband's career than Una Jeffers?" asked Hal with such righteous sadness you'd have thought it happened to him. "Is that the kind of treatment she deserves?"

"It smacks of Mabel," added Bob, now serious. "Jeffers hasn't panned out for her. He's not even considered a very good poet anymore."

"You think Mabel did all that and I helped her?"

Myron was cold sober now. Here was the reason for the party. It was to be an inquisition. It had nothing to do with *The Sisters*, movie or novel. It didn't even have that much to do with him. It was really about Mabel. They were trying to get at Mabel through him.

"You're her boy," said Bob, suddenly sarcastic.

"And you're his boy," snapped Myron, nodding toward Hal.

"Oh?" asked Hal.

"And you better watch your boy, Hal. He's been seen a lot lately hanging around the cathedral's men's room." Myron turned back to Bob, who was getting a reputation for cruising. "A strange way to get religion, Bob."

"C'mon, Myron," said Hal, "let's cut this out."

"You know the story of January and May?" Myron asked. It was a shame. He liked Bob and he liked his poetry. He'd bought several copies of *The Early World* and sent them to friends.

"You really are as nasty as they say," said Hal.

"Not as nasty as some old queen I know."

"I may be nasty," said Hal, now facing Myron, the empty vodka bottle in his right hand. With his height and armed like that, he was a formidable. "But at least I'm not a liar."

"What's that supposed to mean?" Myron was sure Hal was going to bring up Cady again, say something about Myron getting what he deserved. So he was prepared to throw Cliff McCarthy back into Hal's face, another secretary gone bad. He listed them in his head: Spud, Cliff, Lynn Riggs, now Bob.

"Hal," said Bob, shaking his head, "don't."

"You know she's so high and mighty up there in Mabeltown." Whatever he was going to say, it seemed Hal wouldn't be stopped. "If she says nobody tried to kill themselves in her house, then nobody did."

"It's nobody's business," snarled Myron. "Least of all a faggoty old gossip like you."

There was a pause and Hal's eyes were wide with anger. He stepped forward and smiled cruelly. "And if she wants to keep the fact that she has syphilis a secret," he said, his face bright red, "then nobody can say anything about that either."

"What?" asked Myron.

"You heard me! Syphilis! Mabel has syphilis! It was given to her by that other great fraud, Tony Luhan."

"You're beneath contempt," said Myron and flicked his half-full glass of whiskey into the tall man's round, pasty face. Immediately Robert Frost came to his mind. I've been waiting three years to do that, Myron told himself.

"Syphilis!" Hal repeated, his face dripping.

"Let's get out of here," Myron said to Spud, who'd just come into the kitchen. He was all smiles and obviously hadn't heard what was going on. The women chose to stay.

"There's something I want to ask you," said Myron the next morning at breakfast. Last night Myron had waited for Spud to ask what it was all about, but Spud didn't. Perhaps it was for the best. Myron was so angry he couldn't really talk about it. The next day, however, he'd cooled off. If anyone knew anything about it, Spud did. He'd been her secretary, her press agent, her editor.

"What?"

"It's about Mabel."

"What about her?"

Myron hesitated. He still didn't know if he could talk about it. Syphilis was a taboo like incest. At best it was a visitation by a vengeful God on the promiscuous, the loose, the immoral, a punishment with Biblical overtones like leprosy or the plagues visited on Egypt. At worst it was pure disgust and loathing, what had been grouped in his childhood under that most pejorative of words, "dirty." He'd never known anyone who had it but he remembered the "health" movies they'd shown in the army, people with black, rotting holes in their flesh, with no noses and bones wasted away, people in insane asylums mutely staring, their brains gone. Even now it made him queasy. But he came out with it.

"Last night Hal told me Mabel had syphilis," he began. "He said she got it from Tony. Is that true? Or was His Bitchiness just being his bitchiest?"

"Is that why you threw the drink in his face?"

"Yes."

Spud took a deep breath and seemed to make up his mind. "What if I said you owe Hal an apology?"

"I'd say you were crazy."

"Well, you do."

"I don't believe you."

"Hal shouldn't have told you." Spud sighed. It was obviously difficult for him to talk about it. "It's why Mabel goes down to Albuquerque every September. She and Tony have checkups. And she sends blood samples down there once a month. They monitor the disease, which has been in remission for twenty years. It's a tough way to live, having that over your head."

"How do you know this? How does Hal know it?"

"One of the technicians in the lab down there was an old friend of his."

Another secretary? Myron wondered. When does he find time to write? "How long have you known?" he asked.

"Since the mid-twenties. Mabel knew it almost immediately, since 1918."

"What about Hal? How long has he known?"

"I don't know. I found out from him. The technician's been dead ten years. As far as I know Hal never said anything to anyone else before."

"Bob knows."

"He must trust him."

"Does Mabel know that Hal knows?"

"If she does, she's never let on."

"Does she know that you know?"

"I don't know that either. I've never talked to her about it. I try to do what Hal's doing."

"What do you mean?"

"He's kept her secret."

"He told me."

"He shouldn't have. But since he did I hope you'll keep it also." Spud paused. "Whatever you might think of him, Hal's from the old school. He's a gentleman. He's pretty nasty sometimes." He paused again, then went on. "I know he's frustrated with his place in the poetry world. He's second rate and he's beginning to realize it." Spud shrugged. "I love his poetry so I guess that makes me second rate, too. Maybe we're all just beginning to realize what we are."

"I feel second rate, too," said Myron.

"If you are," said Spud, "at least you're making lots of money from it. You know Hal sends out scripts all the time. I'm sure he's jealous that your novel was made into a movie. And I think he did mean to scoff at you. Turned out he couldn't." Spud paused, then wagged his finger at Myron. "But if he ever invites you to celebrate the premier of *May Flavin*, don't go."

Spud had already told Myron what he thought of *May Flavin*.

"But Myron." He was serious again. "Please don't mention it to anyone. It's her secret. Someday she'll have to tell it. But it's hers to tell."

∽

Myron left for New York at the end of October. Over the phone he'd gotten a sublet on East Fiftieth Street. He had to get away. Not that he hadn't been able to work in Santa Fe. He had a good start on a new novel. It would be short, less than two hundred pages. Spud put him onto the idea. Listen to this, he'd said one morning at breakfast, and he proceeded to read Myron an article in last Sunday's *Times* about a man who stood out on a ledge of a hotel in midtown Manhattan for over eight hours before jumping to his death. The article said the event was broadcast on all the local stations and that by the time the man finally jumped there were thousands of people in the street watching. Later it was learned that the man was a mental patient who had attempted suicide many times before. But that wasn't what interested Myron. No, he'd seen something like it in Butte when he was a kid, though that man had finally not jumped. It was the spectators. They were the interesting ones. So he was writing *Anne Minton's Life*, the story of a suicide, as a kind of outdoor Grand Hotel.

After a month in New York he began to think he was through with New Mexico. What was there for him? New York was becoming exciting again. War was breaking out in Europe. It was all over the radio and papers. But if he stayed in the city, he'd need some clothes. So one day he walked over to Brooks Brothers on Madison Avenue and bought a tweed jacket, two pairs of gray flannel pants, some blue button-down shirts, and some striped ties. But the pièce de resistance were English Cordovan leather shoes and new socks to wear with them. Why are these called clocks? he asked the clerk about the design that ran up the ankles of the hose. The young man said he didn't know and confessed that he hadn't even known they were called clocks. Myron asked him to send the packages over to his apartment and gave him his address. The young man brought them himself and Myron offered him a drink. Later, in order to get him out of the apartment, Myron took him to dinner at Maurice's, the French restaurant in the middle of the next block.

Then he got back to work. But as he wrote, his unconscious mind thought its own thoughts. Something was cooking in him, something whose energy he could feel even as he worked on his conscious novel. At times it would come to the surface. It seemed Hal had done him a favor by telling him Mabel's secret. After his initial disgust had come wonder. And he realized Mabel had leaped in his esteem a thousandfold. The woman had unplumbed depths. She was more than a high-class gossip, a clever, self-serving lion hunter, more than a rich interfering bitch. She was facing the possibility of death, of madness and disfigurement, and she was living with the terrible awareness that if her secret ever got out she would be a pariah in the eyes of the world. Myron remembered what he and his fellow soldiers had thought of syphilitics. Yet it was the disease that somehow made her noble, that put everything she'd done since she first discovered she was infected in a new light. Her relationships with Tony, with the Lawrences, with the Jefferses, with the world, all of it had to be seen differently.

Way back in 1914, Rod, Myron's oversexed friend in Joyce Kilmer's writing class made him read Melville's *Benito Cereno*. Myron thought it would be just another book about going to sea. It wasn't. When you finally learned Benito Cereno, the captain of the slave ship, was really the prisoner of the slaves he was transporting, everything that happened before that revelation had to be gone over again in your mind and understood in a new way. It was a book you couldn't help reading a second time, literally a twice-told tale. Myron had been overwhelmed by its effect and later in the twenties, when he was reading for the Selznicks, he suggested it to David as a project. David had loved it but saw no way of producing it at Fort Lee. Now Myron felt this might be the way to tell Mabel's story, keep her secret till the end so its revelation would make the reader reread her life just as Myron was now being forced to do. But in order to do this he'd have to use Melville's device of an observer, a seemingly dispassionate narrator who would be the first to discover the truth.

Then he realized that despite those lurid films he'd been shown as a soldier, he knew nothing about syphilis. So one of the things he would do in the afternoons after his writing day was over was walk down Fifth Avenue to the New York Public Library to do research. Sometimes on these walks things would pop into his head, things that had happened with Mabel. Like the dinner at Marie Garland's. Did you have sex with D. H. Lawrence? What was going on in her mind when she was asked that? I wanted to but I loved him too much to risk infecting him. And what about the Jefferses? Had she for all those years mulled over seducing Robin before hitting on Hildegarde as a substitute? For Myron had decided that she'd probably had sex with no one but Tony since she'd discovered her illness. That must have been a great moment when she realized she had to protect her future lovers against her own diseased sexuality. No wonder she and Tony got married. Still, he didn't know if he could write it. So he just let it percolate and wrote to Mabel that he would again like to rent the Pink House for the summer. She said to come on.

As soon as he arrived she asked him to read something that she'd written that past winter. Myron thought it was going to be a reworking of her piece on Una and Robin, a defense of her actions of the previous summer and an end to that chapter of her life. But that would have needed at most fifty pages. The manuscript she'd brought filled a typing paper box.

"What's this?" Myron asked.

"You said I should try fiction. It's a novel."

"Really? What's it called?"

"*Water of Life*. There's no hurry. I know how busy you are."

Anne Minton's Life was done and soon to be released and he hadn't started the new novel about her. So he wasn't busy. In fact he wasn't sure he would start it. Can you write about a friend that way? Weren't there some things better left unwritten?

"I'll start it tonight," Myron said.

It looked like it would be a chore, at least at first. For one thing Mabel had set her book in, of all places, Hungary. But it wasn't Hungary. It was pure Graustark, a Balkan fantasy. Yet, despite the phony setting, it was also autobiographical. Gaza, the heroine, was Mabel. Full of contradictions and caprices, she went on for paragraph after paragraph ranting about the mediocrity surrounding her, while at the same time recognizing there was something in everyday people she could not fathom. Not until the hero, Gendron, comes on the scene did Myron perk up. He'd expected some version of Tony or Lawrence or Jeffers. It's not what he got.

> *Gendron's eyes were set far apart. They were very black and the outer corners slanted slightly upwards. His lips were full and curling with the lower jaw a trifle undershot and this gave him a strong obstinate self-sufficient look. His nose curved boldly, and he had such thick, inky black shining hair, and the whites of his eyes and his teeth were so white, he gave one an impression of flashing opposites.*

Who's this? he wondered, for he knew it had to be someone from her life. That was the way she wrote. But it didn't look like Lawrence, Jeffers, or Tony. Myron didn't have to read much farther before he got an answer. It was in a conversation between Gendron and his male traveling companion, Ascolar.

> *"She's quite remarkable," Gendron said. "She's not at all the way I thought she'd be. She makes a difference when she comes into a room."*
>
> *"How do you mean?"*
>
> *"She's upsetting. It's as though she makes the earth tremble a little and lets something up out of it. Why's that do you think?"*
>
> *"I think she's a conductor," said Ascolar.*
>
> *"A conductor of what?" asked Gendron frowning and looking ruffled.*
>
> *"Life," said Ascolar.*

Myron remembered that first night in the Santa Teresa house when Cady had remarked about the force of Mabel's personality.

Cady had called her a witch and pulled open the door to catch her. Myron had told Mabel about this later and she'd laughed. Am I Gendron? he wondered. If I am, then she's beaten me to the punch. She was writing about me before I ever thought of writing about her.

> *Gendron stood leaning against the statue and smoking a cigarette. The sun shone on his black, bare head. He stood out as in a painting when the artist sketches with a light, thin wash and concentrates upon a single figure. He seemed so complete he made the stone look vague, the river dim. He was almost too much there, too much air between him and other things. He was brought too far forward for a balanced whole.*

This was a new pleasure for Myron, having his portrait painted. Then it occurred to him that he might be falling into a trap laid by his vanity. Perhaps he was just a model, an actor, an interesting disguise for one of her real idols.

> *Gaza lay on her bed with one of Gendron's books. Until now she had not read anything by him. Why? She had heard of his books, read reviews of them, had them in her library. Now she plunged into an account of his early life, a story of family life in an environment unfamiliar to her. It had a solidity that made real life seem unreal, a vigor and power and passion that shamed her when she contrasted it with her own writing and the thin sophistication of her paradoxes.*

Singermann, he thought. She read it the summer of 1933. It was *Singermann*, she said, that made her decide she had to know him.

> *Life is not the way you have seen it, Gendron seemed to be saying. It is not oddity, or fever, or tension of nerves that make the truest picture. Life is organic, it has a cellular structure composed of endless units.*

The true story of life has the beauty and pathos of the failure or the success of these cells in their effort to grow and to divide. It has deep, steady, onward movement; infinite change but persistent, forward continuity. You've only seen the change. You've missed the wholeness. Your vision is broken and marred.

Myron stopped reading again. Is that what I say? It was amazing. In a declaration of discovery she was writing literary criticism. He remembered all the times when she had questioned him about his beliefs. He finally had to say he didn't know what he believed but that he would not settle for her simplistic sociological and metaphysical explanations. So he'd gotten to her. She'd been listening after all. Myron moved to the next chapter.

The evening grew late and finally they got up to leave each other for the night. They walked through the hall and up the stairs and her long sleeve caught on the newel post at the top and pulled her backward, "Oh, my dear," he exclaimed and bent to help her. It seemed to him this woman was very dear. But in the darkness just before they reached her door, something overcame him, and she, feeling the cessation, began to harden towards him. It was a relief to them both when she found the handle of her door, opened it and switched on the light from inside. They said goodnight like strangers.

Something like this had happened at Marie Garland's after that very first dinner. Mabel had asked him to walk with her to her room. Her sleeve caught on something, and he released it for her, then froze at her proximity. He felt her sexual energy. Then he thought he was mistaken, that he was over-reading the situation just as he had a few nights before with Marie Garland. Obviously his first instinct had been correct. But he knew what had stopped him. What had stopped her? Syphilis? Whatever it was, it was obvious Mabel had done more than just focus on him for her own purposes. Some time during that first summer she'd fallen in love with him. And Myron remembered again the scene in her bedroom when she had stood over him. He smiled. But his good feeling dissipated when Gaza got on the subject of homosexuality.

> *Was this the dear love of comrades that passes the love of women? She remembered a talk she had with a friend, and how they pondered homosexuality. Either it had increased or was more overt. Was it a sign of the weakening of the race? Was the race tired and unable to develop from the undifferentiated sexuality of infancy? Were men losing their essential form and dying out? Was homosexuality really death?*

Here was Mabel's prejudice, and Myron found as he read on that she'd made it the heart of her novel, whose plot centered around her "curing" Gendron. That was where the book failed. In the end the author had to kill him so her heroine would never have to test his sexuality. To do this she turned Taos Mountain (for the landscape described was no longer Hungary but New Mexico) into an active volcano that spewed out a single rock that managed to hit poor Gendron right between his eyes. Prior to this no mention had been made of volcanic activity and, as far as Myron knew, there were no active volcanoes in the Balkans or New Mexico. So here was something to talk to her about. The heroine of the novel cannot be allowed to control its plot. All of the fortuitous, melodramatic crap had to come out. She'd probably faced the same problem in *Lorenzo in Taos*. But reality had controlled that book. Mabel had to accept Lawrence's rejection. Indeed, given her disease, she had probably welcomed it at some level. Now, writing fiction, she thought she could forget reality.

But Myron knew that fiction is where you deal with reality. Reality must control *Water of Life*. Why couldn't her promiscuity with the Tony-like Hungarian nobleman lead to venereal disease as in fact it had with Tony? And why couldn't she share this knowledge with Gendron, who would then become her friend and, in the end, perhaps her nurse? But how could he tell her this? No one was supposed to know about her disease. Were they good enough friends? Perhaps he could write a letter hitting the novel's weak spots and, in showing her how to repair them, lead her to the decision to tell the truth about her life and the horrible thing that had invaded it. He remembered something Bob Davis once said. Tell an author to do something and more often than not he'll reject your advice. Writers want to be original. If you think of it, they won't use it. But if you say that something's weak or boring or isn't working, without saying what has to be done, if they're worth their salt, they'll think of the very thing you want done or something even better.

Then Myron realized that he wasn't going to tell her anything. Her novel about him had given him permission—no, challenged him—to write a novel about her. Why not? Dueling novelists! Sounds Russian. Pushkin and Turgenev. But where was Tony? There was no character like Tony in her book except possibly the Hungarian Count. And how would he get his own character, the truly caring homosexual friend, into it? By becoming the narrator himself. But he would need a disguise, and Myron thought of someone he'd met two years before. Cady was taking him to the village of Los Alamos to see the prep school there. But first they stopped at the teahouse by the bridge. A woman named Edith Warner ran it. Like Mabel she'd come to New Mexico from back east. She sat down with them and at some point Myron asked her if, after living among the San Ildefonso Indians for so long, she had learned Tiwa. No, she'd said thoughtfully. Learning their language would be too much of an intrusion. Myron had loved the answer. Here was someone who trod the earth as lightly as possible. In every way she was Mabel's opposite. Yet the two women were looking for the same thing.

The problem now, however, was saying something about *Water of Life*. He got out a sheet of paper and loaded the Underwood.

July, 39

Dear Mabel:

Here are some remarks concerning your novel.

First, homosexuality is not "death." It's the same as any other kind of sexuality except that which produces a child. Most sexuality is sterile. After all, what is your good friend Margaret Sanger telling us? You yourself say as much in the scenes between Gaza and the nobleman in Budapest. I say this because I think you have an intellectual agenda for your story that doesn't fit the characters you have created.

Here was the place to talk about character. But he would keep it impersonal.

Gendron is a nice character. I like him very much.

He stopped. Someone's written a novel about you. Is that all you're going to say about your character? He went on.

I think the ending twists him out of his natural self into something else for the sake of symbolism. Given Gendron as he is, I don't think he could possibly act as does in the end.

Gendron's is climbing the exploding mountain in order to get to Gaza, who is climbing the same mountain from her side to get to him. They are proving their love by risking their lives in an energetic romantic gesture. The question was why would Gendron, even if he loved Gaza, start acting like her?

Gaza, to me, is a tragic character. I think she was made to search endlessly and never find. In killing off Gendron, you make that point very well. But I can't see how, having described Gendron as you have, Gaza could have found what she sought in him. The irony is in her possession of his dead body.

Over my dead body, Myron thought. Now for the lecture.

I don't believe homosexuals can be changed into anything else without losing their integrity, their pattern and wholeness. You yourself once said this. There are all kinds of love in this world and one man's love is another's aversion. I do not think that love has anything to do with possession; quite the contrary, possession kills love.

There, that says it all. But he went on.

Where I disagree with you most is in the definition of love. I believe giving up is loving; unselfishness is loving. As for the future of the race, I'm sure that will take care of itself in one way or another. Homosexuality is not death. It's simply another form of life. It's always existed and will continue to exist.

Now he found he was getting angry with her.

It seems to me that Gaza, having experienced unsatisfying unions with many men, should have been content to leave Gendron as he was, instead of trying to make him over. I am not going into any defense of homosexuals, but (and perhaps my experience is too limited) I find them good, generous men, sensitive and gifted. I see no reason why they should be distorted into lovers of women so that the race may continue. Women can always find the proper men for this biological exercise.

There, he thought, that ought to do it. But it didn't. He wasn't done. He was, as they say, giving her a piece of his mind.

Why are some people so concerned with "life"? We see it all around us and a lot of it is not very nice. For myself I would prefer to see two Gendrons to every man who recreates. I would leave Gendron free and unattached; and if Gaza thought about it twice, I think she would, too. But being a woman with inflated ideas about life's waters, she wants to capture the poor nice man, put herself in a cage with him and say, "Now, Gendron breed with me, and we'll live, we'll carry on." Carry on what? More wars?

Too harsh. No one wants their sexuality rejected, even a diseased sexuality.

Gaza has life and warmth and the feel of flesh and earth, but I find no tolerance in her. She despises homosexuals. She even despises the nobleman who gives her sexual pleasure. She wants the unattainable. She wants to possess it.

Enough! Let it go. You'll never send it anyway.

Obviously your novel has stimulated me; thanks for letting me read it.

Myron

The next day he called Cady. It was the first time they'd spoken since Myron made the phone call that spared all their lives.

"Hello," Myron said. "It's me."

"Hi Mike," said Cady. "What can I do for you?"

"I'd like to see you. I want to talk to you about something. And I want to show you something."

"You're not going to hit me?"

"No," said Myron and laughed. "I'm sorry I did that."

"Maybe I had it coming." There was a pause. "How about two this afternoon?"

"Good," said Myron. "See you then."

So he drove down and Cady showed him around the place and what he'd done. It was really remarkable, a true adobe compound. And the lyric of a recent popular song ran through Myron's mind, something about a gay ranchero, a caballero. Then they were inside Cady's studio. Myron took Mabel's manuscript from his briefcase, told Cady what it was, and asked him to read some of the pages.

"You always make me read something of Mabel's."

"It's about you," said Myron. "But if you don't want to," and he made a motion as if to take it back.

"No, no," said Cady. "I'll read it.

"It's not much. Just twenty pages."

While Cady read Myron walked around the studio looking

at his latest work. Last October, right before he left for New York, Myron had gone to an exhibit of Cady's and some other New Mexican artists in the state museum. Cady's work had stood out. For one thing, he was the only watercolorist. But what was most impressive was that he wasn't repeating himself. He had moved away from the calligraphic style. His lines now touched, overlapped, and covered the whole paper like topographical caresses. And he had developed a color sense deeper and darker than in his earlier work. Maybe it was the new subject matter: moradas, Penitentes, pueblos. There were more human things in his landscapes. Then Myron was watching Cady read. Where is the anger I felt last year? Just being with him seems to calm me. And Myron wondered if he should tell Cady about how he had waited for them with a gun, and how close they all had come to being dead.

"I'm Ascolar, right?" asked Cady, looking up.

"Yeah. What do you think?"

"I told you she was obsessed with you."

"You were right."

"You know I was so jealous of her. I thought you and she were lovers."

"What?" Myron was shocked. "When did you think that?"

"That first year. Maybe the second, too."

"What gave you that idea?"

"You. You warned me. You put the idea in my head about loving women. And she so obviously was in love with you."

"I'm thunderstruck," said Myron. "I never felt anything like that for her." But even as he said it, Myron sensed that it wasn't quite true, that there was something unresolved in his relationship with Mabel. "She's so much older than me."

"Well, I came to know that. But at first I didn't."

"Does that affect anything now?" Though there were no signs of Cliff in the studio, he knew Cady was still seeing him.

"No."

"I didn't think it would."

There was a long, uncomfortable pause. Then Cady turned to the manuscript.

"I love what she says about me," and he began reading aloud.

Ascolar was used to him and understood Gendron's withdrawals and his need to collect himself, for the reason that Ascolar's own mode was the opposite of this, and he came to himself when he went out to people and to objects, to his canvases as well as his collections of odd, freakish, and beautiful earthforms. Since he was a boy he had collected butterflies, bird eggs, all the curious artifacts of primitive life like flint arrowheads, bone implements, then stamps, and later, rare Japanese prints.

"She's got you," said Myron.

"It's terrific," Cady said and went on:

It was the same with his great accumulation of clothes. For different moods and varying atmospheric changes he had an enormous number of shirts, ties, handkerchiefs, and suits. He never seemed to wear the same things twice, so careful he was to rotate them to develop variety in combination and effect.

"She got you again," Myron said. "Read on," he ordered. "Read the part where she starts comparing us."

Cady put the manuscript down on his drafting table and began turning pages. When he found what Myron was referring to he began again.

To Gendron objects had no importance. He owned little and collected nothing. Ascolar said of him that all he possessed was his typewriter and the manuscript he was working on. His clothes were few and looked well upon him, and he liked his body and spent a good deal of time each day on the care of it.

"That's very nice," Cady said, looking up.

"But go on."

Cady looked down again.

Gendron did not go out to things; they came to him, and

in his consciousness he possessed them even more concretely than Ascolar owned his dear belongings, for Gendron drew into himself the idea of things, the live essence and meaning of forms. With no feeling of possessiveness, Gendron possessed all he came in contact with, and carried with him the impression of everything he passed.

Cady looked up. "This confirms everything I thought about her and the way she felt about you and me." He looked down again and read silently. "It's terrific writing." He looked up. "Is the rest this good?"

"No," answered Myron. "The rest is dreadful. You've read the only good part."

"Twenty pages out of . . . four hundred? What happens to me?"

"You disappear," and Myron proceeded to tell Cady the rest of the novel.

"You're killed?" Cady asked.

"Yes. By a volcano. It takes a whole volcano to kill me."

"You're tough, Mike."

"Yeah."

"So what do you want me to say about it?"

"She's announcing to the world that we are homosexuals."

"I think the world's figured that out by now. At least about me."

"But to put it on paper."

"Have you spoken to her about it?"

"No. That would be an admission that I recognize us."

Cady looked puzzled. "I don't see anything very bad in it, and if it's as lousy as you say it is, it'll never be published. It's just more of the Truth game. So why are you worried?"

"Because I'm writing a novel about her."

"You are?" and Cady broke into a big smile. "Is she going to fall in love with you and get hit in the head with a rock?"

"Not a bad idea." Myron smiled, then turned serious. "I've found out something about her, Cady." He paused again. "It's something nobody knows, something beautiful and terrible." He paused yet again. "It's something that makes her into a great human being."

"What?"

"I can't tell you." Once, he thought, but not now. "Not yet anyway."

"Then when?"

"When I get a good draft. I'll need a reader."

"Okay."

There was a silence. Then Cady spoke.

"Remember telling me once that after it was over between us you still wanted to be my friend?"

"Yeah. It was when I got back from Carmel."

"If you still want to do that, I'd like it."

"I'll tell you what. The last time I was here, I was going to drive you down to Lupe's for something to eat. How about we go there now?" Myron realized once again he was glad just to be with Cady. He wanted to reach out and touch him. There was still that. But there'd be no more of that, not if they were going to be friends. "Better still," Myron said, "how about driving over to the teahouse at the Otowi Bridge for some tea and muffins?"

"Sure," said Cady with a big Martian smile and got his straw hat from the rack by the door. "Let's go."

Myron worked more slowly this time. There was no movie pressure. Rosalind was trying to hawk *Anne Minton's Life* in Hollywood and there was no sign of MGM putting *May Flavin* into production. As for this book, Myron swore Farrar & Rinehart to secrecy about its subject. Not that he wouldn't show it to Mabel before he sent the final draft off. He felt honor bound to do that. But he wanted her to read it when it was as good as he could make it. After all, he was doing her portrait and, if it wasn't going to be flattering in the usual sense, it had to be beautiful in its own way. Myron began work in mid-September, just a little over a year after Una shot herself. If it wasn't for that cruel event, he thought, Hal never would have gotten angry enough to blurt out the truth. Myron then wondered about the letter he'd written Mabel about

Water of Life. He'd surprised himself and sent it. But they hadn't yet talked about it or her novel, which he had returned to her. Just as well, he thought. They'll have plenty to talk about after she sees this. But he wouldn't let himself think about that confrontation. It was too distracting. So he had a hard time going over there. Not only did he not want to talk to her about her novel, but he also wanted to talk about his. He wanted to ask her about what it was like to be sick in the way she was. So he was always on his guard when he was up there, always watching what he was saying.

"Myron, I've changed my mind about the Placita house," she announced one evening when they were alone. "I've decided to sell it to you."

Myron nodded. They were in the Rainbow Room.

"Is that all the reaction I'm going to get?"

"Well, I'm not sure you won't change your mind again."

"I won't."

"May I ask what made you change it this time?"

"I talked it over with Tony. I think I was afraid to sell it to you before because of what happened with Lawrence. Tony never forgave me for letting the Lawrences have the ranch even though it was mine to give. I'd bought it for John but John never liked living up there." She paused. "Tony was angry because I hadn't consulted him. This time I did."

"And he said it was all right?" Myron wanted to tell her she was full of beans, that he remembered that night vividly when he'd asked her to sell him the house. Tony wasn't the reason she'd refused him. He wanted to ask her if she had changed her mind about his being wrong for Taos. That was 1936. Was she in love with him then? And if she was, had she given up on him? And if she had, why two years later, did she make him the hero of her novel? There were lots of questions. But he wasn't going to ask them, not yet anyway.

"He said it was fine. He said you have the money to fix it up. He likes the idea of it being modernized. He trusts you. I don't think he ever trusted Lawrence."

"Do you want me?"

"Yes. I was wrong when I said those things to you." She paused thoughtfully. "I've always wanted this place to be for artists, even those who deny its significance."

"Do you think Lawrence recognized its significance?"

"Oh yes."

"Do you think Lawrence would've liked me?" Myron wondered at his question. He'd never thought about what Lawrence might have thought of him. It must be her writing about me that links us. I may be the last of her failed knights errant, the writers to do her bidding.

"Honestly?" She looked at him.

He nodded.

"No."

"Why?"

"I think he would have resented your success. He never made any money from his writings. Perhaps if he had lived and seen the money coming in as Frieda is seeing it, there would've been room for your success." There was a long pause and she looked at him. "But why are we talking about Lawrence? I've offered you the house you said you wanted. Do you want it?"

"I'm just trying to get my bearings," Myron said. "Tony okayed it, eh? What about the guy you have living there? What's his name?"

"Frank. What about him?"

"What are you going to tell him? If I buy it I want to get working on it right away. I'll put in plumbing and a real kitchen. It means he'll have to get out as quickly as possible."

"He's living there rent free," she said. "He's fixed it up enough to keep the weather out but he has no claim on the place. And I can let him stay in the studio here. That needs fixing up too."

"I thought Brett was in there."

"She's downstairs. But I'm sure she'd love having Frank around. He's very handsome."

There was silence.

"You're still interested, aren't you? We keep getting off the subject. If you're not interested, I'll put it on the market. I'm sure it would go right away."

"I'm still interested." But that wasn't true. He was having his doubts. Did he want to live here? "What would I actually be buying?"

"C'mon," she said and stood. He followed her through the large entry room where Hildegarde had lain unconscious at the bottom of the steps, then a short way down the hall that led to her office. There were papers on the desk. "Read," she said and handed them to him.

Myron was disappointed. Somehow he'd pictured an old Spanish land grant, quill scratches on parchment with the seal of the Viceroy of Mexico or Ferdinand and Isabella. What she handed him was the Taos County Assessor's paper describing the property. The lot with the house on it was 1.135 acres. The other lot that was part of the parcel was .786 acres, which added up to just a little under 2 acres. The house itself was described as a three-room unimproved adobe that had been built in the late 1800s. With the garage its appraised value was a little over two thousand dollars, its assessed value half that. The paper said the north edge of the property bordered on pueblo land, the east edge on Edward and Miriam Bright's small apple orchard and the Catholic Mission that served the pueblo, the south edge on Highway 3, and the west edge on land owned by the Mormon Church. It was more land than Myron expected and though the house had only three rooms, they were large and, with the garage, came to over fourteen hundred square feet.

"There it is," said Mabel.

"How much?" asked Myron.

"I'm asking twenty-five hundred."

"It's only appraised for two thousand."

"We'll split the difference, Myron. Twenty-two fifty."

"Hmmm."

It was only assessed for a thousand. There was a rule of thumb for property in Taos. A hundred dollars a room and a hundred an acre. At least that's what it was two years ago. So this property on the open market would probably bring no more than five or six hundred dollars, a thousand at the most. On the other hand if he paid her what she was asking, he would be square with her. He owed her for all those summers when she'd put him and Cady up for nothing and fed them. It was important to him that he be square with her. After all, he was writing a novel about her. Just like with the Butte miners, he'd owe her more than he could ever pay.

"Okay," he said and they shook hands. "But I want to shake Tony's hand, too. I want him to approve."

"He'll be home any minute now." She stood. "Let's have a drink."

He followed her out of the office, through the entry hall and back into the Rainbow Room where she poured whiskeys and soda. She handed him his and they sat opposite each other, she on her chaise, he on the couch. She was looking relaxed, youthful, the debutante entering old age.

"Heard anything from the Jefferses?" Myron asked.

"We exchange pleasantries and family news."

"Are you still so disappointed in them?"

"Yes," she said thoughtfully. "I had such high hopes for Robin."

He wanted to ask her if she had switched her hopes to him when she was writing *Water of Life*. But he wouldn't. And they were looking at each other. He knew they both wanted to say things. And she was looking so young. How did she do that? Was it the communion dress? She seemed almost virginal. Then he was remembering what he'd once told Cady about where her money came from. Niagara Light and Power. The miracle of turning water into money. And a new title for the novel came to him. He'd been calling it *Florence Gresham*, after her character. Naming a work after an overpowering main character was fine. Myron had done it in *Singermann*. And such a title had been good enough for Melville. But there was so much irony in the idea of Mabel as a virgin that the title of the Henry Adams essay announcing the age of power, "The Virgin and the Dynamo," came to Myron's mind. Why not stand it on its head? *The Dynamo and the Virgin*. And for a moment he was delighted. Then doubts began to creep in. It's too derivative, he thought, too limiting.

"Do you think there'll be a war?" he asked. The Nazis were pouring into Poland. England and France had declared war.

"No," she said. "Roosevelt's not that stupid."

"Cady thinks there'll be a war."

"You know, Myron," she turned to him and said, "Cady has not been the true friend to you that you think he is."

"Oh?" And he waited for what he knew would be an attack.

"When you're gone from here, he immediately takes up with

someone else." And she added pointedly. "He's been doing it for some time."

"Mabel, Cady and I broke up last summer." He was amazed that she didn't know. "We're friends now."

"So you have new affairs?"

"Yes."

"You people," she said and looked away.

"Why should we be any different from heterosexuals?" They were both a little drunk and angry and he wanted to tell her he knew her secret. But he also knew his anger would make it sound wrong. "Are you sure you want to sell me the house?"

"Tony's home," Mabel said.

Myron hadn't heard the front door. But there was Tony in the doorway.

"Myron's taking the house," she announced.

"Good," said Tony. Myron stood. After a moment's hesitation they shook hands, and the three of them spent the rest of the evening discussing what needed to be done to the place and who could do it. Of course Myron would use workers from the pueblo.

Ten

A few days later Myron walked over to the Placita house to meet Frank Waters. He knew Waters was not your ordinary handyman. For one thing, he had published two novels, though for Mabel that was not as important as some kind of mystic affinity she said they had, something about hexagrams and the I Ching. Myron knocked on the door, looked up at Taos Mountain, and counted the cottonwood trees growing along the stream bank. When the door opened, his heart jumped. He managed to say his name, and Frank Waters said his and they were shaking hands. Then Frank asked him to come in. Mabel had already told him that Myron was buying the house. Now he wanted to show Myron the work he'd done, the new doors and windows he'd put in. Myron didn't care. He was remembering what Hildegarde Donaldson had said about Robinson Jeffers. Will this man be fate's reward for my pain? Frank Waters was tall, straight-featured, as handsome as a movie star and, more than that, charming in that western aw-shucks, cowboy way. Now Myron was following the man outside to see the studio he'd made out of the old adobe garage. He'd rehung the garage doors so they'd close, replaced the broken windows, and put in a door for the side entry.

"Can I live out here while the house is being fixed up?" Waters asked. "It'll only be a couple of months. I'm trying to finish a novel, and moving would be real inconvenient. I'll be gone by the first of November."

"Of course," said Myron and realized he needn't have worried about dispossessing him. "Stay as long as you like."

"That's very kind of you, Mr. Brinig."

"Call me Mike."

So what had been perceived as a problem turned out a blessing, an extra bit of excitement the new house was bringing. But because they were both writing so well they didn't see much of each other until the October cold set in. It was then Myron offered Frank the couch in the front room of the Pink House.

"Why sleep in an unheated place?"

Frank agreed. It seemed he'd lived most of his life accepting these kinds of favors from people. Unfortunately, that also made Frank experienced in other ways. So when Myron came into the living room in the middle of the night and stood by the couch as Noel Sullivan had stood by Myron's bed five years before, both men unable to make up their minds, Frank had no trouble making up his. He sat up.

"Don't be mistaken about my being here," he warned. "I'm interested in women and if you persist, I'll move out." Then he added, "I don't want to do that, Mike. I like you, and the setup works for me."

Myron backed off. He hated that kind of thing, forcing yourself on people. He remembered again how he'd felt at Noel's. On the other hand, Frank was so beautiful, so smart, so honest and open, Myron thought he could love such a man, indeed, that he was in love. So the next night when he came home drunk and full of self-pity, he got angry with his guest and took all Frank's pipes and threw them into the fire. The place, he told himself, was beginning to stink. A little while later, when Frank came home and went looking for a pipe, Myron showed him the burned carcasses in the fireplace ashes and told him why he did it, told him that they smelled bad, as if he was being honest. Then he stood before the bigger man smirking like a little kid who'd just gotten even with an older brother.

"You shouldn't have done that," said Frank, and with a sudden upward motion of his right hand, hit Myron on the point of his jaw.

That's all Myron remembered until some time in the middle of the night, shivering with cold, he pulled himself off the floor and lurched into his bedroom. The next morning he went over to the Plaza, bought two new Dunhills at the pipe shop in the La Fonda lobby, and walked out to the Placita House. He guessed that Frank had spent the night on the cot in the studio. He knocked, heard the words "come in," and opened the door. Frank was at his makeshift desk, a door over two sawhorses.

"I want to apologize," Myron said.

"I accept your apology," said Frank.

"It was something we had to get out of the way," said Myron.

"I appreciate all you've done for me," said Frank. Liveright, Frank's original publisher, had gone bankrupt. Myron had read Frank's first novel, *The Wild Earth's Nobility*, then sent a letter to John Farrar recommending him. "I look up to you as a writer, Mike." He hung his head. "I'm sorry I punched you."

There was a moment of quiet, then Myron stepped forward. "Here," he said offering the two pipes in their wooden Dunhill boxes. "Maybe all I wanted to do was get you some new pipes."

They laughed.

From then on they were friends. In the three weeks before Frank left for a Hollywood scriptwriting job, they talked about everything under the sun, things like hard-rock mining, which Frank knew a great deal about, and the ins and outs of publishing, which Myron knew about. And they talked about literature and the books they loved and why they wrote. Frank said he was interested in people's relationships with the earth. Myron thought that sounded a lot like Mabel and had to ask himself if Mabel's vision would have been more palatable to him if she'd been a handsome young man. Then he realized his antagonism wasn't so much to her beliefs as to the way she used them. Frank's beliefs, if you could call them that, seemed to make him humble. In Myron's new novel he'd have to handle this part of Mabel more sympathetically, that is, put a little of Frank into her. For one thing, respect for the earth was the only way to gain respect for the spirochete, the once harmless bacterium that, in its effort to survive, changes into something horrible.

"I'm not sure it's possible for people to relate to each other without relating to the land first," Frank was saying.

"But I'm a Jew," said Myron. "For two thousand years we've had no land to relate to. Mabel says because of that I'm an unformed human being. Has she given you her novel to read?"

Frank shook his head no.

"It's called *Water of Life* and it's terrible. But I'm its hero, the one she tries and fails to make into a human being."

"Have you talked to her about it?" Frank asked.

"Not really. I sent her a letter. But I never acknowledged that the hero was me. I don't want to talk about it until I finish mine."

"Well, I've finished mine," Frank announced.

Myron skimmed it, liked what he read, and sent another letter to John Farrar. He didn't have to. They would've taken it anyway. But Frank thanked him. So they were friends. Not that Myron's libido would take no for an answer. But his sexual forays took the form of talking to Frank as if they were lovers until Frank, in another angry confrontation, told him in no uncertain terms to shut up. Myron did. But after Frank left for Hollywood and Myron moved into the house, he renewed this kind of teasing in his letters, writing words of endearment and double entendre that Frank never would have allowed face to face.

Nov. 5, '39

Dear Frank,

How are you, my dear, sweet fellow? Do you like your new quarters and are you comfortable and hard at work? To say I miss you is putting it mildly. Every departure is a kind of death accompanied by great agony. Nothing has been quite the same; your studio looks so forlorn, even the landscape has changed. Do you think I'm kidding, Pancho? Not at all. My friend, lover, husband, brother, my lord has departed. But he will return . . . or will I come after him, even if I have to slumber in a sleeping bag. Do they make them for two?

Or in the next letter:

Nov. 12, '39

Dear Frank,

You say you feel at home in LA. Fickle fellow! So soon? My skin and bone are thickly coated with the dust and mud of this country and now I am going native. Do come back and keep me company. We will grow old together and I will throw your pipes away. I like to be beaten up every once in a while, like the gin-ridden denizens of Lime house. Perhaps in some other life we were together in London's East end, and you came home every Saturday night and walloped me black and blue? Alas that we live now in a different world—and we are both intelligent artists—or are we? There's so much of the masochist in me.

But he didn't only flirt in his letters. Frank liked to hear news of the local goings-on. He said it made him homesick, something Myron didn't mind doing at all. On November 27, he wrote:

There was another one of those parties at Mabel's though this time she allowed a 'committee' to manage affairs. She loaned the use of her house; everyone else paid fifty cents for liquor. There was a phonograph to dance by; not bad at all; much better than the "orchestra" at your going-away affair. I didn't want to go, but Tinka prevailed. I got drunk, danced with all the gals, especially with Mabel, who was good and tight; Tony was reeling, stumbling over everyone and making a spectacle of himself. The house must have been a shambles the next day, not to speak of wounded shoulders and breasts. There's to be another dance in three weeks. How gay we are!

And there was news about Myron's new friend, Tinka Fechin.

Tinka has been a help to me the past few days with the curtains and furnishings. Some of Mabel's masterpieces did not fit and at least one drape was too gaudy. Tinka substituted monks cloth for the bedroom and the result is really the nicest room in the house. The others are coming along. If Tinka were somewhat less hysterical, somewhat less inclined to nervous, self-conscious giggling, she'd be man's perfect companion.

So Myron's letters were flirty and newsy until Frank did something unexpected for his birthday.

Dec. 22, '39

Dear Frank,

You did send me the soda mixer, did you not? It arrived but with no card and no name or return address. I was puzzled for a minute but remembered you had one in your room, so it must be you. So many thanks and kisses and love and salutations, all of the cheeriest sort, for remembering my birthday. I'm forty-three. Also I got an advanced copy of "Dust Within The Rock" from F&R. The book starts excellently, though I feel sorry for poor March: he's so sad somehow. Is he really you? I do hope you have a best-seller.

Dust within the Rock was the third installment of Frank's family saga centered around Pike's Peak. Myron liked the second book, *Below Grass Roots*, the best. It was about Frank's crazy grandfather who was so obsessed with looking for gold he destroyed his family. Myron called it a miner's *Moby Dick*. But he liked everything Frank wrote, everything he did. He still dreamed of a sexual relationship with the man. And he dreamed actively. Late at night he would do things to Frank that Frank could never have imagined. Yet it was a utilitarian kind of pornography. It allowed Myron to contain his desire and stay at home and keep on with his work. He hadn't worked like this since the twenties, those awful, lonely, great days in Manhattan furnished rooms.

So he wasn't prepared for what happened Christmas Eve. He and Tinka were on the couch in front of the fireplace he'd had built to replace his living room's burned-out kiva. They'd been doing this on and off for several days, just sitting and talking in front of a fire. The place was beautiful but now that it was done, they had little to talk about. Tinka was telling him for the third time about the Bolsheviks and how they had driven her and Nicolai out of their beloved Kazan. But this night turned out to be different. On this night she brought her face in front of his and pushed her lips down on his. "There," she said when she pulled back. "We get married, you and I. We are perfect for each other!"

Myron sat amazed. This was the exact scenario Spud had described. Then he jumped to his feet and said he was taking her home. But it was too late. In the car she was all over him, her tongue in his ear, her hands groping his crotch. Cut it out, will ya? he kept saying as he drove the half mile to her house. Cut it out! The worst was he couldn't believe she meant it. Feigned passion was even uglier than the misplaced kind. So Myron's letters to Frank took a very serious turn.

Jan. 3. '40

Dear Frank,

Tinka continues to be a problem. Yesterday in the post office I smelled out one of her letters, having opened a corner of the envelope I could see her handwriting and I hastily re-sealed it. But as I was about to drop it back into the mailbox, she appeared and stood in front of the mail slot, raising her arms and refusing to allow me to return it. There were several people in the P.O. and to argue would have meant a scene. So I turned and went out and tore the letter up, throwing the pieces into the street. This sort of thing goes on and on and I must just go on trying to ignore her as best as I can. I know she's mad but what can I do? Having her arrested would create more ruction than she's worth. She's one of those people born to create misery for herself and all those near her. Forgive this outburst. It's something I brought on myself.

But Myron knew he had to do something. His life was becoming impossible. He would go out for the mail and if she wasn't at the P.O., there she'd be, when he got home, sitting in his living room knitting an afghan as if she were part of the household. Or, if

Selina, his cook, wasn't there, she would be in his kitchen filling the house with the reek of boiling cabbage. So he took to locking his front door and she took to pounding on it. Then he gathered all the things she had helped him with, the curtains, bedspread, bed linen, and towels, and the next time she pounded, he opened the door and flung them in her face. Yet still she came. No matter what he did, no matter what he said. He even openly confessed to her that he preferred men to women. All she said was that she understood, and that that could be cured with psychiatric help and that they would be very happy. So he ended up screaming at her that she was the one who needed psychiatric help. And still she acted as if she belonged there, as if the banns had been announced and it was only a matter of time before the wedding.

In his desperation, Myron blamed Cady. Cady had refused to help with the decorating. They'd had the first argument of their new friendship over this. When Cady heard Myron had bought a house, he brought Myron the carving of San Isidro that he'd given him a few years earlier. Myron thanked him, said he would treasure it, and asked his friend to go shopping with him. Cady went, and a few days later went again. But the third time Myron asked, Cady let him have it. You've got to do these things yourself! You can't depend on other people doing things you don't like to do! Of course he was right. Myron was lazy about some things and always putting out feelers for aid. But aid is never given without strings. In Tinka's case, the strings turned out to be hawsers. What could he do? He'd brought it on himself. So, having lived in his house only two months, he decided he had to leave Taos, leave New Mexico. The timing was terrible. He loved the house and was writing well. But he called the same friend in New York he'd called last year. This time he got a sublet on East Forty-Fourth Street.

By then Frank had joined Mabel and Tony in New York. Myron had seen a lot of them the year before. This time he wanted to show Frank the sights. But after only a week Mabel put Tony on a train for home, then set out by car with Frank driving. Myron gave Frank the keys to the Placita house and stayed in New York for the rest of the winter and spring of 1940 working on the novel. When he returned in June, Frank was back in Hollywood, and once again he had to face Tinka alone. He tried to do as Spud had done, tough it out, barricade himself in, not answer the door when she pounded, and ignore her when she fell in step beside him on his way to the Plaza. He wanted to talk to Spud about her, ask his advice, at least have someone to commiserate with. Not that Myron had been sympathetic when Spud was the object of her affections. No, it had been a joke then. The trouble now was that Spud was so glad to be rid of her, so guilty for wishing her on someone else, so afraid she might change her mind and come back to him, he avoided Myron like the plague.

"I wonder if I might talk to you about your . . . wife." Whiskey and soda in hand, Myron had seated himself at the man's table. They were in La Fonda's bar.

"You mean Alexandra?" Nicolai Fechin was sipping tea from a glass.

Myron nodded.

"But she is no longer to be my wife. Not for seffen years."

"Oh, I understand that, but I wonder if when you see her, you might. . . . "

"See her? I do not see her. I have this lawyer here in Taos. He see her."

"Well, then it's possible you might be able to communicate with her in some way because . . . "

"But I do not want to communicate with her."

The little man tried to soften what he'd just said by smiling, but his high-cheekboned Tartar face was so thin it was like getting a skull to smile. Myron looked into the skull and saw stark, shining eyes, brilliant with fever. He'd heard that the artist was tubercular and felt bad for bothering him, but he was desperate, and insisted on telling the man all that was happening and how miserable Tinka was making him. After every sentence Myron expected Fechin to say enough, I don't want to talk about her. But he heard Myron out, and when he was done, the artist took a sip from his glass of tea, brought out a box of thin Russian cigarettes wrapped in brown paper, and offered him one. Myron put up his hand. He had given up smoking. Fechin took one for himself and lit it. The smoke smelled like fresh manure and inhaling it shook the man into a violent fit of coughing.

"Yes, that is Alexandra," he said, at last controlling the spasms. "You will not to beliff. . . . " Then he was coughing again.

Myron waited. He could believe anything.

"You will probably not to beliff what a beauty she was. I have put her in paintinks. Haff you seen?"

Myron nodded. She was beautiful once. So what!

"Only after we come to Taos she begin to act stranch. Very stranch. Maybe the altitude, the mountains, the Indians make the women act stranch. Who knows? She have obsession with this man, Spud Johnson. You know him? He pose for paintink. I not blame him."

Myron nodded.

"She give him never a minute of peace. Make scene everywhere we go. So?" He lifted his arms, his wrists seemingly handcuffed to emptiness. Myron had never seen a gesture like it. "I can do notink! No-tink! I say to her, 'Go to psychiatrist.' She will not. All she do is luff."

"Loaf?"

"Luff!" the artist repeated and Myron understood.

"She follow this man everywhere. I say, Alexandra, you make fool off yourself. People laff! She tell me to go away, get out. She say she can no more stant me. My own house! My beautiful house I builted with my own hants! She crazy! She make me crazy. I cannot more stant staying here . . . this Taos I so much luff."

Myron nodded again. After all, he'd spent some time in Fechin's house. There were carved doorframes, lintels, banisters, steps, paneling and mantels in the shapes of florets, sunbursts, birds, leaves, gargoyles, flowers. It was extraordinary, a Russian woodcarver's dream.

"But I must to leaf, not only because other man, but my health. I go to lower altitude. I very happy in California except my health. I sick now, maybe not lonk to liff. I want my paintinks. I never give her my paintinks! Divorce papers say that. But I cannot get them. My precious paintinks. I want to leaf to my daughter."

"Your daughter?" That's right. They had a daughter. Perhaps she could speak to her mother.

"And you know something else," said Fechin, "she jealous of her own daughter, so our chilt have to leaf, too. Only that is not so bad because Eya take care of me in Los Angeles. It is for her I want my paintinks back. I go to court. I have lawyers. Lawyers! They are no goot! So. . . . " His eyes were shining. "You want me to communicate for you when I cannot for myself?" His right hand made a quick, circular movement at his right temple. "She need psychiatrist."

"I don't mean any harm to her," Myron said after he'd nodded agreement.

"You cannot do more harm to Alexandra than she do to herself." There was a long pause. The matter seemed settled. "You say you are writer? I know writers in Los Angeles. Thomas Mann. You know Thomas Mann?"

"No. I wish I did."

"Thomas Mann say, poor Alexandra, she lookink at herself in cracked mirror."

Myron liked the image. There was something fractured about Tinka's doggedly determined courting. There was even something fractured about her face, the way she missed her mouth with her lipstick, her eyebrows with her pencil. She needs glasses.

"Aldush Huxley. You know Aldush Huxley?"

Myron shook his head no, though he'd met Huxley once at Frieda's.

"Very deep writer."

He waited to hear what Huxley had to say about Tinka. She seemed to have been a subject for several great minds. Am I missing something? he wondered.

"Very fine peoples I meet in California." There was another long pause. "If you are a writer, you must to understant Alexandra." He sat back. "But for myself, I cannot to help you." He shook his head. "Poor Tinka."

"What am I going to do?" Myron asked.

Fechin shrugged and the interview seemed over.

But Myron didn't want it to be over. "Most women, once a man rejects them, have too much pride to persist in this way," he said.

Again a near smile in a face so tightly drawn the slightest

twitch had to cause it pain. He's suffered, Myron thought. Once he loved her. You could see it in his paintings. In a way he still did. Like his disease she was devouring him.

"Prite?" the artist asked sharply. "You say prite? You think she fall in luff with you? No! She luff herself. Only herself. Like she liff in a tower. She think she princess. She rule. You obey. You understant? She liff in a tower. Like she put wall around herself. Listen only to herself. Talk only to herself. Like Thomas Mann say, Alexandra look in cracked mirror. The mirror answer yes! Every crack. Always yes! The mirror never say no! That is how she see herself."

Ah, thought Myron and nodded at this explanation. Then he remembered something Tinka had said about making a shrine to Lawrence's ashes and at last feeling she knew him. She needs dead men to love. Aren't Spud and I dead to women? Tinka is a necrophile. We have what she wants in a lover. The dead are mirrors. She sees herself in us. Myron looked at the man and saw that even now he was suffering for her. Poor Nicolai. He couldn't do this for her. As sick as he is, he's too alive. I should leave him alone. I should never have bothered him.

"I admire your work so much," said Myron, trying in some way to thank Fechin for hearing him out and give the man some comfort. "Tinka's proud of your paintings, you know. She'd never sell them. I'm sure they'll be safe with her."

"No!" said Fechin and slammed his fist down on the table in real anger. "I give her house! I give her studio! Paintinks are mine!"

Myron raised his hands. He hadn't meant to defend Tinka. That wasn't why he was there. So he brought the conversation back to himself.

"What am I going to do?"

The question seemed to calm the man. "Ignore," he advised. "Just ignore. Do your work. In a while she fint other man."

"In a while?" Myron asked.

The painter nodded. They sat for a moment.

"Or you could leff."

Myron shook his head no. He'd already tried that. But his stay in New York, which had been almost four months, hadn't been long enough. And he didn't want to go away again. He'd lived in his house only a few months. He was working well, rewriting the new novel into something extraordinary.

"Well then, my frient," Fechin said. "What else? You can marry with her," and his eyes blazed up, "then kill her."

Myron looked into the skull's sockets. Was he serious? Does he want to use me? Does he want to get some kind of revenge and perhaps find an easy way of getting his paintings back?

"Only I think she come back," the artist went on as if Myron's silence meant he was considering the suggestion, "what is the word, haunt? Yes, I think she come back and haunt you."

Fechin obviously meant to be funny so Myron laughed, a cracked laugh for a cracked mirror. Yet wasn't that what she was doing now, haunting him? Underneath the joke was real truth. Fechin had given him a glimpse of how a marriage to such a woman might end. Was there any difference between Una Jeffers's defense of her marriage and Tinka's obsession? Women are crazy, he thought. And he remembered that Frieda had made the same suggestion. Marry her, she said. So had Brett. Only Mabel had warned him. She's always been crazy, she said. And instead of Una, Myron saw Tinka in the tub, a bullet hole in her naked chest. Only the little automatic was in his hand. We are perfect for each other, you and I.

"Thanks for listening," he said and stood. They shook hands and he left the artist with his glass of tea, his thin Russian cigarettes, his terrible cough.

"Myron!"

Myron had gone to bed around four. Now he was being awakened from a deep, dreamless sleep. Someone was at the door. For a moment he thought it was Cady, then Tinka.

"Who is it?" he yelled.

"Frank!"

"Gimme a minute, Frank!" Myron threw on some dungarees, tucked in the polo shirt he'd been sleeping in, and slipped his feet into huaraches. This was the moment he'd been waiting for. He opened the door. There Frank stood, two typing paper boxes in his hands. It was still called *Florence Gresham.*

"I've read it," said Frank once he was inside.

"And? What did you think?" Myron turned on the electric burner under the saucepan. Then he dumped two heaping spoonfuls of coffee grounds directly into the water.

"I was bowled over by it, Myron. I was surprised, shocked."

Myron waited.

"I don't mean that in a bad way. I was totally taken in. And the best thing is it was absolutely right. It was inevitable."

"Do you think the flashbacks are too long?"

"No. Not at all. They're wonderful. We get an old woman here in New Mexico remembering when she was a young, beautiful girl back east and how it was when she first comes to Taos. I know a lot of that is from Mabel's memoirs but it feels so different when you tell it like that. The characters come to life. They're more than Mabel or Tony, Lawrence or Jeffers. And little by little you get what's going on in the present until at the end you find out the woman's secret. She's not old. She's sick. She wouldn't give the earth its due so the earth created something to devour her. The romance of the earth that Florence Gresham demands, you make the cause of her tragedy." Frank took a breath and Myron thought he was done. But he went on. "It cracks the foundation of her beliefs. She was just playing around before. Now she really finds life. It's a monstrous paradox. You make her grow up."

Myron had never seen Frank so excited. He wanted to say enough, you're turning my head. But why stop a person who's raving about you? The coffee was beginning to boil, the room filling with its rich smell. Myron turned it off.

"Is that really what happens with syphilis?" Frank asked.

"Yes. It grows out of a harmless bacterium that, for some reason, changes its shape to a spiral. In the microscopic world it lives in, it finds the spiral a much more effective way to succeed. Scientists call it mutation."

Frank shook his head, then went on with his praise.

"And Dora, Florence's childhood friend, who comes out to New Mexico to escape Florence Gresham's world, and is appalled when Florence shows up, she's the lady who runs the teahouse at the Otowi Bridge. They're perfect foils for each other." Frank was nodding vigorously. "I didn't know you could do a character like that, Mike. I'm envious. I thought that was my kind of character."

"You mean a mystic?" Myron asked.

"Yes. I know you're from Butte but I always think of you as a hard-headed New Yorker." Frank nodded at his own observation, then returned to the manuscript. "And when the disease comes out of remission and Florence moves in with Dora to await that inevitable day when it will finally consume her, it's heart wrenching." He paused again and nodded. "And at the end having Florence begin to slip into madness . . . " He seemed at a loss for words. "And ending the novel with Dora's romantic memory of Florence's beauty when they were young debutantes is wonderful." Frank was nodding vigorously and smiling. "By then you could have made Florence a constellation and I would've believed it."

"So you liked it?" asked Myron.

"Liked it? Hell, yeah, I liked it!" Frank burst out laughing. "I loved it!"

It was Myron's turn to laugh. Then he got two mugs out of the cupboard above the stove, poured the steaming coffee through a strainer, and took the mugs to the table. He put one in front of Frank, kept one for himself, and got out the sugar bowl and a spoon. Then he sat down and pushed the bowl at Frank, who spooned some sugar into his cup. Myron took his black.

"You know Myron, I have to confess I'm not a big fan of your recent books."

"Oh?"

"I loved *Singermann*. It was exotic, about these crazy people called Jews in a crazy place like Butte. I read it when I was working as a lineman in Death Valley, of all places. And I loved *Wide Open Town*. But I couldn't finish *May Flavin*. It promised so much and . . . "

His voice trailed off.

"I regret that book," Myron admitted after a sip. "I rushed it because my agent sold it to the movies for a lot of money. As a writer, that was the worst thing I ever did." He looked up. "Once I had the money I couldn't finish it."

"Well," Frank said, "you redeemed yourself. This book starts in a deceptively usual way, then builds to a marvelous, awful ending."

Myron nodded. Then he asked the question he'd wanted to ask from the beginning. "What do you think Mabel will think of it?"

"You know," said Frank, shaking his head, "I never thought to ask that while I was reading it. Oh, I recognized her right away. But just as quickly I forgot it was her. I was reading about Florence Gresham." Frank looked up and paused. "In fact, I didn't think of it until I was walking over here."

"And?"

"I don't think she'll mind it at all. It's so obviously fiction it couldn't be mistaken for her."

Frank looked up as if something had just occurred to him.

"It's fiction," Myron assured him.

"Then I don't think you'll have to worry about Mabel. I think she'll love it. I give her that. She loves great art." He paused. "The person you might offend is Tony."

Myron nodded. It was a good point. Tony was illiterate and would hear about the novel secondhand. Myron had once asked Mabel if she'd ever read *Sons and Lovers* to Tony to show him what the ranch had been traded for. She'd looked at him as if he was crazy. Of course not, she said. He'd be bored to tears. Then would Tony be bored with *Florence Gresham*? Not if he heard it was about him. Ah Tony. Two winters ago they'd been in New York together and become friends. Mabel was starting her salon again and had given Myron the job of entertaining her husband while she held forth. So he and Tony would take the BMT out to Coney Island, eat Nathan's hotdogs, and race the iron horses around Steeplechase. Sometimes at night they would cab up to Harlem to the Savoy Ballroom to hear the Jimmy Lunceford band. Tony loved it, and the black women had loved him.

"I'd hate to offend Tony or anyone at the pueblo."

"Well, you could do what Lawrence did, move it down to Mexico."

"Maybe. But you know you may be wrong about the book not offending Mabel. She's not the woman she once was. When she was younger she would have been glad to have been written about. Now. . . . " He paused. "You know just the other day she asked me who Madam Egalitchy is."

"She asked me that, too."

"Did she tell you why?"

"I know why. I heard the remark. She'd asked her friend Max Eastman to invite some of the new intellectuals to her place: populists, Communists, people like that. They didn't like her at all. I thought it was funny, but the guy who said it was a jerk."

"In the old days she would've thought it was funny, too," said Myron.

"Maybe you're right," Frank said. "Maybe I'm being naive. She's still very political with lots of enemies who'd love to be able to dismiss her as a syphilitic old bitch. That would destroy any influence she has left. Maybe she won't like it."

"Let me give you another cup." Myron took both cups, poured the dregs into the sink, rinsed them, went to the stove, and turned it on. There was still plenty of coffee in the saucepan. He stood waiting for it to heat up. His mother used to call this findle coffee, though he never knew what a findle was. "How's your work going?" Myron asked as he waited.

"I've just begun a novel about the Pueblo Indian who poached a deer up by Blue Lake. Did you hear the story? He was caught by the forest service and punished by the pueblo."

"Yeah, I heard. You know every so often I do that, take something out of the newspapers and write about it. I did it with *Anne Minton* and my first novel, *Madonna without Child*.

"Haven't read them," Frank admitted. "I read your work about Butte. You were from the Rockies, too. I wanted to write out of my own experience, yet keep it fiction the way you do. Our work doesn't look similar but that's because we've had such different lives. I loved *Singermann*."

"You said that." Myron was thoughtful. "You know, just as I was beginning to write this book I had the same feeling I had before I began *The Sisters*, that I was a failure as a writer. I don't just mean *May Flavin*. I mean even my best books. Take *Singermann*. Somehow I didn't do justice to the material."

"What do you mean?"

"Well, I wasn't fair to my father and mother. I did them as they appeared to me as a boy breaking away."

"But that's what you were."

"No, I was more. It was all right for the boy in the novel to think like that, but not for the real author. I knew from my mother's stories about the old country what kind of life my father had led. He loved the countryside, loved to be in nature, and had to spend his life in a city whose sole purpose was nature's destruction. And my mother. She always called her marriage a marriage of convenience because it got her out of her stepmother's house. But even when I was a kid I knew there was more to it than that. There was something real between them. My mother loved nature, too, and that was his promise to her, that they'd live a life close to nature. She would talk about the old country. *Zeir shein*, she would say and get that faraway look in her eye. What she never forgave him for was taking her to live a life they both hated, a life in the very center of what was really a factory. Yet she also knew it wasn't his fault, that he couldn't help himself. After he was dead, she wept for him and the life they'd lost." Myron shrugged. "That's what I should have written."

He turned off the coffee, refilled the cups, and brought them to the table. They waited for the coffee to cool.

"Stop me if I'm getting too personal, Mike," said Frank at last, "but I often wonder why you haven't written about being a homosexual. I know there's the homosexual in *This Man Is My Brother*, but he treats himself as if he's got an incurable disease. He kills himself rather than face what he is."

"So?"

"Why not show a successful homosexual who accepts himself and who the world accepts, I mean someone like yourself? I think you could do a really revolutionary book about yourself."

"Well, you know," said Myron, feeling suddenly uncomfortable and challenged, "most of my readers know very little about me. And I'm not a homosexual in the true sense of the word. I'm bisexual. I make love to women as well as men." He looked at Frank for a reaction. There was none. "It's part of a writer's job to experience everything. It helps my work too. Whenever I'm in a rut and can't get going, I have an affair with someone of a different sex from the one I've been with." This was a lie but one he'd told many times. "It's like space travel. You change planets, change the air you breathe. It really shakes you up. You ought to try it."

"I don't think so," said Frank, pushing his coffee away, and Myron knew he had once again offended the man. "I have to get going." He touched the manuscript. "It's a fine book, my friend, a fine book. But you're right. It's going to take a lot of courage to publish it."

Myron nodded and sensed Frank was about to leave. "You know what's ironic?" he asked, groping for a subject to keep him there. "I owe you so much and I kicked you out of this house."

"Aw Myron, you don't owe me anything."

"But I feel bad."

"Don't." Frank looked around. "I never thought of this as my house. And you've done a beautiful job. It's not the same house anymore. It's your house."

"You know I travel a lot, Frank. I'm away months at a time. Any time you want to stay here, it's yours. It's good to have somebody in it when I'm not here." They'd gone through all this several times. Frank had already taken him up on it once. "Listen to me," Myron went on. "I sound like a man of property. When I used to stay at Mabel's, I don't know how many people offered me the same deal. People hate to leave their houses standing empty."

"That's true," said Frank. "I've had three offers this month. But I'm going with Mabel and Tony to a conference in Mexico City."

Myron felt a pang of jealousy. Was Frank replacing him in Mabel's heart?

Frank stood.

"I still feel bad about the house," Myron said.

"Don't. After all you've done for me with Farrar & Rinehart, Mike. You know Connie's doing a series about the rivers of America." Connie Skinner was Myron's former editor. They'd parted company after *The Flutter of an Eyelid*. "She wants me to do a book on the Colorado."

"That's great," said Myron and meant it. "Those books never go out of print. You'll be buying your own house soon."

"Not if this war hits." Frank pushed away from the table and stood.

Myron stood, too, and walked him to the door. They shook hands and Myron thanked him again. But when he closed the door he realized his mood had changed. Gone was Frank, whom he could have loved, and gone the elation brought by Frank's praise. In its place was doubt. Why did he ask me about writing about my sex life? Was he implying that if I couldn't write about myself, I shouldn't publish this? But no one would publish a book with a homosexual hero living a homosexual life. It was against the law. They'd sent Oscar Wilde to jail for it. For most people it was the same thing as making love to sheep. Sure he wanted to write such a book. He tried in *This Man Is My Brother* and *The Flutter of an Eyelid*. And full of doubt Myron found himself wanting for another opinion, someone who knew the truth. But Spud was in hiding, and Cady had gone back to Massachusetts to do war work for American Optical. So he called Hal and Bob down in Santa Fe. Last summer, after he made it up with Cady, he'd called them to apologize yet again. He didn't think they'd accept but he had to try. It turned out they felt as bad as he did about what happened.

Myron would spend the weekend. He'd mailed them the novel and a carbon. They were almost done when he got there.

"You've used something told to you in the strictest confidence," Hal complained.

"That's not true, Hal," Bob contradicted. "You told him in anger, not confidence. In fact, I'm not sure you didn't tell him just so he'd write about it. Don't be a hypocrite." Then Bob looked at Myron. "You took your sweet time."

"Still," said Hal, ignoring Bob's charge, "I don't want you to construe my reading your manuscript as condoning what you've done. You understand?"

"I understand," said Myron. "I'll let you finish."

Myron walked down the old Santa Fe Trail all the way to the plaza. He looked at the Indians setting out their silver things under the *portal* of the Palace of Governors, went into Solano's for huevos rancheros, and walked around the town until he noticed the Lensic marquee. *Watch on the Rhine*, with the ubiquitous Bette Davis, was the feature film. But when he got inside, the Kiddie Show was still going on. So he took a seat in the back with some of the parents. There was a Flash Gordon chapter with Buster Crabbe, then an infinity of cartoons. He watched the shadowy children screaming their fear and delight. Then the movie came on. It wasn't *Watch on the Rhine*, but the B half of the double feature and was called *A Date with the Falcon*. Myron perked up when he saw Michael Arlen's name in the credits. He'd met Arlen once at a Hollywood lunch and liked him. It turned out the movie was perfect for its audience, enough thrills popping out of the edge of the frame to keep the kids quiet, and enough of suave George Sanders to keep Myron and the mothers interested. So far he was enjoying himself a lot more than the last time he was here.

Then the main feature came on, and most of the kids took their moms home. A few adults straggled in, but it was a much smaller audience. Adapted from a play by Lillian Hellman, *Watch on the Rhine* was obviously a movie made to show the horror of what was going on in Europe and rouse the audience against the Nazis. Myron thought that for the next few years this would be the kind of thing they'd be making movies about. He remembered John Farrar's recent remark on the oblivion accorded novels released on the day the First World War began. It was his publisher's way of hurrying him. All Myron thought now was that they were calling it the First World War. Would anyone be interested in a novel about Mabel when the Second World War began? But it had begun. Europe was in flames. First Austria and Czechoslovakia, now Poland. A madman was running amok. Depressed, Myron got up before the movie was over and took the long, slow walk back up to Hal's house. They were waiting for him.

"What did you think?" he asked.

"I loved it," Bob blurted out.

Myron wasn't surprised. Not that Bob was an easy reader. But he so disliked Mabel that anything he thought put her in a bad light or gave her pain would be fine with him. Myron waited.

"I agree with Bob," Hal said at last. "It's the best writing you've done in a long time, Myron. Maybe the best you've ever done. By the end, Florence Gresham rises to the tragic heights of your union organizer in *Wide Open Town*." Hal paused, then added, "But your organizer wasn't the main character in that novel. Florence Gresham is in this one. I think this time you've written a real tragedy with a real tragic hero."

Myron felt suddenly faint. Coming from Hal, who was perhaps the most critical man he'd ever met, Hal who'd traveled with Lawrence, argued with Lawrence, loved and hated Lawrence—well, this was the kind of praise Myron had always wanted. He had to sit down.

"What's the matter?" asked Hal, who'd come to his side.

"The walk back up was harder than I thought."

"Get him some water."

Bob already had a glass poured.

"Thanks."

It wasn't water but gin and tonic and it was just what Myron wanted. Then, as he relaxed, he realized that he'd expected Hal—no, wanted Hal—to read him the riot act, to tell him he couldn't publish such a thing. He'd wanted Hal to relieve him of responsibility for his own work. I'm not a young man anymore, he thought. Once I had the courage to take on the monsters of my youth; my family and the Anaconda Copper Company. Have I lost that courage?

"Thank you," Myron finally said. Then he did something really out of character. He began to cry. "Thank you," he repeated.

"So the writing machine's human after all," said Bob.

"Shut up!" snapped Hal and knelt beside Myron. "What is it?" he asked.

"I think I wanted you guys to stop me, to tell me it was awful. I think I'm losing my nerve. She's a powerful woman." He paused. "And she's helped me in so many ways. I've just bought a house from her. I'll probably live here the rest of my life. We're neighbors and friends."

"Then don't publish it," said Bob with sudden coolness. "But not for any of those reasons. Your novel makes her into something I refuse to believe she is, something I don't want her to be."

"What's that?" asked Myron.

"A great woman."

"I wonder if she'll see that?" asked Hal.

"Of course, she will," said Bob and lifted the pile of pages resting on the coffee table to his lap, thumbed through them, found the one he wanted and, to prove his point, began to read.

She sat there listening to his clinical description of what was going on in her body. He was talking about bacteria called spirochetes for their long spiral shapes, and how these shapes were specifically designed by nature to wrap themselves around her long skeletal cells and devour her bones. And she lost her bearings. The categories she'd made the anchors of her life, the sub-headings of race, white, red, yellow, black, shattered completely and she was left with a blurred palette, herself. She was not in the vanguard. She was just another atom in a vast soup of humanity. Then the man was showing her pictures of what was attacking her.

"Myron, that's wonderful writing," said Bob, looking up from the page and over his reading glasses. "If I ever thought of Mabel as some kind of bathroom joke before, I'll never think that way again. You use the disease to explain the stuff with Toomer and the money she gave him. It even explains what she was doing with Lawrence and Jeffers, trying to escape something she couldn't get away from."

"It is wonderful," Hal agreed. "Read ahead to the part when she's alone in the bar after she's left the doctor's office."

Bob shuffled ahead a few pages until he found what he wanted, then began again:

She thought about the spiral of the bacteria. There was something beautiful about it and timeless. She had married Juan with it. They had exchanged it like wedding rings. She would have to tell him. They were married forever now, bound like prisoners to each other. All her life she'd been able to get out of such bondage. Now they had created something between them that neither could escape. The doctor had said they could live a long time with it, that perhaps the symptoms would stay in remission for years. But in the end? she asked. Ah, the end.

"I love it," Hal exclaimed. "Now read the part after she tells Juan!"

Bob shuffled ahead through some more pages, then began again.

At first Juan wouldn't believe her. Not that his people had not experienced the disease. But those who had, had died off and there had been no cases for many years. But Florence showed him the tests and told him what they meant and how it explained the way she had been feeling. When he was convinced, he became contrite. For he was sure he'd given it to her. He talked about a trip he'd made to Colorado and the Ute woman he'd stayed with up there. Florence was tempted to let him think that. Now I'll give you smallpox, she joked. But she couldn't lie like that. So she told about the nefarious Maritan doctor she'd slept with some months before and the letter her mother sent telling her of his ignominious end. That's why I went to the doctor, she told Juan, because of the way I felt and my mother's letter.

Bob stopped, raised his hand, skipped some pages and began again. And Myron realized one of the reasons he'd been so frightened was that he'd gotten inside Mabel's mind. To get inside Mabel, to be her, was to take the same chances she took, to do the very things that made her great and dangerous and memorable. Now he heard his own words as if someone else had written them, as if he was hearing them for the first time and it was frightening.

Florence thought of Dora and her house by the bridge. Once she had called Dora a troll. That had been cruel. But Dora seemed to do nothing but wait for people to pass so she could serve them tea. What a life, she had thought. Now Florence was more isolated than even her friend. How could a person as social as she was, who saw herself only through the eyes of others, live like this? For she realized now that she was isolated even from Juan whose people would take him back, would care for him. The thing was she was more of a warrior than any of them dreamed of being. She wanted to fight what was attacking her, though there were days when she felt weak. Better, she thought on those days, to die in battle than to wait here to be slaughtered on my chaise.

"I love that," said Hal. "That's Mabel. You've got her. She wouldn't ride away to her death passively as Lawrence has her doing." He was referring to Lawrence's story "The Woman Who Rode Away," whose heroine was supposed to be Mabel. "She's no human sacrifice. She's a soldier, a conquistador."

Myron thought of the ways Hal talked about killing her in his play, *Cake*.

"And that's why when she finally moves in with her friend," Hal was saying, "to live by the bridge and let Dora nurse her, it's. . . . "

"Are you going to show it to her?" Bob interrupted.

"I left her a carbon. She's probably already read it."

"She'll never let you publish it," warned Hal. "Not in a million years."

"How can she stop me?"

When Myron got back that night he found a note from Mabel under his door. She wanted him to stop by. But it was late and he decided to call her in the morning. This was the moment he dreaded. Would it be their final confrontation? He didn't want to deal with her yet. He wanted to live a little longer with Hal and Bob's praise. So he slept in and was just thinking about going over to the Big House when there was a knock on his front door. It was a simple, sharp rap with the knuckles, not Tinka's pounding with the underside of her fist. Myron was getting good at figuring out who wasn't Tinka. He opened the door. There was Mabel carrying a briefcase. He let her in and she carried the case to the table, put it down on a chair, and took his manuscript from it. Then she sat down at the table and put the neatly piled pages in the center. So Myron sat down opposite her. There was a silence. She seemed to be gathering her thoughts. He didn't mind the wait. He had expected anger.

"First of all," she said, "I want you to know it's a wonderful novel. I couldn't put it down." She smiled. "I thought I knew everything that was going to happen, but the way you told it, I was as surprised as anyone by the revelation. It was if it had happened to someone else."

"It did," said Myron, and he was about to insist Florence Gresham was a complete fiction when something told him to be quiet and stay alert. Mabel was acting in a much too controlled way.

"I was flattered by your vision of me," she went on. "In my own books I tried to show my growth by dramatizing scenes from my life. But the critics have accused me of editing my life so I could prove the points I wanted proved."

Myron nodded. But he was still suspicious. This was all so measured. He thought of Spud. Had she talked it over with Spud? Had he told her how to act?

"By using the third person, by making it fiction, you've done away with the possibility of that kind of reading. You followed the advice you gave me about turning my life into fiction. Your novel's a writing lesson for me. I can see it now."

"But you did the same thing in your novel."

"Nothing like this." She nodded at the pages, then looked up. "I underestimated you, Myron. I thought you had become a writer of sentimental novels. This, however," and she again nodded at the manuscript between them, "is a fine book, Florence Gresham a great character."

Myron still couldn't believe her. This had to be Spud. She seemed so businesslike and efficient in her use of language. He looked at her. She had on one of her favorite turbans and a long flowing dress, a gown really. It was her Isadora Duncan look from the Villa Curonia days.

"Thanks, Mabel," he said cautiously. "Coming from you that's the best praise this book can get." This was as much as he was prepared to admit.

"But there's something else."

"What?"

"I'm going to ask you not to publish it."

This was what he'd been waiting for. "Why?" he asked calmly.

"There was a point when I was reading it that I got very angry. I felt my privacy had been violated."

"Your privacy?" Myron felt his anger rising. "Who's exposed themselves more than you, Mabel? Your life in its most intimate details is in your books. They're even called *Intimate Memories*."

"I knew you were going to say that, Myron." She paused. "Not my whole life," she added.

He didn't say anything.

"Think of this," she went on. "There will be people who won't read it, who will just hear that it's about me and Tony and that we have syphilis, and they'll judge us. They'll say we deserve it for the way we've lived our lives. For every person who reads and understands the beauty of it, there'll be a hundred who just hear about it and titter over it and have their fun with Tony and me. I could tough it out but I think it would kill Tony. He doesn't deserve that."

"Mabel," Myron began. He would try to match her reasonableness with his own. "I haven't written this to invade your privacy, or to make you ashamed or punish you in any way. In fact, the very mention of syphilis makes the novel fiction. It might look like you for a while but nobody would believe you have syphilis." He thought to mention Frank's reading but decided not to. He didn't want her to know Frank had read it. Not yet anyway. Besides, it was between them.

"This isn't the first time you've written about me," she went on. "I read *Anthony in the Nude* before I ever met you. I was told someone had written a book about me."

He was stunned. He hadn't thought about *Anthony in the Nude* in years. And who would have told her such a thing? He remembered their very first meeting when Cady pulled the car over. Muriel Draper, he thought. That bitch!

"It's a mean book," she went on. "You make fun of that woman."

"No," Myron said. "I don't. She gets what she wants. It's myself I make fun of. I'm the unconscious fortune hunter with the beautiful profile who thinks he will be a great writer someday."

"Yet he ends up loving her," said Mabel.

"And she him," Myron added and wondered what the novel had meant to her. "I wrote that four years before I knew you, Mabel." He looked at her. She looked confused and tired. "It's not the same at all," he went on. "They were small people and I was judging them. I don't do that in this book. I'd be the last one to judge you."

"Then why did you write it?"

"Because it's a beautiful story."

"It is," she agreed. "It's awful in real life but it's a beautiful story." She looked up. "That's why it's so hard for me to ask this. I love great art. It's why I've made this place." She became thoughtful. "One of the things I thought when I finished reading was that perhaps if the venereal disease could be cut, it would be all right. But syphilis is the perfect symbol or process, whatever you want to call it, for what happens to Florence's life. I don't want you to change a word of it."

"But you don't want me to publish it."

"That's right."

There was a silence.

"I don't believe you," Myron said at last.

"Believe me, Myron," Mabel said, a new edge in her voice. "I'm desperate."

"No, I mean when you say that you think it's a great novel. I think you're just flattering me to get me to do what you want."

"If I thought flattery would get you not to publish it, I would flatter you. But I'm trying to be as truthful as I can be. I'm not flattering you. It is beautiful. But I can't let it be published."

"What if I were to tell you I don't care about what you want," and he realized he was again getting angry. "It seems ever since we met we've been playing the Truth game."

"I'd love this to be a game. Unfortunately it's not."

"But I've told the truth. You can't deny it. You and Tony have syphilis." He hadn't wanted to say this. Reality was no way to justify fiction.

"Who did you hear that from?" she asked.

"Several people," he said, and wondered if Spud had told her anything.

"So it's common knowledge?"

"No. I actually heard it from three people who say they've known it for years and have kept your secret. And I'm not going to say who they are."

"But they told you."

"Yes."

"And now you're telling the world."

"Yes."

Her face reddened into anger and he thought she was going to get up and either flee the house or jump at him. She did neither. Instead she reached down into her lap where the briefcase rested, fumbled for a moment, then looked up. When she did, Myron was taken by the depth of her eyes. Was it the way she looked when she made love? he wondered. Then he wondered why he thought of sex with this old women, and he looked away. That's when he saw it. Her hands were clasped around the pearl grip of Tony's Colt .45, both her index fingers on its trigger. She was pointing it at his heart, the spot where Una had pointed her pistol at herself. He thought of the small automatic in the soap dish. A Hollywood prop. There'd been a gun like it in the Saint movie at the Kiddie show. But this weapon was much larger, bigger bored, a cowboy gun. Shiny and new, it looked nothing like the cheap gun he'd bought to kill Cady. Then he remembered that she'd killed him in her novel. This was a much better ending than a stone thrown by a volcano.

"You're changing the rules," he said.

"This isn't a game," she repeated.

"It's better than the stone in your novel, but it's still bad writing." He felt short of breath, as if a .45 caliber hole had already ruined the perfect seal of his chest.

"This isn't a novel either." She looked at him a moment longer, shrugged, and laid the weapon on the manuscript. It was pointed at neither of them. "You see how angry I am. I came here to kill you," she said.

"I don't believe that."

"You bastard!" she screamed. "I took you into my house. I fed you. I confided in you. I trusted you. You bastard!"

He thought she was going to pick up the .45 again, thought to go for it himself. But he couldn't seem to move. Why? Did he think that he deserved to be punished? Or was it because he was disappointed by her reaction? This moment was the culmination of their Truth Game. And he thought he had won. For somewhere inside him he must have been sure she was going to love the novel, sure that she would see the truth of it. That would have given her back her life. How naïve of him. He really did have to believe art could save, that the complicated kind of truth his novel told could make you free.

"I used to think I was above all this," Mabel was saying, "that life couldn't hurt me. Then I got sick." She looked up and their eyes met again. "You have the power now. All I can do is beg you not to use it. I'm asking you to pity us."

"Pity?" The word surprised him. He was the one who was beaten. Why did she think she needed pity? "I've always admired you, Mabel," he said, still trying to catch his breath, "though often you've made me very angry. But after I discovered your secret, I saw you with new eyes. You became almost superhuman to me. You became a true hero. So the one thing I can't do is pity you."

"I think you can and do," she contradicted.

He looked at her. Did pity mean the same thing to them? And why did she suddenly seem so confident? Was it because she knew she was right? He did pity her. He had created her. She was his child. And she was hurt. But who was confusing fiction and reality now? He pitied Florence Gresham, not Mabel Dodge Luhan.

"And I have a contract," he went on. "I live by my writing. I have to publish or starve." It sounded lame and it wasn't true anymore, though he did seem to go through money quickly. "Now you see why I was hesitant to buy this house. How can I live here knowing you feel I've humiliated you? Give me my money back and we'll call it off. The kitchen and bathroom are on me."

"No. It's your house," she said and shrugged. "If anyone leaves it'll be Tony and me." She stood, her confidence seeming to evaporate.

Myron stood also. He didn't know what to say. Was he really driving her out of the one place that had given her life meaning, the place for which she had sacrificed her health? They faced each other across the table. He saw a woman in her early sixties who looked much older. The smooth heaviness of her square face that for years had made her appear girlish now seemed to be falling of its own weight. Though she was thinner now than he ever remembered her being, her nose, mouth, and chin had thickened. She looks like a bruised fighter. Was it the sleepless weekend or the disease? Was the horror beginning?

"You know," she said, "I'm giving my papers to the Beinecke Library at Yale with the stipulation that some of them not be opened until the year 2000." She looked up as if that were a solution. "You could do something like that with your novel."

"Give it to Yale?" He thought of Hildegarde Donaldson. Didn't her husband have something to do with the Yale Press? Were they still together?

"No. Just delay the publication until after our deaths." She thought a moment. "You're almost twenty years younger than Tony or me. Your mother's still alive. You're going to live a long time." She sounded almost envious.

"I don't know about that," he said.

She came around the table and put her arms around him. "It's a beautiful portrait," she said. "I'm proud to have sat for it." Then she stepped back, tears in her eyes. "You showed me things about myself I never knew. I thought what happened to Tony and me was a punishment. I've always felt that. But you've shown me a world that's indifferent to me, a world that couldn't care less if I lived or died. I was always trying to deny that world, always trying to make it into something I could control and make work for me. But the world you present is unfathomable." She shook her head, a motion of amazement. "It throws me back on myself. It tells me there's nothing to be done for me. It tells me that it doesn't care."

He looked at her. Was she going to admit everything?

"The strangest thing is that I find that comforting," she went on. "There is nothing out there that I can know." She looked up and smiled a sad smile. "I thought if I ever admitted this I'd fall into a terrible despair. But all I feel now is relief. I feel I'm . . . cured."

"Of what?" Myron asked, fascinated by these admissions.

"Of . . . of myself. The sickness of myself." She paused, looked down. "After I finished your novel, I called Dr. Brill. I told him about it and how it made me feel." She looked up. "Do you know what he said?"

Myron shook his head.

"He said you'd done me a favor, that you'd given me truth."

"Mabel, we've both written novels about each other." He would finally admit he knew who the hero of *Water of Life* was. "In yours you told the world I'm a homosexual. You invaded my privacy."

"Did you mind?"

"No," he said after a moment. "That part was your best writing. I loved the portrait you painted of me. And of Cady, too."

"But mine isn't the book yours is," she said. "It will never be published."

"Until I read it," he went on, "I never knew how you felt about me."

"And until I read yours I never knew how you felt about me."

He looked at her. She seemed suddenly very dear to him. It seemed to him that though the passion of anger was gone, the affection remained. "I love you, Mabel," he said quietly and was more amazed at his feelings than that he was expressing them.

"And I you, Myron."

"Our poor love," he said and wrapped his arms around her.

"Our poor love," she echoed.

Then she was sobbing against his chest. Why hadn't they said all this sooner? he wondered. Would it have made a difference? No, he had to write the novel. Then he thought of the last time he'd held her like this. It was that night in Carmel when she came to his room soaking wet. Does Gertrude Stein know about her disease? Is that why she felt she had to see her old friend? Then he realized she was talking, her face against his chest.

"You can't imagine how happy he made me," she was saying, "how glad I was to become a part of him and his people."

Myron stepped back and looked at her.

"I didn't blame him," she said and looked down. "You got that right, too. To this day I'm not sure who gave it to whom, who brought this peculiar little snake into our garden." She looked up into Myron's eyes and he wondered again how this dumpy woman approaching her old age could have such an effect on him. "One thing I do know," she went on. "You've written the book I should have written. All the work I did on my own books went for nothing because my last one didn't tell the truth. Yet I could do nothing else. I was afraid. I thought the truth would destroy us. I still think that." She smiled at him. "Tony always said I had to be careful of you, that one day you would write about us."

She turned away, took a step toward the door, then turned back, touched the manuscript, then picked up the revolver, and put it in the briefcase that she'd also forgotten.

"Do what you have to," she said and turned again. "It's a wonderful book."

He watched her through the front window as she got into her car. Then she was gone and he was looking into the dead fireplace. But he was still thinking of her. She'd written a novel about falling in love with him, about trying to make him accept her in the only way she thought she could be accepted. And he'd written a novel telling the world her secret and fallen in love with her, his most beautiful creation. So here I am, he thought, loving a woman so much I'd do anything not to hurt her. But I have to publish it. I owe Farrar & Rinehart a novel. It would be cowardly if . . .

There was pounding on the front door. He looked up. From the sublime to the ridiculous, he thought.

"Go away!" he shouted at the door.

More pounding.

"Please," he pleaded. "Go away!"

More pounding.

Epilogue

Sing Wu's

In January of 1991, a month after his ninety-fourth birthday, Myron Brinig signed a contract with Sweetgrass Books, a press in Helena, Montana, for a paperback edition of *Wide Open Town* to be released the following fall. It was a small press and a thousand-copy print run, but it would be the first time Myron had been in print in over thirty years. His name would be out there. He'd have his headstone although he still didn't feel like dying. He still had George, still made it over to The Closet, though that was a sad place now, and still read books. For his birthday George had given him a collection of essays by the old Jewish writer, Henry Roth, called *Shifting Landscapes*. Roth was the man with the famous writer's block and this was his first book since *Call It Sleep* back in 1936. From an interview at the book's beginning, Myron realized that not only was Roth in control of his faculties, but that he was also working on a new novel. He's got to be near my age. What's with old Jewish men? Are we indestructible? Then he learned from the same interview that Roth was living in Albuquerque. How'd he get out there? he wondered. So he dialed Albuquerque information, asked for Henry Roth's number, got two listings, and tried the one on New York Avenue.

"Hello?" asked a gruff old Bronx-accented voice.

"Henry Roth?

"Yeah."

"How are you today?"

"Lousy. My arthritis is bad. My fingers. My back."

"Sorry to hear . . . "

"So who is this?"

"My name's Myron Brinig."

"Who?"

"Brinig. Myron Brinig."

"Never heard of you. I gotta go."

"No, no! Wait! I'm a writer. Ever heard of a novel called *Singermann*?"

"*Singermann*?" There was a pause. "That rings a bell." Another pause. "It was a long time ago. 1930."

"1929," Myron corrected.

"You wrote that?"

"Yeah."

"Brinig. I remember. You were a big deal then. What happened to you?"

"Tastes change," Myron answered lamely.

"But you're still alive," said Henry Roth, as if that was something.

"I'm ninety-four."

"You make me feel like a kid," the old voice exclaimed. "I'm only eighty-three."

"You are a kid," said Myron.

"You know, Brinig, we used to talk about *Singermann*. I didn't think of doing *Call It Sleep* until I read it. A novel about Jewish life written in English. I thought to myself, I could do better than this."

"Really?" asked Myron, ignoring the insult.

"Yeah." A pause. "What made you call me?"

"I read *Shifting Landscapes*. I was interested in it because it has an article you wrote on Lynn Riggs. I knew Riggs in The Village."

"Ahhh. Then did you knew Eda?"

"Who?"

"Eda Lou Walton. She taught at NYU."

"Yeah. I remember." Myron paused a moment. He did remember. "I think I once went to her apartment. She had poetry readings there, right?"

"Yeah. We might've met," said Roth.

Then, like young people who discover they have more in common than they ever imagined, they were talking about Greenwich Village in the twenties and writers they knew and left-wing intellectuals. And when that was exhausted, Myron asked Henry Roth how he could write if his arthritis was so bad, and Roth went into raptures over an invention called a personal computer.

"The keyboard has such an easy touch even I can use it. You should see. The words come up on a little television screen. Then you press another key and what you wrote is saved on a disk and can be printed later."

Myron said he'd heard of these things and thought they were hard to operate. Roth said they were, but he had the high school girl next door come in every morning before she went to school to open it up for him. "At the end of the day, she stops in and takes my disk to her house and prints up what I've written. I hardly have to pay her anything. You should get one."

"A high school girl?"

"Wise guy. You know what I mean."

"Yeah."

Then there was silence, and Myron thought they'd run out of things to say. He was going to say goodbye and it was good talking to him and maybe they'd talk again, when Roth cleared his throat.

"You know, Brinig," he began, "I owe you."

"What do you mean?"

"There's a scene in *Singermann* that's always stuck in my mind. I think it was the germ of *Call It Sleep*, and who knows, maybe it's the reason I'm writing what I'm writing now."

"What scene?"

"The one where the young boy is awakened by his older brother who's having a wet dream. They share a bed. Did that really happen?"

"Yeah," said Myron. "I was the boy. But it wasn't *Singermann*. It was in a short story I published in *Munsey's*."

"Whatever! I was bowled over by it, the force of it, the sheer animal urgency. I wanted to do that in *Call It Sleep*. But most of that book's an evasion. Sometimes, through those years when I couldn't write, I'd think of your scene and tell myself I had to be as honest as that."

"What's the new book about?" asked Myron, suddenly very interested. Roth's voice had become young in its excitement.

"Incest," he announced. "For most of my teenage years and into my twenties, I was lusting after my mother and screwing my sister."

"Really?" Myron didn't know what to say. He'd gotten a lot more from this call than he bargained for.

"I owe it all to you and your honesty. If this book ever comes to anything, it's because of you."

"What's it called?"

"*Mercy of a Rude Stream.*"

"Shakespeare."

"Yeah."

"I hope I live long enough to read it," said Myron.

"I hope I live long enough to write it," said Roth.

"*Kalichas,*" said Myron. It was his mother's expression for feeble old men.

Henry Roth laughed and said goodbye and that they should stay in touch. Myron agreed and they hung up. But he was still thinking about Roth. Surely *Call It Sleep* was earning him more fame and money with each passing year. Why wasn't he satisfied? Because he'd written only one novel when it was obvious his urge to write was overwhelming. So let him write. If it turns out to be only foolishness, who cares? There's always the possibility it might be good. Hadn't the man said he was trying for something big? I'm going to rewrite my life as it really was. I'm not going to evade anything. And Myron began to think of the things he'd evaded. He went to his bookcase, the shelf that held his novels, and pulled down *All of Their Lives*. It was all he had. There were no copies of *Florence Gresham*. Long ago an angry lover, an affair of only a few months, had burned all of his manuscripts.

Myron opened the published novel to the beginning of the last section, the part where Florence first meets Juan.

"I beg your pardon!" called Florence. "Are you going to Santa Fe?"

The Indian looked down at her as from a great height. For some moments he regarded her with an expressionless stare. His visage was indeed noble, the great American head, so great that white Americans have pressed the lines and features into that commodity they respect most highly.

"Yes, I go to Santa Fe."

"Will you take me, please?" asked Florence.

She looked petite and cool and pretty from where he stood above her; and undoubtedly there were other qualities that caught his attention and fancy. Small as she was she had personality and power. He had known a good many white women and did not think much of them; but he suspected that this particular lady was different. He was a purely instinctive creature and acted from within.

"Yes, I take you," he said, and smiled.

Florence had never beheld such a smile. It had the sweetness, the all-embracing goodness of fresh earth, fragrant after the rain.

Myron liked what he read. It was a wonderful beginning to the rest of their lives. Will you take me? Yes, I take you. But the page was all written over. At some point he must have toyed with the idea of rewriting it. Many of the lines were penciled through and there were margin notes. "His visage was indeed noble." Myron pulled the book close to his face and read what he'd written in the margin. "Right out of Fenimore Cooper," it said. "Can't get away with that today." Myron nodded and skipped to the next line with a pencil line through it. "There were other qualities that caught his attention and fancy." He looked at his note in the margin. "No!" he'd written. "Flabby euphemism for sexual attraction!" Myron sat back and reread the section without the offending lines. He nodded, then continued reading further. But it was slow going for he stopped whenever he ran into a lining-out to read his correction. Then he got to the part where Florence gets dropped in Santa Fe by Juan. She wants him to take her all the way to Taos, which Myron had called Ramos.

Obviously he hadn't liked that name for he had begun crossing it out as soon as it appeared and written the word "Taos" above it.

"Too Spanish," he'd written in the margin. "Taos is better. A mysterious, talismanic, oriental sound to it." Myron had to agree. It was one of those myths perpetuated by Mabel, that the Pueblo Indians were descended from Chinese mystics. Myron read on. In the next chapter he'd switched to Dora's point of view. There was a long note in the margin. "This Dora's nothing like the original. She's the opposite of Florence but in a different way than Edith Warner. She's bloodless, envious and possessive." And as he turned pages he realized he had crossed out all of Dora's lines. So he skipped to the next chapter, where Florence buys land and hires Juan to build her a house. In the margin he'd written, "Expand! Florence should watch them lay on the mud as if it were a living substance, as if it were the flesh of a woman." Myron knew what he'd done. By cutting out the building of her house, he'd essentially cut Juan out of this version of the novel.

"As if it were the flesh of a woman," he said aloud.

Then he put the book down. No amount of rewriting would help. It would never be anything but lousy. Why did it even exist? Because he'd convinced himself he could write a second novel based on the first to satisfy his contract, and publish the first one later. What a problem solver he was. With the wisdom of Solomon he'd given himself a choice any decent mother would have rejected. Now the baby was dead. Why'd he do it? Was it egotism, cowardliness, kindness? And how his publishers had wailed! They'd wanted *Florence Gresham*. It's going to make your reputation with the critics, John Farrar had pleaded. It'll put you over the top. But Myron was adamant. Now he sat, tears in his eyes. Was this why he'd been forgotten, because he'd censored himself? Whatever the cause it was years too late to do anything about it. Then Myron thought of Frank Waters. As far as he knew Frank was still alive. If he was, he would be an old man. What if he's senile? What if he doesn't remember me? After he left Taos, Myron never saw Frank again, never even called him. So he dialed Taos information and was surprised when they gave him a number.

"Hello," said a dry voice.

"Frank, is that you?"

"Yes. Who's this?"

"Myron Brinig." There was a silence. "You remember me?"

"Of course I remember you, Mike. I'm just overwhelmed."

"You thought I was dead, eh?"

"No. In fact I've been thinking about you. I ran into Lois Rudnick a few months ago at a lecture out here. We got to talking about you and she told me how angry you were about her book."

"What did you think of what she said about me?" Myron was suddenly happy. Some place in the world people were still talking about him.

"I thought it was great that someone was remembering you."

"As a member of Mabel's faggoty chorus line!"

Frank laughed. Then there was silence.

"What do you look like now, Frank?" Myron asked to fill the silence, then thought, my god, I'm flirting.

"I've got huge pouches under my eyes and I'm a skinny wreck." Frank laughed. "What do you look like, Mike?"

"I've gone totally white." He paused. "Aside from that, pretty much the same."

There was another moment of silence, then they both burst out laughing. But after the laughter the silence returned. Myron had to fill it.

"You remember *Florence Gresham*?" he asked.

"Of course," Frank said. "It was wonderful."

"You ever read *All of Their Lives*?"

"No. I started it but I . . . " There was a pause, then Frank went on. "Don't take it the wrong way, Mike. You know what I thought of the other version."

Now it was Myron's turn to go silent.

"Why didn't you publish it after they died?"

Mabel and Tony had died within months of each other in 1962. They were in their eighties. Penicillin had given them more years than they'd had a right to expect. And by then Myron had ceased publishing.

"I tried," said Myron, "but nobody was interested in her anymore. Or me."

"I wish you had called me. After Rinehart dropped me, I went with the Swallow Press. Small presses are good. My books have been in print ever since."

"That's great," said Myron. He didn't want to admit that he'd tried several small presses.

"You know," Frank was saying, "Mabel used to talk about you. Both she and Tony were pretty much alcoholics by the end. But sometimes if I went over there early in the day I could still have a conversation with her. Sometime it would come around to you and your novel."

"What did she say?" Myron asked.

"That she never should've interfered with you, that you made her into someone great, that you immortalized her. That was the term she used. Immortalized. Then she would begin to cry. It was pretty bad there at the end."

Myron felt tears coming, which was odd because he hadn't felt anything when he was told of Mabel's death.

"Why don't you bring it out now?" asked Frank. "I'll bet someone down here would be interested. The University of New Mexico Press, some place like that. There's lots of local interest in her now."

"I can't."

"Why not?"

He hesitated. Oh, what the hell, he thought. "My only copies of the manuscript were destroyed in a fire."

"Really?"

"Yeah. That's why I'm calling you, Frank." Myron thought he sounded pathetic. "Did Mabel ever mention having a copy of the book? The reason I ask is that when I left Taos, I had the original and two carbons. I know I made three. Did Mabel ever mention anything about that?"

"No," Frank said. "Not to me. But if she had a copy it would be in the Beinecke Library at Yale where her papers are. Why don't you call them?"

"That's a good idea, Frank," and Myron felt excitement. "If somehow she had a copy, they'd have it."

"Yeah," Frank encouraged.

"Are you still writing?" asked Myron.

"Yeah. I'm doing a little memoir now. You're in it. Just some of the dinners at Mabel's." He paused. "Is that all right?"

"Sure."

"What are you doing besides looking for your manuscript?"

"Next fall a small press in Montana is coming out with a paperback of *Wide Open Town*."

"That's terrific," said Frank. Then there was a long pause. "We've got to keep in touch," he said.

"Yeah," Myron agreed.

So they exchanged addresses and he gave Frank his phone number and they hung up. Then Myron called the Beinecke Library at Yale and they read him a catalogue of Mabel's papers. *Water of Life* was there. She'd never tried to get it published. But there was no mention of *Florence Gresham*, though they told him that a lot of her papers were being held from public view until the year 2000. After he hung up Myron asked himself why she would weep over his novel if she had a copy. She didn't have it, he decided. It's gone.

He picked up San Isidro, who stood on the coffee table. The room had grown dark and he could feel the saint better than he could see it. The original had not felt nearly as good. It had angles made by a primitive carving tool. It was these angles that gave it the look of folk art. In 1950 when Cady donated his collection to the Museum of New Mexico in Santa Fe, he asked Myron for the original back so it could go with the rest. Twenty years ago on a trip to Santa Fe, Myron took Steve to the museum to show him the saint. It must be worth thousands, Steve said, implying Myron had been dumb to return it. But Myron didn't care. Things like that are better off in museums. Besides, he liked this one. It was smooth and felt better and was done by a professional who'd signed his name. Lopez, it said at the base. Cady had bought it for him to replace the first one. They'd shopped for it together. Ah Cady. Mabel was wrong. Among the three of them, Cady was the real talent. Yet he was forgotten too. We all had our flaws, Myron thought. Cady's was his need to help people.

That's why he volunteered. I have to do it, he said. He was thirty-six when he went in. Yet he served in every major campaign in Europe. He even saw the death camps. When he got back his femininity was gone, as well as his joy. He told Myron that he couldn't stand living near Los Alamos so they found him a studio behind Becky James's house on Dent Street. But that didn't work and Cady moved far away to the Virgin Islands. But that didn't work either and in a year he was back at Jacona. The way he painted had changed yet again. His new work looked like aerial photos of battlefields. Beautiful in their own way, they didn't come to life until he began to experiment with color. And that's when Myron began to believe his friend was coming out of it. But it was too late. There'd been too much snow, too much mud and death. In 1952, when Cady was only forty-eight, he suffered a heart attack, and two years later on November 15, his fiftieth birthday, he died in Saint Vincent's Hospital in Santa Fe. At what should have been the height of his career, Cady was gone.

Myron squeezed the wooden saint. In his more self-pitying moods, he would talk to it as if there was some intelligence there. Sometimes he would ask it for release as if it had authority over him. Let me go, he would plead. I want to die. Then he'd recite the beginning of Tennyson's "Tithonus" to it.

"The woods decay," he began now in the darkening room, "the woods decay and fall. The vapors weep their burthen to the ground. And after many a summer dies the swan." He took a breath. "Only me," he wailed, "cruel immortality consumes."

He stopped. He didn't really want to die. Who did? He thought of Carmen. Poor Carmen. He never knew what hit him. And so many of the others. This was a terrible thing, this AIDS. He shook his head. Ah death. Then he thought it would have been better if Cady had lived to a ripe old age and gained the reputation he deserved and produced the kind of work he was bound to produce. If I had died in 1954 I still would have been one of America's leading writers. That was the year Stanley Rinehart, who broke with John Farrar after the war, joined forces with Henry Holt and dropped Myron from the new Holt Rinehart list. His career ended the year Cady died. Of course, he didn't know that. In a few more years he would sell the Placita house and come back to New York to be closer to the publishing world. He would publish one more novel and all through the sixties he would go on writing. A writer who publishes twenty-one novels doesn't just stop. Only in the seventies did he slack off, and even then . . .

"Myron! What are you doing sitting in the dark?"

The light came on. Myron's white piano, the only piece of furniture left from Taos, glared at him. It took up most of their tiny living room, and George wanted to sell it. After I'm gone, Myron would say.

"I didn't hear you come in."

"C'mon," said George. "I don't feel like cooking. Let's go out to eat. What would you like?"

"How about Chinese?" asked Myron.

Chinese meant Sing Wu's down on Second Avenue and Tenth. They'd catch a cab on Second, zip down, eat, then walk over to First Avenue and zip back up. There'd be time for a nightcap.

"Yeah," George agreed. "That'd be good."

"Let's go," said Myron.

They started with sizzling rice soup. As much as for its taste, they loved the ceremony. The waiter would deliver a tureen of steaming shrimp broth to the tray stand, then, with a flourish, uncover a steel serving dish full of crenulated rice cakes. He'd let their smoke rise a moment, then, with metal serving tongs, grab two or three, flourish them in the air, then place them in the tureen, where they'd go off like muted firecrackers. During the winter of 1938, Myron brought Tony here and they always ordered this dish. So it was Tony who first pointed it out. "China man look like Mabel," he said. Myron immediately saw what he meant. It was Mabel when she was burning pine boughs to drive out stale air. Even now, as Myron watched the waiter, he could see her doing her little dance with the burning piñon. It's so stuffy in here! she would say as she ran from one corner to another waving the crackling smoke. It's so stuffy!

But here in Sing Wu's the aroma wasn't piñon. It was onion, garlic, and shrimp. Myron looked around. The nearby diners were staring wide-eyed. Though the waiter had finished filling the tureen, the rice was still popping. Not until it quieted did the man begin ladling the shrimp broth and rice into two smaller bowls. The people at the other tables, realizing the fireworks were over, broke into applause, and the Chinese man stopped for a moment to smile and bow. Then he put a bowl of soup in front of Myron, then George. When he left everyone in the room turned to their food except Myron. He was looking at George. His friend was nearly seventy now but still a handsome man. His birthday was coming up soon. What can I get him? Thirty-two years we've been together. It's been a good time. And Myron thought of a perfect gift. They had talked about getting one before. George had a nephew who knew about such things. Myron would call the man tomorrow.

"What is it?" asked George, finally realizing he was being watched. He put his porcelain spoon down in the bowl and leaned back.

"You know what I did today?" Myron asked.

Afterword

"UNLESS YOU EXPLAIN IN A PREFACE WHO Myron Brinig was, readers will think you made him up," my editor warned after seeing an early draft of this novel. "They'll think he's some kind of gay Forrest Gump."

I laughed. But the more I thought about it, the more I worried. One of my reasons for writing the novel was to bring Myron Brinig back into the public eye. Had I done the opposite, turned him into fiction? After all, when I first heard of him I hadn't believed he existed. It was spring of 1978 and I was in the University of Montana Bookstore talking to a man so old he'd been credited with founding our English Department. Professor Emeritus H. G. Merriam had written a history of the Missoula Valley, and I had just bought a copy and he had just signed it. I wasn't particularly interested in the subject, but you had to respect a nonagenarian who was still publishing. So there I was, making literary small talk. Who do you think is the best native Montana novelist? I'd just asked him.

"Myron Brinig," he answered without batting an eye.

"Who?"

Montana was so new I could think of no really good native Anglo novelist, and I thought he would have to cite a Native American like D'Arcy McNickle or James Welch. I should have known better. In the twenties Professor Merriam had founded and edited *Frontier*, the first—and for years, the only—literary magazine in the Rockies. And he had a reputation as a curmudgeon who suffered fools not at all.

"Brinig," he repeated. "Myron Brinig," he said, then added, "He's not really a Montana writer. He's a Butte writer. There's a big difference."

"Never heard of him," I admitted.

"He's Jewish," Professor Merriam added as if I, one of two Jews on the English Department's staff, had been doubly remiss in my ignorance.

"Really?" was all I could muster.

"You ought to read him," he directed. "His books are in the library." And he turned to the next in line.

Five minutes later I was on the fourth floor of the Mansfield Library examining a shelf of twenty-one novels. From the number and sound of the titles, *The Sun Sets in the West*, *Wide Open Town*, I wondered if Professor Merriam wasn't losing his grip. They sounded like pulp westerns. I took down *Wide Open Town* and checked it out. Two days later I was back for *Singermann* and two days after that, *This Man Is My Brother*. Who is this guy? I asked myself. Only then did I think to go to the library's copy of *Twentieth Century Authors*. There he was. A whole column. It said he was born in Butte in 1900 and currently lived in Taos, New Mexico. I flipped to the front. The edition was twenty years old. I flipped back and looked at the photo. Brinig looked like Oscar Levant.

Probably dead, I told myself. Still, when I got home I dialed Taos information. There was no listing for him. But I kept at it and called Taos City Hall. Someone there remembered him. They said he'd long ago sold his house and moved but they didn't know where or if he was still alive. I tried Butte information. They found a Brinig listing. I dialed, and over the phone I was told by an old lady, who said she was his cousin, that if he was still alive, which she didn't think was the case, he would be living in Los Angeles. I dialed LA information. There was no listing for him in LA or its environs. I gave up. He would be seventy-eight. Probably dead, I decided.

In the fall of 1979, I attended a conference in Butte on the rebuilding of that city. I was there as an observer for the conference's sponsor, the Montana Committee for the Humanities, but I took every chance I got to ask people about Myron Brinig.

Several members of the Butte Historical Society remembered his books, and the next year I was invited to a Myron Brinig film festival at the Montana School of Mines. The festival consisted of one film, *The Sisters*, starring Bette Davis and Errol Flynn. Not a bad movie, I thought, and seeing Hollywood's version of Butte was fun. But the most important thing that happened was my meeting a reporter for *The Montana Standard* who was interested in Brinig. Andrea McCormack had a reputation as a good investigator but I never expected she would find what she did. Just a few months later, the winter of 1981, she called to tell me that he was alive and living in New York City and that she had his phone number.

He's in his eighties, I told myself as I dialed. Don't expect too much. What I got was an intelligent, articulate man who was delighted by my interest. So that summer, on a University of Montana summer school grant, I flew to New York to meet him. Handsome, active, with a full head of white hair and alert eyes, Myron Brinig seemed happy to talk about his past. It turned out he was born in 1896 in Minneapolis and came to Butte when he was three. So he was not only older than *Twentieth Century Authors* said, he was also, strictly speaking, not a Montana native. But the most important thing that happened was that at the end of the meeting he gave me his memoir. I want to see what you think, he said. I took it back to Montana, read it, and thought that with editing, it might be publishable. It never was published, but eventually it would be the basis for several scenes in *The Taos Truth Game*.

In the fall of 1982 I was asked to another conference in Butte, this time to speak about Brinig. One of the good things that came from this conference was the restarting of the Butte Historical Society's publication, *The Speculator*. Its winter 1985 issue included the opening chapter of Myron's memoir and an excerpt from *Wide Open Town* entitled "A Night on Big Butte." For the first time in thirty years, Myron Brinig was in print. He called me after he got his copy. It's a far cry from Farrar & Rinehart, I said. He didn't seem to care. And two years later, when he learned that he was being included in *The Last Best Place*, the now famous Montana literary anthology that came out in 1989, he called me again.

"When I was young, I never wanted to be considered a Montana writer," he said. "I didn't want to be thought of as provincial. Now I'm proud to be one."

He was happy. But I wasn't. He was a novelist. Excerpts didn't do him justice. His best novels had to be reprinted. But this didn't begin to happen until 1991 when Montana's Historical Society opened their reprint series of Montana writers with *Wide Open Town*. Unfortunately, three months before the novel came out, Myron Brinig had passed away. He was ninety-four.

So there's the answer. He existed. But this raises another question. Why has he been so forgotten that there's still a chance he could be mistaken for fiction? Neither I, nor any of my English Department colleagues, had ever heard of him. I had stood in front of a shelf of his novels and been ready to dismiss them as junk. But they weren't junk. Several of them are very good, and their goodness was recognized by the reviewers of that day. It was the later critics who let him down. They were supposed to write the articles that would have put him in a context so he could be talked about. But there aren't any articles about him. He's not even criticized as bad. He's never mentioned at all. He's simply not there.

But he has to be there. Brinig was one of the earliest Jewish novelists writing in English about Jewish immigrants. The first novel of this kind, *The Rise of David Levinsky* by Abraham Cahan, was published in 1917. The next, published in 1923, was Samuel Ornitz's *Haunch, Paunch & Jowl*. The third, published in 1929, was Brinig's *Singermann*. A year later, 1930, Mike Gold's *Jews without Money* came out. Then came *Call It Sleep* in 1935. Yet if you look at any anthology of Jewish writing in print today, though the others are there, Brinig's name is nowhere to be found, and if you look to the great critics of Jewish writing in America, Irving Howe, Leslie Fiedler, Saul Bellow, his name is never mentioned, his books never discussed.

Brinig also wrote one of the first Depression novels about labor strife. In 1931 *Wide Open Town*, about a Butte miners' strike, the major incident of which is the lynching of an IWW union organizer, was published. This book alone should have entitled him to be remembered by scholars of thc American labor movement. The seminal study of the literature of that movement is Walter Rideout's *The Radical Novel in the United States, 1900 to 1954*. In a section he calls "Strike Novels," Rideout cites several obscure works written in the 1930s. But Brinig is never mentioned. You'd think, if for no other reason than scholarly thoroughness, that a novel about a strike like the one described in *Wide Open Town* would be represented. It isn't.

Only the gay critics are beginning to deal with him. Brinig was the first writer from the West to write about being gay. In *Singermann* there are not one but two homosexual sons in the Singermann clan. One, Harry, would rather dress windows than marry. The other, the youngest, Michael, dreams of becoming a writer and is happiest in the company of his English teacher, a middle-aged spinster. In *This Man Is My Brother*, the *Singermann* sequel published in 1932, the main character is an older Harry, who is now in charge of the family department store. Michael, now a writer, comes home to Butte to tell the story of his older brother, who never comes to grips with his homosexuality and is driven to suicide by his feelings. In *Footsteps on the Stairs*, published eighteen years later in 1950, Brinig writes about an overt homosexual experience. Jimmy Joyce, youngest son of a wealthy Butte Irish family, goes to San Francisco, where he has a one-night affair with a man he picks up in a bar. It's a beautifully rendered scene, unprecedented at the time in the bravery of its presentation. But this was 1950, the beginning of the McCarthy era, and such a character and his author were to say the least, not appreciated.

Perhaps the most wonderful thing about this story is that when Brinig died thirty-five years after he stopped publishing, he left me himself in the form of his memoir. It was called *Love from a Stranger* and we had edited it so it would stress the years he lived in Taos, my thought being that because he had known so many famous people there, it would be interesting to publishers. If we can just get your memoir published, I used to tell him, I'm sure your novels will follow. But in the eighties no one was interested in the memoir. So I took another tack and eventually got Montana historians to publish his labor novel. After his death and the release of *Wide Open Town*, I thought my obligation was over. But I still had *Love from a Stranger* that he and I had worked on.

In the spring of 2001, about a year after I moved to Albuquerque, my wife and I drove up to Taos to look for the house Brinig had told me he once owned. I had no other purpose, or so I thought. It was just sightseeing. So I went up to Mabel's Los Gallos and asked a lady who worked there if she knew where Brinig had lived. Amazingly she knew of Brinig and directed me to where she thought the house was. Beyond Spud Johnson's house, she said. They're both bed and breakfasts now. I found the place she meant and the owner happened to be there so I asked him if he knew to whom the house once belonged. Yes, he said, Mabel Dodge Luhan. I said that was true but that I thought it also once belonged to a writer named Myron Brinig. Never heard of him, the man said, repeating that it had belonged to Mabel Dodge Luhan, and walked away. I was amazed by his abruptness. I shouldn't have been. He was saying there was no profit in the place having once been owned by a forgotten writer, that to be remembered the dead must in some way serve the living. We didn't stay around long after that. But on the trip back to Albuquerque, *Love from a Stranger* came to mind. I hadn't looked at it in fifteen years. When I got home I got it out and began reading, and a few days later I started *The Taos Truth Game.*

Earl Ganz
Albuquerque